UNTAMED
HOPE TARR

Tarr pegs Victorian-era London perfectly...
poignant and romantic."
—*Romantic Times Book Reviews*

Medallion Press, Inc.
Printed in USA

DEDICATION:

To Sandra Durfee, "world's best" English
teacher, a former mentor and forever
friend, with affection and respect.

Published 2008 by Medallion Press, Inc.

The MEDALLION PRESS LOGO
is a registered tradmark of Medallion Press, Inc.

Printed in the United States of America
Typeset in Adobe Garamond Pro

10 9 8 7 6 5 4 3 2 1
First Edition

ACKNOWLEDGMENTS

Untamed is the final book in my "Men of Roxbury House" trilogy. Closing the chapter on the series affords me many satisfactions, as well as the opportunity to thank those special persons I may have missed acknowledging in the previous two books.

To Paul Lewis, executive director of the Fredericksburg Athenaeum housed at the Wounded Bookshop, 109 Amelia Street, Fredericksburg, Virginia, my heartfelt thanks for your friendship and support over the past six years (and counting) and for all you do to keep the arts and letters not only alive but thriving in our historic downtown.

Also to Beatrice Paolucci and Hamilton Palmer, Raymond and Dana Herlong, Rudi and Elsa Van Leeuwen, and Paul O'Neill, my friends and fellow Fredericksburg "rabble-rousers," for fighting the good fight, as well as stepping out to read their first romance novels—mine. Thanks to you all, I've learned that in the end it's not winning or losing that counts, but the friendships forged along the path.

Finally, to the fabulous folks at Medallion Press for their ongoing commitment to excellence in turning out yet another splendid package, as well as their patience in waiting for the manuscript to be "born." By way of embracing what my buddy Kim Castillo of Romance Novel TV calls "shameless self-promotion," I hope readers who enjoy Rourke and Kate's story will look for the previous trilogy books, *Vanquished* and *Enslaved*, on bookstore shelves. Excerpts are posted online at www.hopetarr.com.

Wishing you fairy-tale dreams come true . . .
Hope Tarr
Fredericksburg, Virginia
October 2007

PROLOGUE

ourke's Rules

   Rule Number One: ne'er let them see you cry. If they do, they'll only hit you that much harder, pound your body and will into bloody pulp.

   Rule Number Two: watch, listen, and wait. Sooner or later your luck is bound to change, so mind you keep a sharp eye out and a canny ear cocked.

   Rule Number Three: when your chance comes, take it. Cut loose and run as if hell's own hounds chased you. And dinna ever look back.

   Never look back.

CHAPTER ONE

"... the law is a ass ..." [sic]
—CHARLES DICKENS, *Oliver Twist*

London Central Criminal Court
Old Bailey Sessions House, 1875

From the front of the courtroom, the judge called out, "Bailiff, read the final case if you please."

Heads swung to the back of the room. The defendant, thirteen-year-old Patrick O'Rourke—Rourke—swallowed against the twist of fear knotting nooselike about his throat. Unlike the poor blubbering bugger called up for sentencing before him, who'd pissed a steady stream to the prisoner's stand and then promptly puked, he swore to hold onto his tears, his bladder, his breakfast—and above all, his dignity.

Never let them see you cry.

The bailiff nodded. "The defendant is one Patrick

O'Rourke, late of St. Giles parish but no known address. The accused is a minor child aged thirteen years or thereabouts, and orphaned. Two prior arrests, the first for vagrancy and the second for petty thievery; for the latter, he was sentenced and did receive fifty lashes."

Rourke gritted his teeth as he had six months before when they'd tied his hands to the whipping post and laid into his back. The humiliation and pain were branded on his brain, but lest he forget, the cross-hatching of white scars scourging his shoulders was there to remind him. The whipping had been good preparation for last night.

Seemingly satisfied, the judge nodded. "Let the prisoner come forward."

Having been brought up two times before, Rourke recognized his cue. He stumbled out into the aisle between benches, the robin's egg-sized lump beating a tattoo on his forehead, the scabbed blood forming a cowl over the left side of his face, the shouted questions ricocheting like cannon shot inside his brain.

"What made you set out to off the prime minister?"

I didn't know he was the PM, and I didna set out to off anybody.

"Are you in league with the Fenians?"

I'm not a Fenian. I'm not even Irish. I'm Scots! If I'm in league with anybody, it's Johnnie Black, but his game's running street scams, no politics.

"Did Disraeli's supporters put you up to this?"

Who the devil is Disraeli?

"Are you counting on the court to show mercy because of your youth?"

Mercy for the likes of me—fat chance of that!

Sweat broke out on his forehead. The room suddenly seemed to sway. He drew a steadying breath and willed himself to keep moving. By the looks of it, half of Fleet Street had turned out to pack the court, and he had too much pride to let himself be written up as a fainter. Finally he reached the front of the room. Stomach pitching, he sidestepped the puddle of vomit. Even with his left eye swollen shut, the latter was recognizable at close range as that morning's prison porridge. The bailiff grabbed hold of his sleeve and guided him up the few slippery steps to the prisoner's box. The hinged door slammed closed, sealing him in like a coffin.

"Order in the court. *Order,* I say!" The gavel's cracking down muted the din to a murmur. The judge settled back into his thronelike seat and reached up to right his crimped periwig. "Let the charges be read."

The bailiff cleared his throat. "Mr. Rourke stands accused of robbery and assault, possession of a deadly weapon with intent to harm, and possibly treason, though the latter charge remains to be answered."

Treason! He'd entered the courtroom fully expecting to forfeit some portion of his future to picking oakum, beating hemp, or working the water pump, but treason was a capital crime, a hanging offense. How was he to have known that the mark whose pocket he'd set out to pick the night before was none other than William Gladstone, the prime minister? Gladstone hadn't looked particularly ministerial. Traipsing about in the greenish haze of fog swathed in a top hat and caped greatcoat, he'd appeared much like any other well-heeled older gent out for a twilight stroll about St. Paul's, not the most advisable after-hours trek, but no doubt he'd reasoned the walking stick he carried would protect him.

He'd been wrong.

Rourke's partner in crime was Johnnie Black. The flash-house leader was a scarecrow of a man in his early twenties with a fringe of black hair that hung over his eyes in greasy strings and a gold front tooth he liked to polish with the pad of his thumb. They'd shadowed the mark for several streets, and then taken cover against a boarded-up building to size up the situation.

Johnnie turned to Rourke, his voice a low rasp. "I'll distract him, and you pinch his purse. Got it?"

Back flattened against the bricks, Rourke whispered back, "Piece o' cake."

And so it should have been. The mark was an older gent, tall and solid-looking, but then there were two of them to his one. The walking stick worried Rourke a bit, but with Johnnie running interference and his own nimble fingers, he'd be in and out before the gaffer even knew his pocket had been picked.

Seemingly satisfied, Johnnie shoved away from the

wall and beckoned for Rourke to follow. They started down the street, walking out in the open this time, Johnnie shoving his hands into his pockets and keeping up a low whistle.

They caught up with the mark at the lamppost, and Johnnie sidled forward. "Begging your pardon, guv, but my little brother and I were wondering if we might trouble you for the time." He followed the request with a toothsome smile.

The man didn't smile back. From beneath bushy brows, his gaze went from Johnnie's pocketed hands to Rourke, who barely reached his big "brother's" shoulder. Apparently deciding they were harmless, he reached inside his coat for his timepiece. Lifting it to the lamplight, he squinted as if struggling to make out the numbers on the face.

The action brought his coat pocket gaping. Rourke moved in, sliding his right *working* hand inside the gap. Wool tickled his palm. Using his index and middle fingers pincer-fashion, he clamped onto cold, smooth metal cinched about wadded paper—a money clip? Holding onto his prize, he started to withdraw.

The man's gloved hand snapped out, banding Rourke's wrist like a prison manacle. "What the devil do you think you're about?"

Rourke shot up his head. The thunder in that jutting brow had him trembling in his shoes. Next to him, Johnnie let out with, "Bugger it, we're screwed," and peeled off. Cold panic struck him. He was all alone.

"Leave off!"

Rourke ducked, ramming his head into the mark's middle. The man fell back. He hit the post hard, cracking his crown. His hat flew off, and he folded to the ground. Rourke stared down at the slumped figure at his feet. Knocked out cold—blimey, what luck! Home free, he picked up the dropped money clip and turned to run. A dripping sound stalled him. Blood? Dread threatened to turn his bowels to water. Crikey, had he just killed a man? Even though he was breaking the cardinal rule of street boys—no looking back and no going back, either—he had to know.

He swung around to have a look. "You all right, guv?"

The mark didn't answer. Blood ran down the side of his craggy face, trickling through his salt-and-pepper side whiskers and collecting in a puddle on the pavement. Rourke dropped down beside him and laid two fingers along the pulse point at the side of the whiskered neck. The thrumming beneath his fingers was steady and strong. Relief flooded him. He wasn't a murderer! For a moment, he considered celebrating his good fortune by nicking the timepiece, too, but then decided to let the gaffer keep it. If he snaffled it, he'd only have to turn it over to Johnnie, and the gang leader's desertion didn't sit well with him.

The blare of a bobby's whistle sent him shooting to his feet. His head whipped around. The two blue-suited policemen stood a street away, pointing. Shoving the money in his pocket, Rourke turned and ran. Huffing breaths and pounding footfalls sounded behind him. He picked up his pace, running faster than he'd ever run before, his lungs burning and his heart poised to pop. It was no use. They were closing in. His fleeting attack of conscience was about to cost him dearly. He'd broken the sacred rule of street boys.

Never look back.

Before he knew it, the pair was upon him. The heavyset one twisted his arms behind his back while the other cracked the club down upon his head, the butt opening up his forehead. Nausea hit like an invisible fist. He spiraled to the ground. Hard hands patted down his limbs, torso, and groin, and then slid between his legs and squeezed.

"Take your filthy mitts off me!"

Bright lights danced before his eyes. Warm stickiness ran down his face, lining his mouth with the taste of metal. Laughter rumbled above him. He tried getting up, but it was no use. They had him pinned. They yanked off his boots and then his stockings, and the object he'd until then forgotten all about clanged onto the pavement. His knife, they'd found it.

"Well, well, what have we here?" The gloating face of the club-wielding officer he recognized as Taggert hovered above him. "I have you red-handed, Rourke. This time it's sure to be prison stripes for you, my lad."

"Have you anything to say for yourself, Mr. Rourke?" The judge's voice called him back to the present.

Rourke thought for a moment. "The name's O'Rourke, milord." If he was doomed to swing, then at least let the papers print his name proper. "And I'm no traitor."

The judge's bland look suggested innocence was a trifle with which he preferred not to be troubled. He looked to the bailiff. "Before sentencing commences, is there any evidence to be considered?"

The bailiff replied, "We have the sworn testimony from the two police officers who made the arrest, as well as this knife recovered from the prisoner's shoe." He picked up a box from the evidence table.

The judge nodded, and the bailiff carried the box over to Rourke, tilting it so he might see inside. Rourke's blade lay on the green baize lining. He swallowed hard.

The judge shifted his gaze to Rourke. "Officer Taggert has gone on record as stating that this weapon is yours. Do you deny it?"

Heart thumping, Rourke hesitated. Perspiration broke out on his forehead and pricked his pits. He carried the knife for protection only. He'd never so much as shown it to a mark. He'd never set out to hurt anyone. Until last night, he never *had* hurt anyone.

"Is the blade yours or is it not? Speak up, boy, I haven't all day."

Knowing that his life well might depend on what answer he gave, Rourke fought to hold his voice steady and his mind clear. "Aye, milord, it is, but—"

"That will be all." The judge looked down on the court recorder seated below at the small side table. "Let the record reflect the accused answered in the affirmative."

"I am afraid I must object."

The deep-timbered voice drew a collective gasp from occupants of the courtroom. Heads swung about to the back of the room, Rourke's included. His mark from the night before, Prime Minister William Gladstone, strode down the aisle toward the witness stand, greatcoat billowing behind his tall form like a ship's sail. Other than a small bandage applied above his left eye where his brow must have scraped the sidewalk, the legendary statesman looked surprisingly hale.

Rourke cast the judge a sideways glance out of his still-working right eye. "Prime Minister, your presence does this court great honor, but it is not required. We have the sworn testimony from two trusted witnesses, officers of the Metropolitan Police Force, as well as the assailant's weapon, which he himself has just identified."

Gaining the witness stand, the prime minister stepped inside. "Be that as it may, I wish to bear witness for the defendant."

The judge's salt-and-pepper brows rose to reach the hairline of his wig. He leaned forward. "It is highly irregular for a victim to testify on his attacker's behalf."

Gladstone nodded, his craggy countenance betraying no emotion. "Highly irregular though it may be, it is

11

perfectly legal. The presumption of innocence until guilt is proved beyond a reasonable doubt is the golden thread that runs throughout the web of English criminal law, is it not so, my lord judge?"

The judge gave a grudging nod. "Very well, milord, pray proceed."

The prime minister folded his long arms behind his back as though preparing to address Parliament. "The lad did not attack me, as you say. He did, indeed, attempt to pick my pocket, but that is all. It was only after I set hands upon him that he did shove me. My coming to harm was pure accident, hence the charge of robbery must be reduced to the lesser crime of thievery. With me lying on the ground and my money clip in his possession, there was nothing to keep him from running to ground. Instead he elected to remain and render me aid—not to assassinate me as some today have alleged. It is the inherent morality and selflessness of that choice that brings me to speak on his behalf."

The judge scowled. "The boy is an orphan who makes his home in the St. Giles rookery among his fellow thieves and vagabonds. Reformation through incarceration is his only hope. Thrice now he has demonstrated he cannot be left to his own devices, that he must be removed from the society to which he is a danger."

Watching closely, Rourke saw Gladstone shake his head, then wince as though the gesture caused him pain. "Prison will only push him over the precipice to destruction. The company he keeps there will murder all that is good in him and nourish the little that is bad."

The judge fingered the sleeve of his robe. "In that case, pray tell us, what is it you propose, sir? Surely you do not suggest this court should simply set him free?"

"Let him be sent not to prison, my lord judge, but to school."

"School!"

School? Rourke had never attended a real school, but the Methodist do-gooders at the Christian Mission on Whitechapel Road held classes sometimes. Whenever he could, he sat in. The backless benches were hard on a bum, but the lesson part was all right. He liked the ones to do with numbers the best. His sums almost always came out right, and he could carry impressively large figures in his head.

Gladstone continued. "There is a Quaker orphanage in Kent known as Roxbury House. The institution has an impressive record of rehabilitating troubled boys and girls. I sit on the board of directors. Remand the boy to my custody, and I assure the court he will be found a place there."

The judge removed his spectacles and kneaded the bridge of his nose. "And if he runs away?"

"I will settle a surety of one thousand pounds upon him to vouchsafe that he will not."

A thousand pounds! Rourke felt his jaw drop. He could scarcely fathom such a sum, let alone himself worthy of the trust it implied.

He swung his gaze back to Gladstone. "I believe in this young man. I believe he possesses sufficient goodness and power of will to turn his life about. But to do so he must be given a chance."

An hour later, Rourke found himself unchained, released, and bundled into Gladstone's well-appointed carriage, the soothing scents of leather, cigars, and bay rum filling his nostrils, a wool carriage blanket wrapped about his shivering form. His benefactor sat on the opposite seat, his large gloved hands resting atop his gold-tipped walking stick. So far he'd not spoken since depositing Rourke inside.

Uneasy with the silence, Rourke looked from the thumbs he'd been twiddling. "I didn't mean for you to fall and crack your crown—honest."

Gladstone nodded. "I know that."

Rourke plucked at a loose thread in the blanket's weave. "Are you going to hit me? I shouldn't blame you if you did."

From beneath the bandaged brow, gunmetal-gray eyes honed in on his bloodied forehead and bruised face. "I rather suspect that in your short, miserable existence, you've been struck overmuch as it is."

Rather than answer and risk turning into a "rat," Rourke pulled back the leather window curtain and looked out. His left eye was badly blurred, but if he kept it closed, he could see well enough with his right. The snow-covered streets were far wider and straighter than the narrow, winding warrens of the East End. They must be headed westward to the fancy part of town where the toffs lived.

"How much farther is Roxbury House?"

"Roxbury House is in Kent." The prime minister's voice held a trace of surprise. "Tomorrow morning we shall take the train there together. Tonight we shall stay at my house."

Rourke let the curtain drop and turned back inside. "You're taking me to Number Ten Downing Street! *That* house!" Patrick O'Rourke to hobnob with the inhabitants of the ministerial residence, who would have thunk it!

The corners of the older man's mouth twitched in what might have been the beginnings of a smile. "Quite. Once there, my good wife shall see that you receive a wholesome meal, a hot bath, and dressings for those wounds. The future will look a good deal brighter after a night's rest in a bed all of your own."

Yawning, Rourke wasn't so certain about the bath part, but the bit about supper and a bed sounded grand. After a year of living off maggoty meat and bunking on a musty mattress with three other boys, Gladstone's description of the hospitality to come seemed like heaven on earth. Truth be told, he was more than ready to fall asleep where he was. Outside, the air was sharp as a knife, but cradled within the gently rocking carriage, he felt snug as a bug in a rug. Suddenly it seemed an effort to hold open even one of his eyes. He snuggled against the leather squab and considered that for the future, he might want to alter his rule of no looking back.

Looking back might not always be such a bad thing after all.

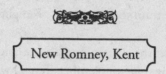

New Romney, Kent

Some thirty-odd leagues from London, on an estate set upon the wide, flat plains of the Romney Marsh, a little girl of a like age but markedly different birth was having her own trial of a day.

Straw and stable mud sticking to her riding boots, eleven-year-old Katherine—Kate—raced into her family's breakfast room, skidding to a stop at the foot of the linen-covered breakfast table. "Papa, Papa, someone's stolen Princess. She's not in her stall. She's not anywhere in the stable or in the paddock, either."

Arthur Lindsey, third Earl of Romney, lifted red-rimmed eyes from the raw egg he'd just dropped into his glass of beer and scowled. "Katherine, do cease cater-wauling. It's scarcely ten o'clock."

Kate halted at the table's foot. Loud sounds at any time of day always made Papa cross, but particularly so in the mornings. Displays of "vulgar emotion" did not set well with him, either. Chest heaving, she tried calming herself as best she might, given the monumental nature of the current calamity.

Princess was very precious to Kate. The mare had been a birthday gift, the last birthday her mummy would live to help her celebrate. Since Mummy had gone to live with the angels the summer before, the horse had been Kate's closest confidante, best friend, and principal playmate. She loved her little sister, Bea, certainly, but you couldn't really play with a toddler. Nor had she ever understood why so many other little girls fancied dolls. She'd found dressing and undressing them to be a bore, but then she scarcely cared for clothes herself. As for stuffed animals, why bother cuddling a cloth-covered bear or satin-sewn pup when there were so many real live animals to love who could love you back?

Be the weather fair or foul, every morning Kate sprang out of bed, pulled on her riding boots, and rushed out to the stable where she headed straight for Princess's stall. Kate couldn't imagine a lovelier start to the day— or a worse beginning to this one.

"I'm sorry, Papa, but Princess's gone missing. She's not in the stable or the paddock, either. Someone must have stolen her in the night. We have to do something, call in the magistrate, organize a search party, post a reward . . . *something* before the thieves get any farther away."

"Calm yourself, Katherine. The horse isn't stolen. It has been sold."

Sold! The unfathomable horror of that single word sent Kate staggering. "S-sold?" Her stomach couldn't have hurt any worse if he'd stood from the table and struck her.

Her father nodded, and then winced as if the minor movement must cause him pain. "I'm sorry, Katherine, but there was no help for it. I got into a . . . spot of trouble the other night, and family honor called for putting Princess up as collateral."

Family honor? "You wagered my horse in a card game?"

His gaze shuttered. "It is not the place of children to question their parents." A curtain of frost closed over his face. "I know you're fond of the beast, but a pony is property to be purchased and sold, not unlike this table upon which our breakfast is laid out or the chair upon which I sit."

Princess wasn't property, not to Kate's way of thinking. Property was an object, unthinking and unfeeling, whereas a horse was flesh and blood. And Princess was so smart. She'd learned all sorts of clever tricks over the past year. But she didn't only think. She felt things, too. Whenever Princess caught sight and scent of her mistress, she nickered and came trotting over, rubbing her head against Kate and sometimes even trying to groom her. Imagining how frightened and bewildered her friend must be feeling now, Kate caught her reflection in the pier glass in time to see a tear squeeze out of her eye and slide down her cheek.

Even knowing she was fighting a losing battle—grown-ups always had the upper hand no matter how canny and capable a child might be—Kate's sense of justice compelled her to go on. "If that's true, then she's my property, not yours. You and Mummy gave her to me. Taking back a gift is wrong."

"That will be quite enough." Papa's red-rimmed eyes hardened, and his mouth thinned. "You would have outgrown her in another year or two. Once our . . . finances are more robust, we shall go to London and take a drive to Tattersall's in Knightsbridge Green. You may select any mare you fancy." Apparently considering the matter settled, he raised his breakfast pint, tipped it back, and downed the ovum in a single swallow.

"But I don't want any horse. I want Princess."

Gagging, he set the glass aside. "You are being deliberately obstinate. A horse is a horse is a horse."

Not to me, Papa.

Proud though Kate was, for Princess's sake she was prepared to plead. She edged toward his chair and caught at his sleeve. "Buy her back, Papa, please do. If you do, I'll be the best, most obedient daughter in the whole world, I promise."

He shrugged her off and reached for the napkin to blot his mouth. "I'm afraid it's too late."

Too late meant Princess was, indeed, gone. The hollow feeling in Kate's stomach matched that in her heart. There was nothing left for her to lose. She stared up at her father, his elbows planted on the table and head held between his slender white hands, and felt hatred curl like a garter snake in the pit of her belly.

"I hate you! I hate you! I *hate* you. I wish you were the one dead and not Mummy." If he was, Kate felt certain it wouldn't be the angels he lived among.

Upset as she was, it wasn't temper that compelled her to tell her father she hated him. It was the truth. Her mother wouldn't stay out all night getting into "spots of trouble," and then come home afterward reeking of cigar smoke and perfume and another bad smell that belonged to a grown-up drink called brandy.

He slammed a fist atop the table, sending the empty place setting rattling. "Katherine, these tantrums will not be tolerated. Such public displays of spleen are not only unladylike, they are common. Go to your room and do not dare come out until I say you may—*now!*"

Kate turned and ran from the breakfast room, into the front hall, and up the stairs. Halfway up, she tripped, coming down hard on her knees. The bruising pain felt right somehow, solid. She pulled herself up by her hands and scrambled to the top, nearly plowing into the sweet-faced, blond chambermaid, Hattie, polishing the landing rail.

"Miss Kathy, you gave me a fright. Are you all right?"

Normally Kate would have stopped for a chat—they were friends, after all—but today she pushed past. She didn't stop running until she reached her bedroom at the back of the house. She entered, slamming the door behind her. A shriek drew her attention out the window, curtains fluttering in the spring breeze. Her window looked out onto the stable, paddock and pasture beyond, the main reason she'd years ago chosen this room as hers. She hurried over and yanked the chintz aside.

Her heart lurched. A groomsman wearing dark green livery trimmed with yellow piping emerged from the pasture, pulling Princess in tow. Even from a distance, Kate saw the pony's posture had a forlorn air, ears flattened toward the back and tail tucked. She dug her nails into her palms, helpless to do more than watch as the man walked Princess down the drive leading to the main road. Several times the horse dug in her heels and turned her head back, but the groom jerked on her bridle, forcing her forward. A stranger looking on might have dismissed the horse's behavior as obstinacy, but Kate knew full well what it signified.

Her friend was searching for her to say good-bye.

Kate hadn't cried since the day Bea was born. Her mummy had laid the squalling bundle in her arms and made her promise to be both mother and sister. Now she balled her hands into fists and scrunched them against her eyes, thinking to stop the tears from flowing like the little boy in the fairy tale who'd plugged the hole in the dyke with his thumb. It was no use. Water spurted from her eyes and slid down her cheeks and neck, the salted droplets dissolving into her collar. Her throat felt raw, and her chest burned as though she held her breath underwater and was coming to the end of her endurance.

Only Kate wasn't coming to the end, not nearly. She might be drowning in sorrow and thrashing in fury, but she was only at the beginning. Sobbing, she fisted a hand into her hair and tugged hard, fighting the urge to turn her futile anger inward and rip out great golden brown chunks.

I'll never forget you, Princess, and I'll never stop loving you. Not now, not ever. And I'll never forgive you, Papa, or forget. Not now. Not ever.

Some time later, calm descended. She scrubbed her fists across her eyes and turned away from the window, her decision made. Never again would she open herself to such heavy heartache, such wrenching loss. Whether Papa won at cards or lost no longer mattered. She wouldn't be accompanying him to Tattersall's no matter how "flush" he might be. She was done with horses, done with losing precious things she loved, done with loving period. The cost was too dear, the result too painful to bear repeating.

The lesson, bitterly learned, would follow Kate into the ensuing years.

When you loved someone, they always, *always* went away.

CHAPTER TWO

> "And I have thrust myself into this maze,
> Happily to wive and thrive as best I may."
> —WILLIAM SHAKESPEARE, Petruchio,
> *The Taming of the Shrew*

Covent Garden Opera House
February 1890

Rourke squinted out into the ballroom where guests were penned in like so many Shetland sheep. "You swore she'd be here."

Stepping back amongst his friends, Harry and Gavin, he yanked at his collar, the starched points of which had been stabbing into either side of his jaw for the past hour. If seen, the gesture would betray his commonness, but it couldn't be helped. It was hot. Hot as hell, or best make that hot as *Hades* as his newly fashionable former Roxbury House friends, Gavin and Harry, had schooled him to say. The enormous crystal chandelier suspended overhead wasn't solely to blame. Heat from incandescent burners spilled out from the tiered opera boxes, wilting the elaborate floral arrangements and glittering guests, thickening the air with the rank sweetness of dying flowers and ripening flesh, the stench calling to mind the undertaker's front parlor where once he'd worked as a mourning "mute."

Since leaving the Roxbury House orphanage at sixteen, he'd worked any number of menial jobs—ditch digger, chimney sweep, and lastly railway navvie. The hard labor had broadened his shoulders and strengthened his back, as well as his will to make something of himself. When he'd entered the pub's prize fight on a lark and stepped over the ropes to duke it out with the reigning contender, no one, including himself, had expected him to hold out for the requisite three minutes. He'd not only held. He'd won.

What irony that his present abject misery owed to how very far he'd risen in life. And yet at times such as this, when he found himself rubbing elbows with jewel-festooned females and their mustached husbands and beaux, the latter sporting shiny gold watch fobs and fat money clips, he felt the telltale tingling creeping into his palms and the fingers of his right hand, his *working* hand, starting up with the old familiar flexing jig.

Forcing his fingers still, he reminded himself he didn't need to be that person anymore. He *wasn't* that person. And if the prospect of a pearl-studded brooch or gold tie clasp still had the power to make his hands prickle, the delectable yet-to-be-met "she" brought another very particular part of him to life with the beginnings of a long-unsatisfied ache.

"She" was Lady Katherine Lindsey, daughter to the Earl of Romney and one of London's preeminent Professional Beauties, young ladies of rank who condescended to allow their pocket-sized photographic portraits, or *cartes postales,* to be displayed for sale in shops such as his photographer friend, Harry's. She was also the woman whom the day before Rourke had announced to his two friends he meant to marry.

Harry Stone, known to the public as Hadrian St. Claire, sidestepped the protruding plumes of the grand dame in front of him and directed his gaze out onto the milling crowd. "And so she shall. She may have arrived already."

Standing on Rourke's opposite side, his barrister friend, Gavin Carmichael, added his calming voice to the fray. "Mind how long it took us to get through that receiving line. Guests are still arriving. Have patience, Rourke. If she's here, we'll find her."

If Rourke lacked patience, and admittedly he did, it was with good cause. After years in Scotland, he'd come back to London with one purpose: to find a blue-blooded Englishwoman for his wife. He wasn't looking to make a love match. That would take longer than the fortnight he had left to woo and win. From what he could tell, like Happily Ever After endings, love was the stuff of fairy tales. Once he found a woman of proper pedigree, pleasing looks, and breeding age, he would consider his search ended and his posterity well served. A highborn mother meant that his future children would never be on the receiving end of "the cut direct," that canny knack aristocrats had for looking through you as though you were made of glass, *dirty* glass, and then flaring their nostrils and curling their lips as horses did when they smelled something rank.

In the social whirlwind of the past two weeks, he'd so far encountered prim debutantes, brash American heiresses, and randy widows; the latter promising to provide any number of carnal delights. None of them had moved him to give more than a glance or smile in passing, certainly not a proposal of marriage. Determined though he was not to go home empty-handed, he couldn't stretch out his stay indefinitely. He'd neglected his railway company in Edinburgh far too long. The railway business was as cutthroat as any street scam, the threat from rival companies calling for constant vigilance, the opportunities for swallowing up the smaller fish boundlessly lucrative.

Discouraged, the other day he'd set out for a wee stroll, his meandering footsteps leading him to bustling Parliament Square. That was where he encountered "her," or rather her likeness in the form of a pocket-sized hand-tinted photograph resting atop the velvet-covered shelving inside Harry's shop window. The photograph was shot in profile, the woman's slender hands resting demurely in her lap, her wavy, honey-colored hair drawn up to display the sweet contour of high-boned cheek, lush mouth, and softly rounded chin. Unfortunately the shop was shut up, the shades drawn, the sign turned to closed. Rourke had stood still as a statue in the bracing cold, his face pressed up to the glass, his good eye employed in memorizing every detail of that lovely fine-boned face.

Once he got back to Gavin's flat, he hadn't lost any time in asking after her.

"*There's a photograph of a young woman in Harry's shop window. Dark eyes, light brown hair, hands folded in her lap. Do you know her?*"

Gavin had looked up from his open copy of the *London Times*. "*That would be Katherine Lindsey. She's one of Harry's PBs, Professional Beauties, and by far his best seller. They've worked out an arrangement where she sits for him exclusively. Don't scowl so. It's all done in the best of taste, and for the most part, the husbands don't mind.*"

"*She's married, then?*" On the walk back to Gavin's, he'd tried tempering his enthusiasm. For all he knew, his mystery lady might very well be married, engaged, or otherwise beyond his touch. Still, hearing the confirmation sent his hopes sinking like a body weighted with stones tossed into the Thames.

Gavin shook his head. "*If you bothered to read anything beyond financial reports, you'd know the lady has made something of a reputation for herself. She's been engaged three times, and each time she has cried off before the banns were read."*

Intrigued as much by her story as her face, he'd found himself making excuses to stop by Harry's shop for a second, third, and even a *fourth* look. Finally he'd swallowed his pride, plunked down his guinea, and purchased a copy of the portrait. It sat propped upon his bedside table, hers the last face he looked upon before sleeping and the first upon rising.

But there was no substitute for the genuine article. The opportunity to encounter Lady Katherine in the flesh had brought him here tonight. Apparently she had some affiliation as a volunteer for the Tremayne Dairy Farm Academy, the charitable recipient organization of that night's ball. Reckoning that the dance card of a beauty, and a "professional" one at that, would be among the first to be filled, he'd taken up strategic position on the periphery of the dance floor.

"That's her over there." Harry's voice brought him back to the present. "Standing amidst the half-dozen penguins in Lord Dutton's set. You can't miss her."

Excitement gripped Rourke. He felt like a child on the eve of all those bountiful Christmases he'd heard of but never once known. Craning his neck, he scanned the ballroom, the muzzy figures melding into one glittering mass of jewels, plump bare shoulders, and swirling satins and silks. But the trouble with rich people was they tended to speak, move, and dress so very much alike.

Exasperated, he turned back to his two friends. "Point her out to me."

Gavin spoke up, "It's a society ball, Patrick, not Billingsgate Market. Pointing is not quite the thing."

Harry let out a huff. "Hang your pride and put your glasses on, man."

That was an easy enough recommendation for Harry to make. Handsome Harry, they'd called him back in their Roxbury House days, and with good reason. Blessed with height, blond good looks, and two working eyes, Harry had been coaxing girls out of their knickers before he was old enough to shave. Likewise, tall, dark, aristocratic Gavin had drawn his fair share of female admiration since they'd entered the ballroom. Barrel-chested, blunt-featured, and with a shock of auburn hair that no amount of Makassar oil could seem to tame, Rourke's rough-hewn looks were less likely to recommend him to a delicate London lassie like Lady Katherine. Having a dodgy eye to boot hardly seemed fair, but certainly he wasn't the only man in the room wearing glasses. He slid a gloved hand inside his tailcoat's inner breast pocket and pulled out the detested spectacles. Shoving them on his crooked bridge of a broken nose, he leaned forward.

Like an oyster opening to reveal the pearl sheltered within, the clutch of evening-attired "penguins" parted, bringing their prize into view. Lady Katherine Lindsey peered out from her sanctum and smothered a yawn behind her slender gloved hand.

The first thing that struck him was how very tiny she was. Barely reaching the shoulders of the men ranged about her, she was also slight as a fairy. Following on that thought was that she was far prettier than her picture. Harry might be one of the best photographic portraitists in London, but the photograph he'd taken didn't begin to do her justice. But then, how could an image imprinted on paper and tinted by hand begin to capture the creaminess of that pale oval face; the wicked, willful flash of those dark eyes; and the wonderful mobility of her lush mouth, berry ripe and fashioned for kissing? The only conceivable flaw he could find was her nose. Seen full face, it was thin about the bridge and slightly longish. An aristocrat's nose, no doubt it tended to point north, and yet the delicate pinkish tip begged to be tweaked—and kissed.

She must have sensed him staring. Shifting to the side, she cast her gaze over one gentleman's shoulder and their eyes met. The jolt of sexual awareness struck like a thunderbolt splitting a placid springtime sky, the tingling heat sliding down his spine and settling in his cock. Suddenly glad of the concealing crush, he lifted his champagne flute in silent salute and then knocked back a sip. Warm as piss, just as he'd known it would be, and flat, too. Holding her eye, he choked down the froth and then made a deliberately droll face.

The corners of her mouth lifted ever so slightly upwards, affording him a flash of straight white teeth and two devilish dimples bracketing her bottom lip. As if remembering herself, she feigned a yawn and covered her hand over her mouth once more, only this time Rourke knew it wasn't boredom she sought to smother. It was a chuckle.

"I think she fancies you, mate." Harry nudged him in the ribs, but Rourke ignored him, refusing to be distracted.

Emboldened, he sent his gaze on a lazy downward glide, the shadowed hollow of her slender throat inviting mouths and tongues to linger. Her cream-colored gown was of obvious quality though simple in style, the décolletage low but not indecently so, just low enough to allow a teasing glimpse of cleavage. Elbow-high white satin opera gloves sheathed arms that were both slender and shapely.

Imagining those lovely arms wrapping about his neck as he peeled away her gown, he asked, "What's she like?"

He sensed Harry shrug. "She has a reputation as a shrew, and honestly earned from what I hear, though she's civil enough to me. Always keeps her pose without any fuss or fidgeting, though she's not much of a talker. Brings her younger sister along to our sittings, no doubt to keep things on the up and up, not that she need bother."

Irrational jealousy caused Rourke to look away at last. He stole a sideways glance at the handsome photographer, but his friend's attention was fixed not on Lady Katherine, but instead on a tall, curvy brunette sipping champagne and chatting to several goggle-eyed gentlemen on the far side of the room. Rourke recalled Harry earlier introducing her as Caledonia Rivers, not a PB, but one of his commissioned portraiture subjects, as well as a leader in the women's suffrage movement.

Harry scraped a gloved hand through his silver-blond hair and scowled. "She's off-limits, Rourke."

Ordinarily Rourke's tastes ran to buxom women with big breasts and long legs. His former mistress, Felicity, was as tall as he, as well as a proper armful. Striking though Miss Rivers was, his thoughts kept turning back to the pocket-sized Venus on the other side of the room.

Happy to have his handsome friend's interest elsewhere engaged, he clapped Harry on the shoulder. "Dinna fash, man. Bonny as your Miss Rivers is, I've set my cap elsewhere."

Setting his cap for Lady Katherine was but the first step in winning her. In his hard-scrabble experience, winning anything meant fighting for it. Whether he found himself in a London opera house, a pugilist's ring, or a railway laborer's hut sleeping three to a bed, jungle law prevailed.

He divided his gaze between his two friends. "If you'll excuse me, there's a lady who's promised me the next dance . . . only she doesna know it yet."

Gavin and Harry exchanged amused looks. Gavin's

dark brows rose. "Pardon me for asking, but since when do you dance?"

It was a reasonable question. What little grace he possessed was centered in his nimble-fingered hands; otherwise, he'd been born with two left feet.

Rourke grinned and handed Harry his champagne flute. "Since now."

Blood pumping as though he was once more ramping up to step into the ring, Rourke shouldered his way through the throng. From the pit, the orchestra struck up a waltz. He smiled. The dance had three features to recommend it to a tangle-toed clod such as him: it required moving in step with only one other person, its tempo was slow, and it afforded a man the chance to lay actual hands upon a woman in public without being slapped.

Approaching his quarry, he ran his gaze over the competition, assessing his most likely point of entry. Of the six men assembled, he recognized two by name. The tall, lanky blond was Henry, Lord Dutton, and his porcine and prematurely balding young friend was Sir Cecil Wesley. The latter's slouch betrayed him as the weak link.

Aware of Lady Katherine watching him, Rourke summoned a sunny smile. "Good evening, gentlemen, milady. I trust there are no objections to my joining you?" Without awaiting an answer, he clapped Wesley on the shoulder. Fingers sinking into the young baronet's sponginess, he moved him aside and stepped forward, thrusting himself dead center into the circle.

He made Lady Katherine what he hoped was a serviceable bow. "Lady Katherine." Straightening, he caught a whiff of her scent, orange blossoms and some other fresh but as yet unidentified fragrance that had him thinking of sunshine and balmy spring breezes. Ignoring his rivals' furious faces, he honed his gaze on her coolly curious brown eyes. "I've come to claim my dance, milady." *I've come to claim you.*

For a few seconds, her aloof mask slipped, and he caught a flicker of surprise in her eyes, the pupils widening ever so slightly. She hesitated, glancing down at the arm he extended. "Yes, I do believe this dance is promised to you."

Lord Dutton scowled, his bottom lip protruding like a sulky child whose gingerbread was about to be taken away. "But how can that be? This is the first waltz of the evening." He turned to Lady Katherine. "As I'm sure you will recollect, I bespoke this dance when I brought you your glass of punch."

Tiny though she was, she held her ground. "You are mistaken, sir." She circumvented Dutton and came to Rourke, laying her small, gloved hand lightly atop his arm. "Gentlemen, if you will excuse us." The latter was not spoken as a question.

Chest swelling, Rourke led her away toward the dance floor, his triumph a trillion times more potent than snaffling a watch or pinching a purse. In this case he'd stolen something far more precious, a diamond of the first water, a pearl beyond price, straight out from under the toffee noses of his supposed betters.

As soon as they were out of earshot, she leaned in and whispered, "I suppose I should thank you for rescuing me. Dutton and his set, ugh! What a lot of bloody bores." She angled her face to his profile. "By the by, who the hell are you?"

For a lady born, she certainly cursed a blue streak, not that he was one to mind. "Patrick O'Rourke, though my friends call me Rourke. Actually, my enemies call me Rourke, too, as well as do my business colleagues. Come to think of it, everyone does. I'm Scottish," he added for no particular reason.

"So I gathered from your burr."

He nodded, unsure of whether to feel complimented or put out. "The *O* in my surname confuses some. My father was Scots-Irish from Ulster, but my mother was Scots born and bred. Her people are in Cromartyshire. That's in the far Highlands." Jaysus, they hadn't even reached the dance floor and already he was blathering like a dimwit.

Lady Katherine sent him a cross look. "Yes, yes, I am well acquainted with the location of the Scottish counties. No doubt you surmise I am one of those silly females content to wallow in utter ignorance of geography, but I assure you, I possess both a globe and a map of the British Empire."

Her snappishness stunned him. He hadn't pegged her as silly or ignorant. That she apparently consulted maps didn't unduly surprise him. He opened his mouth to say as much, but instead something very different came out. "You don't much care for people, do you?"

She shrugged, which did interesting things to the creamy flesh edging out of her bodice. Small though she was, she wasn't small everywhere. "I find people in general to be quite tolerable. It's arrogance and ill manners I cannot abide."

He opened his mouth to remark upon the questionable wisdom of pots calling kettles black, but by that time they'd reached the thronged dance floor. She let go of his arm. Lumbering behind her, Rourke's broad shoulders clipped couples on either side. Clearing a space for them, he turned to take her in his arms. It was then that he was minded of the proverbial fly in the ointment.

He couldn't actually dance.

She looked up at him and cleared her throat. "You did invite me to dance, did you not?"

Sweat pricked Rourke's brow, and his glasses fogged from heat, but this time he couldn't blame the overabundance of people and lamps. His arms hung at his sides as if once more weighted with prison irons. "Aye, I did."

She let out a sigh as though suddenly weary. For a heart-stopping few seconds, he thought she might turn on her heel and walk away, leaving him to stand there alone, a buffoon, a laughingstock. Instead, she reached down, clasped one of her hands about his wrist, and carried it around to rest on the small of her slender back.

"I won't bite, I promise." Under other circumstances, Rourke considered a well-placed nibble to be a most pleasing occurrence, but he held off on voicing such a naughty thought so soon and instead concentrated on his stiff legs and shuffling feet. "Place your other hand in mine—yes, the *right* hand, there's the way. Now all we need do is to carry off some semblance of keeping time with the music. One-two-three, step in, step close. Mind how we are making a small circle?"

Staring down at their toe-to-toe feet, her slipper-shod ones making his seem like elephant hooves, Rourke nodded. Her waist beneath his hand felt supple and impossibly small, the warmth from her silk-sheathed skin pouring into his palms.

The lady's scowl confirmed she was not pleased to find herself in the arms of an amateur. "Do try not to lift your feet quite so very high. We are not cantering, Mr. O'Rourke, we are dancing, or at least attempting to. The proper move is more of a glide than a step."

How on earth did a woman who barely reached his shoulder still manage the trick of seeming to stare down the tip of her nose at him? Finding his voice at last, he asked, "Will there be any further instructions, milady?"

"Just one. You needn't squeeze my hand like a tourniquet. I assure you, I've no notion of escaping."

He grinned. She was warming to him, he could tell.

"You don't?"

"No." Expression pained, she shook her head. "Your foot upon mine has me most securely pinned."

He lifted his foot, and her expression eased. "Bullocks. I mean, forgive me, milady. You're so slight, I barely felt—"

She looked up at him and released another sigh, her cool, peppermint-laced breath wafting up to kiss his cheek. "Pray do not apologize. I find apologies to be bloody boring."

Rourke found himself fighting a smile. "You're a very good teacher." He was looking forward to teaching her a trick or two, only *off* the dance floor, but there was a whole fortnight of wooing to be got through before that happy event occurred.

She shrugged, apparently oblivious to his carnal thoughts. "It's one thing for you to look a fool, but I can't very well have you making me look foolish, now can I?" Caught up in staring at the kissable tip of her nose, he stumbled, clipping what must be her big toe. "Ouch! You really don't dance, do you?"

"This is only my second go at it, actually. Seems like a great deal of trouble." Not to mention potentially crippling to his partners.

"Why did you ask me, then? You needn't have. I was hardly in danger of turning into a wallflower. Dutton was correct. This dance was promised to him."

"Would you believe I fancy meeting pretty girls, and dancing seems the best way to go about it, at least in London?"

She hoisted her chin. "I'm hardly a girl. I'll be seven-and-twenty in another few months."

So she was only about two years younger than he. That surprised him. Still what surprised him most was that she'd so readily owned her age. Most women on the shady side of twenty-five would sooner lie down on a bed of nails than admit it. And yet she still satisfied his third requirement: she was young enough to breed. With the first two requirements well met, Rourke considered he had a green light to move forward with his goal.

Eager to get on with the wooing, he said, "By the by, has anyone ever told you that you have verra beautiful eyes?"

She rolled her eyes at him, her *beautiful* eyes, and then shook her head. "As a point of fact, sir, I have been told so many times, not because they are particularly handsome—they are plain brown and quite ordinary, in fact—but because complimenting a lady's eyes is the sort of trite blandishment gentlemen seem to think we fancy hearing."

He smiled, secretly pleased she wasn't easily won. "On the contrary, they are neither brown nor plain. Amber, I think, for sure it is I'm a dragonfly caught up in the sticky resin of your gaze."

"The sticky resin of my gaze!" She threw back her head and laughed, the rich throaty sound putting him in mind of coarsely woven silk. "Tell me, are the girls in

Scotland snared by such tripe?"

Careful to keep the requisite six inches between them, if only to keep his cock stand from brushing her belly, he said, "Some are, enough I suppose. In your case, however, any compliment I give is no less than true. My mate, Harry, scarcely did you justice."

Looking down on her upturned face, he could appreciate all the dazzling little details the photograph had missed or muted—the thick fringe of smoky lashes rimming her almond-shaped eyes, the single beguiling freckle touching the top of her upper lip, the small white scar riding her left cheekbone, which he suddenly very badly wanted to lick.

That got her attention. "How are you acquainted with Mr. St. Claire?"

"We spent part of our childhood together."

After Gavin's grandfather had surfaced to reclaim him and their friend Daisy had been adopted by an older theatrical couple, their Roxbury House Orphans' Club had halved to two, he and Harry. Though they'd sometimes fought like cats, the future photographer was the closest he had to a brother.

"In London?"

He shook his head. "No, in Kent, near Maidstone."

He paused, wondering if he might have given too much away. It was early days as far as wooing was concerned, and it wouldn't do for her to find out he was an orphan. And yet, of all the places he'd so far lived, some more than once—London, Edinburgh, Kent, and now Linlithgow in Scotland—Roxbury House was the only one he ever thought of as home.

"I grew up in Kent, as well." Lady Katherine's voice pulled him back to the present. "Our seat is in Romney."

"Your father is an earl, is he not?"

She nodded. "The peerage isn't terribly old. My father's only the third Earl of Romney. It started out as a courtesy title, a life peerage granted to my great-uncle for some dubious personal service rendered to the Crown and then . . . Oh, well, it scarcely matters now. Suffice it to say, the Lindsey name is very old, very proper." She said the last bit while making a face as though to suggest that while her family was proper, she was less so.

"Where do you bide in town?"

"I beg your pardon?"

"You keep a house in town, do you not? What is your direction?"

Her gaze shuttered. "Sir, must I remind you that we've not yet been introduced. You should have had your friend, Mr. St. Claire, speak for you. Even a Scotsman must have some sense of protocol. There are rules about these things, you know."

He bent his head to the soft velvet of her cheek. "Ah, well, rules are a hard thing for a rough fellow like me to hold in mind when I've a bonny lass in my arms, the heat of her skin pouring into my palms, and the scent from her hair filling my nostrils and leading my thoughts astray to all manner of foolish fancies."

It was her turn to stumble. "You are beyond forward, sir. I would be well within my rights to slap you."

He grinned, enjoying himself more by the moment. Not only did Lady Katherine meet his requirements for a bride in terms of title, looks, and breeding ability, but she exceeded them. Unlike the other milksop females he'd encountered in the past weeks, she had a mind all her own.

"Aye, you would be, but you willna. Slapping me would cause what you highbrow folk fear above all else: a scene."

She didn't seem to have an answer for that. They completed another turn, and then the waltz segued to a close. He let his hand linger in the curve of her back a moment or so after the music stopped. Imagining holding her thus the first time he lowered her onto their marriage bed, he withdrew and stepped back.

He led her to the edge of the floor. "I claim the next waltz as mine whether you've promised it to that dolt, Dutton, or not." He would gladly claim the next dance as his and every one thereafter, though he didn't think bravado alone would carry him through the complicated figures of a reel.

She opened her mouth as if to answer with some cheeky retort when her gaze snared something beyond his left shoulder. The beguiling mischief drained from her face, a darker emotion—fear, horror—taking its place.

"No," she whispered, and for whatever reason he didn't think she addressed him.

He took a step toward her. Improper though it was, he laid his hand on her arm. "Lady Katherine, Kate. . ."

Her eyes found his. Like a subject of mesmerism coming to from a trance, she blinked and then shook her head as if to clear it. "Delightful though it was to have my head planted in your breastbone and your feet flattened atop mine, I cannot dance with you again."

Just when he'd fancied she was warming to him, she turned chill as ice. "And why is that?"

She glared up at him. "A lady is not required to give a gentleman her reason, nor is it his right to demand one. I bid you good evening, sir."

Before he could think what answer to make to that, she curtsied, turned, and swept away.

Heart hammering, Kate exited the dance floor. She felt the Scotsman's angry emerald eyes stabbing like twin sabers into her back and quickened her pace. Reaching the doors leading out to the lobby, she shot a glance over her shoulder to make certain he hadn't followed her. She was equal parts disappointed and relieved when she saw that he had not.

Deserting a gentleman on the dance floor counted as

abominably rude even for her. For a few mad snatches of seconds, she actually considered retracing her steps to apologize. Kate Lindsey apologizing to a man, or at least considering it! Dear Lord, what had come over her? Manners or the lack thereof aside, she hadn't the luxury of time. For once, *this* once, she wouldn't have minded dallying.

He wasn't so much handsome as . . . imposing. When he'd approached her to dance, the virility he'd exuded made the other men about her seem suddenly puny and weak. For a brief moment when he'd held her close, she'd feared she might swoon from being pressed against the force of his muscled heat. Once her hand had accidentally brushed his bicep, and she'd felt her knees go weak. Until now, she had thought such an overblown reaction only occurred between the covers of romantic novels. If any real-life woman had described having a similar experience, Kate would have been quick to proclaim her a dolt.

But the reality could not be denied. Patrick O'Rourke had made a most definite impression upon her. Rough manners, quaint speech, and utter lack of dancing ability aside, she was powerfully, dangerously, *carnally* attracted to him. When she'd first taken his hands and placed them upon her, she'd suddenly found it hard to breathe, though her laces were but loosely tied. Looking up at him, she'd had the sudden urge to strip off her gloves and run her fingers through his thick auburn hair, to fall into the emerald sea of his eyes and surrender her lips and all the rest of her to his will.

She'd wanted to kiss him in plain view.

In the grip of that shocking, titillating thought, she admitted that never before had she felt such a powerfully physical reaction. Even the diamond winking at her from his left ear appealed, if only because it made her think of a pirate—bold and sexual and dangerous. When he'd called her pretty and remarked upon her eyes, she'd pretended affront, but she'd been secretly pleased. No doubt he made a habit of doling out such blandishments to women all too ready to lap up his praise like hungry cats presented with a dish of cream. And yet the manner in which he'd run his gaze over her, his eyes darkening to deep emerald, she could almost believe he'd meant it, if only a little. And to have finally found a man who could not only flatter but banter, what bliss!

But like all good things in life, *hers* at least, the exhilarating interlude had ended far too soon. She'd chanced to look over Mr. O'Rourke's shoulder—his thrillingly broad, powerful shoulder—and glimpsed her father leaving the ballroom with his crony, Lord Haversham. She'd pulled the pair from any number of gaming clubs that past year. A few hours in Lord H's dubious company invariably left her father's purse lightened and her burdens increased tenfold.

As always, duty took precedence over pleasure. She had to find her father. His departure from the ballroom in the company of that particular gentleman could only mean one thing—trouble of a particularly costly kind. Fortunately she didn't have to waste valuable time wondering where they would go. Having volunteered on the event-organizing committee, she recalled that a casino meant to be a miniature of the famous gaming rooms at Monte Carlo had been set up as part of the evening's program of entertainment.

In the case of her scapegrace parent, anticipating the worst wasn't paranoia. It was a survival skill hard learned over the years. They'd enjoyed a full month's respite, during which her father had kept his promise and stayed away from the gaming halls. She'd even made some small headway in paying the monthly household accounts. But if she didn't wrest him from Haversham in the next few minutes, the vicious cycle would commence anew, and all her hard work would be for naught—again. Her father would pick up where he and Haversham had left off months ago—the heavy drinking, the deep play, and the staggering sums lost. Invariably it would fall to her to come up with a plan for setting the situation to rights, for raising the required funds quietly, discreetly. She'd been most creative so far, but still, she was not a magician. She couldn't make money grow on trees or pull it rabbit-fashion out of a hat, more was the pity.

Outside in the lobby, she flagged down a passing server and asked for directions, then headed right down the sconce-lit hall. By the time she reached the suite of rooms transformed into a casino for the night, she was herself once more, Capable Kate, perennially out-of-sorts shrew who could plot and plan as bloodlessly as any man.

She stood on the threshold, surveying the scene inside. Sconces were anchored at intervals on the flocked wallpaper, and a cloud of cigar smoke hung low over the room. Across the carpet, a dealer in a white shirt and silk striped vest presided over a Trente et Quarante table, doling out red and black chips to the clutch of dark-suited gentlemen ranged about the brass rail. A roulette wheel occupied center stage, presided over by a pretty young woman in black feathers, opera gloves, and a low-cut gown, her throat glittering with a collar of paste diamonds and pearls; otherwise Kate was the only female in the room.

Aware of heads turning her way, she hesitated, and then, remembering herself, hoisted her chin. Tonight was hardly the first time she'd entered a gaming establishment with the purpose of finding her father and leading him out. In the present case, gaming was but one of several entertainments offered, the guests all top-drawer, the monies marked for charity, the surrounds imminently more respectable than the seedy, smoke-filled gaming halls on Leicester Square; the latter she'd been obliged to enter more times than she cared to count.

"Can I assist you, miss?" Kate turned to see the tuxedo-clad casino clerk, betting book in hand, draw up beside her. "If you wish to take part in the play, the entry fee is twenty pounds."

Twenty pounds. Kate mentally calculated the quantities of mutton chops, cartons of eggs, and bottles of milk twenty pounds would purchase. The wages for Hattie, their maid-of-all work, amounted to a mere twelve pounds per year inclusive of bed and board, and even that pittance was embarrassingly overdue.

Still, she couldn't find it in her heart to begrudge Lady Stonevale's fallen girls the funds to make a fresh start in life. The charity, for which she served as a volunteer, was near and dear to her heart. She only hoped her father hadn't gambled away their futures to the point where she and Bea would have to seek out places in the parish poorhouse for themselves.

"Players agree to divide any winnings equally with the house, which in the present case is Lady Stonevale's charity school." The clerk's explanation ended Kate's woolgathering. "May I conduct you to a private table, or would you prefer to try your luck at the roulette wheel?"

Spotting her father at one of the circular card tables, she shook her head. "Neither, I'm afraid, but thank you."

She started down the narrow aisle between tables, navigating her way around the butler circulating with a tray of brandy snifters and a box of cigars. Coming up on her father's table, she took in the pile of chips heaped upon the green baize-covered tabletop and felt her spine stiffen and her hackles rise. She lifted her gaze and locked eyes with Lord Haversham. The last time her father had been lured into deep play by his dissolute friend, her mother's pearl choker had gone missing.

Tamping down her anger, she said, "Lord Haversham, I see you have once again blown across our path like an ill wind."

Unlike her father, sagging in his seat, the fifty-something viscount appeared clear-eyed and lance straight. He pushed back his chair and rose. "Lady Katherine, you are as sweetly disposed as ever I remember you and even lovelier with that becoming flush to your cheeks."

Kate glanced at the diamonds winking from his French cuffs and had no doubt where the money had come to pay for them. Lord Haversham might be a peer of the realm, but he was also as canny a card shark as they came.

"I have your measure, sir." Rather than say anything further and risk a scene that would be gossip by the morrow, she turned to her father. "Come away before you lose any more. I will find a porter and call for our carriage."

He twisted his head around to look at her, his bleary gaze confirming he was three sheets to the wind—no great surprise there. "Not now, Kate. Havy and I are playing a friendly game of euchre. 'Tis for charity, mind."

In the popular gambling game, the twos and sixes were removed from the deck, and each player was dealt five cards. To be euchred was to get fewer than three tricks. By the looks of things, her father had played at least one hand—and lost.

Resuming his seat, Lord Haversham chimed in with, "Indeed, Artie, those poor fallen women need all the aid we can render." His ironic tone suggested he'd helped a girl or two to her fall from grace and was proud of it.

Seething, Kate didn't bother stripping the scold from her tone. "Given our situation, I dare say charity begins at home, which is where I am taking you."

He lifted shaking hands and batted her away as though she were an insect of which he wished to be rid. "Have someone flag down a hansom for you if you must, but the carriage remains here until I am ready to leave."

"You would have me take a hack?" Even by the low standard he'd set, this was bad behavior, indeed.

She glanced down to the beaded reticule, a slight weight dangling from her wrist. In it she carried a handkerchief, small pocket comb, and her house key, but nary a coin. Just like the rest of her life, the accessory was a shiny display with little of substance.

Dropping her voice several decibels, she admitted, "But I haven't any money with me."

He shrugged. "In that case, return to the ball and enjoy yourself until I am prepared to leave."

Shame heated her cheeks. He addressed her as though she were a child—and before her nemesis, no less. She was humiliated. Worse still, she was trapped. She couldn't go back to the ballroom and risk encountering Mr. O'Rourke. After her hasty and, yes, rude departure, he was the very last person she felt up to facing. Nor did she feel inclined to pick up the thread of the inane prattle perpetuated by Dutton and his set, something to do with fox hunting and the latest cut of riding coat. Under the circumstances, there was only one place a woman of her pedigree and position might go to pull the thorn from her paw and lick her wounds.

The ladies' retiring lounge, otherwise known as the loo.

CHAPTER THREE

"I know she is an irksome, brawling scold;
If that be all, masters, I hear no harm."
—WILLIAM SHAKESPEARE, Petruchio,
The Taming of the Shrew

Watching Lady Katherine peel off toward the lobby doors, Rourke hesitated and then started after her. The little snob had drawn him out and then cut him, and he wasn't having it.

But more than his pride stood at stake, and in the dim reaches of his soul he owned it. Lady Kate was different, he could feel it. Despite her recent rudeness and generally sharp tongue, she both intrigued and moved him. Before deserting him on the dance floor, she'd looked almost as though she might cry. No, something had happened to send her haring off, something far more serious and distressing than suffering through his abominable dancing.

Cutting his way through the throng, he was halfway to the doors himself when a hand landed on his shoulder, hauling him back. For a few dizzying seconds, instinct took over, and he was once more a purse snitch pursued by club-wielding officers of the law. He swung about, fists at the ready. A half-dozen furious male faces glared back at him, Lord Dutton and his porcine friend, Wesley, leading up the pack. Remembering where he was and, more importantly, *who* he was now, he unclenched his hands and dropped his arms to his sides.

Sweat prickling his collar, he summoned a chuckle. "What can I do for you gentlemen?" He honed his gaze on Lord Dutton.

Glancing down at Rourke's hands, dangling benignly from his sides but still big as hams, the lanky lord swallowed hard. He cast an over-the-shoulder glance to his companions, as though making sure they were still there to back him up.

Apparently assured of their support, he turned back to Rourke. "That waltz was promised to me."

Rourke shrugged. "You may have bespoken the dance but no the lady. She's no your property, mind."

Wesley, piped up. "As a matter of fact, they were promised only . . . Well, the nuptials have been put off in deference to . . . Lady Katherine's shy sensibilities."

"Shy sensibilities, indeed." Rourke couldn't help it. He tipped back his head and laughed. "I've no met a less shy woman in all my days."

His mind left that thought and pivoted back to the principal point. Dutton was one of the jilted fiancés. Small wonder the man seemed so peevish. Jaysus, what a wean he was. Small wonder Lady Katherine had given him the heave-ho. What surprised him was that she'd apparently considered marrying him at all. Rourke wondered if the other two would-be grooms were also present. Fashionable London, he was discovering, was a wee world.

He made the rounds with his gaze. "But with all respect, Lady Katherine is a wilding. If a man hasna the—" balls, guts "—*skill* to tame her, 'tis best he step aside and set her free."

Dutton lifted his thin upper lip and snickered. "And I suppose you fancy yourself the better man for the job?"

Not wanting to give away his matrimonial intentions so soon in the game, Rourke mustered a nonchalant shrug. "Who's to say?"

"Care to make a small wager on it?"

Intrigued, Rourke answered, "That depends upon what you have in mind."

This time Dutton shrugged. His expensive evening clothes hung from a scarecrow's frame, putting Rourke in mind of a more polished version of Johnnie Black. "You have the next five days to coax a kiss from Lady Kate, a kiss in public, with at least one reliable witness present. The loser forfeits a hundred pounds. To keep things aboveboard, we'll inscribe it in the betting book at White's."

Since coming to London, Rourke had passed by White's famous bow front window while strolling St. James's, but a glimpse from the sidewalk was as far as he'd gotten. Membership in the legendary gentlemen's club was exclusive, meaning closed to the common likes of him.

"And you can't force yourself on her," Wesley interjected. "She must kiss you of her own accord."

Rourke regarded the baronet with an icy eye. "I have never forced myself on a woman in my life, and I dinna mean to begin now."

"So you accept, then?" Dutton asked, narrow eyes gleaming like a rat's in the night.

Rourke hesitated. He had no need of money, and a hundred pounds was a pittance these days. Beyond that, despite her less than civil treatment of him, he had no real wish to humiliate the lady.

He shook his head. "I've nay wish to take your money, gentlemen, nor to compromise the lady."

"Not so fast." Dutton's high-pitched drawl stalled him in his tracks. "If you're so confident of your prowess, then prove it by putting up some of that shiny *new* tin from your pockets—or is your Scotch boasting a great lot of hot air?"

The latter was a less-than-subtle allusion to the fact that Rourke's wealth was earned and not inherited. In a new nation such as America, being a self-made man was a point of pride, but not so in England. Here an honest, hard-working man was ground up and spit out like so much factory pulp while the most despicable ne'er-do-well was exalted so long as he bore a title.

Rourke whirled about. "I believe you must mean *Scots*. Scotch is a whiskey, mind."

To a man, they shrugged, indicating it was all the same to them.

Lord Dutton cast him a sly look. "*Dinna* say the Bull of Bow *hasna* the balls for a *wee* wager." He grinned, obviously pleased with his cleverness as a mimic.

So they'd found out about his pugilist's past. It was hardly a secret, though it was coming on seven years since he'd last stepped inside the ring. Unlike many professional pugilists addicted to the blood aspect of the sport, Rourke had known when to quit. He'd purchased his first few shares of railway bonds with the prize money won by knocking down the reigning contender, Big Jim O'Malley, and then signed on to a railway crew as a navvie and begun working his way up the ranks. He'd bought the railway company lock, stock, and barrel two years before and had since amalgamated a second—and a third.

And yet to this lot he would never be more than a Scottish guttersnipe from the East London stews. It struck him that perhaps Lady Katherine wasn't the only one of her kind in want of a working man's lesson.

"Verra well, gentlemen, you're on. I accept your terms, only to make things more . . . shall we say, interesting, let us not limit ourselves to a paltry hundred pounds. What say you to a thousand?"

He rested back on his heels to wait. It was no great secret that Lord Dutton lived on his expectations, tied to his papa's purse strings in the form of the ubiquitous quarterly allowance. To be fair, that state of perpetual dependency was shared by many a society male. In Dutton's case, however, he had borrowed against his yet-to-be realized installment. In short, his lordship was in debt up to his bulbous eyeballs. Ratcheting up the wager to one thousand pounds changed the stakes considerably.

Predictably, Wesley's plump cheeks lost their ruddy glow. "A . . . thousand pounds?"

"Aye, unless you *gentlemen* suddenly dinna feel quite so confident of the terms."

"No, no, we're on. A thousand pounds it is. That is . . . if you will accept my marker?" Dutton gulped again. A thin sheen of perspiration appeared on his high brow and long upper lip.

"Of course, milord. We are all . . . *gentlemen* of our word, are we not?"

The supper bell rang. Smiling, Rourke turned and continued on his way. Out in the lobby, he headed for the coatroom instead. Gavin and Harry would have to finish the evening without him. The brief interlude had changed his mind about haring after Lady Kate. No doubt she expected him to do just that. The better strategy—and, indeed, what had started out as a wooing was rapidly segueing to a war—would be to give her the rest of the long, dull evening to wonder where *he* had gotten to.

Lady Kate, you may not yet know it, but you've met your match in me.

❦

Face hot, Lord Dutton followed the Scotsman's departure with his eyes. He hadn't given up on marrying Kate quite yet, not entirely. Ordinarily an earl's eldest daughter would be beyond his touch, but reliable rumor had it the Lindsey sire suffered from the gamester's disease.

As soon as the Scot was out of earshot, Wesley turned his pudgy countenance on him and demanded, "What the devil are you about?"

Dutton waited for the other three men in their party to drift away before turning to answer. "What do you mean?"

"Correct me if I'm mistaken, but you're not precisely flush these days. Only last night you admitted to borrowing against your next quarter's allowance. You hadn't enough tin in your pockets to pay the hansom driver."

Dutton didn't deny it. "I couldn't turn down the chance to tweak that boxer's broken nose and teach him a lesson in the bargain. Who the bloody hell does he think he is, mixing freely with his betters and calling

58

himself a gentleman as though he is our equal? Stealing away Kate Lindsey stands as the final straw."

"He hardly stole her. She might have turned him down, only she didn't."

Dutton scowled. "The bitch is merely playing hard to get. She'll come 'round, you'll see. In the meantime, I've no intention of letting a bounder like Patrick O'Rourke have the first slice of a yet-to-be-cut cheese— *my* cheese."

Wesley's eyes bulged. "You're likening Lady Katherine to cheese?"

Dutton felt his mouth forming a grin. "Soft, ripened cheese, for she'll melt in my arms—and my mouth—just as soon as I come in hers."

It seemed Kate was not the only one having a bad time of it at the ball. She stood within the enclosed lavatory stall, blotting her eyes, while outside in the main powder room the row between four women spiraled to climax. Grateful to have gotten inside the stall before they'd started up, she was nonetheless trapped into waiting out their leaving.

Peeking out the crack of the mahogany door, she confirmed that two of the four combatants were the Duncan sisters, Isabel and Penelope. A pair of nastier bitches one would be hard-pressed to find. The smirking blonde in the pale pink that matched the faded fabric covering the settee, Kate recognized by her sallow face only. The statuesque brunette was Caledonia Rivers, of course, president of the London Women's Suffrage Society and one of Kate's personal heroines. She'd spotted her earlier in the evening making the rounds with Hadrian St. Claire, her escort for the evening and, judging from the intimate gestures and warm looks passed between them, perhaps quite a bit more.

Sounds coming through the stall door were muffled, but Kate heard sufficient to gather that Isabel had made some snide remarks about Miss Rivers's form and apparel, both of which Kate found to be exceptional. The sleek black gown with its jeweled evening straps was clearly inspired by Sargent's portrait of Madame X. Its classical simplicity made a stunning statement, of which Kate heartily approved. For herself, she'd always avoided frills and bows and flounces, feeling as if such fussiness made her look not only childish, but frumpy and, above all, short. As for the suffragette's full figure, Kate would do all but murder for such lovely height and curves. Clearly jealousy was the driving force for the Duncan sisters' attack. They were not the most attractive of girls. Still, three against one was hardly fair odds. Were Kate's eyes not still damp and her face flushed, she wouldn't have thought twice about bursting out from her hiding place to provide the suffragette with backup. Fortunately, it seemed the otherwise soft-spoken lady could more than fend for herself.

Miss Rivers swung about to the viperous trio like an avenging Valkyrie. Kate missed the start to what the suffragette said, but as her throaty voice rose to crescendo, she caught the splendid finale. "And so I am allowing myself the liberty, the *pleasure*, of telling you all to go to the devil."

Isabel—or was it Penelope?—sniffed. "Well, I never . . ."

Several pairs of feet padded across the tile work toward the exit door. Kate waited for the lounge door to bang closed. It did. She pulled down on the brass chain to announce her presence to the room's remaining occupant and stepped out.

"Brava!"

Miss Rivers swung around from the mirrored counter where she was dabbing at slightly watery eyes with a bunched handkerchief. "Excuse me?"

Wondering how her own face fared, Kate walked over to the marble-topped sink to wash her hands. "What a pack of bitches. Were I you, I shouldn't mind a single word any of them said."

She glanced into the gilded mirror, checking her reflection. Her eyes weren't as swollen as she'd feared, nor her cheeks especially spotty. Until the flames faded, she suspected most people would assume she'd simply been overgenerous with the rouge.

Feeling more confident, she accepted a linen hand

towel from the attendant. She blotted her hands dry, tossed the used towel into the receptacle, and turned to Miss Rivers.

"I don't believe we've been introduced. I'm Katherine Lindsey, only do call me Kat. That is how my family and friends address me, and I have a suspicion you and I will be great friends, indeed." She extended her hand.

The tall woman hesitated and then dropped the hankie and clasped Kate's hand in a reassuringly firm shake. "I'm Caledonia Rivers, but I prefer Callie. Caledonia sounds rather fierce, I think."

Breaking hands, Miss Rivers crossed to the settee and sank down on the velvet-covered cushion. Eying it, Kate confirmed it was, indeed, the same drab pink as the smirking blonde's ugly gown.

"Then it suits you. You were fierce—and splendid." In no hurry to leave her hideaway to return to the madding crowd, Kate settled onto the cushion beside her. "We're both rebels in our way, you because of your politics and I because of my refusal to become leg-shackled to some man simply because every woman of a certain age and station is told she must marry."

Shoulders drooping, Callie admitted, "True enough, only I feel such a fool. I shouldn't have lost my temper as I did."

Kate resisted the impulse to wrap her arm about the woman's shoulders as she would have done her own sister. But alas, they were British, after all, and the nearest thing to strangers.

"Nonsense, you'd every right to give that lot the dressing-down you did, but then again, I'm known to have a bit of temper myself." There was an understatement. The past month, she'd smashed a crockery bowl and two vases after learning of her father's latest spree. "As to the rubbish about your gown and looks, pay it no heed. You've managed to draw the undivided attention of every male in the room—the breathing ones, at any rate."

Turning to face her, Callie sent her a knowing look. "Not quite every male, I should think."

Kate felt warmth rush to her cheeks and knew the flush had nothing to do with her earlier tears. She was blushing.

"If you're speaking of Mr. O'Rourke, I assure you I've done nothing to encourage him." It seemed being a mature woman of almost twenty-seven hadn't yet afforded her the invisibility she'd hoped.

Callie shook her head and smiled. "It would seem you need do nothing at all. He is quite clearly smitten."

Kate tapped her gloved finger against her lips, thinking yet again about how nice it might be to kiss him, only not in the middle of a ballroom floor, but rather someplace private—and dark. Rather than risk betraying herself, she shifted the subject to her new friend. "Hmm, I rather think the same could be said of Hadrian. Mr. St. Claire, I should say."

The suffragette's green eyes widened, the irises a

slightly paler shade than Mr. O'Rourke's, more of a jade color, whereas the Scot's were a deep, rich emerald. Dear Lord, was she truly mooning over a man's eyes? How unlike her. She could almost believe he'd used their brief time on the dance floor to hypnotize her. She wasn't acting at all like her capable, practical self.

"That's why you look so familiar. Why, you're one of his PBs, Professional Beauties, aren't you, his best seller?"

Kate shrugged, not sure whether to be flattered or embarrassed at being so recognized. A bit of both, she supposed. "It's a great deal of stuff and nonsense, but then again, it pays the accounts."

Uh-oh. She must be off her game, indeed, to let that last bit slip out. Ladies in her position weren't supposed to permit sordid matters of custom entry into their pretty, empty heads. Fearing she might give more of herself away if she lingered *a deux*, she popped up from her seat. "Shall we go back in? I for one could do with a drink."

Once she'd gotten home and deposited her father, fully dressed, into bed for the night, Kate had hoped to find solace behind the closed door of her bedroom, but such was not to be. Crossing the threshold, she found Beatrice, Bea, waiting for her inside.

Long legs tucked beneath her night rail, her sister scowled at her from the foot of the bed. "It's not fair that you got to go and I didn't."

Resisting the urge to point out that life, strictly speaking, wasn't required to be fair, Kate bypassed the bed and crossed to the bow-front dresser. Peering into the mirror atop, she said, "We've had this discussion until I at least am blue in the face. You're not out yet. You have four months before you turn eighteen, and then you may attend all the dreary formal functions you desire."

"But four months is an eternity."

Kate smothered a smile and reached up to remove her earrings. "It seems so now, but the time shall fly by before you know it."

In the interim, there was at least one more payment due her from Mr. St. Claire. Sales of the *cartes postales* continued to be brisk, and of the PBs whose photographs he stocked, she remained his best seller. She hoped that would continue. Those yet-to-be realized funds were already marked for the dressmaker. To come out, a young lady must be properly turned out. Even if family pride was not at stake, she wouldn't see her sister go about looking like someone's country cousin or poor relation. The good news was she doubted Bea would require more than one season before a match was made. Coltishly tall, slender, and blond like their mother, Bea was a pretty girl who promised to bloom into a beautiful woman. If only she might grow some sense to accompany her fine looks.

She finished taking out her earrings, the pearl drops her sole remaining legacy from her mother, and flipped the lid on the rosewood jewelry box. Laying them to rest in the velvet-lined compartment, she said, "You should have been in bed hours ago. It's almost one o' clock."

Reflected in the mirror, Bea hugged her tented legs and leaned forward, resting her chin atop her knees. "Very well, I'll go, but first I want to hear all about it, every delicious detail."

Delicious details such as their father getting drunk —again—and gaming away funds they didn't have—again? Tonight's loss was limited to fifty pounds. Where he'd gotten his hands on the blunt to play, Kate couldn't begin to know. Tamping down her anger, or trying to, she plucked the pins from her hair. As much as she tried to shelter Bea from the truth, she was beginning to wonder if keeping the girl in the dark wasn't doing her a disservice.

Where *had* he gotten his hands on that kind of money? A horrid thought struck her, and though she wanted to believe it was only her paranoia at play, she couldn't go to bed until she'd settled her suspicions one way or the other. She pulled the dresser's top drawer all the way out, emptied it of handkerchiefs and under things, and turned it over to examine the sliding drawer at the false bottom.

Bea unfolded her long legs and rose from the bed. Walking up behind her, she frowned. "Kat, what are you doing?"

"Hush."

Kate slid the compartment door back and felt around the hollow for the pouch secreted within. It was there still. She sighed, this time in relief. She loosened the drawstring and pulled the folded money out, counting quickly. Her "nest egg," one hundred pounds, was thankfully all there.

Bea's eyes popped. "Why, Kat, it's a fortune. Where did you get—"

"Hush!" Kate spun about and grabbed her little sister by the shoulders. "Bea-Bea, mind me, you are never to tell Papa about this money, do you understand?"

Goggle-eyed, Bea nodded. Dropping her voice, she said, "All right, but what's it for?"

"It's my . . . pin money from posing for Mr. St. Claire, and that is all you or anyone else need know."

Kate turned back about, shoved the wad back in the pouch, and replaced it in the drawer. She slid the drawer back inside its cavity and turned back to Bea, once more seated on the bed. Moving to the bed, she sank down on the edge next to her sister.

Twisting her long blond braid about her index finger, Bea turned to her. "Since you're not going to say what the money's for, at least tell me about the ball I missed."

"Well, I met a most interesting woman, in the ladies' retiring lounge of all places. Her name is Caledonia Rivers. She's a famous suffragist, and she's about the same age as I. I have an inkling we're going to be very great friends."

The brief interlude in the ladies' room had brought home just how much Kate had missed having friends. Most of her school chums had gone their own ways years before. The few with whom she'd kept in touch were married with families of their own. She didn't accept many social invitations because to do so would have obligated her to return the hospitality in kind. She'd only attended that evening's ball because her volunteer work for the charity school afforded her free tickets.

Unfortunately their cozy chat had been cut short by the appearance of Mr. St. Claire, who had come in search of Callie. The warm, urgent looks passing between the pair stood as Kate's cue to make her excuses and leave. She'd headed off to the supper room, half-hoping she might encounter her waltzing partner, but there was no sign of the sexy Scot. She told herself she should feel relieved. No doubt he'd found some other poor woman to trod upon and hold far too close. Instead she'd felt a keen sense of disappointment—followed by a surge of irrational jealousy. She'd spent the remainder of the evening dodging Dutton and company and standing by the potted palm pushing canapés about her plate.

Bea blew out a bored breath. She dismissed the promise of female friendship with a flick of her long-fingered hand. "I meant the men, Kat. Did you meet anyone . . . interesting?"

Kate hesitated. *Interesting* seemed such a paltry

word to describe him. *Intriguing*, *mesmerizing*, and *exasperating* even, but surely not *interesting*. Hours later, she still found herself marveling over how she could be so powerfully attracted to a man who in no way matched what she thought of as her "type." He wasn't even good-looking, at least not in the traditional sense. Before now, Kate had fancied tall men with lean builds, similar to Lord Dutton's. Mr. O'Rourke was several inches shorter than her former fiancé, and yet he'd somehow managed the trick of seeming the tallest man in the room. Beyond that, the arm she'd laid her hand atop had been granite-hard, the bulging bicep threatening to rent the sleeve of his obviously expertly tailored evening jacket. The coat had fit his broad shoulders, barrel chest, and trim torso like a glove.

But more so than his rough-hewn looks, it was his manner that attracted her. Never before had a man dared talk to her in so frank and . . . earthy a fashion. And the way he'd swooped in like a great beast of prey to claim her for their waltz had excited her mightily. The mere recollection excited her still.

Had she been a young miss of Bea's age, rather than an older, unmarried sister considered to be on the shelf, their dancing so intimately without first being introduced would have been scandalous. But other than a few raised eyebrows and a disapproving look or two from the matrons lining the wall, they'd been left alone. Invisibility was one of the dubious benefits of a woman growing older, she supposed. In a few years she would be thirty, and then she would no longer have to worry about what people thought at all. With Bea's future settled, Kate would be free to do precisely as she pleased. Until now, her future freedom had taken the form of chocolate eating and novel reading, but it occurred to her to wonder if she might not supplement those relatively tame carnal delights with an indulgence of a wilder, more primal sort.

Might she also find herself free to take a lover?

Before tonight, such a scandalous thought had never so much as crossed her mind. Now that it had, her mind quickly mapped out a mental picture of her prospective partner in illicit pleasure. Who better to dive into sin with than a big, buff Scotsman with emerald eyes; a sexy, lopsided grin; and a fancy for whispering naughty bits in her ear?

Feeling her face heat, Kate shook her head. "No, I didn't meet anyone. Why do you ask?"

Bea shrugged, the smocked night rail's square neck sliding off one slender shoulder. "You seem . . . well, different somehow. Your cheeks are pink, and your eyes are all soft and . . . glowing."

Kate dipped her head. "I'm sure it's just a result of becoming overheated in the crush."

If she was so transparent to her baby sister, what must those who'd seen her during the ill-advised waltz have concluded? Had she been making calf eyes at her dance partner? She hoped to God not. Perhaps it was a good thing Mr. O'Rourke had left early, presumably to gather his rosebuds elsewhere. If he was a typical man, and Kate was coming to believe there was precious little variation in the gender, he was likely disporting himself in some brothel at that very moment, oblivious to her mooning.

Bea's voice called her back to the present. "I shouldn't like to think of you all alone once I leave. Don't you want to marry, Kat? Oh, I know you say you don't, but goodness, if you don't, what *will* you do with yourself once I'm gone?"

Fondness washed over her. Bea was such a child still. She reached behind and slid her arm about her sister's slender shoulders. "In the main, I shall eat plate upon plate of lovely chocolate trifle and grow fat as milcher and merry as a clam, and I shan't care a jot for what anyone thinks of me ever again, truly I shan't."

What she didn't add was that her particular notion of spinsterhood didn't include continuing to play keeper to their drunken lout of a father. Once Bea was flown from the nest and settled into a fine feathered one of her own, Kate meant to go, as well. The details of how she would support herself in her independence remained to be fully worked out, but that was not to say she didn't have a plan. For years now, she'd kept a journal and written in it almost daily. Much of what she'd scribbled was dreck, but she fancied some of her recent compositions, mostly poetry and short stories, were quite good, perhaps even . . . publishable. How much money a published author might earn was as yet unknown to her, but once Bea was settled, she meant to find out.

In the meantime, the money trickling in from Mr. St. Claire's sale of their *cartes postales* was amounting to a tidy sum. Had she not used the money to pay the accounts, she would have far more than one hundred pounds tucked away. Fortunately, more work was on its way. Recently the photographer had approached her about coming in for another sitting. This time he fancied a setting from classical mythology with her attired as Artemis. The Greek goddess of the hunt was also the patroness of unmarried women, a sign from the Powers That Be she was headed in the proper direction, it must be!

Until she found a way to make a living by her pen, she must leave off indulging in too many sweets. A PB could ill afford pimples or a gain in girth. Kate deemed the sacrifice well worth it.

As scrumptious as chocolate was, freedom would taste far sweeter.

* * *

Two days later, Patrick O'Rourke turned up on Kate's doorstep.

It was her "at-home day," that one day midweek when the lady of the house turned up her door knocker and prepared to receive callers. For Kate, the weekly ritual was also the cornerstone of her campaign to keep up the appearance of prosperity. Given the sad state of their finances, that was a considerable challenge. Whereas ordinarily a lady of her station living in London would think nothing of provisioning her tea tray with exotic delicacies purchased from Fortnum and Mason, Kate did her own baking. This week's selection was buttered tea cakes and Scotch shortbread. The humor of the latter hadn't hit her until she was rolling out the dough. After her thrilling but brief interlude with the stimulating Scot, she must have his birth country on the brain.

Pulling her thoughts back to the practical, she'd modified the recipe to add a few strips of candied orange peel, which she fancied would prove to be a nice touch. Certainly the simple fare was nothing of which to be ashamed. On the contrary, the bone-china teapot had a rather large chip in the curved handle, which explained why the pawnbroker had given her such a very good price. Fortunately, most of her callers would be older ladies whose eyesight was no longer the best. To stay on the safe side, she'd camouflaged the damaged spot with a hand-knitted cozy.

Congratulating herself on her ingenuity, she was dusting the gilded hallway mirror when the knock sounded. Hattie, their maid-of-all-work, was in the kitchen putting the final touches on the tea tray, including setting doilies beneath each serving plate. Kate glanced down at the watch pinned to her bodice. It was as yet only nine thirty. So-called morning calls never commenced before midday, and usually not until after luncheon.

She dropped the feather duster in the umbrella stand, tore off her apron and shoved it inside, as well, and peered out the peephole. Mr. O'Rourke stood upon her front steps, clapping his great hands together and blowing crystallized rings of breath into the cold.

Kate flattened her back against the door and considered what to do. Part of her hoped that if she waited, he would grow discouraged and go away, and the other part of her hoped he would remain. Leaving it to fate, she started counting slowly to five. One, two, three . . .

Another, harder knock sounded, the pummeling causing the wood at her back to shake. Drawing a deep breath, she turned about and opened the door.

"What the bloody hell are you doing here?"

From the step below, he doffed his bowler and smiled up at her. "Good morning to you, too, milady." His gaze snaked around her right shoulder to the door, the turned-up knocker an undisputed indicator she was "at home."

Kate let out a huff, if only to distract from the pitch of her suddenly fast-beating heart. "I suppose you might as well come in." Knees wobbly, she stepped back to admit him.

He entered, his broad shoulders seeming to fill the narrow foyer, his presence dwarfing the delicate furnishings, making them seem almost doll-sized. Turning about, he announced, "Actually, I'm here not to come in so much as to take you out, if you will, that is. I have a friend for you to meet."

Even for a Scot, he must be the most indecorous man she'd ever met. "I scarcely know you."

He had the audacity to wink. "We could remedy that, and we *shall* remedy that, but first let me introduce you to my friend."

Mentally calculating whether there would be sufficient tea treats to serve two hungry men, she glanced beyond him but saw no one about. "Very well, invite him in."

"My friend is a 'her,' actually."

Kate's heart dropped. She might not want him, she most certainly did not want him, and yet she'd been flattered to think he might want her, if only a little. The other night at the charity ball, she'd been certain he was flirting. Could she have misread him so completely?

He shook his head. His eyes were beaming. "And I'm afraid that's not possible. The friend is rather large for a town house."

So, his lady friend was fat! Kate knew it was bad of her to feel so positively buoyant about that, but Lord help her, she did.

"I find that difficult to fathom. Surely you exaggerate. Do invite her in."

He gestured toward the door she was reaching to close. She followed his gaze out to the street where two horses, a chestnut mare and a black bay, were tethered to the hitching post.

She turned back to him. "Your friend is a horse?"

He nodded. "I find that horses are the best sort of friends. Treat 'em right, and they're loyal as the day is long. Even better, they canna talk, yet they seem to understand fair near every word I say."

He grinned at her, and Kate felt her lips twitching. She'd rather die than admit it, but his brash charm was winning her over. Seen in the broad light of day, he was better looking than she recalled, almost handsome, in fact.

"Oh, very well, but I can only come out for a minute."

She grabbed her coat off the hall tree and shrugged it on, not giving him the opportunity to do the gentlemanly thing and aid her, and then followed him out. A wrought-iron fence bordered the frost-parched patch of front lawn. He held open the gate for her, and she walked up to the post where the two horses were tethered.

Drawn to the mare because she had a look of Princess, she held out her palm. Soft nickering and then nuzzling confirmed the horse was ready to be friends. Kate pulled off her glove and reached out to stroke the white blaze marking the space between the animal's dark, intelligent eyes.

"Well, hullo, sweetheart, and what is your name?"

Rourke let the gate swing closed. He stepped out onto the sidewalk, drawing up close to Kate. "Her name's Buttercup, at least for now. I'm considering buying her. Her present owner said I might borrow her for the day.

We're trying each other out, Buttercup and I. What do you think of her?"

Kate couldn't imagine why he should care for her opinion one way or the other. As far as he knew, she might be wholly ignorant of horses. She wasn't, of course, but that was beside the point. Nonetheless, she stepped back to run her gaze over the animal.

"She appears to be healthy and well cared for," she said at length. "Her eyes are clear, she seems calm and of good disposition, and her coat lies flat and appears smooth and shiny. I don't see any markings to indicate parasites or bruising."

Healthy skin was elastic. To test, she reached up and gently lifted a fold of skin from the horse's neck and then let go. The fold disappeared immediately, a good sign.

She turned back to Rourke, wondering if he might be gulling her. She supposed he was more than capable of telling a good horse from a bad one. Given his wealth, the purchase of one mare wouldn't count as a major setback.

She found his gaze riveted upon her face. His thickly lashed emerald eyes had little flecks of gold bordering the irises. She'd never before seen such extraordinary eyes on a man, but then again she'd never before found herself standing dumbstruck on a sidewalk staring up at one, either.

Kate was accustomed to being chased by packs of men, but not to being the object of any one man's single-minded regard. The former was akin to how a fox must feel when the hounds closed in, whereas the latter felt . . . well, very different. For once, she wasn't eager to get away. In point, there was nowhere else she'd rather be. The bracing air aside, she would have been happy to stare back at him for hours on end.

But, of course, that would be folly. Her object was to marry off Bea, not embroil herself in that dubious state. With her ill luck, she'd likely land a scapegrace like her father. The men with whom she was acquainted had done little to raise her estimation of their sex. Beyond that, she wasn't convinced Mr. O'Rourke was the marrying sort. That she even found herself thinking of him in those terms sounded an inner hue and cry.

"I think Buttercup here is a sound investment. Of course, to render a complete opinion, I would have to observe her move." Cursing the quaver in her voice, she averted her gaze to safer territory, Buttercup. She caressed the animal's coat for a lingering moment, crooning endearments as once she had to Princess. "Yes, you're a beauty, a fine lady, aren't you?"

The mare nuzzled her, searching for treats, and she laughed at the wonderfully cold, sloppy press of that seeking nose. She'd all but forgotten how much she missed having a horse.

Mr. O'Rourke laughed with her. "In that case, come out riding with me. Afterward you can render a full report."

She looked up to find him smiling at her, a slow,

lazy smile that set her pulse hammering. Despite the cold, shame heated her cheeks. Dear God, he must have fancied she was fishing! And perhaps she had been, if only just a little.

"I can't," she said, the declaration coming out more sharply than she'd intended. Softening her tone, she added, "As you can see, this is my day to entertain callers."

"I'm a caller, am I not?"

She couldn't help smiling at that. "Not an official one. Had you waited until this afternoon to drop by, you might have been invited to stay for tea."

His eyes locked on hers. "I'm no all that fond of tepid tea or stale cakes—or empty conversation. And I loathe waiting."

Kate couldn't blame him, especially about the waiting part. Still, she had a reputation as a shrew to uphold, and so far that morning she hadn't been doing her part.

"For the record, my tea is not tepid, but piping hot, and my cakes are freshly baked."

She almost added *by her*, but stopped short of giving herself away. Whatever rumors had made the rounds about her family's finances, an earl's daughter admitting to baking her own tea things would more than confirm them.

"Come anyway."

She stepped back from the horse, ashamed by the depth of her longing. "I can't."

She was tempted, she truly was. But she had an obligation to Beatrice to play hostess. If Bea was ever to land a suitable husband, they had to keep up the semblance of genteel living.

He fixed his gaze on her, one of those long, lingering looks that made her feel as though she were standing before him in her shift—or nothing at all—rather than bundled into a sturdy winter coat. "Can't or won't?"

One roan-colored brow hedged upward to almost reach the small white scar riding low on his forehead. She hadn't noticed it the other night, but she did now. For a mad half moment, Kate badly wanted to reach up and press her lips against the blemish, to trace that tantalizing half moon with the very tip of her tongue and press his palm against her breast.

Dear God, what is coming over me?

Whatever was the matter with her, it was all the more reason she must not give in and go. "In this case, they are one and the same." She heard the wavering in her voice and knew by the sudden gleam in his eyes he'd heard it, too.

He shrugged, and Kate's gaze riveted on how the breadth of his shoulders pulled at the broadcloth of his coat, stretching the fabric to its limit. Her heart gave another of those strange little flutters.

"Why not let your callers leave *their* cards this once and instead come with me?" He leaned forward suddenly, so close that she could smell the spiciness of his shaving soap and feel the brush of cinnamon-spiced breath on her face. "I would have wagered you're a woman who does exactly as she pleases. But then again, if you're set on spending such a fine day indoors with a pack of old biddies, I canna stop you. I'll just be on my way then."

The invisible devil perched on her left shoulder urged her to cast her cares to the wind and go with him, this once overruling the dutiful angel perched on her right. She reached around him and turned the door knocker down. "I can only come out for a few hours. I'll need to be back by two o'clock at the latest."

"Agreed."

"And I'll need to change. Give me ten minutes."

"Make it five. Buttercup is growing restless and so am I."

Almost to the door, she stopped and cast a grinning glance back at him over her shoulder. "Ten, and you will be waiting when I come out again."

She disappeared inside the house, leaving him standing at the curb with the two horses—and his guilt-burdened conscience. Luring her into kissing him in public would leave her irreparably compromised. Once she was, her choices were to accept his suit or live out her days as a social pariah. At least that was how he understood these matters to work. Looked at in that light, the wager was a godsend to his purpose, and yet if he had the choice to make again, he would refuse and let nature take a gentler course.

He salved his conscience by reminding himself how rudely she had treated him the other night. Still, it was a pity he must make public sport of her. What sport passed between them in private once they were wed would be a horse of a different color.

In the meantime, he would wait for her. Though he wasn't patient by nature, he'd learned there were some things in life, treasures precious and rare, that made waiting worthwhile. The night before he'd made up his mind that Lady Katherine Lindsey was one of them.

CHAPTER FOUR

> "'Tis a world to see
> How tame, when men and women are alone,
> A meacock wretch can make the curstest shrew."
> —WILLIAM SHAKESPEARE, Petruchio,
> *The Taming of the Shrew*

An hour later, Kate and Rourke walked their horses around the sandy track of Hyde Park's Rotten Row. Other than a few stragglers, they had the area to themselves. At the height of the season, the park would have been crammed with riders on horseback and ladies and gentlemen parading about in small, fashionable conveyances, but it was still February and most members of the ton remained rusticating on their country estates. The situation suited Kate. If she was going to fall upon her face in the dirt, she'd sooner not have her peers as witnesses.

She hadn't been on a horse since Princess, and then

she'd rarely ridden sidesaddle. At first she'd worried her equestrian skills might have eroded, that she might not be able to keep her seat, but the mare showed herself to be docile and responsive to her somewhat rusty commands. They'd started out at a walk, building to a canter. Several circuits around the track, Kate's confidence had returned sufficiently to try a gallop. After the first few circuits, she relaxed, feeling as though she were floating on clouds, of one mind with the mare.

She ventured a glance over to Mr. O'Rourke. It struck her that he wasn't wearing his spectacles today. She supposed he must only need them for reading or other close work. Mounted on the bay beside her, he looked dapper in a double-breasted driving coat of black-and-white wool houndstooth check and gabardine trousers. His riding boots, she couldn't help but notice, were polished to a high gloss.

So far, his behavior had been as perfectly correct as his clothing. He had shown himself to be both a gentleman in bearing and an obliging companion, content to let her set the gait and pace, solicitous of her comfort and safety but not fawningly so. Kate had spent more than half of her life serving as a keeper to her father and a mother to her little sister. In recent years, placating creditors and dodging would-be suitors angling for an earl's daughter had consumed what little free time she'd had left. Before today, she'd forgotten how good it felt to release her responsibilities for a few hours and simply enjoy herself.

"This is lovely," she said for no particular reason. "I could almost fancy us in the country."

He turned to her, and Kate found herself pinned beneath the force of that breath-stealing emerald gaze. "You're not much for London, are you?" Not precisely a question.

She hesitated, weighing her words. "Like most places, it becomes tedious after a while. The same people, the same gossip, the same . . . Well, what you said earlier about stale cakes and empty conversation, I feel like that sometimes. As though the longer I'm here, surrounded by everyone gorging themselves on beautiful things and decadent pleasures, the emptier I become." She stopped herself from saying more. Why was she telling him these things?

"But you do like horses." Not a question this time, either.

He had the habit of framing declarative statements as questions—questions to which he apparently already knew the answers. She tried telling herself that was only a mannerism of speech, an artifact of his Scots dialect, but the gleam in his gaze and that canny, crooked half smile told her it was a great deal more. On some level, he was testing her.

"I like them well enough." *Too much enthusiasm, Katherine. Tamp it down before you give yourself away.* "But it's a great deal of bother to keep a horse in town."

Stabling a horse in London was, indeed, an expensive proposition. When her mother was alive, there'd been money for such luxuries, but not now. Even if they'd had the funds, she would have declined. After Princess, she hadn't been able to risk falling in love with another horse.

He fixed her with that unnervingly steady gaze. "The way you handle Buttercup, I would've wagered you were too mad about horses to find anything about them bothersome."

"I had a pony when I was a child, a frisky little filly I named Princess. I got her for my birthday when I was ten, and for a little over a year, she was my best friend."

She stopped herself. Once again she'd volunteered more than she should, a great deal more. Kate's pride couldn't risk him finding out just how poor her family was. Princess hadn't been the last casualty of her father's gaming. They'd only let the town house in Mayfair because Kate had calculated that to do so was less costly than keeping a grand house open year-round. Few people outside of Romney knew that the servants had been dismissed, the few unsold furnishings buried beneath Holland covers, and the house boarded up. Beyond the income from the harvest and rents—and Kate wasn't certain what they'd do if this proved to be another bad year—they had no money to speak of, nor property to barter, sell off—or lose.

"What happened to her?" Mr. O'Rourke's deep

timbre drew her back to the present.

Throat thick, she looked away, cursing herself for having started down this path. "I . . . outgrew her."

As if sensing her need for a change of topic, he reached across and patted her mare's neck. "Buttercup has more than passed any test I might have given her. She's shown herself to be an ideal mount for a lady. Docile and sweet as honey, aren't you, lass?"

Kate snapped her head back around. "Is that how you fancy females—docile and sweet?" Dear Lord, whatever had possessed her to say such a thing aloud?

Heat flooded her face. Any hope she'd had that he might let the remark pass died when he looked over at her. Green eyes brushed over her face, and then drifted lower to the vee of her throat not covered by her coat's open collar.

"That all depends on the particular female—and the manner of sport in question."

A blast of sexual heat hit her, stoking a heavy throbbing between her thighs. Suddenly Kate needed to feel *terra firma* beneath her own feet. "I think I need to walk for a while."

He nodded, and she led the horse over to the side of the track. Grabbing a fistful of mane, she slid her foot from the stirrup and started to dismount.

Hands, warm and strong, braced about her waist. Mr. O'Rourke eased her down to the ground, his breath striking the side of her face.

Shaky, she turned about to him. "Thank you, but you needn't have bothered."

"It wasna a bother."

He kept hold of her waist a moment more before handing her the reins and stepping back. They walked in silence for a moment more, the horses following.

At length, Kate asked, "Why did you ask me here?"

It was an honest question. In her experience, men pursued a woman for one of two reasons: money or sex. Unlike her other suitors, Patrick O'Rourke couldn't be after her supposed fortune. It was common knowledge he'd made a killing by buying up railway stock, purchasing a Scottish railway company several years before and then amalgamating smaller, vulnerable companies with his own. She was given to understand his company held the monopoly on lines traveling the northwest route from London to Waverly. Likely he was one of the wealthiest bachelors circulating about town, which went a long way in explaining why men like Dutton despised him so.

Might he be angling to make her his mistress, then? But, no, rough though his manners were, surely even he was aware that one did not approach an earl's daughter with that sort of proposal, even if she was almost seven-and-twenty and as good as on the shelf.

If not to marry her for money or take her into keeping for sex, then what *did* he want with her?

"I wanted to get to know you. I saw the knocker was up and thought I'd take a chance. Betimes, had I paid you a proper call, would you have come out?"

"Probably not," she admitted.

"Why did you come?" How neatly he had turned the tables on her, and yet Kate found herself considering what answer she would give if she dared.

Because my father's house feels like a prison. Because before you came, I was lonely, lonelier than usual. Because after the other night, I desperately needed a morning off from being me—and a friend.

Because there's something about you unlike any other man I've known before that draws me like a moth to a flame, though I know in my head, if not my heart, that I should stay away—far away.

Rather than admit such shameful truths aloud, she shrugged. "As you said, it's too fine a day to spend indoors. I should be getting back, though."

She said the latter with a true sense of regret. Until now, she'd been having such a good time, she'd all but forgotten that Mrs. Billingsby and her son, Hamilton, were to drop by after two o'clock. Since the other night's "spot of trouble," she had her hopes on that young man coming up to scratch. Hamilton Billingsby was pleasant and presentable. He came from money, and Kate hoped his family might be willing to overlook Bea's paltry dowry in exchange for marrying their son into one of England's top-drawer families. Certainly Bea could do far worse for herself. If she became engaged, there would be no need to go to the trouble and expense of financing a come-out. But it was early days yet. There was no telling whether Bea and the young man would suit. As eager as Kate was to see her sister settled and herself free of familial obligation, she wouldn't push Bea into a union that might make her miserable.

His gaze, so rarely serious, turned so now. He scoured her face. "Have I gotten you in trouble, then, by whisking you away on your at-home day without so much as a by-your-leave?" His tone conveyed true concern. "If you'd asked me in to stay, I might have met your father and asked proper permission."

Ask permission of her father—that was rich. Her father had been still abed when she'd left. Assuming he'd risen, he would be having his beer and raw egg about now. Afterward he would go to his study and drink steadily throughout the day. Fortunately he never became loud or foul-mouthed or violent, as she was given to understand some men did. Mostly he stayed out of their way, especially on her at-home day when callers arrived. If it wasn't for his proclivity for entering into deep play when he was in his cups, Kate could have resigned herself to leave him be.

"Not yet, but the park will become more crowded as the day lengthens. It wouldn't do for us to be found alone together without a chaperone. The gossips would have a field day."

It was no less than the truth. She didn't give a jot what people thought of her, but she wouldn't do anything to harm Bea's chances.

He snorted. "I hadn't realized I was in need of a chaperone." His eyes sparkled, though he kept a straight face. "That eager to have your wicked way with me, are you now? Mind you hold your gaze high and your thoughts pure, milady, for I've nay defense against your wiles."

Kate couldn't help it. She burst out laughing. Since meeting Patrick O'Rourke, she had done more smiling and laughing than she had in the past year.

He touched his hand to her shoulder. "Ah, Katie, good it is to hear your laughter, to see your smile and know I had some part in bringing about that glow."

Kate sobered. She glanced down at his hand on her arm. Touching in public between the sexes was verboten. "You haven't the right to call me familiar, and even if you did, my given name is Katherine. As matters stand, we scarcely know one another." She shifted to the side, and he let his hand fall.

His smile, however, stayed fixed in place. She couldn't say why, but the lopsided curve of his full lips and bright flash of white teeth muddled her thoughts and sent her insides twisting with longing. "We could remedy that. Coarse though I am, you want me, Kate, you know you do."

Kate ran her gaze over him, feeling her heart pounding in that wild way it only ever did when he was near. "I wouldn't wager on that were I you."

Her choice of words sent his smile slipping. "Oh,

you want me a'right. Why else are your eyes bright as beads and your cheeks afire?"

"If my face is pink, it's because of the cold. And if my eyes are dark, it's because I'm shocked—livid, in fact."

"Not so very shocked or livid as you might care to let on." He reached down and cupped her cheek in the buttery kid leather of his gloved hand. "When was the last time you were kissed, milady? Really kissed?"

She backed up, bumping into the horse. "That is none of your affair."

"And that isna an answer." He slid his foot between hers, his leg tenting her skirt and pressing against the inside of her thigh. "I ken you're a woman who wants for kissing. Some women don't, mind, but you're not one of those. Cold though you pretend to be, there's a fire inside you that willna be banked nor denied. You don't only want for kissing, milady. I'd say you're fair near starved for it."

She jerked her chin and looked up at him. "Why you arrogant, insufferable, coarse . . . wretch . . . And I suppose you're the man for the job?"

"Mayhap I am. I fancy I know a thing or two about what a woman like you needs."

A woman like her! Dear God, was he suggesting she was on the shelf, past her prime? She hadn't hesitated to proclaim the same any number of times, and yet for some unfathomable, illogical reason, hearing the confirmation uttered from the lips—the sensual, kissable lips—of the very attractive, if utterly unsuitable Mr. Patrick O'Rourke had her heart turning from featherlight to cannonball leaden and dropping hard and heavy to the tops of her booted feet.

"Of course, there's only one way to find out for sure." He moved to cover her.

Kate backed up a step, but there was nowhere else for her to go. The tethered horse was directly behind her, the Scotsman at her front. Though he was of average height, still he eclipsed her.

"Dinna fight pleasure for pleasure's sake, Katie. 'Tis said to be what separates us from the beasts."

The wild pounding was worsening, her heart threatening to slam through her chest. And then there was the warm, fluttery feeling between her pressed-together thighs she couldn't explain away as anger or fear or any emotion other than what it was—desire.

Angrier with herself than him, she lashed out, "I think you are a beast, a great coarse, common beast."

He smiled as though she'd paid him the highest of compliments. "If I am, then only think what a challenge it would be to tame me. You fancy a challenge, don't you, milady?"

His lips hovered a hairsbreadth from hers, his breath a balmy breeze on her cheek. The latter was cinnamon spiced. Like a fine, oak-aged Scotch, it hinted of intoxicating delights buttery rich and delicious.

Kate tried catching her breath and then lost it

altogether. For once in her life, no ready response came to mind. Words clever or otherwise quite simply refused to come. She was struck dumb, mesmerized. His mouth was a mystery she longed to explore, his darkening green eyes beacons from which she could not look away.

And yet she couldn't give up control, not yet, not entirely, not like this. "Step back, sir. You stand too close."

Holding his ground and her gaze, he shook his head. "*Improperly* close, would you say?"

A trickle of moisture slid down her thighs. Even though it was full winter, her body beneath her riding habit felt feverish, hot. "Yes, I would."

He slid a single gloved finger down her chin to the hollow of her throat. "Good."

Kate gulped. "Good?"

His hands slid to her waist, the palms anchoring to her hips. "Aye, for it makes it easier to do this." He pulled her flush against him and covered her open mouth with his.

***

Any thought of the wager flew from Rourke's mind the moment their mouths met. Her mouth was spiced with mint, her untutored tongue moist and quite simply delicious. Lost in Kate's kiss, it wasn't until he touched his tongue to hers that it struck him. He'd won. He might even take pity on that dullard, Dutton, and neglect to collect his winnings. The only prize he craved was Kate.

He registered the very moment the last of her resistance gave way. Her lips parted on a sigh. She slid her hands up his chest, wound her slender arms tight about his neck, and rose up on her toes. Dutton, the bet, besting his betters, all receded to the far reaches of Rourke's mind. For the next few minutes, reality narrowed to the small, slender female enfolded in his embrace—the soft hitch of her breathing; the feeling of firm, urgent fingers digging into the tops of his shoulders; her mouth firing off thoughts of how delicious she must taste, not only there but everywhere else.

He pulled her closer, flush against his thighs, and rolled his hips, letting her feel his hardness, his strength. Her one arm left his neck, her open hand sliding down the front of his coat, fingers plucking at the brass buttons. For a moment Rourke wondered if he hadn't let things go too far. He'd only meant to kiss her. He hadn't counted on such rapid surrender, such a beautifully unbridled response.

Against his mouth, she murmured, "I can't seem to stop kissing you."

He angled his head and nuzzled her neck. "Who's asking you to stop?"

She had the front of his coat open. Her small hand found its way inside. Glancing at her, he confirmed her eyes were still closed. If he had one unfulfilled wish to make the almost-perfect moment even more so, it was that she would open them, look up at him, and say his given name—Patrick.

He pulled her scratchy wool collar aside and nuzzled the side of her neck. "So sweet you are, my Kate, so sweet and soft."

Covering her, he slid his hand inside her riding jacket. He found her breast and palmed it through her shirtwaist, bringing the nipple to pebbling. "But, Katie, we canna bide here. We should go somewhere . . . a hotel."

A hotel! The sordid suggestion snapped the spell, bringing Kate back to full consciousness of where she was, what she was doing, and worse still, what more she'd been about to do.

Shaking, she shoved against his chest and stepped back. "How dare you paw me so in public!" She took a shaky step back.

Heat fisted him in the face. "Pawing you, is it? I had the impression you fancied the feel of my hands on you, big and coarse though they be. But now I see that those wee moans and hard teats stabbing into my chest werena you enjoying yourself at all."

When she didn't answer, he stripped off his gloves to show her his bare hands. The palms were square and callused, the blunt digits both long and thick. He turned them over to show her the white scars thickening his knuckles. "They're boxer's hands, Kate, a railway navvie's hands, coarse and rough and ridged with scar. And yet it's gentle they can be when I choose it. It's gentle I'd be with you."

She shook her head, the corners of her kiss-swollen mouth shaking. "Take me home." As much as she wanted to believe it was the cold air stinging her eyes and making them water, she owned the true cause: tears.

He nodded. "I can be patient when I must. I'll take you back to your father's house—for now." He slid a step closer and lifted her chin on the shelf of his battered knuckles. With his other hand, he used his big thumb to swipe the wetness from beneath her eyes. "But know this, my wild Kat. I mean to wed you and bed you and make you mine in every way. And once I do, my Katie girl, sure you'll purr like a kitten in my arms and ne'er think to leave again."

Holding back by the stand of trees, the rider waited until Rourke and the tiny brunette remounted and turned their horses toward Hyde Park Corner. Once they had, she walked her rented gelding out toward the open track.

Lifting off her man's hat, Felicity Drummond shook out her head of flame-colored hair, sending pins flying. Ah, better. Given her height, dressing as a man didn't present any undue difficulty, but she'd be damned if she'd cut her hair.

Raking her bare hand through the tangles, Felicity allowed that for a supposed frosty-tit, Lady Katherine had exuded considerable sexual heat. The wagered-upon kiss had quickly become much more, until Felicity had wondered if the pair wasn't halfway to rutting in the park. Watching them from her hideaway, the moist mouths and urgent hands and grinding hips, she'd felt her own cunt beginning to cream.

But before she took care of Mother Nature, she must take care of business. Dutton and his friends wouldn't like learning they'd lost the wager, but there was one other gentleman whom she knew for a fact would be most pleased. Lord Haversham couldn't wait to see his crony's meddlesome daughter married off, and if she was packed off to Scotland afterward, so much the better. Felicity had her doubts. More than doubts, she fully expected Haversham's scheme to backfire, which was why she was so willing to help. That and because he was paying her, of course. Compromised or not, from what she'd heard of Lady Katherine, the shrew didn't seem the sort to wed a man who'd made her a public laughingstock.

Rourke might have come to London trolling for a well-bred wife, but Felicity was determined he would go back to Scotland empty-handed.

Back to Scotland—and back to her.

Kate left Rourke standing by the lamppost in front of the town house, the reins of both horses in his hands. He speared her with his determined gaze. "The next time I call on you, it will be to speak with your father."

Kate didn't answer. She wasn't certain what to say. Her brain bade her act in one way, and her body in entirely another.

His hands found the tops of her shoulders; his gaze searched her face. He drew her to him, gently this time. It was as though her bones were made of butter, her spine a jellied eel. She had no will or desire to resist. Even after their harsh words in the park, she was as malleable as melting metal on an overheated forge.

"My actions today may not have been honorable, Kate, but my intentions are. I meant what I said before. I want you for my wife."

Kate shook her head, her thoughts still in a fog. "I won't marry you or anyone else."

The words lacked her usual conviction. She sounded almost as if she was trying to convince herself more so than him. But then she wasn't herself, not really. The fever that had broken over her once they'd begun kissing had been unlike anything she'd ever before known or imagined. It wasn't as though she'd limited herself to a brief ladylike peck. Like a child tasting her first chocolate treat, one small nibble hadn't been nearly enough. The feel of his firm mouth moving upon hers had been an exquisite sensation, as had been the breadth and pressure of large, warm hands anchored to her hips, the heat from him searing the wool. How good his touch had felt, how warm and solid and reassuring to lean in and surrender to his strength. And when he'd stripped off his glove and showed her his scarred hand, she hadn't felt revolted. What she'd felt was powerfully, wantonly aroused. Imagining those big thumbs flicking over her swelling nipples, the long, blunt fingers doing lovely, unspeakable things to the aching wetness between her thighs, she felt as if her body would burst into flame.

And then there were her own hands, shameless in their eagerness to lay him bare and explore shape and texture, scent and yes, taste, too. Had his sordid suggestion not snapped her back to sense, who knew how far her wicked touch might have taken them both?

He frowned. "We *will* marry, Kate. For the rest of this day I'll leave you in peace to accustom yourself to the notion."

Peace, Kate had precious little of that left. Thanks to him, to his kiss, her world had been torn asunder, her neat, orderly plan for her spinsterhood set at sixes and sevens. She opened her mouth to consign him to the devil from whence he'd obviously come when he angled his face to hers, his breath and body warming the space between them. Dear Lord, he smelled . . . good.

His hands found the tops of her shoulders. His gaze softened, and he shook his head. "Ah, Kate, who could have known it would prove so verra hard to let one wee lassie go on her way?" He brushed his lips over her forehead and then dropped his hands and stepped back.

His gaze swept her face, settling on her lips. "You'll like being married to me, sweetheart, I promise you will."

Disappointment flooded Kate. Even in the midst of her annoyance, she craved his kiss, the crushing of his mouth and mating of his tongue with hers. And yet even that slight caress had its effect. Trembling, she backed away. Shaken, she turned and stumbled toward the house. Aware of his eyes following her, she stepped inside, pulled the door closed behind her, and then bolted it. Everything she was or knew herself to be seemed to have altered in a scant few hours. She couldn't be quite sure the soles of her boots even touched the ground. For all she knew, she had floated inside.

Lost in the maze of her thoughts, she barely had time to change back into her gown when Hamilton and his mother arrived. The visit was pleasant enough, and Bea behaved with perfect decorum, but still Kate found herself distracted. Her thoughts kept drifting back to the morning. Patrick O'Rourke was the hands-down most arrogant, infuriating man she'd ever met—and the most compelling. Up until the confusing kiss, it had been one of the more pleasant outings she'd had in a very long time.

As soon as their guests took their leave, Kate seized the chance to go to her room. Hattie could handle the dinner. Even if she burned it to ash, Kate needed time alone to think. She'd just sat down on the bedside when the knock sounded outside her door. The determined rapping announced her visitor as Bea, of course.

The door cracked open, and her sister poked her blond head inside. "Kate?"

Kate swallowed a sigh. The morning, which had started out so pleasantly, had shaken her badly. The experience of kissing Mr. O'Rourke—Rourke—had challenged everything about herself she had assumed to be true. She'd never before considered herself to be a wanton or even close, but she was beginning to wonder how much further matters might have gone had they had been in a more private place. She needed time alone, a few minutes at the very least, to sort out her muddled thoughts and tangled feelings.

"The point of knocking is to seek *permission* to enter, not to simply barrel in."

Bea rolled her eyes, the same china blue as their mother's, and entered anyway. Pulling the door closed behind her, she asked, "Who was that man you went riding with?"

"So you've been spying again?"

Bea shrugged. "I may have chanced to glance out the window."

"Uh-huh."

"Well, don't keep me on tenterhooks. Who was he?"

"His name is Patrick O'Rourke."

Kate hadn't expected the name to mean anything to Bea, but it seemed she was mistaken. "*The* Patrick O'Rourke?" She stared at Kate, bug-eyed.

Kate nodded. Lord help her if there was more than one. "How do you know him?"

Bea shook her head. "I know *of* him. They say he has buckets of money and a castle somewhere in Scotland. A *castle,* Kat, can you imagine?"

"A lady does not remark on a gentleman's assets. It is vulgar."

Bea rolled her eyes again and huffed. "Oh, for heaven's sake, Kat, we're in your bedroom with the door closed. There's no one to hear us. Papa went out hours ago, and you know what that means. Besides, it's not as though you don't talk about money. You talk about it all the time."

"If I do, it's only because of the need to impress upon you and Papa the necessity of not frittering away what little we have left."

She plopped down beside Kate. "If you married Mr. Rourke, we wouldn't need to fret about money at all. We'd all be rich as Croesus."

"His surname is *O'Rourke*, by the by, and it is he who would be the rich one. We'd still be poor as church mice, only I'd be leg-shackled to him for life. At any rate, it's a moot point as I have no intention of marrying him or anyone else."

Bea crossed her arms. "Very well, then. I suppose I shall just have to marry him."

Kate was unprepared for the jolt of jealousy that announcement brought about. Dear Lord, was she . . .

jealous?

"Don't be absurd; you're not even out yet, and even if you were, I'd lock you away myself before I'd let you marry that coarse, conceited, ill-bred Scotsman."

Bea stuck out her chin. "I don't think he's coarse. From what I saw of him through the window, I thought he was rather dashing and . . . *virile*." Bea punctuated the pronouncement with a sigh.

Kate snapped her head about to her sister's dreamy-eyed profile. "Where on earth did you happen upon such a word? No, don't tell me. You've been reading those penny dreadfuls again, haven't you?"

Knights in shining armor and Prince Charmings were best left to fairy tales. In the real world, a woman had only herself to rely upon. The sooner Beatrice accepted that decidedly unromantic fact, the better it would be. In light of the earlier episode in the park, Kate would do well to remember it herself.

Bea turned to face her. "They're romantic novels, and there's nothing dreadful about them. You should borrow one sometime, sister dear. You might learn something."

Kate privately considered she had learned quite enough for one day. Regardless, she did not greatly care for her sister's tone, even less for the unflattering implication that she was in want of romantic tutelage—even if that was indeed the case. Thinking of her enthusiastic but clumsy response to what had been a most smoothly executed sensual assault had the tips of her ears heating.

"Beatrice, I'll not have you talking like a light skirt."

Bea rolled her eyes again. "*Beatrice,* is it? I must have touched on a nerve, indeed."

Kate only called her by her full name when trouble was brewing, and they both knew it. They exchanged looks, and all at once burst out laughing.

The bedroom door swung open, crashing against the wall and bringing both women to their feet. Their father stood on the threshold, his coat unbuttoned, his cravat askew, and his eyes wild. It was obvious to Kate he was not only drunk, but furious. Her heartbeat quickened to a canter. To give the devil his due, he'd never before raised a hand to them, but there was always a first time. She slid a protective arm about Bea's shoulders.

His red-rimmed eyes narrowed on Kate. "I never thought I'd live to see the day when a daughter of mine would so disgrace the Lindsey name."

Heat fisted Kate in the face. She'd been found out. Someone must have seen her kissing Mr. O'Rourke in the park and reported back. She'd thought they had Rotten Row to themselves, but apparently that was not the case. One of the "stragglers" must have watched them with an avid eye.

Out of the corner of her eye, she slid a look to her sister. Now which of them was the light skirt? What sort of example would her bad behavior set? Were it not for her father blocking the door, she would send Bea off beyond earshot.

"I've just come from White's. There is quite a flurry about the betting book."

White's was a sore subject on any day. Even had the exclusive gentlemen's club not presented yet another opportunity for her father to game, membership was a luxury they could ill afford. Ordinarily Kate would have seized on yet another opportunity to make that point, but the ferocity in his gaze had her holding her tongue.

"Apparently a certain Scotsman by the surname of O'Rourke wagered Lord Dutton and several other gentlemen a thousand pounds that he could seduce you into forgetting yourself and submitting to a public embrace. The conditions of the wager gave him five days to do so, but it seems he required but two."

To be the subject of a wager, and one inscribed in the betting book of White's, was beyond humiliating. Horrified, Kate dropped her arm and moved away from her sister.

My actions today may not have been honorable, Kate, but my intentions are. I meant what I said before. I want you for my wife.

His show of earnestness had moved her. She'd been halfway to believing he might actually care something for her beyond the challenge of bringing her to heel. But now she saw him for what he was: a heartless manipulator, a devious seducer.

Bea lightly touched her sleeve. "Are you all right, Kate? Can I bring you some tea?"

Her father answered for her. "Tea will not repair your sister's soiled reputation." Shifting his gaze back to Kate, he said, "If you care nothing for your own good name, only think of how this will reflect upon your sister. What chance will she have at making a decent match with a spinster sister who goes about kissing strange men in public parks?"

She opened her mouth to point out that, thanks to him, there were as yet insufficient funds for Bea's come-out, but glancing sideways at her baby sister's fresh face and guileless eyes, she held her tongue. Instead, she said, "He's not a stranger. We met at the other night's ball."

"And so, of course, you let him take you riding without a chaperone."

Kate slid a hand into her hair where a headache thrummed. She shook her head. "We will speak of this later. Please leave me."

Lord Lindsey let out a huff. "I am master here, and your father. We'll speak of this when I say, and I say now."

Too numb to fear him, Kate looked up and speared him with a steady look. "I will not have this discussion with you when you have been drinking. Kissing Mr. O'Rourke puts me beyond the pale, to be sure, but if anyone has disgraced our family name over the years, it is you, Father."

"You are obviously overwrought." He hesitated and then backed away. "I will leave you to think on your folly."

Bea scarcely waited until the door was drawn. She

turned to Kate and took jiggling hold of her arm. "Did you really do it, Kat? Did you really kiss him?"

Miserable, Kate shrugged free. Subsiding onto the bed, she clapped a hand over her eyes and nodded.

"Well?"

Eyes squeezed shut, she said, "Well, what?"

"What was it like? I mean, was it . . . nice?"

Kate opened her eyes and peered up at her sister through tented fingers. "It was all right, I suppose. Oh, I don't know, I scarcely remember."

Liar, liar, pants afire . . .

"Are you going to kiss him again?"

"No!" Not a lie that time, but a sacred promise. "Oh, do stop badgering me and go to your room. Better yet, why don't *you* bestir yourself for once and see if Hattie needs help with the supper?"

"But—"

"No buts. Off with you."

Bottom lip sticking out like a spout, Bea rose and shambled over to the door. Reaching it, she turned back inside. "Wager or no, I think it's grand you kissed Mr. O'Rourke. I mean, you are coming up on seven-and-twenty. This may be your last chance."

That sealed it. Kate dropped her hands to her lap. "Go!"

Alone at last, Kate moved to the velvet-covered chair by the window. The view overlooked the walled garden, and though there wasn't much in bloom in winter, at least the boxwoods stayed green year-round. The topiary wanted for trimming and the statues badly needed hosing down, but still it was a pretty scene. An oyster-shell path led to the gazebo at the very back. The thatched roof showed signs of rotting. Several boards needed to be replaced, if not the entire roof. Small acts of maintenance and repair, and yet all cost money.

The subject of money had her thoughts winding back to Mr. O'Rourke. She had her answer now. He hadn't pursued her for money or sex, but for sport. He'd made sport of her! It was not to be borne. She would not bear it. In kissing her on a wager, a very public wager, he'd struck at her most sensitive spot—her womanly pride. Sitting there staring outside, she felt her heart hardening into something approximating genuine hatred.

The present situation called for "an eye for an eye and a tooth for a tooth" if ever there was one. Staring out into the garden, a plan began taking shape in her mind. At first it struck her as incredulous, but the more she considered it, the more certain she became that it just might work.

According to the Bible, pride went before a fall. Well, she would contrive a scheme to deal Mr. O'Rourke's pride such a mighty blow that the Scot took a fall worthy of Humpty Dumpty. Like the nursery-rhyme character, once Rourke fell off that wall, there would be no chance of cobbling together the shattered bits.

CHAPTER FIVE

"If I be waspish, beware my sting."
—WILLIAM SHAKESPEARE, Kate,
The Taming of the Shrew

One Week Later

Your invitation to tea came as a rare surprise."

Ensconced in the wing chair across from her, Rourke, as Kate was coming to think of him, leaned over to take the cup and saucer she held out. The bone china looked impossibly small and fragile in his big hands. Remembering how gentle yet skillful at giving pleasure those hands could be, Kate felt shame shoot into her cheeks.

"A welcome one, I hope." She leaned over the tea table and stirred a third lump of sugar into her own steaming cup. Perhaps it was the bitter taste of humiliation from which she still suffered, but she couldn't seem to get the brew sweet enough.

"Aye, most welcome. When you didn't return my messages, I thought you must be avoiding me."

He had one leg thrown over the other in a manner in which no born gentleman would ever think to sit. The pose stretched his trousers taut over the cast-over leg, displaying its muscled breadth. Recalling the thrilling feel of being hauled up hard against his rock-solid thighs, Kate drew in a shaky breath. Even in the throes of conspiring to send him to rack and ruin, she couldn't stop her thoughts from turning back to that astonishing kiss.

Focus, Kate, focus.

"Not at all." Kate reached for her slice of seed cake and broke off a small piece, not because she was hungry, but because now that she'd poured out the tea, it was something to do. "I have been busy with my volunteer work, and, of course, my sister has a come-out soon."

It had taken a full seven days to coordinate all the details of her scheme. So far her plan was playing out perfectly. Even better, he appeared to have no notion that she knew of his disgusting wager. Only why must he look so heart-stoppingly handsome? Was that the devil's way of tempting her, she wondered. His tweed jacket, silk-striped vest, and gray flannel trousers showed off his muscular form to advantage. A cravat pin set with a good-sized emerald brought out the deep green of his eyes. She'd hoped that upon seeing him again, the flame she'd felt before would have fizzled, or better yet, died and been replaced by disgust, but such was not the case. She was still powerfully attracted to him, more attracted than ever, and as much as she hated him for that, she hated herself more.

"I've missed you, Kate. Your photograph, though a fair-enough likeness, makes for a poor companion." From the window seat, their "chaperone," Bea, let out a soft snort. "I haven't been able to get you out of my thoughts all week. You are even lovelier than I remember."

He ran an appreciative eye over her, and she fancied she did look rather fine. She wore her hair pinned up into a chignon in the French fashion. She'd deliberately left a few curls loose to brush her throat. Likewise, her rosewater-silk tea gown was a deliberate choice. The elbow-length leg-of-mutton sleeves showed off her slender forearms to advantage, and the low V-neckline and fitted basque waist made the most of her petite figure. It was like dressing for a play and setting the stage, though whether the outcome of her afternoon's labor turned out to be a tragedy or a comedy depended upon where one sat—literally.

She affected a shrug. "I have been thinking of you, as well, most especially what you said when we last parted."

His face fell. He leaned forward and lowered his voice. "If it was about the hotel, I'd hoped you would have forgiven me that ere now."

"Oh, that. Consider it water under the bridge. I do." Kate dismissed the subject of her near ruin with a flick of her hand.

Looking relieved, he settled back in his seat. "In that case, what is on your mind, lovely?"

That was Kate's cue to lean forward. She set her plate aside and concentrated on affecting the earnest expression she'd been practicing in the mirror for a week now. "Were you serious about marrying me, or was that only foolish wooing talk?"

Expression sobering, he shook his head. "Nay, I meant every word, Kate. I want you for my bride. Why do you ask?"

"Because I have been doing a great deal of thinking this past week, and I find my position on marriage has altered—considerably." She punctuated the latter with a fluttering of lashes and a simpering smile.

"You have?" He set his teacup and saucer on the marble-topped table by his elbow and leaned in. "Is that true, Kate?"

She answered with a bright-eyed bob, or so she hoped. Like the teapot, she felt steam rising from her head. "It is said to be a woman's prerogative to change her mind, especially where matters of the heart are concerned, and I have done just that."

A broad smile broke over his face. "In that case, milady, I can have a special license warming my pocket within a few days."

"A special license!" Kate nearly dropped the plate she was holding. Good Lord, but he must be eager.

He nodded. "I canna stay away from my business all that much longer, and my mate, Gavin, is a barrister on the Queen's Counsel. But to do things proper, first I must speak with your father. When do you expect him home?"

For a smattering of seconds, panic flared. If he spoke to her father, the game would be up. Beyond that, now that he'd won the bet, why on earth would he wish to marry her?

From across the room, Bea called out, "Papa is ministering to the, uh . . . fallen women at Lady Stonevale's academy. There is no saying when he will return."

Kate sent her sister a grateful glance before returning her gaze to her "mark." "Special license or not, I am afraid I shall require more of a proposal than that."

He swept the napkin from his lap and rose. "Forgive me, sweeting, of course you deserve better."

Rounding the tea table to her, he went down on one knee. Furious though she was, there was something enormously stimulating and more than a touch wicked about a big, brawny Scotsman kneeling at her feet.

Emerald eyes lifted to her face, the sight and his nearness bringing her breath to hitch. "I'm a plain-speaking man and not the poetry-spouting sort, but I'll be a good husband to you, Kate, and a good father to whatever children the Lord sees fit to give us."

Ah, so that was it. He wanted a brood mare to help him set up his nursery. The realization was akin to dousing her with chilly water. No doubt he figured she would do as well as the next woman, even better for being an earl's daughter. It was all she could do not to rise up and dump the teapot's contents, not tepid but quite scalding, over his head.

Reining in her temper, she focused on putting the wheels of her scheme into motion. "Ever since I was a very little girl, I've carried about a particular romantic notion of how my future husband would propose."

"Tell me, then."

She feigned hesitancy. "You will think me silly."

"Nay, I willna." Under any other circumstances, she might have found his eagerness touching, but not so now.

"Why not?"

She dropped her voice to a whisper. "You might even say it is a fantasy of mine."

"A fantasy, you say?" Clearly that got his attention. His eyes lit, and he lowered his voice, as well, making Kate wonder what it might be like to hear that throaty burr whispering to her in the dark. "Tell me, milady. I swear I'll make it come true, or as close to true, as a mortal man may." He reached for her hand and twined his big, blunt fingers through hers.

The slight contact sent desire shivering through her. Gooseflesh rose on her upper arms; her nipples pebbled. "Very well, then." Determined to stay on course, she cleared her throat. "My beloved and I wait until darkness falls."

He winked at her. "I fancy the dark." His big thumb stroked her palm, drawing forth the familiar fluttering from the far reaches of her lower belly.

Furious at him though she was, it was dashed difficult to concentrate on recalling her rehearsed lines with him touching her like . . . like *that*. "Once it is quiet and pitch-black, we set out for a moonlit stroll in the garden, a garden very much like the one at the back of this house."

He turned her hand palm up and bent to press a kiss into the sensitive spot just inside her wrist. Kate shivered again.

Lifting his head, he smiled up at her. "I always fancy a moonlit stroll. Go on."

"My intended takes my arm, and we stroll down the path to the farthest reaches of the garden, far away from the house and the eyes and ears of anyone within."

He whetted his lower lip, and Kate remembered how succulent his mouth had tasted, and his tongue, too. "Aye?"

"I let him lead me to a darkened corner hidden by hedge and sit me down on the stone bench. Thus seated, I ask him to grant me a very special, very private favor."

She looked over to the window seat where Bea appeared to have her nose buried in a book. Kate knew better, of course.

His eyes found hers, snaring her gaze and drawing it back to him. He lifted her hand again, this time drawing her middle digit into his mouth, so warm, so wet. "I'd grant you any boon you ask, you must know that."

His mouth wasn't all that was wet. Moisture spurted between her thighs. Without looking, she knew that the crotch of her silk panties would be soaked through. Squeezing her legs tightly together, she focused on regaining control. "I ask him to kneel at my feet, lay his hands most daringly upon my . . ."

"Milady?"

"My . . . *person* and . . . Well, I can't very well finish telling you here, now can I?" She jerked her chin to the window seat where Bea sat with her head cocked and her hair tucked behind her upturned ear.

He nodded his understanding. "Very well, when, then?

"Meet me later tonight a few minutes before midnight. The house will be abed, and we will be quite alone."

"Kate, are you certain?"

She nodded quickly. "Yes, quite. Come through the alleyway behind the mews. I'll meet you at the gate and let you in."

"Why must we wait 'til then?"

Kate let out a huffing breath, releasing the tension building within. Lord, was he to argue with her already? "We just must. Who knows, maybe it has something to do with midnight being the witching hour. I don't know. Do you want to hear the rest of it or not?"

He nodded. "Aye, I do. Go on."

"There is a bench at the far end of the garden. I want

you to take me there, go down upon your knees as you're doing now, and ask me to marry you—in a song."

His brows shot upward. "You want me to sing to you?"

"Yes, I do."

"What difference can it make for me to sing the words as opposed to simply saying them?"

"I'm not sure. It just does. That's why it's a fantasy, I suppose. Fantasies aren't bound by reason or regular rules. Singing just seems so . . . romantic. I confess I can feel my heart fluttering and my knees trembling just imagining it. But if you'd rather not . . . I mean, if singing goes against the grain of some cherished principle, well, then, please forget I ever mentioned it. We can carry on as we are with a more traditional leisurely courtship—weeks, months, even years, if you wish."

"Nay, if it's singing you fancy, then it is singing you shall have." Leaning closer, he whispered, "I can't wait to have you, Katie. I'm half-mad with wanting you." He leaned in to kiss her.

Not trusting herself, Kate jerked back. "And have me you shall, sir, only wait you must, at least until midnight."

She flattened both palms against his chest, intending to stay him. She'd forgotten how hard-muscled and big and strong he was, not only to look upon but also to touch.

"But, Kate—"

She cut him off by laying her index finger across his protesting lips. "Please, Rourke, I've dreamt of this day, this moment, since I was a little girl. I want everything to be just right, simply perfect." Lord, but she was laying it on with a trowel.

He looked dubious, yet resigned. "If it means that much to you—"

She cut him off with a flutter of her hand. "It does, I assure you it does."

He nodded. "Then I'll sing to you, of course. But be forewarned, I have a fantasy, too."

"You do?" Even in the midst of playing coy, her body betrayed her, the slow strumming of her sex aching for release.

"Aye, I do. Someday, sweet Kate, I'll want you to look into my eyes and call me Patrick."

Rourke showed up at the back gate five minutes in advance of the agreed-upon meeting time. The sky above him was a canopy of grayish white, and the air held the knife sharpness that usually portended snow. The moon peeped out from a bank of clouds, its bleached rays breaking over the walled garden. Touched by its translucent light, the statuary shapes within seemed more ghosts than cold stone.

Stamping his feet and clapping together his gloved hands, he considered Kate's odd request. A singsong marriage proposal was an odd romantic fantasy, but if indulging her whim meant her saying yes, then so be it. Betimes, the garden was deserted. It would be only the two of them. With no one but his future wife and the moon and stars to witness his folly, there was no good reason not to simply throw himself into the spirit of the thing.

And yet something beyond the fear of looking foolish wouldn't let go of him. Earlier that day she'd seemed entirely too eager for a woman who but a week before had declared she meant never to marry. Sitting in her snug parlor sipping tea, suspicion had flared, but he'd tamped it down by telling himself his guilt must be reflected back to him. Damn the wager, damn Dutton, and damn him for letting himself be goaded into accepting. He'd been looking over his shoulder ever since accepting Dutton's marker. Assuming the young lord made good on his word, Rourke meant to give the money to charity, either the Tremayne Dairy Farm Academy or Roxbury House, whichever institution's need was greatest.

Had someone not spotted him and Kate in the park and reported back—and he'd yet to discover who that creditable source was—he would have gladly allowed the wager to die. He hadn't let his guard down all week. Sooner or later, word must get back to Kate, and once it did, he could only imagine her fury—yet another reason he felt in such a rush to finish up this wooing business and wed. If his luck held, he'd have her wedded and bedded and them both on their way back to Scotland before any gossip found its way to her ear. If he was truly fortunate, she might never know.

The soft crunch of footfalls drew his attention inside the gate. Lantern light bobbed like an apple dangled on a string, starting at the house and coming ever closer. Kate? Eagerness gripped him. Anticipation had his pulse picking up pace and his cock throbbing.

She met him at the gate, a fairylike figure attired in a fur-trimmed cape, its hood drawn up to cover her hair. "You came." She pulled back the hinged gate door, and he stepped inside.

"Aye, did you doubt I would?"

"No, I would have *wagered* you'd come."

There it was again, the word he'd come to loathe. Tamping down his guilt, he reached inside his coat pocket for his spectacles to better see. He had his proposal speech—or rather, song—in his pocket, as well, but without glasses, he hadn't a prayer of seeing it.

Kate's small hand shot out to his arm. "No, don't. You look ever so much handsomer without them. Take hold of my hand. I could lead us through that garden blindfolded."

"That would be the blind leading the blind, indeed."

She made a face, or at least he thought she did. It was altogether too dark to tell. "You do trust me, don't you, Rourke? Trust is the most important ingredient to a marriage, or so I've been told."

"Aye, I trust you."

Her small hand wrapped firmly about his wrist. Given that she was the woman with whom he meant to wed and spend the rest of his life, that ought to have been a comfort. So why was it he felt the hairs pricking the back of his neck and a feeling of dread dropping into his belly?

They entered the garden. He ran his free hand along the edge of the stone wall. His other hand remained in Kate's. She held the lantern aloft and steered them along. They stepped off the path and cut across the frost-parched grass. Feeling his way through the darkness with his future bride and her lantern as his guidepost, it occurred to him he must really care for this woman; otherwise he would never have opened himself up to this vulnerability.

Out of the corner of his good eye, he glimpsed the sparse scenery in passing—a dilapidated gazebo, chalk-white statues, a boxwood hedge, and assorted topiary shapes, the latter grown shaggy for want of shears.

"We are here," she announced in a carrying voice, letting go of his hand.

Feeling his way to the cold slab of stone seat, he wondered why she spoke so loudly. Surely the point of all this moonlit meandering was to evade calling forth attention from the house. "Indeed, we are."

She set the lantern on the ground at their feet and took her seat beside him. "All alone."

He moved closer, his thigh brushing her hip. "Aye, all alone."

Cold though it was, her closeness was making his

blood heat and his pulse hammer. Once he got through the business of making his proposal, and her accepting, he meant to take her in his arms and pick up where they'd left off in the park. After a week apart, another nibble of forbidden fruit, dare he say, a larger bite, was due.

But beyond any pleasure gleaned from the moment, it was the future he couldn't wait to embark upon. Sitting beside Kate on the bench, he realized he was very much looking forward to taking her to his home. The castle he'd acquired was a shambles still, the steward he'd hired making slow but steady progress. Rourke had instructed him to focus his attentions on the grounds as his first priority, but now that he was bringing home a bride, he would need to alter that plan.

He found her shoulders with his hands, careful not to grip too tightly. That day in the park he'd forgotten himself and been rough with her, not that she'd seemed to mind. Still, he vowed to treat her with kid gloves from thereon. Slowly, gently, he turned her in his arms.

"I've always fancied the dark." He leaned in, intending to claim her with a kiss. Only this time Kate didn't open for him. Her lips, stiff and dry with the cold, remained locked. He drew back. "Shy, sweeting? I wouldn't have thought it from your boldness the other day."

She nodded, though he couldn't read her downcast eyes. "That was daytime boldness. Things have a different face at night."

He glanced at her sharply, wishing he could better

see. Her voice sounded choked. He wondered if she, too, might be nervous. There would be time aplenty for kisses later.

"I suppose there's no time like the present." He stood, took off his hat and laid it on the vacant seat, and went down on his knees. He reached inside his pocket, for his spectacles or his song or both she couldn't know.

She grabbed hold of his elbow. "I've changed my mind. It was only a silly schoolgirl fancy that has passed. Let us forget I ever mentioned it. There's no need for you to sing your proposal. I'd rather you didn't."

He groaned. "You must have heard me before." There was a flutter of white as he shook out a folded piece of paper. "But I've been practicing all afternoon."

I've been practicing all afternoon. Hearing those words, Kate felt her heart thaw. He'd been practicing to please her. The very thought made her throat thick and lumpy and her false smile wobble. She couldn't recall the last time anyone had tried to please her, let alone put so very much effort into doing so. It was entirely possible no one ever had. Her memories of her mother had grown misty with time, but what images she could piece together presented a picture of a parent who was kind but either too ill or distracted to pay her much heed.

"You went to all that bother for me?"

He looked up from the paper he held. "Pleasing you isna bothersome to me, Katie."

Kate stared down at him, feeling as though she were

seeing him for the first time. Lantern light splashed
across the sheet and his face, casting the blunt features
into sharp relief. Until now, she hadn't fully appreciated
what a thoroughly beautiful man he was. Moonlight ha-
loed his hatless head, casting the proud high brow, lean
cheek, and strong chin into sharp silhouette. Her gaze
strayed to his mouth, and she recalled how soft yet firm
his lips had felt upon hers the time they'd kissed. Close
as they were, the musk of him filled her nostrils. A rich,
peaty flavor that brought to mind fall bonfires and buttery whiskey swirled about her like an Avalonian mist.
If only they might set aside her plan for revenge and his
for marriage and simply be a man and a woman taking
romantic refuge in a secluded garden. Beyond anything,
she wanted him to lay her upon that cold slab of stone
bench, lift up her skirts, and teach her about pleasure.

But it was too late for that. The plan was in motion.
An eye for an eye . . . Only now did she see that the only
aim revenge would accomplish was to render them both
blind.

Rourke cleared his throat. "I canna say my singing
voice will do justice to the lyrics, but here goes:

My dearest Kate,
Of amber eyes and lips so sweet,
Of honeycomb hair and satin skin,
Of sharpest wit and tart-spiced tongue,
Say you'll come live with me and be my wife, my love?"

Kate swallowed against the knot in her throat.

The last line was purloined from one of Shakespeare's sonnets, but otherwise the clumsy lines were heartwarmingly original.

"My servant Ralph helped me write it." He paused. "What say you, Kate?"

Kate stared at him. She tried to answer but couldn't seem to muster her tongue. She was helpless to do more than shake her head.

As if influenced by the moon's magic, the statuary and topiary shapes shifted and then sprang to life. Men and women popped up from their hiding places, putting forth peals of laughter.

Rourke leapt to his feet. "What the devil . . ." He turned to Kate, who'd also risen.

Kate brandished the lantern. "Consider yourself had, Mr. O'Rourke."

Blood pounding in his ears, Rourke turned to face the half-dozen or so "statues" advancing zombielike on him. They weren't statues or specters, but living, breathing, *laughing* people. The little shrew had made a public fool of him, and in that collective laughter Rourke heard the echo of every childhood taunt he'd worked so hard to put behind him.

He whipped his head back to his would-be bride. For someone who'd just put one over on him, she didn't look particularly pleased with herself. She looked nearly as miserable as he felt.

Even with the proof of her betrayal staring him in

the face, he found it difficult to credit that such a small, adorable specimen of femininity could orchestrate mean-spirited mischief. But orchestrate it she had. The treachery involved in meting out such humiliation to another human couldn't be excused by a sharp tongue or shrewish nature. It couldn't be excused at all. There was only one state of being that could drive a woman like Kate to do that which she had just done to him.

The woman must be pure evil.

"Mark me, Kate, you'll pay for this." Sidestepping a toga-clad Lord Dutton, face and half-bare chest powdered white, he could only hope the viscount caught his death.

She shot up her chin and threw her shoulders back, rising to her full if diminutive height. "My name is Katherine. Lady Katherine Lindsey."

Watching Rourke stalk away, bumping into statues—real ones—and walking into boxwood hedge as he fumbled for his glasses, Kate reminded herself she ought to feel triumphant. Her plan to humiliate her latest and most persistent suitor had gone off without a hitch. No man in his right mind would continue to pursue a woman who had done to him what Kate had done. She should feel happy, relieved, elated even.

Kate felt none of those things. Though she couldn't know for certain, she suspected she felt at least as bad as her victim and quite possibly worse. Looking about the crowded garden, she realized she was the only one not laughing. Watching Rourke stalk away, his broad back disappearing into the mist, she didn't feel triumphant. She didn't feel elated. Instead she felt empty—and very much alone.

A smirking Dutton sidled up beside her. "Aren't you going to thank me, Kate?"

"Actually, I'm not."

Looking beyond him, Kate glimpsed the Duncan sisters, sheets draped over their gowns and laurel wreaths in their hair, snickering amongst themselves. Cold reality crashed down over her. *I'm no better than any of them.* For someone who'd secretly fancied herself a cut above the company, the realization was humbling, indeed.

Fat face painted green and silk leaves sewn to his coat, Cecil Wesley shuffled up to her other side. He looked more like a chubby bean stalk than a boxwood bush, not that it mattered now. "Good show, Kate. You put that Scottish bloke in his place."

"Oh, shut up, Wesley."

She turned to stride up the path leading back to the house. With the two principal players gone from the garden, a sense of anticlimax filled the air. The crowd began to disperse.

Watching her go, Wesley stamped his cold-numbed feet. "Dash it, you'd think after all that she might have invited us in for some refreshment—tea and cakes at the very least. Hang the tea, a glass of port would be just the thing to knock off the chill." He rubbed at bare, hairy arms.

Dutton rolled his eyes. "Don't be an ass, Wesley."

"What'd I say?"

"The wrong thing or too much of the right thing—either way, you've managed to chase her off—*again*."

"Bullocks, I did, didn't I?"

Watching the ball of lantern light that represented Kate disappear into the house, Dutton shook his head. "Words and women, Wesley—how many times must I tell you the two mix about as well as oil and vinegar?"

Sitting in Gavin's parlor, Rourke lifted his glass of whiskey—his fifth or was it his sixth?—and knocked back another scorching swallow. Ordinarily he wasn't much for drowning his sorrows in drink. Growing up, he'd witnessed firsthand what befell a man who let whiskey and gin gain the upper hand. When sober, his father had been a decent sort and a hard worker, but once the spirits took over, he became another creature entirely not unlike the high-minded Dr. Jekyll transforming into the murderous Mr. Hyde. Any woman, child, or animal unlucky enough to cross Seamus O'Rourke's path when he was in his cups had better either run fast or take cover. But for one of the rare times in his life, Rourke was prepared to break his rule and get rip-roaring pissed.

He shook his head, which was just beginning to ache. What a fool he was to ever think that a woman like Lady Katherine Lindsey could see beyond his blunt-featured face, coarse hands, and plain speech to the man beneath. He'd actually chalked up her odd behavior earlier to proposal jitters. When he'd first glimpsed Kate at the gate, his heart had fisted with gladness. Fool that he was, he'd fancied she was as bloody glad to see him as he was her. What had come over him to so let down his guard? He could almost believe some mischievous fairy had sprinkled him with pixie dust the potency of opium.

Seated in a leather armchair nursing a sherry, his first, Gavin said, "I gather she found out about the wager?" Wearing a belted dressing robe and leather mules, he still managed to maintain the dignity of a top-notch barrister.

"Aye, so it would seem. Still, it's hardly the same thing. I never set out to hurt her."

"Did you tell her that?"

"Well . . . no."

"Maybe you should."

The laughter from the garden still buzzing in his ears, he clenched his free hand at his side. "Kate Lindsey can go to the bluidy devil. I'm done, finished, washing my hands." He illustrated the latter by chafing together his palms. Only the tumbler of whiskey he held had entirely slipped his mind. Whiskey sloshed onto his trouser legs and dribbled spots on the carpet.

Suddenly the whiskey hit, blurring his already

blurred vision and causing Gavin to grow a second head. A sigh broke from the opposite side of the room. Blinking, he glimpsed his friend rise from his chair and cross toward him.

Gavin hooked a hand under his arm and hauled him to his feet. "Up you go."

"Where . . . where are you taking me?"

"To bed."

Limp as a rag doll, Rourke felt himself being ferried toward the door. He dug in his heels. "Dinna wanna go to bed. Well, no with you leastways."

He cast Gavin a sideways glance and dissolved into guffaws. Suddenly everything seemed funny—*almost* everything.

Expression droll, Gavin shook his head—heads. "I appreciate the clarification, but for the record I wasn't offering."

The restless energy that had driven him ever since leaving Kate's garden suddenly deserted him. Like a windup toy someone had forgotten to tend, he could only seem to function in slow motion. Speech was an effort, the resulting words garbled as though he spoke through a mouthful of marbles.

"Dinna . . . wanna . . . be a . . . burden."

"Nonsense, you're not a burden."

Somehow they'd gotten out into the hall. "That's what you say now. What is it they say about houseguests and fish?" Not waiting for an answer, he delivered the punch line. "Both s-stink after . . . the first day." A crack of laughter broke forth from him. Bowled over by his own cleverness, he doubled over, gripping his sides. Suddenly the corridor began to pitch and sway. "Gav?"

"Yes?"

Rourke gulped, the pendulum like motion picking up pace. He pressed a hand to his pounding temple and reached out his other to find purchase on the chair rail. "I'm verra sorry."

"What on earth for?"

"For . . . this."

Rourke dropped to his knees and vomited.

Sitting at Gavin's breakfast table the next morning, Rourke sipped his second cup of black coffee and avoided looking at his friend's plate of deviled kidneys and buttered eggs as best he might. For someone who was three-quarters Scots and one-quarter Irish he really ought to have a stronger stomach, along with better tolerance for spirits. His ancestors on both sides must be turning in their graves to see what a lightweight they'd weaned.

Thinking aloud, he said, "I haven't given up on marrying her, you know."

Seated next to him, a freshly ironed and still-folded copy of the *Times* between them, Gavin shot him a horrified look. "You can't mean to marry someone out of spite."

Rourke shrugged, reached for a sweet roll, thought better of it, and then set it back on his plate untouched. "I don't know why not? Lust and beauty fade, but a good, solid hating has a hold that stands the test of time."

"What of love?"

Rourke was fond of Gavin. More than fond, he loved him like a brother. Still, at times such as this, he couldn't help finding his friend something of a sop.

He shook his head, which proved to be a very large mistake. Gripping the table edge, he waited for the dull pounding and black wave of nausea to subside. Sweating, he pushed his coffee cup and saucer aside and reached for his water glass instead.

Taking a small swallow, he asked, "What of it?"

"I was under the impression you held a tendre for Katherine, some fond feelings at the very least."

Katherine. The way Gavin spoke the name, it sounded as though he and Kate were long-standing friends. After the previous night, Rourke might detest the woman, he *did* detest her, but she was still his woman. Regardless of what he might have said about washing his hands of her, in the *sobering* light of day, he wasn't yet ready to relinquish his claim on her, though, admittedly, forging a future with her seemed about as likely as strolling the moon's surface or uncovering the ruins of Atlantis.

But Rourke had been pulling himself up by his bootstraps nearly all his life. When it came down to it, Kate Lindsey was just another challenge to be faced, not terribly different from overtaking a rival railway company or boxing half-blind. Whenever the prize was in sight, Rourke always, always managed to find a way.

Kate, you've nay notion o' the just desserts I'll be dishing up.

CHAPTER SIX

"By this reck'ning, he is more shrew than she."
—WILLIAM SHAKESPEARE, Curtis,
The Taming of the Shrew

November 1891

Kate sat by the parlor window, the curtain drawn to allow looking out onto the rain-soaked street, the road itself dyed to deep obsidian, the sidewalks glittering like glass where ice from the previous week's snow had melted and then refroze. Today, however, it rained. Every so often a carriage rattled by, splashing mud from the gutters onto the curb, but so far none had stopped. Her journal lay open in her lap, the pages blank, the fountain pen abandoned to rest in the binding crease. She wasn't feeling especially creative, but then, these days she wasn't feeling much of anything at all.

Looking out onto the deluge, she wondered if later in the day the precipitation might turn to snow. She hoped so. Growing up in the country, she used to adore snow. Snow at least served some purpose. You could *do* something with snow—make snow angels, and snowballs, and, yes, snowmen—but rain in the winter only made things soggy and miserable.

Today was her at-home day, and the fact of slippery roads and raw winds might be marked by some hostesses as bloody bad luck. Beyond that, it would be Christmas in another few weeks. Anyone venturing out would be most likely to head for Selfridge's on Oxford Street or Harrod's in Knightsbridge, where they might shop the myriad departments while staying snug and dry. She doubted she'd have any callers to eat the currant buns and seed cake she'd taken pains to bake, and then decided she didn't really care. As she did every week, she thought back to that long-ago "at-home day" when Patrick O'Rourke had shown up unannounced on her doorstep and persuaded her to go riding with him. Of course, riding wasn't all he'd persuaded her to do. That memory seemed almost to belong to another person, and yet coming on two years, she recalled every blisteringly vivid detail.

She reached up and traced her mouth with her index finger, scratching the nail lightly over her bottom lip, reliving the magic of that moment, the gentleness of his kiss, and her own hungering response. Even with so much time passed, she marveled at her former boldness. She brought her hand down to her lap, examining the small white palm and slender pink-tipped fingers with a sense of disbelief. Had she really employed that very hand to unbutton his coat and run it down the length of him, mapping the terrain of strong neck, broad shoulders, and hard muscled chest—and in a public park, no less! That she'd taken him by surprise was clear—he'd only bargained, or rather *wagered*, for a kiss, after all—but she'd also astonished herself. Who would have imagined Capable Kate Lindsey, supposed ice maiden, self-avowed spinster, and proud-to-be shrew, might contain such a wealth of . . . passion?

The miracle was that she seemed to have escaped a scandal, or at least much of one. The whole White's betting book episode seemed to have blown over in a week's time, no doubt eclipsed by some more savory scandal broth. As for the garden scheme, from what she gathered, those who'd participated must have been too ashamed or too bored by its lackluster result to speak much about it. Of course, she didn't go about in society much, less and less if she could help it. There'd been one episode where she'd chanced to cross paths with Isabel and Penelope Duncan on Bond Street, their gloved hands laden with parcels from an obviously successful day spending their papa's money in the shops. The sisters had looked straight through her, their pinched noses pointed north and thin mouths sneering, and then swept past. She hadn't minded all that much. It hadn't been empty bravado when at Lady Stonevale's charity ball she'd counseled Caledonia, Callie, not to mind a single word they said.

The suffragette and Hadrian St. Claire had married. Surely they would have heard about the cruel trick she'd played upon their friend. When she'd stopped into Mr. St. Claire's photography shop to stage the Artemis sitting and to collect her latest installment from the previous quarter's sales, he'd treated her civilly but had not been overly friendly. It was no better than she deserved. She hadn't seen Callie since their brief meeting at Lady Stonevale's charity ball. Though she thought about her a great deal, she'd been too ashamed of her behavior to renew their acquaintance—yet another loss.

Outside, she heard a carriage pull up, the wheels screeching as the driver halted on the wet road. It seemed she was to have a visitor after all. Not certain if she was glad of that or not, she closed the journal, set it aside, and got up. Not terribly curious, she opened the door without looking out.

Patrick O'Rourke—Rourke—stood on her doorstep, shaking rainwater from the crown of his hat. Rain plastered his hair to his high brow and lean cheeks, the drenched locks looking more black than auburn.

"Thursdays are your at-home days, are they not?"

Kate could only stare. She couldn't seem to find her tongue. She hadn't expected to ever see him again.

Though he occasionally came to London, and had purchased a house in Hanover Square, they hardly ran in the same circles. She hadn't heard he was back in town.

"Are you going to invite me in?"

She found her voice at last. "Yes, of course, I . . . Do come in." She stepped back to let him enter.

"Have you other guests?" He set his hat atop her banister and looked past her into the parlor.

"No, I haven't. Just you, if you'll stay, that is."

Now that the shock was wearing off, she realized she was pathetically glad to see him. "I hadn't heard you returned from Scotland." *You never said good-bye before you left.*

She led the way into the parlor, mentally cataloguing its shabbiness. Even for so-called old money, they were putting on a poor show of it these days. Keeping up appearances was harder and harder. The money Kate had been saving for Bea's come-out had "mysteriously" disappeared from its hiding place, and she had to believe their father was the culprit. It was beyond depressing.

He followed her inside. "I just got into town yesterday. I bought a place, a town house in Hanover Square."

"Yes, yes, I heard. That's nice, very fashionable. Do you like it there? Will you take some refreshment?" Dear Lord, she was babbling like a brook.

He stared at her, emerald eyes raking her face. He looked the same and yet different somehow, older she supposed. Fine lines had chiseled their way into the corners of his eyes. If they'd been there before, she didn't recall them.

Finally, he said, "I can't stay long."

"It needn't be tea," she added quickly. "I'm sure we have some sherry or brandy about." She was tempted to add, *If Father hasn't drunk it all*, but held back. As much as she'd missed him, she wouldn't stoop to using pity to win him back.

Hat in hand, he stood stiffly by the door. "Nothing for now, thank you." He glanced to the armchair, the same he'd occupied the first and last time he'd taken tea with her, the cushion slightly more worn. "May I sit?"

"Please do."

She perched on the edge of the settee, doubly glad she'd thought to close the journal. Today's pages might be blank and the ones from the day before, as well, but not so for the long days and months after he'd first gone.

Silence descended. They traded glances, and Kate wished she'd thought to put on a more becoming gown. The chocolate-colored satin might bring out her eyes, but the fabric was rather faded, she was afraid.

"Do you come to the city often?" Mentally she kicked herself. What an inane thing to ask.

"If by the city you mean London, then aye—or rather, yes, I do. I hold property in the north, in Scotland, and it was grouse season, after all. But as you see, I am returned—like an ill wind, you might say."

Kate didn't care for his cryptic tone. Her pleasure

in seeing him again began to fade, replaced by a sharper version of the earlier unease.

"What brings you into town?" His affairs weren't any of her business, but she was at a loss for what to say.

Rather than answer, he said, "This isna a social call, Kate. Forgive me, I meant to say Lady Katherine."

Rather than answer and open up that particular wound, she asked, "If not, then pray what manner of call is it?"

"A business one."

"In that case, I'm afraid my father is indisposed."

He seemed to find that amusing. One side of his mouth quirked upward, not the good-natured grin of her memory, but an unpleasant smile, a snide smile, a smirk. "I don't doubt it."

Something of her father's reputation must have reached him. The earl had come home that morning just as she and Bea were sitting down to breakfast. Ordinarily he was unabashed about his nocturnal carousing, but this morning he'd been unwilling to look her in the eye. Though she was always on pins and needles when he went out, his unusual sheepishness had set off an inner alarm. He'd poured himself a glass of lemon water from the pewter pitcher and stumbled upstairs to bed. It was coming on two o'clock, and he'd yet to emerge.

"My business is with you, not him—unfinished business, you might say."

His cryptic tone sent Kate's heart thumping. "How

can that be? We have not spoken since—"

He cut her off with a shake of his head. "Humiliating me in front of half of London hardly seemed conducive to keeping up our acquaintance."

She resisted the pettiness of pointing out that "half of London" had been only a half-dozen people. Whether she'd enlisted one confederate or legion, what she'd done was wrong. She'd hoped he would have forgiven her by now. Apparently he had not.

She folded her hands in her lap to hide their shaking. "You should know that I was . . . that I am very sorry about how things ended between us."

"Is that an apology, milady?" He regarded her beneath raised brows.

"Yes, yes, it is only . . ." She left the sentence unfinished, unsure of what more to say.

A year ago, she would have seized on the opportunity to add that the humiliation meted out had cut both ways, but that only now she found she did not care so terribly much. The wagering episode struck her as more in the way of a schoolboy prank than mean-spirited mischief. From the little she'd cobbled together of Rourke's upbringing, she suspected he'd been lured into accepting Dutton's challenge more to prove his worth than to humiliate her. Looking back, it was difficult to believe she'd mustered the upset she had, but then appearances had come to mean less to her than they used to. She wasn't nearly so angry anymore. In point, she wasn't angry at all.

He frowned at her. "I didn't come for an apology."

"Then why did you come?"

The feral glitter in his gaze had her palms perspiring. "I came to collect my winnings."

He slid a big hand into his inside coat pocket. Drawing it out, he produced a small folded slip of paper. Holding it out, he asked, "Do you know what this is?"

Kate felt her stomach drop. Without rising to examine it, Kate more than knew. His reference to "winnings" was a dead giveaway.

"It is my father's marker, I dare say." Still, she waited for his reply, dread pinning her to the chair.

Rourke nodded. "Aye, it is. I happened upon the earl at one of his haunts in Leicester Square the other evening."

Pinned no longer, Kate shot to her feet. "You lured him into deep play."

He scoffed at the suggestion. "I hardly had to lure. He and his mate, Haversham, were already in over their heads. When I offered to stake your father for the evening, he willingly accepted. I didna have to offer a second time."

Numb, she heard her voice as though it were an echo inside a tunnel. "How much?"

He turned his face up to look at her. "Five thousand pounds."

Kate staggered back a step. Feeling the edge of the

chair at the backs of her knees, she sank back down into her seat. Five thousand pounds was a small fortune. She scoured her brain for what he might possibly hope to collect from them in the way of recouping so large a sum. Apart from the estate, thankfully entailed, they'd no property. The town house was let, the carriage on its last spring, the two horses long past their pasture age, the silver and fine china long ago sold. She touched the pearl drop dangling from her left ear. Dear God, not Mama's earrings. The matching pendant hung about Bea's throat. The thought of giving up precious mementos pierced her heart.

She reached up to slide the backing of the earbob out of the hole in her lobe. "Take these until I can find the means to come up with the rest, only pray allow my sister to keep her necklace. It is all she has of our mother."

He sent her an incredulous look. "What am I to do with a pair of earbobs?"

Her gaze honed in on his pierced ear, sporting a small ruby today to match his crimson cravat. Humble origins or not, he really was a most stylish man. "Wear them or sell them. Oh, I don't know."

He shook his head. "Keep your baubles, milady. The prize I've come to collect is dearer than those."

"What is it you mean to collect?"

"You."

"You want me as your mistress, then?" If he'd set out to humble her, to bring her low, he couldn't have hit upon a better way.

Rising to stand, he shook his head. "I don't need to buy a mistress, and if I did, I could set one up for far less than five thousand pounds." His tone might have cut glass.

Kate stood, as well. "Then what do you want with me?"

"The same thing I wanted two years ago—marriage, children to inherit the legacy I've built, a hostess to preside over my dinner table."

Kate shook her head. "But you can have those things with any woman."

He speared her with a dagger-sharp look. "Not every woman is the daughter of an earl."

So it was her blue blood he was after. The thought had crossed her mind two years before, but for whatever reason she'd set it aside.

Kate felt on the verge of throwing up her hands. His kissing capabilities aside, she'd no intention of marrying a man who plainly loathed her. "Mr. O'Rourke, we've been through this before. As deeply as I regret the circumstances of our last . . . parting, I cannot, and will not, make amends by marrying you."

He shook his head. "You have a choice, milady. You can marry me or see your father hauled off to debtors' prison. That would cause you and your sister quite a scandal, I should think."

Kate felt as if invisible hands cinched about her throat, cutting off her breath. Chest heaving and head reeling, she regarded him, fighting for control, fighting for air.

She hauled up in front of him, hands fisted at her sides. "The first time I set eyes on you at Lady Stonevale's ball, I thought you resembled a pirate. Now I see you don't only look like a pirate. You *are* a pirate."

He shrugged. "Aye, I am, just as you are a mean-spirited, sharp-tongued shrew. Given the defects in both our characters, I wouldna be surprised if we didn't rub along well enough. Be that as it may, I will send word as soon as I have the special license. In the meantime, I advise you to begin packing what things you wish to bring with you."

"Bring with me? Where am I going?"

"Why, home to Scotland, of course."

"Scotland isn't *my* home."

"It is now."

A throat being cleared had her whipping about. Her father stood on the threshold. By now she should know there would be no aid from that corner, and yet she so desperately wanted to believe. Thoughts ran through her head, ghosts of a little girl's pleading.

This once, Papa, show yourself to be a better man. This once, let the bad news be a mistake, or at least not so very bad as it seems.

Instead, Kate rounded on him. "You lost me in a card game!"

He hung his head and nodded. "Essentially, that is so."

"You staked me like. . .like chattel. Of all you've done, this deed puts you beyond the pale."

He acknowledged Rourke with a nod and then crossed the room toward her, moving at a crawl as an old man might, though he couldn't be much past fifty. "All will be well. These things have a way of righting themselves in the end."

These things have a way of righting themselves in the end. How often over the years had she heard that tired excuse?

"Mr. O'Rourke has agreed to pay off our debts and to settle a dowry on your sister. We can reopen the house at Romney, pay our creditors off, and even give Bea her come-out in grand style."

Kate's lower lip trembled. His lack of remorse was dispiriting at best, infuriating at worst. "And what of me, Papa, what shall I have?"

He drew up in front of her. She could smell last night's spirits on his breath. "A wealthy husband who can give you a fine home and children is not to be lightly dismissed. You are not growing any younger, my dear." He reached out a trembling hand to pat her shoulder, but she pulled back.

"Pray don't add hypocrisy to your long list of sins

by pretending for a moment that any of this has to do with me."

She turned away in disgust. Her gaze alighted on Rourke. She'd expected to find him gloating. Instead he stood silently looking on, green eyes grave and mouth unsmiling.

"You've your revenge on me at last, sir. You must be mightily pleased with yourself."

He didn't answer. Something flickered in his eyes, pity perhaps? But no, such a villain must know nothing of pity or remorse, either.

She looked between the two men, hard-pressed to know which of them she hated more. Her father, she decided, for he was supposed to protect her. Mr. O'Rourke, on the other hand, had put forth his predatory claim in the most straightforward of ways. He had never pretended to be ought than the bounder he was. Not a bounder, but a pirate.

"Very well, Mr. O'Rourke, since you leave me no choice, I suppose I shall marry you."

Later that evening, Kate sat on the edge of the settee, holding her head in her hands, looking glumly on as Bea paced the rose-patterned carpet and her father stood at the wine table by the window quaffing glass upon glass of port. Marrying a man who plainly loathed her and meant to make her miserable was a bitter pill to swallow, but there was no help for it. Rourke held her father's marker, and, without the funds to redeem it, she could either marry him or see her father imprisoned, her baby sister left dowerless, and her family name forever besmirched.

Bea pivoted to their father. "I don't mind the marrying part, but I don't want Kate to go to Scotland. I need her here to coach me for my come-out."

The earl turned away from the window and dealt his youngest a distracted pat. "Don't fret, my dear. We'll find you a sponsor, your Aunt Lavinia, perhaps."

"Oh, Papa, not that old biddy, please! She'll put me in hoops and feathers, and I shan't have any fun at all."

Kate couldn't take much more. "Oh, have done, both of you. Bea, mark that I am present in the room, so you needn't discuss me in the third person as though I was in Scotland already. And, Papa, while you're pouring the better part of that decanter down your throat, pray spare a glass for me."

Bea's mouth formed a shocked circle. She cast Kate a scandalized look. "Kat, really! Ladies don't drink port! Ratafia or sherry perhaps, and certainly champagne, but never port."

"Ladies, little sister, do not find themselves sold like livestock or traded like horses." As it turned out, she'd had no more say in her future "master" than had poor Princess.

Her father poured in silence, and Bea passed over

the short-stemmed glass with a huff.

Ignoring them, Kate knocked back the port in a single swallow, then coughed, throat ablaze. Really, how did her father manage to drink as he did day after day? She thought the sensitive skin inside her mouth must be peeling and a hole burned at the back of her tongue.

Bea drew up toward her. Her gaze dropped to the empty glass in Kate's hand and then snapped up to her face as though expecting a Jekyll-Hyde transformation to take place at any time. "You're supposed to sip it, aren't you?"

Kate shook her head. Now that the fire was dying, she felt a mellow acceptance taking hold.

"Not if you mean to get drunk, you don't." Kate held out her empty glass. "Hit me again."

Rourke was sitting down to breakfast in his Hanover Square town house the next morning when the sound of a throat being cleared called his attention to the half-cocked door. He looked up from the buttered kippers he'd been pushing about his plate. Ordinarily he brought a hearty appetite to the breakfast table, to any table, but leaving Kate near tears the night before seemed to have set him off his food.

Ralph Sylvester, his "butler" and former flash-house friend, poked his sandy blond head inside. "May I, *sir*?"

Rourke beckoned the former-felon-turned-respectable-butler inside.

Coming up on the table, Ralph presented the usual precisely folded and still-warm copy of the *London Times*. "It came late today, but it's hot off the presses and fresh off the iron just as you fancy it—*sir.*"

"Thank you." Rourke added it to the stack of newspapers at his elbow, which he'd as yet to give so much as a glance.

As no one was about, Ralph helped himself to a cup of coffee and pulled up a chair. "I have something else for you, a wee wedding giftie, as you might say." He slid a brown-paper-wrapped parcel across the cloth-covered table.

Among his many talents, Ralph Sylvester was a first-rate mimic, which was why he'd been so invaluable to Johnnie Black. He could affect just about any accent, including that of a plum-in-the-mouth English butler. The kicker was, he really was a crack butler and a marvel of a valet. Rourke hadn't read an unironed newspaper or put on a wrinkled shirt since taking his old friend into his employ.

Rourke pushed his plate away and reached for the parcel, lifting it to assess its weight. The novelty came from growing up without ever receiving a single present, no doubt, but for whatever reason wrapped parcels always made him feel like he imagined a child must feel on Christmas morning.

"What do you suppose this is?" He held the package

up to his ear to see if it rattled.

Ralph sipped his coffee with a casual air. "I'm certain I couldn't say, *sir*. Perhaps you might contemplate opening it?"

He tore the paper away and lifted out the contents. The smell of buttery new leather, all but untouched by human hands, wafted up to greet him. "It's a book."

"How novel."

Glancing at the title, *The Taming of the Shrew*, Rourke couldn't resist. "Actually, it's a play."

The valet rolled his eyes. "I think you might find it to be more of a marital-advice manual."

"A marital-advice manual, hmm?" Turning the volume over, he examined the very familiar binding. "Why, Ralph, I'm touched. If I didn't know better, I'd say this came from my very own library." He'd ordered several hundred books, all bound in rich morocco leather, the tooled spines and gilded page edges mostly for show.

Ralph swiped a kipper off the discarded plate and popped it into his mouth. "Ah, well, what to get the man who has everything?" Licking butter from his thumb, he added, "Since you're hell-bent on being a bastard to your bride and making a hash of your marriage before it's begun, I thought you might as well get it done right and proper—the bastard part, I mean."

Ralph didn't know the half of just what a bastard Rourke had become. Kate's father's weakness for cards had afforded him the very opportunity for which he'd been waiting. It had been a simple matter of asking 'round to learn what establishments the earl frequented. Once he'd tracked him to Leicester Square, he'd begun making the rounds of the main gaming halls. The earl was already deep into his losses and his cups, a pretty opera dancer perched upon his knee and sliding red chips down the front of her frock. Rourke had paid the girl to go away, enough to keep her in gin for the next several nights, and sat down to watch the play. By the time dawn lit the sky, he'd had the old man's marker warming his pocket.

Telling Kate was supposed to have been the center-piece of his revenge, only he hadn't particularly enjoyed doing so. Actually he hadn't enjoyed it at all. There'd been one moment when he thought she might cry, and he'd been hard-pressed not to go to her. Collecting his hat and walking back out into the rain, he'd felt as soiled as the leavings of tire-tracked snow.

He reminded himself that the little shrew had made her bed that night two years ago in the garden, and by God, he meant to see her lie in it. His only worry was that she would insist upon doing so alone. The whole purpose of their marrying was to beget heirs; otherwise his railway legacy would die with him.

Rourke cracked the cover and flipped through. At first glance he found the Italian names off-putting, but the variations of the shrew's name—*Katherina, Katerina, Katherine*, and, of course, *Kate*—were easy enough to track. The shrew in Shakespeare's play had the same name as his bride.

Intrigued, he reached for his reading glasses. His tastes in reading material ran to newspapers and railway stock reports, not to literature and certainly not Shakespeare, and yet . . . Despite what he'd said to Gavin after the garden incident, he didn't care to spend the rest of his life at odds with his wife, but trust on both sides had been badly breached. He didn't see how a play written hundreds of years before could remedy all that, but reading it was a small investment of his time.

Might a "marital-advice manual" masquerading as a play be the very thing he needed to steer his and Kate's relationship back on course? Skeptical though he was of any advice offered between the covers of a book, he supposed it wouldn't hurt to have a look.

Rourke put on his spectacles, cracked open the play's cover, and settled in to a morning's read. Engrossed, he didn't look up when Ralph left, drawing the door closed.

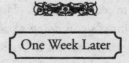

One Week Later

Kate awoke on her wedding day to a gray drizzle outside her window. How appropriate. Her trunk had been brought down from the attic the night before, all but her wedding gown and traveling costume neatly folded and laid inside. It sat in the corner of her room, ready to be brought below when the time came to leave. Packing had driven home how very little she owned. Her clothes, books and journals, a few mementos, and her mother's pearl earbobs summed up her worldly possessions. For being eight-and-twenty, she hadn't much to show for her life. Certainly she had no "legacy," railway or otherwise, as did her fiancé.

Hattie came early to do her hair and help her dress, offices Kate usually performed for herself, but as the maid pointed out, it was her wedding day. Petite and blond and far younger-looking than her forty years, she'd been with the family since Bea was born. Kate considered her more relative than servant.

"I don't mean to talk out of turn, milady, but I'm not so sure your going off to Scotland is such a bad thing." She stepped behind Kate to do up her laces. "Only I wish there'd been time to have a proper wedding dress made. You're a good girl. You deserve to wear white."

Were hers a love match, Kate would have agreed. But Rourke wasn't her choice for a husband, rich though he was. He didn't want her for herself, but for the social status her blue blood would bring. He'd blackmailed her into this marriage, foisted himself on her in the vilest of ways. She told herself that whatever misguided spark of attraction she'd once felt for him had died the moment he pulled her father's marker from his pocket. Until she saw him again, at the church, she had no way of testing whether or not that would prove true.

Kate shrugged. "The brown silk will be fine. It's not too terribly out of fashion, and the hat with the silk roses should look well enough with it."

At Hattie's insistence, she glanced at herself in the mirror. A pale, pinch-faced woman with enormous medium brown eyes stared back at her. There were purplish shadows beneath the eyes and faint cracks about the corners. It occurred to her that for once, her father was correct. She really wasn't getting any younger.

The first person she saw upon coming downstairs was her father. He looked up from the foot of the open staircase, a glass of port in hand. "You look lovely, Kat." He leaned forward to buss her cheek.

Kate pulled back before he could. "I left the house keys with Bea, as well as directions for the laundry and recipe receipts with Hattie." She would have liked to have taken Hattie with her—at least that way she could ensure she received her wages on time—but with Bea's come-out approaching, her sister would need a maid.

He opened his mouth as if to say more, and then closed it on a nod. "We will manage."

Kate took leave to doubt it, but for once held her peace.

Bea trotted down the stairs behind her, looking fresh and lovely in one of the new gowns purchased from Rourke's largesse. "Shall we go?"

Rourke had sent a private carriage and driver to fetch them to the church. Even though Kate felt more like she was being abducted than driven somewhere, she had to credit the consideration of the gesture. The carriage pulled up at precisely a quarter 'til ten. Looking out the front window, Kate saw that the conveyance was the flashy sort, meant to turn heads, a broad, shiny, black-lacquered beast with gilding on the trim.

The smartly turned out young driver met them at the door, a big black umbrella held aloft. "Mr. O'Rourke left very specific instructions you weren't to be late." He bowed. Rising, his gaze riveted on Bea crowding into the doorway.

Noting the answering blush riding her sister's cheekbones, Kate pushed her back inside and out of view. "In that case, let us not delay."

An hour later, Kate, Bea, her father, and Hattie sat in the front pew of the chilly church, tapping their toes upon the flagged floor. After the first few minutes, Hadrian and Callie rushed inside.

Callie settled her gaze on Kate. "Katherine, it's so lovely to see you again. I was so afraid we would be late." Callie's gaze left Kate to scan the other pews. Turning back to Callie, she asked, "Where is Rourke?"

Arms folded, Kate shook her head. "Where, indeed."

Apparently Rourke had asked his two friends to stand as witnesses to the wedding. Callie explained that their other two childhood friends, Daisy and Gavin, were occupied with opening their newly restored theatre. Apparently the pair had wed the spring before.

The newcomers settled in to wait. Desultory conversation made the rounds, mainly remarks on the recent spate of foul weather and voiced hopes for an early onset to spring. Hadrian broke away to set up the camera and tripod he'd brought along, apparently at Rourke's direction. Several more minutes ticked by. After a while, the rector rose, stretched, and announced his intention to go next door to take a cup of tea. Hattie's brown bonnet drooped, her cheek coming to roost on Kate's shoulder. The driver, Ralph Sylvester, scratched his sandy blond head, paced up and down the aisle, and periodically fired off profuse apologies for his master's lateness and assurances of his goodwill. Kate took note of how very often the driver's hazel eyes danced their way over to snare her sister's blue ones and of how often a pink-cheeked Bea looked back. If her supposedly eager "bridegroom" didn't arrive soon, there might well be a wedding that day, only not hers.

Clearly Rourke was not yet done with humiliating her. His latest lark sent steam rising kettle-style from atop her head. She was about to rise to leave when the vestibule door flung open, the crash echoing up to the rafters. Heads turned in unison to the back of the church.

Rourke strolled down the aisle between pews, emitting the soft tinkling of bells. Jaws dropped and eyes popped.

Hattie snapped upright and muttered, "Oh, dear." On Kate's other side, Bea giggled behind her glove.

Kate was not amused. She rose, stepped out into the aisle, and ran her gaze down the length of her bridegroom, then back up again. A jester's cap perched upon her soon-to-be husband's head, and his big feet were stuffed into pointed slippers such as a clown might wear. A musty scent rose from his suit of clothes, patched with a potpourri of materials from gabardine to crimson silk. He must have acquired the costume from a rag-and-bone shop or raided the poorhouse closet. A pirate's enormous gold hoop hung from his pierced ear.

"What the devil do you think you're about, dressed in that bizarre fashion? You are out to make a fool of me, and I will not have it." Kate marked the shrillness in her tone but was too furious to care.

His craggy face split into a broad grin. "We are all fools in love, milady." He reached out to take her hand, but she snatched it back.

"Some of us are more foolish than others." Aware of the others looking on, she folded her arms across her chest and dug in her heels. "If you wish to marry me, first you shall have to change into a decent suit of clothes. And take off that ridiculous hat and those shoes."

Her gaze drifted over to Hadrian and Callie, a silent appeal for support. In contrast to the bridegroom, the photographer was dressed to the nines in a pale gray wool flannel suit. Likewise, Callie was smartly turned out in a princess-cut carriage costume of dark green wool trimmed with lace appliqués repeated on the matching muff. Neither member of the couple would meet her eyes. Clearly she would get no help from that quarter.

She swung her gaze back to Rourke. He stared at her for a disconcertingly long moment. A ginger-colored brow hedged upward. "Do clothes make the man, milady? As for the bells on my toes, I promised you as much the other day. Betimes, the celebration of a marriage is meant to be a joyous occasion, is that not so, Reverend?"

In the midst of the chaos, the rector had returned. He strode down the aisle, sucking at his teeth, the Bible tucked beneath his arm, a white substance that looked suspiciously like frosting lodged in the corners of his mouth.

Drawing up to the marrying pair, he turned to Rourke. "Have you the special license?"

"Aye, I do." Rourke reached into his pocket and handed it over. Kate would not have been greatly surprised to see moths fly out.

The priest gave the paper a perfunctory glance. "I have a baptism in an hour. Shall we?" He gestured to the front of the church.

Kate dug in her heels. "No."

Rourke gripped her arm and stepped forward. "Yes." He turned to her, patted his patched pocket, and mouthed the word, "Marker."

Kate felt her face flush. Despite the draft wafting in through the vestibule, she felt her skin prickle with heat. To taunt her with the cause of her downfall, and on their wedding day, no less! What manner of monster was she marrying? Patrick O'Rourke wasn't only an ill-bred churl. He was pure evil.

Teeth gritted, she leaned in and whispered, "I hate you."

Taking hard hold of her elbow, he steered them both toward the altar rail. "Dearest Kate, I wouldna have it any other way."

CHAPTER SEVEN

> "I must, forsooth, be forced
> To give my hand opposed against my heart
> Unto a mad-brain rudesby, full of spleen,
> Who wooed in haste and means to wed at leisure."
> —WILLIAM SHAKESPEARE, Kate,
> *The Taming of the Shrew*

Do you, Katherine Elizabeth Lindsey, take this man, Patrick Donald O'Rourke, to be your lawfully wedded husband, to love, honor, and obey him . . ."

Standing at the altar in the nondescript little church, Kate was hard-pressed to believe this was her wedding day. It seemed more a nightmare than a celebration, or, barring a nightmare, certainly a farce. Standing beside her, Rourke shifted feet, setting bells tinkling. Kate suspected he did so on purpose to distract her. She repeated her vows through gritted back teeth, her jaw screwed so tight it stood in peril of popping. Casting him a sideways look, she didn't miss the wicked glint in his eye when she stumbled over the dreaded *O* word.

"I now pronounce you man and wife." Looking relieved, the rector closed his Bible with a thump. His pale gaze lifted to Rourke. "You may kiss the bride."

Aware of eyes watching them from the pews, Kate tensed when Rourke turned to her to claim his kiss. She meant to give him only a quick buss and step back, but he captured her face between his callused palms and kissed her hard. The bruising assault was as unlike the previous kiss in Hyde Park as an embrace could be, and yet Kate felt herself swept away by it, her body melting against him and her mouth opening to receive his thrusting tongue. He dragged the tip along the roof of her mouth, and liquid heat splashed her inner thighs, her nipples swelling inside her gown's tight-fitting bodice.

Clapping broke the spell. He released her, and Kate took a shaky step back. She opened her eyes to his grinning face. "There's nay need to be bashful, sweeting. We're wed now in the eyes of God and man."

Her palms itched to slap away that smug smile and replace it with her handprint, but they were in a church, after all. Mindful of her surroundings, she let him lead her down the few steps to where their small party spilled out into the aisle. A makeshift receiving line formed, and subdued congratulations made the rounds.

Shaking Hadrian's hand, Rourke announced, "We must have a photograph to remember this happy day."

More than content to forget, Kate shook her head. "I won't stand for a photograph with you wearing that ridiculous costume."

He backed up to the front pew. "Is that your final answer?"

Spoiling for a fight after that morning's ill treatment, she tossed back her head. "Yes, it is."

"Will you sit for one instead?"

Kate opened her mouth to answer in the negative, but before she could get out so much as a syllable, her husband's arm wrapped about her waist like a whipcord, pulling her down. They fell back against the bench, Rourke buffering the impact and Kate landing hard atop him. Slung across his hard-muscled thighs, the edge of his forearm circling her waist, Kate had never before felt so humiliated, so powerless to direct her fate. Skirts bunched, feet dangling, and hat sliding forward over one eye, she could only imagine how ridiculous, how comical, she must appear.

"Let me up, you great ox. I won't be . . . photographed in . . . disarray." She tried pulling herself upright, but his arm bracing her waist held her fast.

He pulled her closer, stealing her breath. "You canna deny me this memento of our nuptials, my sweet."

"I can and I will."

"Nay, I'll be wanting this image of my angel on our special day. I insist."

"And I insist you shall not."

"Mind, mere minutes ago you swore to obey me in all things." His voice was a warm hiss in her ear.

Kate hissed back, "Like rules, there are some vows made to be broken."

"Not that one." His head swiveled to the photographer. "Take the bloody photograph, Harry. We'll want a memento of this sacred moment to see us through the fifty-odd years of bliss ahead."

Fifty-odd years; it might as well be a prison sentence. Feeling frantic, Kate shouted out, "Mr. St. Claire, don't you dare so much as lay a finger on that striking cord!"

Clearly torn, Hadrian hesitated. He looked from the groom to the bride and then over to his wife. "Callie?"

She lifted her shoulders and shrugged. "I'd say you're damned either way, darling."

"That was my assessment, as well."

Hadrian ducked behind the camera. His silver blond head disappeared beneath the black cloth. A moment later, the flash flared. Black spots skittered before Kate's eyes.

Lifting the cloth, the photographer looked out, "That one might come out a bit blurred because of all the, uh . . . kicking. Shall I take another?"

"Aye!"

"No!" Kate managed to work one arm free. Using her elbow, she dealt her new husband a sharp backward jab.

Behind her, he stifled a groan. "My blushing bride is only shy of having her picture taken."

"Don't be absurd. I have sat for Mr. St. Claire any number of times." She stopped herself, but not soon enough.

Her husband's chuckle tickling her ear confirmed she'd made his point for him. "And so you shall again, my sweet."

Kate stilled. Submitting to having a second picture taken in that ridiculous pose was a serious blow to her badly wounded pride. She hoped that jab had hurt him, a little at least. Better yet, she hoped it left a large and painful bruise. She expected she'd find out later that night unless he slept in a nightshirt, which she doubted. In a matter of hours, she would see his naked chest along with all the naked rest of him. The prospect raised a powerful, primal ache.

Dear God, I'm no better than a harlot.

It had taken this moment, this definitive epiphany, for Kate to learn something new about herself, something dark and shameful, and until now, quite secret, even to her. Where her new husband was concerned, she was a wanton. What other explanation was there for wanting to lie with a man who treated her so ill?

Matters worsened as the morning wore on. They'd scarcely crossed the threshold of the town house where the wedding breakfast was to be served when Rourke announced they must leave after the first toast was drunk. "Most patient, virtuous, and sweet wife, it is time for us to away."

"Don't be absurd," Kate snapped. "It's not as though

Scotland is going anywhere, though one can always hope. For the present, I mean to enjoy this lovely breakfast along with our guests, if for no other reason than it cost a fair piece."

She could calculate the cost of her bridal breakfast down to a single toast point topped with crab if only because, like everything else, she'd directed the menu. She congratulated herself she'd struck a near-perfect balance between keeping up appearances and not sending them all to the poorhouse. Bankrupting them was her father's bailiwick, not hers.

Strolling into the dining room where the food was laid out, Kate scarcely spared him a backward glance. The array of lobster patties, pastries, and strawberries with clotted cream made her mouth water and her stomach rumble. For the past week, she'd subsisted mainly on worry, weak tea, and wafers. Now that the deed was done and her doom sealed, she discovered she was famished.

Every dish looked and smelled enormously appealing—all save for the bridal cake. Set on a cloth-covered table to the side, its trio of tiers frosted with almond cream and festooned with candied fruit in the shape of orange blossoms, it had been delivered the night before. The topmost tier served as the stage for two figurines, a miniature bride and groom. The bride's painted porcelain face looked smiling and content, the groom's equally blissful.

"There is a dining car on the train." Rourke's voice

sounded beside her.

Picking up a plate from the stack, she waved him away. "Go if you must. I will take a later train and meet you."

To drive home her point, she used a pair of silver serving tongs to lift a lemon-curd tart from the pastry platter onto her plate.

"You would have us spend our wedding night apart?" She fancied he sounded a trifle hurt.

Kate was careful not to let her indecision show. As much as she dreaded being alone with her new husband "in that way," the prospect of going to her bridal bed alone brought a sharp stab of disappointment.

She cloaked the latter in a devil-may-care shrug. "If we must, then so be it. As you said, we likely have fifty-odd years ahead."

"Bonny Kate, it is I who say whether or not we must spend this night apart, and I say we must not. Faith, I'd no sleep a wink without my turtledove tucked 'neath my wing." He swooped in, his arms going about her back and waist.

"Leave off." The plate slid from her fingers and bounced onto the carpeted floor. She tried shoving him away, but to no avail. He remained as immovable as a boulder. "We have spent every night of our lives apart ere now. Surely one more will do us no harm. And I am most certainly not your turtledove. Why on earth are you speaking in this strange, stilted fashion?"

He hauled her over his shoulder. "Come, my love,

we must away. Our love nest awaits us, and I mean to sleep beneath my own roof this night."

Kate's head hung like an upside-down anchor, her bum pointed due north, and her legs dangled weightless, one satin slipper falling off and striking the floor. She kicked out at his legs and pounded her fists upon his back, all to no avail.

He bore them steadily toward the door, family and guests clearing an aisle to the exit. On the way there, he paused to shake hands or receive a wink or a pat on the shoulder from one of the males in attendance.

"Mr. St. Claire, make him set me down." Mouth twitching, Hadrian looked away.

Her gaze alighted on his suffragette wife. At last an ally, perhaps even a champion. "Callie, help me. Surely you of all people cannot countenance what amounts to an abduction."

"You might be surprised," Rourke murmured. Apart from being slung over his shoulder like a sack of meal, she was doing her best to ignore him.

Callie shook her dark head. "Nor can I halt it. You are married now, and the current laws give Rourke dominion over you. We are petitioning Parliament to have the unjust laws governing marriage altered for that very reason."

"But I haven't time for petitioning Parliament. I need help—*now!*"

Callie shifted her shoulders to indicate her helplessness. "For the present, there is not much that may be done."

Hanging upside down as she was, Kate couldn't be sure but she thought she glimpsed a small *Mona Lisa*-like smile touching the brunette's mouth. "And you call yourself a feminist."

In her present predicament, maintaining one's dignity was a losing battle. She twisted her head to look back at Rourke. "Set me down, you bloody ox. Have you taken leave of your senses?"

He gave her buttocks a less than gentle squeeze. "Mayhap I have, milady, but as I said before, we are all fools in love."

***

They boarded a northbound train to Scotland from the station at King's Cross. On the way to the station, Rourke stopped off at his Hanover Square house and changed out of his wedding attire and into normal clothes. He hadn't minded the bells overmuch, but those pointed slippers had begun to pinch.

Kate had waited in the carriage. She hadn't spoken a word to him since he'd carried her out of her father's house and deposited her on the red leather carriage seat. Fortunately her little maid had raced after them with her carpetbag of immediate essentials, and Ralph, with Harry's help, had loaded her trunk into the carriage boot.

Standing on the platform, he'd found himself wishing they were lovers headed for a honeymoon in truth.

By way of breaking the ice, he'd offered up some of the history of the station.

"Legend has it King's Cross is built on the site of Boudica's final battle, or else her body is buried beneath the platforms. There are passages under the station her ghost is said to haunt."

"Fascinating." She turned her back on him.

And so began their first day as husband and wife.

Occasionally some of the uniformed workers who passed them by recognized Rourke, but he tapped the side of his nose, signaling them to silence. Before stepping onto the first-class car, he turned over their trunks to a porter with some very special instructions.

They settled into their first-class compartment. Silence descended. Leaning back against the tufted leather seat, Rourke glanced over at his bride. Seated across from him, her white-knuckled hands wrapped about the handle of the unwieldy-looking carpetbag in her lap, she was so far keeping her own counsel. Silent as the sphinx, was more like it. Though the train had yet to leave the station, she'd fixed her gaze out ever since they'd first sat down.

Ordinarily he wouldn't have minded. In his opinion, most people prattled too much as it was. The ritual of silent prayer meetings at Roxbury House had touched his soul in a way that traditional church services never had. Had he been born in an earlier era, the medieval period when his castle had been built, he might have made a fair monk, not because he was especially godly or religious, and certainly not because he was interested in celibacy, but because he liked the idea of living in a community where people reserved speaking for those times when they truly had something to say.

But in this case the silence felt more leaden than golden, the dull weight of it making the waiting time stretch out. Rourke felt as though they'd been sitting stalled on the tracks for hours, though, of course, that was not so. Wondering what time it was, he pulled out his timepiece, and then remembered he'd left his glasses in the pocket of his discarded "wedding" suit. That was going to be a problem.

He stretched out the fob chain to his wife. "Can you tell me the time?"

She swiveled her head from the window. "Of course, I can tell time. Do I seem a simpleton?"

Rourke sucked in a breath. While he'd rather enjoyed the antics at the church and the breakfast, too, he could already see this taming business was turning into hard labor, a labor of . . . love. "I asked if you would read *me* the time. I havena my glasses."

"Oh." She gave the watch face a quick glance as people with perfect vision might do. "It's coming on a quarter 'til one."

"How close to coming on?"

Amber eyes flashed to his face. "A minute or two, give or take? Why, are you in some sort of rush? Is someone *chasing* us?"

Actually, Ralph Sylvester was secreted in one of the second-class cabins. Once they disembarked at their destination station of Linlithgow, Rourke intended to give the butler-cum-valet-cum-coachman a head start to the castle. The latter was crucial to setting up the next act of his personal play.

But beyond any behind-the-scenes machinations, Rourke was a man who ate, slept, and rose by the clock. He took considerable pride in the fact that, according to the latest timetable report, his trains never veered off schedule by more than a minute. Perhaps it came from having little or no structure as a child, but living according to rigorous routine felt more a freedom than a restraint or imposition. Once he'd left Roxbury House, he'd missed the bells that had regulated meals, lessons, recreation, sleeping and waking, and even worship.

He glanced across to Kate, her head once more turned to look out onto the platform. Rourke wasn't fooled. He didn't for a moment doubt that she was every whit as aware of him as he was of her. Unfortunately for him, she was also just as stubborn.

Leaning back in his seat, he found himself studying the woman with whom he would share not only his bed, but also his life, the next fifty years of it at least. From the few embraces they'd shared, he knew her skin really was that petal soft, her hair that sweet smelling, her lips and tongue as delectable as a ripe peach. Were circumstances different and theirs a normal marriage, he might well choose this moment to draw the car's velvet curtain all the way closed and reach for her. He'd never made love on a moving train, or a stalled one, for that matter. Given that he owned the whole bloody railway, that fact struck him as both ironic and a shame. He had the urge to reach out and lift his bride onto his lap to straddle him, tunnel a hand beneath her skirts and finger her, the honey from her sex trickling like treacle onto his hand, covering his mouth over hers to muffle her first soft moans and then her throaty cries. The fantasy, vivid, brought on one hell of a cock stand.

He shifted in his seat. Inadvertently his knee bumped her leg.

She swiveled her head around and pinned him with a glare. "Must you fidget so?"

Fidget—Jaysus, if only she knew.

He reached into the brown paper bag of food items he'd bought from the vendor cart back at King's Cross. "Apple?"

"No, thank you."

"If you fancy a hot meal, there's a dining car a few compartments down from this one."

He ought to know. The northbound line on which he'd booked their seats was one of his, the shiny black and red steam locomotives the finest of his fleet, the blueprint of their interior laid out in his head.

She shook her head.

"Are you certain? We dinna disembark 'til Linlithgow. That's almost an eight-hour journey, mind."

"Yes, Mr. O'Rourke, so the printed ticket said."

"I have a name, you know. It's Patrick." For whatever reason, he still very badly wanted to hear her call him by his given name.

"I am aware of that. And a middle name, as well. Donald?" Her lips twitched.

"Donald was my mother's da's name."

She cocked her head to the side. "Perhaps I'll call you Donald. You just might look like a Donald."

She was teasing him, but at least she was talking to him again. "Dinna dare. If you won't call me by my given name, then call me Rourke as my friends do."

Her brows lifted. "Ah, yes, and you and I are such great friends, aren't we?"

The sarcasm wasn't lost on him, but for the time being he would do his best to ignore it. "As we're wedded now, here's hoping we're no enemies."

Back in London, two former Roxbury House friends-turned-married-lovers stood in the crowded greenroom of their newly renovated theatre, sipping champagne and shaking their heads at their friend Rourke's extraordinary telegraphed news.

Kate and I wed. STOP.

Taking train to castle in Scotland. STOP.

Come up for Gav's birthday next month. STOP.

The telegram arrived before Daisy stepped out onstage as Hermia in *A Midsummer Night's Dream*. Fortunately Hadrian and Callie, both witnesses to the hasty wedding and sworn to secrecy until now, had arrived before the final act to fill in the glossed-over details. Apparently not only had their brash friend coerced Lady Katherine into marrying him, but once she had, he'd swept her off her feet and carried her away—literally.

Gavin took a sip from Daisy's champagne flute and then passed the glass back. "Rourke wedded to a blue-blooded shrew; there's a play in that, as well as ample poetic justice. If I hadn't helped him get the special license, I might think he was playing a practical joke on us."

"Why, darling, that brilliant mind of yours isn't only for legal matters, is it?" Catching his blank look, she elaborated, "As Shakespeare might say if he were still alive, the play's the thing. In this case, the play's already written and has been for several hundred years."

Gavin's gaze connected with hers, and a broad smile broke over his face. "You don't mean *The Taming of the Shrew,* by any chance?"

She nodded. "Indeed. I'd say given the circumstances, a special wedding gift is in order, wouldn't you? You never know, but it might make for . . . *instructive* reading."

Gavin rolled his eyes. "That depends upon Rourke actually reading it. I've yet to see him pick up anything that wasn't a newspaper or railway financial report."

"You assume Lady Katherine is the one in need of taming."

He sent her a tolerant smile. "In that case, I'll post it first thing in the morning."

She reached out and swiped her thumb over the champagne bead resting on his sexy lower lip. As much as she loved a party, she was very much looking forward to their private celebration after the guests had gone.

"Perfect, my love, pray do."

"Married!" Felicity pulled her head from the musky space between her latest keeper's tented knees and looked up into his strained face. "Why didn't you tell me before now?"

On the cusp of climax, Lord Haversham raised his perspiring head from the pillow. "It just happened this morning. Lindsey said O'Rourke refused to stay for the wedding breakfast. Threw the little shrew over his shoulder like a sack of corn and carried her off to the train station. God, I would have loved to have seen the bitch's face. With luck, that meddlesome package will be out of my hair. Good riddance. The younger chit is biddable enough. She should present no problem at all."

His heavy hand landed at the back of her head, pushing her down, but Felicity reared out of reach. "You should have told me."

His lordship scowled. "What's it to do with you?"

Swinging her long legs over the bedside, Felicity shrugged. She hadn't even known Rourke was back in London, but then these days she hardly traveled in West End drawing-room circles. "I fancy my information as much as the next person. I've certainly helped you to yours a time or two."

Considering the question, she padded over to the chipped dresser, moving slowly to give him time to appreciate her buxom backside and delicious curves. Of all her lovers, a considerable number particularly as she was just twenty-three, there was only one man who'd ever truly possessed the power to not only satisfy, but enslave her. Patrick O'Rourke—Rourke—had always given her as good a shagging as he'd got. Felicity wasn't prone to self-reflection, let alone regret, but this once she had to admit she'd been a bloody fool to let him loose. Given time, she might have brought him around to the idea of their marrying. Even if he'd held the hard line—and Felicity's mouth watered at the memory of just how very hard he got and how very long he remained that way—being his mistress had brought its own rewards.

But beyond the carnal delights he could deliver, Rourke was a rich man and a generous one. He'd purchased the former Palace supper club to help out a friend, but he'd yet to reopen it. Before its closing, the popular Covent Garden nightspot had launched the careers of several stars of the stage, including the actress formerly known as Delilah du Lac. The music-hall chanteuse, whose real name was Daisy Lake, had gone on to debut in a proper play at Drury Lane. With her new husband, also a friend of Rourke's, she was about to open her own theatre in the East End.

Felicity's stage career was progressing at a considerably slower pace. She'd left Edinburgh for London two years ago, and by now she really ought to be a top liner somewhere. Instead she was stuck dancing in the chorus at the Royal Alhambra Palace on the east side of Leicester Square. Most of her fellow dancers seemed to have no ambition beyond trolling the canteen between performances and flirting with the gentlemen patrons for pairs of gloves and shots of gin. Felicity aspired to better, but she was coming to wonder if "better" was, indeed, on the way. The present shabby suite of rented rooms where Haversham had set her up was fast losing its charm.

Haversham called to her from the bed, "Surely you don't mean to leave me now, like . . . this?"

In the rust-spotted mirror, she caught a glimpse of his tortured face and smiled. The sadist in her loved that she was leaving him aching.

Folding her arms across her berry-tipped breasts, she turned about to face him. "That all depends on how cooperative you show yourself to be."

He scowled again and braced his hand about his cock. "What the devil? I'll play any game you fancy, only come over here and finish this first."

As much as Felicity enjoyed toying with the whips and paddles and silk ties tucked into her bedside table, she had more important matters on her mind. "All in good time, ducks, but first tell me everything you know about the younger Lindsey sister—and I mean *everything*."

Kate nodded off shortly after they crossed the border into Scotland. She awoke to Rourke pressing on her shoulder. "Kate, wake up, this is our stop."

Muzzy-headed, she nodded and got up. She collected her carpetbag and followed her new husband out into the train vestibule. It was dark when they stepped down onto the open-air platform.

Kate looked about, the station lights illuminating winter white sky and gray drizzle. The rural station was a far cry from the splendor of King's Cross, but then King's Cross was in the heart of London whereas Linlithgow was a much smaller town. It stood to reason a castle wouldn't very well be in the city. What had she been thinking?

The obvious answer was, she hadn't been thinking. She hadn't thought things out at all. She'd trusted Rourke to take care of their travel plans, to take care of her. She wasn't used to putting her fate, her person, in anyone else's hands, particularly a man's. That she had, and without conscious thought, brought about an odd and disconcerting mix of feelings.

Following him through the knot of disembarking passengers, she found himself admiring the way the cut of his coat showed off his broad shoulders and tapered waist. Whatever his faults, she couldn't discount the obvious. Her new husband was a fine figure of a man.

That a man who always dressed so meticulously would have shown up as he had to a wedding, his, baffled her. Obviously he'd set out to annoy her—he had annoyed her—but why he would choose to do so by dressing as a clown baffled her.

He positioned her by one of the benches on the platform. "Wait here, Kate. I'll go and fetch our luggage, and then we'll be on our way."

For once Kate was too fatigued to argue. Beyond that, she sensed she was in good hands. Kate had only ridden the train a few times before, but her husband owned railways. She hadn't missed the respectful looks lanced their way by the stationmaster and porters back at King's Cross. He more than knew what to do.

Kate took a seat on the bench. A gust of winter wind found its way inside her coat. She shivered and pulled the collar closer. This far north, the winters were far colder than what they'd left in London. If she stayed on, she would have to purchase a heavier winter coat than her fashionable, if thin wool one.

If she stayed on. She caught the implication that she had a choice and shivered with a different sort of chill.

She was married now, leg-shackled as it were. Like it or not, her place was with her husband.

Returning footsteps had her snapping back to the present. She looked up at Rourke's sober face. "I'm afraid our luggage has gone missing."

"Lost!" Kate popped up from her seat.

"Aye, I'm afraid so."

"How can that be? I stood beside you on the station platform in London when you turned it over to that porter."

His nod acknowledged that was so. "It seems he omitted actually loading it into the baggage car. It may be sitting on the platform still, provided it hasna been stolen."

"Stolen!"

"It's possible, but hopefully not. If it was recovered, they'll send it on the next train in another day or two."

For a man who'd also lost his luggage, and on his own railway no less, he seemed remarkably resigned. Had Kate been in his place, heads would have rolled.

He cocked his head to the side. "Actually, it's all for the best."

She glared at him. All this cheeriness really was beginning to grate. "How so?"

"The cabs are all off for the evening."

"Meaning?"

Beneath the hazy glow of the platform lights, his smile seemed to broaden to a jack-o'-lantern's grin. "We'll have to walk."

She looked beyond the platform where the drizzle was fast building to a full-scale downpour and felt her spirits dampening along with the weather.

"But it's raining—hard." She didn't have so much as a parasol with her, let alone an umbrella. All she owned at the moment was contained in the upholstered carpet-bag lying on the bench seat.

He tucked her arm in his. "Dinna fash, Kate. As neither of us is particularly sweet, we've nay worries of melting."

"How much farther is this castle of yours?"

Rourke cast a backward glance to his bride limping along the roadside. The mud had sucked off her left shoe a while back, and in bending down to retrieve it, she'd slipped and fallen face-first in the mud. She'd lost her hat, as well. A gust of wind had made short work of it, blowing it into a frost-parched field where it landed in a pile of dung. Wet hair trailed down her back and plastered her cheeks and neck. Every so often, she reached up a hand to smooth it back, smearing even more filth on her face. Poor lass, if pride preceded a fall, Kate had fallen twice now and still she managed to hold on to her dignity. Under other circumstances, he might have found himself admiring her. Damn it, he did admire her, though he had no intention of altering his course.

Every time he was tempted to take pity on her, he forced his thoughts back to the escapade in her father's garden. The mental picture of those jeering faces, Kate's among them, brought him back swiftly to his purpose—taming the shrew trailing behind him.

He pretended to consider, though he knew the distance exactly. "Och, another league, I'd say."

Breathing hard, she hauled up beside him. "But that's an hour's walk at least. And we've walked so far already. Are you quite certain you know the direction?"

"Dinna fash, lass. I ken these roads like the back of my hand."

She shielded her hand over her eyes and peered out onto the hedgerow-bordered roadway. "I'm not, uh . . . fashing. I was only wondering where we are. I could almost imagine we're turning in circles."

Rourke hid a smile. They had done a loop or two, as a matter of fact. His castle was less than a league from the train station. On a fine day he sometimes walked to the station simply to enjoy the exercise. They might have been there by now, only he'd deliberately taken her the most rambling, roundabout route of rutted country lanes.

Likewise, their luggage going missing was no happenstance. He'd arranged with the porter to have their trunks "lost." The man had looked at him oddly, but as Rourke owned the railway, what was he to do but comply? This taming business was proving to be bloody hard work. He only hoped Kate broke and soon. Until she did, he had no choice but to suffer along with her.

To annoy her, and hopefully speed matters along, he made a point of thickening his burr. He wasn't the ace mimic that Ralph was, but he tossed in every Scots colloquialism he could. She hadn't remarked upon it yet, but he suspected before long she would.

"Was there no one who might have met us at the station?"

"Aye, only we werena expected 'til tomorrow."

That news had the predicted effect. She swung her head about. Even in semidarkness, there was no missing the murderous look she lanced him. "Tomorrow! Do you mean to say we might have stayed for our wedding breakfast and taken a train in the morning?"

"Aye, so we might have—only I found myself so bowled over by your sweet temperament and pleasing ways in the church, darling Kate, that I couldna bring myself to wait another day to bear you back to my own home—and bed."

Rather than answer that, she said, "Are you quite certain we haven't missed it, some entrance road or drive . . ."

"That eager to begin the honeymoon, are ye?"

She screwed up her face as though a foul smell had wafted their way. "If I'm eager for anything, it's a hot bath and a hot supper and a night's rest—*undisturbed* rest."

"In that case, Katie, forward ho. The hospitality of my hearth awaits my lady's pleasure."

CHAPTER EIGHT

> "This is a way to kill a wife with kindness,
> And thus I'll curb her mad and headstrong humor.
> He that knows better how to tame a shrew,
> Now let him speak—'tis charity to show."
> —WILLIAM SHAKESPEARE, Petruchio,
> *The Taming of the Shrew*

By the time they reached Rourke's castle, Kate's teeth were knocking together, and an unshakable chill streaked the length of her spine. She'd swallowed her pride and accepted Rourke's coat a while back if only to silence his persistent offers. Still, with their clothing soaked through, the extra layer scarcely helped. Limping up the drive beyond the stone gatehouse, curiously devoid of a keeper, she was too fatigued, dispirited, and bone-chilled to give the crenellated battlements and cone-topped towers more than a passing look. There would be plenty of time for exploring in the days ahead—those "fifty-odd years" came to mind. For the present, all she wanted was to get inside where it was dry and presumably warm, or at least *warmer*, and have a hot bath and a hot supper, the latter in no particular order.

They stepped inside, and Kate found herself in the vestibule of a medieval great hall. Torches burned from cast-iron brackets anchored at intervals on the stone walls, providing patches of flickering light. Something tickled her nose, and she looked up. A tapestry of spiderwebs hung suspended from the vaulted ceiling. Judging from the size and intricacy of the webs, they had been there for some time, a graveyard for flies and other insects, as well as home to more spiders than Kate cared to think about.

Kate hated spiders.

A stone fireplace took pride of place at the far end of the hall. Basking before it, a large brindle-colored mastiff rose from a plaid pallet covered in fur and ambled over to greet them, or rather Rourke.

Kate's gaze swung back to her husband. Other than horses, she hadn't realized he might have animals purely as pets. "Ho, there, Toby, I missed you, too." Leaping up on his hind legs, the dog planted his forepaws on Rourke's chest.

Kate eyed the animal, more miniature horse than dog. Standing upright, he was very nearly as tall as she. "That is *not* a dog."

"Oh, aye, he's a dog a'right." Rourke scratched the beast about the ears, sending the long, black spotted tongue lolling out one side of his mouth.

Kate hung back by the door. Ever since one of her father's hunting dogs had knocked her down face-first on the bricks, leaving her with the small white scar on her cheek, she'd been hesitant around dogs, large ones at least.

"What, uh . . . kind is he . . . other than large, I mean?"

Rourke shrugged as though the question of his pet's pedigree had never occurred to him before now. "Part mastiff, wolfhound, and mayhap wolf. In the main, To-by's a mongrel like me."

"I see."

The dog subsided to the floor on all fours, and Rouke brushed at the paw prints fronting his jacket. "Don't let his size fool you. Toby is as gentle as a lamb. He wouldna harm a fly. Now a thief or a poacher, well, that's a different story. Once he gets used to you, he'll be your best friend. He'll even sleep at the foot of your bed."

Given that the dog was not only large but rather matted and smelly, Kate heartily hoped to be spared the delight of having Toby as a bedmate. Still, if they were all to live together, and it appeared Toby had the run of the castle, it behooved her to make friends.

She slowly set the carpetbag inside the door—no sudden movements!—and stretched out her hand. Toby trotted over, sniffing and then slobbering her palm in search of treats, no doubt. Like everything else she'd so far seen, he could benefit from a good scrubbing.

"I'll bring you a bone from the kitchen next time." She made a mental note to see about his grooming in the coming days and pulled her hand away. Swiping it on the side of her mud-caked skirts, she asked, "Where is the kitchen, by the way?"

Rourke shrugged. "Dunno, exactly. Somewhere below stairs."

Kate heartily hoped that wherever it was, it was in better condition than what she'd so far seen. Thinking back to the sumptuous wedding breakfast she'd missed, she asked, "Can you point me to the pantry at least? Once I wash my hands, I'll cobble together a cold supper."

He startled her by stomping his foot. "There'll be no cold suppers for my bride! My Kate shall have a feast to rival all feasts—stewed mutton and kidneys, roast goose, capon, and new potatoes."

She hadn't exaggerated when she'd called the castle shambling. That was possibly too generous a description. If the main rooms had been permitted to descend into such a state, Lord only knew what awaited her in the kitchen. She doubted the necessary foodstuffs were in store. Even if the larder was stocked, preparing the dishes he called for would take hours. Kate needed food now.

"And for dessert, let there be plum pudding and bride cake. Why, 'tis our wedding day, Kate. We must have cake." He grasped her wrists and raised her joined hands to meet his smacking kiss.

She jerked away. "If you'll recall, we had a lovely

189

cake at the breakfast you insisted we leave."

Rourke softened his voice. "You've only to name your fancy, Kate. Ask for what you want, and it shall be brought forth as if by magic."

As she'd so far seen no servants about, Kate doubted it. Late though it was, ordinarily someone—a housekeeper or butler—would have risen to see to their needs.

All at once, he stalked off, calling, "Cheevers! Cheevers, where are you, you lazy lout?"

"Rourke, really, is that necessary?"

Before now, he'd always been so soft-spoken. Even when he'd carried her off from their wedding breakfast, he'd never once raised his voice. Now that he was home in Scotland, however, it seemed bellowing was his preferred method of communicating—another facet of married life to which she could look forward.

Hands covering her ears, Kate followed him into what apparently served as a dining room these days. A long wooden trestle table, of the sort once used in monastery refectories, dominated the room, a dozen or so carved high-backed chairs thrust around it at intervals. A heavy epergne sat in the center, several of the wax candles melted to stubs. From what Kate could see, there was no electric or even gas lighting. It was as if she'd stepped back into the Middle Ages.

An old man emerged from the shadows and ambled forward, hunched over and dragging one leg behind him, Quasimodo-fashion. "Here I am, sir, milady?" Brownish eyes, remarkably clear and lively for one so decrepit, lifted to Kate's face.

Rourke banged a fist on the table's edge. "Send word to the kitchen that I am arrived with my bride and that no time is to be lost in bringing forth the feast."

"The, uh . . . feast, good master?"

"Aye, our wedding supper, and be quick about it."

Given Rourke's humble beginnings, Kate was shocked to hear him barking at a servant, and an elderly one at that. If she didn't know better, she might suspect he'd been drinking. She tried reasoning with him.

"At this hour, surely the cook must have retired to bed long ago and the kitchen maids dismissed for the night, as well."

Her tentative tone took her aback. She scarcely recognized herself. It wasn't like her to mince her words. Good God, was she settling into wifedom already?

Her husband's gaze hardened. He slammed a fist upon the table, sending one pewter candlestick crashing onto its side. "Then we'll rouse them, by God, the lazy lot."

Kate sighed. Even she could see it was pointless to argue. Let him call for the food and discover for himself that what he bespoke was impossible. Perhaps then he would believe her and let them sit down to a simple but filling cold supper. Even bread and cheese would do at this point.

Dividing her gaze between the men, she said, "If one

of you would point me the way, I'll go and wash up and be back down in time for supper." Given the primitive state of everything else she'd so far seen, she doubted the bedchambers were outfitted with plumbing, but perhaps there was a water closet somewhere in the main area.

Rourke reached for her hand. Apparently oblivious to muck and slobber, he carried it palm side up to his lips. "You seem fresh as a daisy to me." He held on to her hand.

A daisy dipped in mud, perhaps. "Nonsense, we are not animals, at least I am not. I will sit down to sup as soon as I wash the filth of the road from my face and hands." She tugged her hand free. "I shall be a few minutes at most. If you cannot stave off your hunger that long, then by all means begin without me."

"Are you suggesting I would sit down to our nuptial feast without my wife?"

Kate let out a snort, an unladylike gesture to which under the circumstances she felt fully entitled. "Our nuptial feast, as you call it, was this morning's breakfast, which, thanks to you, I missed. It is too late in the hour, sir, to profess a gentleman's manners."

She would find a place to wash on her own. Mustering as much dignity as she might under the circumstances, she grabbed a fistful of her skirts, fast drying to a stiff mess, and hobbled toward the staircase.

Watching her go, the dog opened his mouth and yawned, the sound emerging as a cross between a sigh and a whine. Rourke held in a chuckle. What a woman he'd married. He couldn't help but admire her. Even his dog admired her, which was saying a lot, as Toby was as big or bigger as she.

Tiny though she might be, her petite frame housed a lioness's heart. Since that morning, he'd tested her sorely, and yet still she kept her chin up and her back straight—and her spirit unbroken. Subjected to similar circumstances, most London misses would be watering pots now. Not so his bold, brave Kate. *His* Kate—when had he begun thinking of her as his? To do so was folly, for she had yet to so much as say his given name.

He waited until "his Kate's" footfalls disappeared down the corridor, and then whipped about to Ralph. "Bring the food in and be quick about it. The devil only knows how soon she'll be back. Hurry, man!"

Ralph reached up to the white beard slipping partway down one side of his face. In retrospect, he really should have been more generous with the spirit gum, but thanks to the slow-moving cabbie he'd taken from the train station, he'd been pressed for time.

"I am hurrying, sir, but it's difficult to be quick about much of anything with my leg strapped into this brace."

Fortunately he need not go all the way down to the kitchen to fetch the food. The prearranged meal waited in covered serving dishes on a cart in the adjacent room.

Rourke scowled. Ordinarily he was the most good-natured of employers. Ralph could tell this taming business must have him on edge. "We all have our crosses to bear, Sylvester, and mind I'm paying you handsomely to bear yours. Now, go."

Heading off, Ralph was beginning to regret bringing the play to his old friend's attention. Rourke's lady didn't strike him as a shrew in need of taming so much as an overburdened young woman inclined to snappishness. The younger sister, Beatrice, was positively sublime.

"If you'll pardon my saying so, *sir*, playing pranks upon one's wife hardly seems the way to go about celebrating a marriage."

Rourke snorted. "Whatever gave you the notion this is a celebration? It's war."

At wit's end, Kate lifted one of the tapers from its bracket and set out to find her own way. After several minutes of aimless wandering, she came upon a set of backstairs. The stairs led to a dormitory-style suite of rooms that must have most recently served as the servants' wing, though the beds were stripped and empty now. The bare-bones amenities included a water closet with a sink and crude crank. She'd used her few remaining pins to put her hair back up as best she could and then washed her face and hands with the rusty water.

Her exploration took longer than she'd hoped, but eventually she found her way back down to the main hall, and from there the side door leading into the dining room. Given the snail's pace at which the game-legged servant moved, not even a cold meal could have been made ready in her short time away. She heartily hoped someone had thought to set out some refreshment to ease the wait. A glass of sherry would be lovely, as would a hot cup of tea.

She stepped inside, the lit candles in the candelabra camouflaging the dirt and dust and adding an ambiance of mellow warmth. Her new husband was ensconced in a thronelike chair at the head of the table, a napkin tucked into his collar and a plate of chicken bones set before him.

Seeing her, he smiled and beckoned her over but made no move to rise or pull out a chair. "Ah, Kate, there you are. I feared you might have taken a wrong turn."

"I did take a wrong turn, several." She glanced at the drumstick in his hand. "I see you started without me after all."

He paused to take a nibble of the meat. "Started and finished, as a fact."

"Finished! You can't mean to say you ate it all?"

He shook his head. "We Scots have hearty appetites to be sure, but I couldna eat all that bounty nay matter how many breakfasts I missed."

"Where is it, then?" Kate would gladly sit down to sup in the kitchen.

"I had it carted away and tossed in the rubbish bin."

"All of it?"

"Aye, every last morsel. The boiled round of beef was tough as leather and the roast chicken dry as bone. The salmon wasna all that bad, though. It was rare tasty, in fact."

"There was salmon?" Kate was very partial to salmon.

"Aye, served up with buttered green beans and some sort of nuts atop."

"Almonds, perhaps, slivered?" Kate's watering mouth was poised to drool like the dog's.

"Aye, I believe it was. Rough fellow that I am, such poorly prepared fare is good enough for me, but no for my lady wife."

"But I haven't eaten since last night's supper. I need food—now!" Her voice, she realized, had shot up rather shrill.

"Nay worries, I saved some for you."

"You did?"

Staring at the chicken leg in his hand, so little meat left that the bone showed through, it was all she could do to keep herself from lunging forward and wresting it away.

He pulled the meat off and fed it to the dog. "Aye, I did." He dipped a hand into his pocket, pulled out a small green apple, and tossed it to her.

She caught it between both hands. "You are the soul of kindness, sir." She rubbed it against her dirty gown and then bit in.

"Mind that forked tongue of yours, Katie, or tomorrow's breakfast may well go the way of tonight's supper."

The apple to her mouth, she pulled out a chair for herself and sat down. "You cannot starve me—not for long at any rate." Kate had never before spoken with a full mouth, but the present circumstances called for an exception.

"Dinna fash, Katie. I'm no out to starve you. You've scarce sufficient meat upon your bones as is." He reached around and slapped her thigh, not hard enough to sting, but the surprise made her start. "Were I to feast upon your smile, were you to serve up a honeyed word every now and again as opposed to only vinegar, sure I'd see that the best of my larder and wine cellar were laid out for your pleasure."

"I'd rather starve than cozen up to you."

Rourke shrugged. "Suit yourself."

The apple whittled to its core, she set it on the plate of bones and pushed back from the table. "Never fear, I shall, starting by going to bed." Picking up her sodden skirts, she stomped toward the door.

"Whose bed is it you mean to go to?"

The question stopped Kate in her tracks. Slowly, very slowly, she turned back to face him. Planting her fists upon slender hips, she dug in her heels and glared.

"If you think to bed me after the brutish treatment you've so far dished out this day, then you'd best think again, sir."

"That randy, are we?" He raked his eyes over her.

Having just glimpsed her reflection, she knew full

well what he was seeing—dirty hair, dirty face, dirty gown, dirty . . . everything, as well as pale and hollow-eyed—hardly the most provocative package.

Returning his gaze to her face, he smiled. "Nay worries, Katie. I can find the willpower to resist your charms for the night at least."

"I intend to lock my door all the same."

Kate's eyes blazed with defiance, challenge. Rourke tore off the silly napkin and rose from the table. He moved toward her, closing the gap between them in three long strides until he stood before her, so close he had to be careful not to tread on her feet, the shoeless one especially. A lesser woman—make that most women—would have backed down or at least backed up a step or two. Not so Kate. She neither moved a muscle nor budged an inch. Drenched, filthy, and foodless, still she held her ground, tipped back her head, and met his gaze head-on with a fierce, unflinching look of her own.

Captivated in spite of himself, he reached down and lifted her chin on the edge of his hand. Given the drenching she'd endured, he'd expected to find her flesh cold as marble, but instead it was warm and glowing and impossibly soft. He couldn't resist. He wrapped his hands about her forearms, reed-slender yet strong, and bent to brush his mouth over hers.

He drew back. "Make no mistake, lass, when I decide to claim my husbandly rights, no wee lock shall keep me from you."

Mutinous eyes glared up at him. "Is that a threat?"

He dropped his hands and stepped back. "Nay, sweeting. That is a promise."

After the impromptu kiss, Kate hadn't stayed to test Rourke's promise to leave her alone for the night. She grabbed her candle and dashed from the dining room in search of a bed. Surely in a castle this size, if she kept opening doors, sooner or later she would come upon a suitably equipped bedroom.

At some point the dog, Toby, joined her. Like his master, he had a full stomach and apparently nothing better to do than plague her. After opening more doors, including closets, than she cared to count, she found a cubby-sized room. Like the other rooms she'd so far peeked into, the bed was stripped of both linens and mattress, but there was at least a heavy, carved chest in the corner. Holding her candle aloft, she checked the ceiling. Aside from one cobweb in the opposite corner, she didn't see any evidence of spiders. And the door had a latch.

Encouraged, she crossed the room. She stuck the stub of candle into an empty candlestick holder and then knelt to open the chest. The lid was heavy. She had to use both hands. She heaved it up on screeching hinges, sending dust clouds flying. Eyes watering, she rifled inside. She pulled out a heavy tapestry coverlet that had seen better days and a smaller, lighter blanket. She dragged the coverlet over to the fireplace and laid it out, then rolled the blanket to serve as a pillow. A squeak drew her attention to the door, as yet unlocked. The dog nosed his way inside and lumbered over to her. She tried leading him out by the collar, but he stiffened his legs and stood his ground. Kate was too tired to argue.

"All right, you can stay, only not in my bed, such as it is. You can sleep in that corner." She pointed him to the corner without the web.

Tail thumping, he stared up at her with liquid brown eyes and stretched out on the coverlet anyway.

Kate sighed. She crossed to the door and slid the rusty bolt in place.

When I decide to claim my husbandly rights, no wee lock shall keep me from you.

Shivering, she lightly touched fingertips to her lips and returned to her makeshift bed. The coal bin was near empty. She scrounged the last few bricks and made a piddling fire, which the dog seemed to appreciate. He rolled onto his back and poked all four paws up in the air, displaying a white ruff and speckled belly to go with his otherwise brindled fur.

"You really are a mongrel, aren't you?"

Kate gave the belly a gingerly pat and then tried nudging him over to the side, again without success. For a woman used to being in charge, she wasn't having much luck being listened to today. She sat down on the vacant patch of the coverlet not covered in dog and held her hands out to the heat. Pins and needles pricked her numb fingers back to life, but her nails were still alarmingly blue.

What if I died here?

Setting aside her remaining shoe along with that morbid thought, she stretched out on her side. *Ah, lovely.* The floor beneath her was cold as a marble tomb and just as hard, but the dog at her back was warm and pliant, if somewhat stinky. So, she supposed, was she. Even if her accommodations left something to be desired, she'd never before taken such pure pleasure in lying her body down for the night. She curled into a comforting ball, tucked her hands beneath her head, and focused on going to sleep.

But with her eyes closed, the bizarre wedding day played again and again in her mind. How fortunate that she hadn't any preconceived notions, romantic or otherwise. Most women of her acquaintance expected their weddings to be . . . well, beautiful. Thinking back on the farcical nuptials and the aborted wedding breakfast, she couldn't imagine anything less beautiful. Tired as she was, she felt a sob building at the back of her throat. She rolled onto her back, the tears sliding from her temples and melting into her hairline.

The ruckus had her rocketing upright, the dog with her. The would-be musician with a string instrument stood in the hallway just outside her door. It was Rourke, of course, strumming the score to what vaguely resembled "Greensleeves" and singing the lyrics at the top of his lungs. Kate dragged a hand through her tangled hair and dried her eyes on her crusty sleeve. It seemed her wedding-day torments had yet to end. Along with freezing and starving her, he apparently meant to deprive her of sleep and bleed her ears.

Directing her voice to the closed door, she called out, "Are you mad? It's past midnight."

The bellowing abruptly ceased. "We are all fools in love, milady."

So he'd said several times earlier. The line he quoted was a famous one. Exhausted as she was, she found herself racking her brain for the author. Be it prose or verse, that he quoted any literary source was itself odd. He didn't strike her as the poetry-reading sort. Who *was* the author? Dryden? Poe? Swift? Ordinarily she would have known it off the top of her head—she *was* the poetry-reading sort—but she was beyond exhausted, not to mention halfway to ill with hunger and chill.

Kate's temper rose apace with her voice. Glaring at the door, thankfully locked, she shouted, "You are most certainly a fool, but we are not in love! And it's bloody late. Go to bed!"

"Nay, if music be the food of love, I think I'll play on a while. Betimes, I recall how you fancy being sung to."

So that's what this was about. He still hadn't forgiven her for making him look foolish that night in the garden. As misbegotten as her plan had been, he really ought to let bygones be bygones. She had just opened her mouth to say so when the din started up again.

"What the devil is it you're playing?" Barring bagpipes, she couldn't imagine a more offensive instrumental.

Pitching his voice over the music, he answered, "The hurdy-gurdy. Do you play?"

"No."

He paused as if thinking that over. "Meaning not the hurdy-gurdy, or no instrument at all?"

"I play the piano a little." Could they really be having this conversation through a closed door at this hour?

"I could teach you to play the hurdy-gurdy and the Scottish harp, too." His voice was almost boyish in its enthusiasm.

"No, thank you." She was coming to wonder if her new husband might not be a bit, well . . . *off*.

"Do you fancy favoring me with a song, then?"

"No!" She turned and punched the makeshift pillow. If she was of a mind to "favor" him with anything, it would be her knuckles to his nose.

She settled once more on her side. The strange serenade carried her thoughts back to his caterwauling that night in the garden. Beyond all reason, she smiled. He had the most dreadful voice of any man she'd ever heard sing, and yet thinking of the effort he'd put forth to please her back then sent her heart squeezing in on itself.

A wistful sigh escaped her.

"Kate, do you sleep?"

She wasn't sure why, but the thought of him just outside her door made her feel safe, not threatened. To think she'd been on the cusp of crying herself to sleep mere minutes ago. "If I said yes, would you go away?" She smiled into the "pillow" and closed her eyes.

There was a long pause, and then he said, "I'll bid you good night, then." Was it her imagination, or did his tone hold the slightest trace of regret—and hope?

For a mad minute, Kate considered rising, unbolting the door, and pulling him inside to join her on the makeshift pallet, his big, strong body a buffer to both loneliness and the floor. But that would be not only mad, but impractical. Hungry and dirty as she was, more than any other creature comfort, she desperately needed sleep.

Yawning, she slid her tented hands beneath her head. For whatever reason, she gave in to the temptation to call out one last time. "Good night, Rourke."

When he didn't answer, she supposed he must have already gone to seek his own bed.

Outside Kate's door, Rourke lowered the hellish instrument, which someone had left forgotten in the attic to warp, and flattened his back against the wall. *Good*

night, sweet Kate.

And she was sweet, or at least she could be. He'd seen glimpses of her kindness and her caring over the past week and before that, always for others, though, never for him. She'd only married him to save her scapegrace father and spoiled little sister, after all. So far she'd asked nothing for herself, though he would gladly shower her with the world's riches, or his share of them, at least.

And she could be stoic, his Kate. Throughout the day, he'd been relentless in testing her mettle, and yet every time he had, she'd shown herself equal to the challenge. Braw and beautiful and bold, she'd bellied up to that wet, bone-chilling trek from the train station like a seasoned foot soldier rather than what she was, a wee woman in a muddy, sodden gown, a woman so small he could easily span her waist with his two clumsy, coarse hands. *Ah, Kate . . .*

Earlier he'd known a moment's guilt—more than a moment's. When they'd reached the castle and she'd stood before him, teeth chattering and slender shoulders shaking, he'd almost lost heart for carrying out the rest of his plan. He hoped she hadn't caught a chill—or worse. Petruchio might have set out to kill his Kate with kindness, but not so Rourke. He only wanted to teach his new wife a lesson, to soften her spleen so they might have a somewhat happy life, but not to harm her—no, never that.

What is it you dream of, my Kate?

Given the trials he'd put her through, he suspected her dreams would be filled with sumptuous foods and feather-soft beds and bottomless baths with steaming water that never cooled. Imagining her in a copper hip bath and nothing else, the water pearling over bared moon-pale skin, he felt his pulse quicken and his cock harden. *Ah, Kate . . .*

He didn't have to think twice about on what, or rather who, his dreams would center. Kate. That earlier brief kiss alone had left him aching for her. Assuming his restless body permitted him the luxury of sleep, he would dream about his beautiful bride and the wedding night that should have been theirs. Even looking like a cat pulled from the bottom of a bog, she stole his breath and touched his soul. Suddenly Rourke owned that taming her wasn't going to be nearly enough.

Someday, my Katie girl, I want your dreams to be filled with me.

Owing to Toby scratching at the door, Kate rose early the next morning. Crossing the room to let the dog out, she had an unpleasant awareness of every bone and muscle in her body. On the way back to "bed," she sneezed, once and then three times in a row.

I'm coming down with a head cold—bloody lovely.

After the previous day's sodden trek, an onset of

pneumonia wouldn't greatly surprise her, but the genesis of the sneeze was more likely the dust. With sunlight pushing its way through the window's dirty leaded-glass panes, she saw that the thick white powder blanketed everything within eyeshot. Instead of the furniture being buried beneath Holland covers or put in storage, it apparently had been left out uncovered for an indefinite period of time. Dust sheathed every flat surface and infiltrated every carved nook and cranny; dust motes floated like fairies in the close air, and dust bunnies apparently reproduced exponentially beneath every piece of furniture, much like the animal for which they were named. Lord only knew how long such a sad state of affairs had endured, but it was about to end.

Other than the old man Cheevers the night before, she hadn't encountered a single servant. Her new husband might be an industry magnate on par with the American robber baron, Scots-born Andrew Carnegie, but he obviously knew next to nothing about what was required to run a large household. Fortunately Kate did. Though it had been a long time since she'd had occasion to put that particular talent to the test on a grand scale, she hoped it would be akin to riding a bicycle—once learned, never forgotten. And if she fell off, she'd simply get back up, brush herself off, and try again.

Be it riding bicycles in bloomers or managing households on shoestrings—compared to marriage, such pursuits were cakewalks.

CHAPTER NINE

"I am as peremptory as she is proud-minded.
And where two raging fires meet together
They do consume the thing that feeds their fury.
—WILLIAM SHAKESPEARE, Petruchio,
The Taming of the Shrew

The next phase of Rourke's taming regimen called for waking his bedraggled bride before the cock crowed. Unfortunately Kate wasn't the only one he'd exhausted the previous day. He rose from his cot, heavy-lidded and stiff-kneed, as well as later than usual. Depriving Kate of creature comforts had meant depriving himself, as well. It occurred to him that having Ralph—Cheevers—stow all the mattresses and bedding might not have been the best of ideas.

He dressed in his stiffened clothes from the day before, shaved with the dull razor he found in the washstand drawer, cutting himself and bleeding like a stuck pig, and finally combed his hair with his fingers. Where the devil was Ralph? At the train station, he hoped, seeing about springing their "lost" luggage from the storage bin. Clearly the past several years of ironed newspapers, expert tailoring, and servants to wait upon him had rendered him soft. He almost wondered if his bride might not be made of sterner stuff than he. For an earl's daughter, she struck him as remarkably self-sufficient.

He headed to the small room in the south tower Kate had claimed as hers. The door stood open.

"Kate?" He stepped one foot over the threshold, strangely shy of venturing inside.

A buck-toothed chambermaid looked up from the bed she was making up. The four-poster seemed to have grown a mattress overnight.

"Where is my lady?"

"Up and gone."

Up and gone! Panic flared through him. Could Kate have found her way back to the train station and left him? She wasn't familiar with the area; still he knew her to be a highly resourceful woman. They'd been married just a day, but their union was yet to be consummated. With at least one servant, the plain-faced maid, to bear witness to that less-than-flattering fact, she would have little difficulty obtaining an annulment. The garden escapade would be nothing compared to the laughingstock he'd be when word got 'round that Patrick O'Rourke hadn't bedded his bride. But beyond any damage to his reputation, it was the sinking sense of failure, of being abandoned yet again, that had perspiration soaking his brow.

"She's in the front hall reviewing the staff." She returned to her task.

Like a balloon receiving the prick of a pin, panic and the breath he'd been holding rushed out of him in a whoosh. "In that case, why aren't you there?"

"I'm not a reg'lar. I just help out me mum from time to time."

"I see."

Halfway down the stairs, he heard Kate's voice from the hall below. "In managing a household, be it small or large, one must have a clear understanding of one's priorities."

Intrigued, he stopped on the landing above. Setting his hands atop the dusty rail, he looked down. Kate addressed his servants standing in queue before the stairs. As she spoke, she strode back and forth along the length of the line, which from his vantage point resembled more of a squishy semicircle. Back lance straight and hands folded behind her back, she reminded him of a general reviewing the troops.

A quick glance confirmed the "troops" weren't much to see—a few footmen, a trio of housemaids, and a big, red-faced woman whose stained apron proclaimed her to be the cook. His stable manager, Hamish Campbell, was there, too, mud and hay sticking to his boots, his unshaven face wearing an expression best described as shell-shocked.

A small man with a monkey's face followed behind Kate, scribbling notes into a pocket-sized black book. Rourke suspected the little man was his steward.

The ragtag crew had more or less conveyed with the property, holdouts from the previous owner. Other than the stable manager, Rourke couldn't say who they were or what they did exactly. Since acquiring the estate at a foreclosure several years before, he'd channeled all his energies into making improvements on the land and buying breeding stock for his stable of racers. He'd given the castle nary a thought. Judging from the conversation in progress, Kate was bent on changing that—hell-bent.

Rather than continue on down, he held where he was, feeling as though he was watching a play in progress. Kate's "costume" hadn't changed much from the night before, though it looked as if she'd brushed the dried mud from her gown. She must have found someone to bring her washing water, as well, because she'd obviously cleaned up beyond the previous night's hasty ablution. With her pretty, shiny hair pulled back from her face and secured with a strip of ribbon and the sleeves of her shirtwaist rolled high above trim elbows, she scarcely resembled the haughty society miss and PB he'd waltzed with nearly two years ago.

Rourke ran his gaze over those slender bare limbs and felt his mouth go dry. Before now, he'd never thought of a woman's forearms and elbows as especially erotic, but the sight of Kate's had him hardening. Lusting after her for nearly two years must have made him hungry for every bit of bare flesh he could glimpse—that and the fact that he still hadn't bedded her.

Beyond that, she looked adorably domestic and utterly at home—far more at home than he felt in this drafty mausoleum, truth be told. He might have held the deed for several years, but he was still getting used to the place, still getting lost amongst its maze of drafty, poorly lit corridors, still tempted every now and again to head below stairs to the bright, homey kitchen (aye, he knew where it was) and put his feet up among the people who not so long ago would have been his peers. What an odd and uncomfortable sensation it was, this feeling of being an interloper in one's own home. So much for being king of one's castle. And yet with the morning of her first day merely hours old, his new bride wasn't only making herself at home, she looked well on her way to conquering it.

"Housemaids, your first duty of the day, in the winter months especially, is to open the shutters of all the lower rooms and take up the hearth rugs for beating." Kate paused before two redheaded maids, clearly twin sisters. "Ashes from the grate are to be swept and deposited in the cinder pail for sifting. Twice a month, furniture is to be polished with my special receipt of linseed oil, vinegar, and spirits of salts, the precise proportions of which I shall write down for you. We'll start with the great hall and then work our way up to the top." Addressing the first twin, she said, "Jenny, I am appointing you captain of what we shall call the East Tower Team." She pivoted to the second twin. "Millie, you shall head up the West Tower Team. Agreed?"

Eyes bugging at what must be their first taste of authority, the girls bobbed curtseys in unison. "Aye, I mean, yes, ma'am."

"The members of the winning team, the team that completes its territory first and to best satisfaction, will earn an extra half day of a week with pay for the term of their tenure, understood?"

The latter obviously got everyone's attention. Shoulders shot back, and chins lifted. The queue went from wobbly arc to almost-straight line. From the back, someone said, "An extra half day and paid, too. Gorm!"

The third maid's hand tentatively lifted. At Kate's encouraging nod, she said, "What's to be done about the master's study, milady? It's in neither wing."

For the first time since Rourke had come upon her, Kate seemed to falter. "I shall tend the cleaning and airing of that room myself." Brightening, she ran her gaze over the group. "We will convene at this spot every Monday at this time to report on our progress, as well as to discuss any difficulties that arise. You may go now, but if you've any questions, please don't hesitate to ask. Until I can employ a proper housekeeper, I shall be working right alongside you."

Rourke waited for the assembly to disperse, and then

continued down the stairs. Reaching the bottom, he cleared his throat to warn her of his approach. "Good morning, Kate." Heart thrumming, he stepped off the landing.

She started anyway, swinging about. "Good morning." The look she lanced him suggested that his uninvited presence had rendered the morning decidedly less so.

"I see you're settling in." It was an inane thing to say, but well, he had to say something, didn't he?

She frowned. "I am trying to, only I cannot seem to locate Mr. Cheevers. When I asked after him this morning, everyone acted almost as though they'd never heard of him."

Rourke hesitated. "I'm sure he's, uh . . . rattling about somewhere." Preferably any "rattling" had taken him to the train station to retrieve their luggage.

Kate sighed. "This place is a shambles." She frowned up at the ceiling. "We had a leak last night. I set Jenny to mopping it up. I'm beginning to wonder if those cobwebs aren't all that's holding the roof on."

Slipping back into character, Rourke summoned a jaunty smile and clapped her on the back just hard enough to knock her slightly forward. "Sure, a wee bit of dust and cobwebs aren't beyond the ken of a crack housekeeper such as you. Betimes, Kate, is that any way to speak of our home? It's here we're to spend our first days—and nights—as man and wife." He dropped his voice and added, "My mum always said a woman remembers the bed where she lost her maidenhead all her days."

She shot him a quelling look. "Must you be so coarse this early in the day?"

Arm about her, he leaned close and dropped his voice, his lips falling just shy of brushing that delectable shell of ear. "We are married now, Katie. The sooner you accustom yourself to my rough Scots ways, the better it will be for both of us."

She jerked away. "I saw quite enough of your rough ways the other day to last me a lifetime, certainly the next fifty-odd years at the very least. And while we're on the subject, please cease calling me by that inane nickname. My name is Katherine."

He grinned, pleased to be getting under her skin. "Not to me, it isna."

She huffed. "You are impossible, but I suppose since you're here, you might as well have breakfast."

That took him aback. "There's breakfast?" As if on cue, his stomach rumbled. Other than the chicken wings he'd quickly plucked clean the night before, he hadn't eaten all that much.

She nodded and started toward the dining room, apparently expecting him to follow. On her way, she said, "I hope to be up to serving a full breakfast by the end of the week, but for now we'll have to make do with cold pastry and pie." She ushered him to his seat and turned to go.

Rourke paused at the door, amazed. A clean linen tablecloth covered last night's bare boards. On the far side of the chamber, the ancient sideboard appeared to have been dusted, and several covered chafing dishes set atop. There was a pot of what must be coffee set on the table where a single place had been set. From the hearth, the freshly *swept* hearth, a cheerful fire blazed.

Stepping inside, he swung his gaze back to Kate. "This is bounty."

Rather than acknowledge the compliment, she said, "You'll have to serve yourself. Until I can hire more servants from town, I can't spare a footman to wait at table." She turned to go.

"You're leaving?" For whatever reason, the prospect of sitting down to breakfast by himself as he normally did, struck him as a grim thought. "Aren't you having breakfast, or are you still full from last night?"

He'd half-expected her to slap him. Instead her lips twitched. "I've had mine already, thank you." So that explained the return of the brightness to her eye and the bloom to her cheek.

"Then stay and bear me company while I have mine."

She hesitated, nibbling at the bottom lip he'd barely tasted last night. "I'll stay for a bit."

Satisfied, he moved to the sideboard. Uncovering the dishes, he found scones, a dish of marmalade and another of clotted cream, and a cold pie that Kate informed him was steak-and-kidney.

Sitting down, he bit into the flaky crust of a scone while Kate poured the coffee. "This is good. The cook knows how to do some things properly."

She set the silver pot down. "Actually, I made that dish."

"You bake?"

She nodded and turned away to busy herself with arranging the dishes on the sideboard.

Glancing back over his shoulder, he found himself on eye level with her pretty bottom. Almost choking on crumbs, he asked, "Since when does an earl's daughter bake?"

She shrugged and turned about to face him. "Household management has long been a passion of mine. I'm a great disciple of the late Mrs. Beeton."

She strolled over to the table and picked up the coffeepot to top off his cup. He was almost finished with his first scone, and she'd yet to sit down.

Lost in looking at her—surely she had the most elegant neck he'd ever seen—it took him a moment to catch up to the conversation. "I'm sorry, but who is Mrs. . . . Beeton?"

"*Was*, actually. Sadly she died at only twenty-eight." Though she didn't say so, he sensed she was thinking that was her own age. "Isabella Beeton is the author of *Mrs. Beeton's Book of Household Management.* It was first published several decades ago but has since fallen out of print. It's a wonderful book, full of all sorts of useful information and recipes for everything from boot blacking to sponge cake. Unfortunately, my copy was packed in the trunk that's gone missing."

She looked so forlorn that Rourke found himself resisting the urge to reach out and take her small hand. "I have a feeling our luggage will be returned to us soon, mayhap this very day. But please, won't you sit, for a minute at least?"

Unlike the night before, when he'd studied to be rude, he rose and pulled out the chair beside his.

She hesitated and then slipped into the seat, and he resumed his own. She looked over at him for a long moment and then said, "I know you own railways, or at least one very large railway, but beyond that, I don't really know what you do. For good or ill, we are married now. I want to understand what it is you do, truly. Were you a squire, a gentleman farmer of some sort with tenants raising sheep and corn, I would have some sense of it, but commerce is something about which I know next to nothing."

He opened his mouth to assure her he wasn't a gentleman of any sort, but clamped it closed again. Sarcasm was the very last thing that was called for, not when she was showing herself prepared to at least meet him halfway. More than halfway, for he doubted many women of her station cared overmuch for how the money that paid for their gowns and jewels and servants came about so long as it did.

Warmed by her interest, he explained, "In general, the larger railway companies seek to amalgamate the smaller, independent ones. For the acquiring company, this is good business in that it results in raised profits and dividends for the shareholder. For the individual traveler, it depends. In some cases, a monopoly causes fares to be raised and service to decline. In our case, however, I fancy travelers benefit, as well. Acquisition of smaller lines has allowed our company to extend its scope of service. By way of example, before we acquired the Edinburgh-Glasgow Railway, we would have had to disembark and change trains yesterday, always an inconvenience, but especially so in the winter months. As it was, we were able to stay warm and dry in our seats the entire eight hours."

He'd expected her to point out that they'd hardly stayed "warm and dry" once they'd reached their destination. Instead she said, "The train we rode yesterday was one of yours?"

"Aye, it was." The locomotive with its state-of-the-art steam engine and shiny black-and-red-trimmed cars was a particular point of pride. "Once I took over . . . acquired controlling stock in the Edinburgh-Glasgow, my first action was to get rid of the old trains and outfit new ones with dining cars, water closets—" He stopped for fear of boring her.

Kate looked anything but bored. Her gaze honed in on the diamond stud winking from his left ear. "So you really are a pirate, then?"

The twinkle in her eyes told him she was teasing. Still, for whatever reason, he felt himself minded to give a serious answer. "Aye, I suppose I am. It's a rich man's world, Kate. For those not born to privilege, pillage and plunder are frequently the only avenues for bettering our lot."

To his surprise, she didn't challenge him but answered with a mild nod. "My father has done nothing with the fortune he was born to other than squander it. Were the estate not entailed, there would be nothing left at all. Our blood may run blue, but it is tainted with the gamester's disease. There are only so many economies one may make and still keep up appearances. At some point, money must be earned." She bit her lip and looked down, the fingers of one hand plucking at a loose thread on the linen.

Guilt stabbed him, for her father's gaming had been the agent by which he'd blackmailed her into marrying him, after all. And then it hit him like the proverbial thunderbolt from above. What a bloody fool he was to not have seen it ere now.

"That's the reason you let Hadrian take your picture for those wee photographs, isn't it? Modeling wasn't a pastime, but a means to earning money. He paid you, didn't he?"

Until now, he'd assumed her modeling for Harry must be a hobby only, a pastime to satisfy a secret vanity. What an ass he was, as well as a hypocrite. As much as he railed against those who prejudged others based on appearances, he was guilty of doing the very same.

Amber eyes ablaze, she started to push back from

the table. "Whatever arrangement I made with Mr. St. Claire is a private matter."

Rourke's arm shot out, his hand covering her small one, not to capture but to comfort. "For what it's worth, Harry's kept a closed clapper. But I'm not wrong, am I?"

She blew out a breath and settled back in her seat, her hand for the moment resting still beneath his. "He didn't pay me a salary, if that's what you're implying. PBs—Professional Beauties—never take money, but in my case we struck a bargain. In return for my sitting exclusively for him, he remanded to me half of the proceeds from every *carte postale* bearing my image sold in his shop. It wasn't a lot of money, but it was enough to cover the household accounts and keep our creditors if not precisely happy, then at least not so angry that any one of them would go to the trouble of taking Papa to court. It was strictly a business arrangement," she added, glancing up as though she might be reading his mind.

Absurd as it was, he resented that Harry had been the one to come to her aid and not him. When she'd begun modeling, Rourke hadn't yet met her. Even if he had, she projected such an abundance of confidence and self-possession he doubted he would have bothered to probe beneath the surface to discover her true situation. The woman with whom he'd waltzed at Lady Stonevale's charity ball had hardly seemed in need of rescuing.

He hid his niggling jealousy behind a smile. "I meant to marry a lady, but to marry one who is also a

Professional Beauty, well, that is quite . . . something."

She shook her head, her gaze pointing down. "Professional Beauty is the moniker given to all ladies of society who sit for portrait photographs to be sold. I'm hardly anyone special. Common and middle-class people like to look at us and imagine how grand our lives must be. If only they knew . . ."

Her voice drifted off. She blushed and dropped her gaze. On any other woman of her age, such an action would equate to simpering, but on his Kate—and he really had begun thinking of her as his—it was genuine modesty. The physical effect was enormously appealing. The pink rising in her cheeks only made her amber-brown eyes appear darker and more luminous.

"Ah, Katie, such slender shoulders to bear such a great burden." *Kate, Katie, let me bear your burdens. Let me share your life.*

She flashed him a quick, tight smile, but her eyes looked bleak. "But then I'm known as Capable Kate for reasons obvious to all." As if reading his silent question, she supplied, "My mother died giving birth to Bea. Until marrying you, I was the de facto mistress of my father's household and mother hen to my sister. Capable Kate, they both call me. I've been stuck with the moniker since I was ten. I hated it, then. I fancied myself a princess like . . . my horse, but I've grown used to it over the years. You must admit, it fits."

So that explained her almost feverish industry. Kate

had grown up believing she was valued only for what she could do for others, rather than feeling loved and loveable for herself. Until now, he'd always assumed his being orphaned was the equivalent of drawing the short straw. But based on what he'd just heard her say, he was no longer so sure about that. Unlike him, Kate hadn't seemed to have had a Harry or Gavin or Daisy to show her otherwise.

Gentling his voice, he asked, "Is there nothing you want for yourself, Kate?" His hand on hers still hadn't moved, nor had she drawn it away.

She shook her head. "Don't go thinking I'm selfless, because I'm not." She swallowed hard, setting off a visible ripple in the lovely long column of her throat. "I wanted so very many things for myself—my independence, the time to write my silly drivel and perhaps someday find a publisher to do something with it, chocolate, a horse."

He couldn't help but notice how she used the past tense, not *want* but *wanted*, as though because of marrying him all her dreams were dead on the vine. Rather than tackle that topic now, he said, "I didn't know you wrote." Genuinely curious, he asked, "What sort of things do you write—if you don't mind my asking, that is?" Kate's literary aspirations were a new wrinkle, but she seemed such a private person he didn't want to unduly intrude.

She shrugged, and he let his hold on her slide away.

"Short stories mostly, the occasional poem. Someday I'd like to try a novel. Small dreams, perhaps, and undoubtedly selfish of me, but they were mine and I cherished them, and now none of them will ever come true."

He felt as though he were back in the boxing ring and had just fallen for his opponent's sucker punch to the gut. "And you think marrying me means you must give them all up?" Did she really see him as such a brute?

Her silence was an answer in itself.

He shook his head. "I have a stable stocked with horses, several Arabians, including a mare about to foal. There's no reason you can't ride any of them, well, all but one." His most recent acquisition, a splendid stallion, Zeus, wasn't yet broken to the saddle. "And you can pen your poems or whatever else it is you wish to write and have them published by whomever you please. I don't ken much of such things, but I'll beat down the publishers' doors with my bare fists if that's what it takes to have your work read."

"You really don't mind?"

He shook his head, ashamed it was such a marvel to her that he might be reasonable, let alone kind. "Why should I? Just as I go about my business during the day, so can you. As for chocolate, have as much as you please. There's a sweet shop on High Street with hoards of the stuff, some of it imported from Belgium, mind."

That thought quickly led him to another. Ralph had yet to show his face, and he was coming to wonder if his manservant might have met with some snag over the luggage. Until it was retrieved, his bride had but one dress, the sad little sack hanging from her slender shoulders. A stop by the station might be just the thing.

He lifted his hand from hers at last. "I'm headed into town myself on some, uh . . . business. What say you to accompanying me? We can buy you the biggest box of chocolates they have—and at least one wee dress."

Dividing his gaze between the two gowns the dress-shop owner held up, Rourke shook his head. "The green one is too garish, and the rose too girlish. My wife is a lady born, you see, and though admittedly very tiny, she is a woman grown."

Standing in her shift and a borrowed robe from the dressing room, Kate considered that for a man who claimed to know next to nothing about female fashions, her new husband had no shortage of opinions. As for his pointing out her small stature, true, she was slightly built but not freakishly so. Doubtless her husband was accustomed to stout, raw-boned Scottish lasses who could plow a field and birth a baby in the same day.

The dressmaker, Mrs. MacBride, answered with an injured sniff. "I assure you, sir, these colors reflect the latest fashion, from Paris no less."

Kate heartily doubted the high-necked green gown

with the tartan underskirt hailed from farther than the next county, but for once she held back from speaking her mind. Until her baggage arrived—if, indeed, it ever did—all she had to wear was her ruined traveling costume, the hemline still encrusted with grime despite that morning's vigorous brushing.

Impatient to be on their way—she'd agreed to come along only after he'd said she might stop by the office of the local gazette and place an advertisement for a housekeeper—she tapped him on the arm. "Perhaps we could purchase a bolt of fabric and one of those pattern books over there." She gestured to the wall where several fashion publications sat in the wooden display rack.

"You sew?"

She nodded. "A little."

Actually she sewed a lot, not as a pastime but as a necessity. If only he knew how many of her and Bea's gowns she'd stitched from patterns she'd created after pouring over the fashion plates in *The Queen Magazine*, *Sylvia's Home Journal*, and *Harper's Bazaar*, he wouldn't be so quick to dub her a snob.

"My lady wife to sew her clothes like a common mantua maker, I wouldna dream of it!"

There he went again, his mood sliding from reason to lunacy in the blink of an eye. Kate drew in a deep breath and gritted her teeth. "Please."

Please must be the magic word, indeed. All at once, his gruff expression softened and the wildness left his eyes. He turned to her, and the heat of his gaze resting on her face had Kate forgetting to breathe. "Verra well, then, if that is what you wish."

Their purchases made and loaded into the carriage—it seemed he had a carriage house, as well as stables—they stepped out of the dressmaker's shop onto the old cobbled street. "The sweetshop is next, I think," Rourke said.

Ever since their talk at breakfast, he'd been suspiciously accommodating, even nice to her. Resolved to take advantage of his good mood for however long it lasted, Kate said, "Do you think the proprietress will let me place one of these signs in her window, as Mrs. Mac-Bride did?"

She glanced down to the stack of hastily made advertisement posters in her arms. If she was going to return to her writing, that housekeeper couldn't be brought aboard soon enough.

He stopped in his tracks and smiled down at her, eyes smiling, too. "If you look at her as you're doing now, I canna fathom her saying anything but yes."

Self-conscious, she reached up and touched the bonnet they'd just bought to make sure it was on straight. "How is it I'm looking?"

He caught her hand and carried it to his lips, his warm, moist, kissable lips. "Adorable, lovely, that mouth altogether sweeter than any confectioner's treat."

The wildness was returned to his eyes, only Kate didn't think it was lunacy this time, but rather . . .

passion. "Rourke!"

His giant step brought their bodies brushing. "Kiss me, Kate."

She pulled back, gaze darting to the street beyond either of his broad shoulders. Several shoppers passed by, one girl goggle-eyed and giggling. She swung her gaze up to her husband's. "But we're in the middle of the street."

He spanned her waist with his hands, and against all reason Kate felt herself melting into the warmth of those big, broad palms. "Aye, so we are, but we're married now. Kiss me, anyway. Kiss me as a lover would, as though you mean it."

Kate stood rooted in place. Her heart skipped, her breath hitched. And between her thighs, a slow, honeyed heat was making its presence known.

"Are you ashamed to be seen with me, then?" Despite the glint in his eye, she had the feeling that this once he posed a serious question.

She shook her head. "It's not that."

"Then what is it? We're no in London anymore. Any passersby will see a pair of newlyweds showing a bit of fondness for one another on the street."

"A bit of fondness, is that what you call it? Twice now I've let you cajole me into kissing you in public, and only look what has come of it."

"What, indeed." He drew her to him and leaned down, his lips matching to hers.

"How now, what luck is this?"

They broke apart. Cursing beneath his breath, Rourke dropped his hands from Kate's waist and turned about to the hansom cab drawn up at their side.

His London servant, Ralph somebody or other, leaned out from the open carriage window. Snapped back to sense, Kate said, "Did you just come from the train station? We are on our way there now to see about the missing luggage. Had we known you were coming, we might have met you."

Struck by the number of *we*'s that short greeting included, she glanced over to Rourke, wondering if he'd noticed. Storm clouds rode her husband's high brow, and his jaw seemed quite set.

"Yes, Mr. Sylvester, had you seen fit to share your plans, we might have met you, indeed."

"There's no need, milady. I have it right here." He pointed to indicate the carriage boot.

"You have my trunk!" Clapping her hands, she said, "That is happy news. I suppose we can all ride home together, then?"

"Aye, so it would seem."

Standing at his washstand later that day, Rourke picked up his freshly stropped razor, and made the first downward swipe through the shaving soap on his face. "You couldna have held off hailing me for one wee moment?"

Ralph handed him a towel—a freshly laundered towel—and shrugged. "It was a case of now or never. That hack was headed down High Street at full-steam speed. Besides, I thought you'd be happy to have your missing trunks back. Lady Kate, or rather *Mrs. O'Rourke*, certainly seemed so." He winked, but Rourke refused to be teased out of his foul mood.

Scowling into the mirror, he tossed the towel over his shoulders and wiped the blade on the cloth. "*Bon vivant* as you fancy yourself, did it no occur to you that I might be in the middle of something important, so to speak?"

Ralph set the bottle of bay rum on the washstand next to the pitcher and basin. His hazel eyes found Rourke's in the mirror. "She's your wife. You can kiss her anytime . . . can't you?"

Rourke didn't have an answer for that, at least not yet. As Kate's husband, he had the legal right to do far more than kiss her. But eager as he was to bed her, to make love to her in every way she would accept, he realized he wanted more from her than simple sex. Taming her willfulness was one thing, seducing her by force entirely another. Standing on High Street, his lips lowering to hers, he'd understood that a physical claiming would no longer suffice.

Along with sex, he wanted some small place in what he was coming to see as a truly beautiful soul.

Ralph drifted over to the trunk. From the vicinity

of the bed, he called back, "By the by, your luggage isn't all I picked up at the train station."

Ever since opening Ralph's "marital-advice manual," Rourke was beginning to be wary of unasked-for gifts. "Open it for me, will you?" He turned back to the mirror and finished shaving.

He'd just washed the last of the lather from his cheeks when a crack of laugher sounded, followed by Ralph's exclamation, "This is too rich."

Red-faced, Ralph walked over to him, holding up a small leather-bound book. "You'll never believe what your friends Daisy and Gavin sent you as a wedding gift."

Rourke didn't have to put on his spectacles to read the title on the weathered cover. Somehow he knew. He just did. "A copy of *The Taming of the Shrew*, perchance?"

Ralph nodded. "As the Bard wrote, mate, it seems the play's the thing."

CHAPTER TEN

"Such a mad marriage never was before."
—WILLIAM SHAKESPEARE, Gremio,
The Taming of the Shrew

One Week Later

The next week was a whirlwind of activity as Kate worked to put her new home in some semblance of order. Though the hoped-for housekeeper had yet to appear, she'd hired one or two additional helping hands from the village. The existing servants, the twin maids especially, seemed to have good hearts and a genuine eagerness to learn. By the end of the week, everyone seemed to have slipped into a reasonable routine. The appearance of the main chambers in both towers was markedly improved, the grates swept and blackened, the curtains and rugs beaten free of dust, the furnishings and silver polished. Thanks to the return of her trunk, she had Mrs. Beeton's book in her possession once more. Along with Toby, who scarcely allowed her out of his sight, the well-worn tome was her constant companion as she made her daily rounds.

Her other "companion," her husband, was a great deal more complicated to sort out. She tried keeping up her end of their verbal sparring, but coming up with fresh insults was beginning to feel like a great deal of bother. She almost fancied they were becoming friends. Over the course of early-morning breakfasts and late-night suppers, the confidences had trickled out. When she'd admitted that she hadn't ridden regularly in years because her father had lost her childhood pony at cards, he'd dried the tear trickling down her cheek with his own hand. Likewise, he'd told her a bit about his being orphaned and running afoul of the law and finally being sent to an orphanage in Kent, Roxbury House. There he'd met his three best friends, Harry, Daisy, and Gavin. The Roxbury House Orphans' Club, they'd called themselves. The name had made Kate smile while plucking at her heartstrings. From the stories he'd so far shared of their secret attic meetings and sundry adventures, they sounded to have been a merry little band, more family than friends. That her husband had risen from such destitution to his current wealth humbled and amazed her.

She was growing fond of her big, bluff Scottish husband. Whereas she first saw him as a madcap ruffian, a social climber, a bully, the charming, hard-working man she was coming to know and like didn't fit any of those preconceptions. Whether watching him deliver a foal with his big, gentle hands or pondering investment reports with his wire-framed spectacles slipping down his broken nose, the very last thing she wanted to do with him was scold.

She wanted them to make love.

Since that first night, there had been no more midnight "serenades"; indeed, no nocturnal visitations of any sort. Their mad marriage was a puzzle to Kate. She knew Rourke had married her for her blue blood and breeding ability, not unlike the prize Arabian he'd recently acquired for his stables, but sleeping apart scarcely seemed the way to go about bringing forth the future generation. Tired of waiting to be asked, she'd had her things moved from her cubbyhole room to the larger bedchamber adjoining his. She couldn't know if he was pleased or annoyed. For all she knew, he hadn't noticed at all. The adjoining dressing-room door remained closed if unlocked, on her end at least.

In the midst of it all, a surprise visitor arrived from London. Kate was in the front parlor trying to decide whether she should replace the velvet draperies at once or wait until spring when they would come down anyway and be replaced with a lighter fabric, when a throat clearing drew her attention to the doorway.

"You have a visitor, milady." The maid Jenny bobbed a curtsey and stepped back to await her answer.

Kate ran an approving eye over the girl, feeling an inner satisfaction. Hair combed, nails clean, and eyes bright as buttons, like the castle, she was showing marked signs of improvement. Though the smart new uniforms she'd ordered from Mrs. MacBride had yet to arrive, the servants seemed to go about their duties with a new dignity.

When Jenny told her the identity of her mystery guest, Kate felt a smile break over her face. "Bring her up at once, please."

Another few moments passed, and then Kate's friend and former maid, Hattie, materialized at the door. The older woman looked very smartly turned out in a plumed hat and wool carriage dress, but then it was Hattie who'd taught Kate to sew.

"Hattie!" Kate rushed across the room and enfolded her friend in a hug.

Hattie hugged her in return. After a moment, she stepped back. Holding her former mistress at arms' length, she ran her gaze over Kate's face. "Miss Kathy . . . I mean, milady . . . I mean, Mrs. O'Rourke . . . Oh, I can't say as I know what I mean exactly, but Lud, it's good to see my girl again."

"It's good to see you, too. Won't you sit?"

Hattie hesitated and then took a seat on the edge of a heavy velvet-covered sofa. They spent the next few minutes with Hattie catching Kate up on the latest news from home.

Interrupting her, Kate asked, "How go the preparations for Bea's come-out?"

The maid pulled a face. "Your Aunt Lavinia's brought on some fancy Frenchie to serve as ladies' maid, and sure the chit knows more of hair dressing and fashions than I ever will." Her gaze dropped to her gloved hands clenched in her lap. "I thought I might come and see if you needed help setting up housekeeping, but of course, you would have servants of your own now." Gaze downcast, her smile slipped, and she shook her head. "Like as not I should have telegraphed ahead, but . . . Truth be told, milady, I needed to get out of London for a while."

Rather than pry, Kate said, "Of course, you are welcome to stay as long as you like." A thought dawned, and sudden though it was, she realized it made perfect sense. "How would you fancy taking the position of housekeeper?"

Hattie's head snapped up. Jaw dropping, she said, "From maid-of-all-work to housekeeper, well, that would be quite a step up."

Kate agreed it would. "Still, you must admit it makes sense. Having performed the duties of all the other positions yourself, you'll be ideally suited to supervise. And you'd be doing me a service." As much as she enjoyed the work—housekeeping was equal parts art and science—she was looking forward to getting back to her writing.

"All right, then, I'll do it."

In the days that followed, they quickly fell into a routine, commencing with an early-morning cup of tea taken in Hattie's own room. Close as they were, after the first morning Kate could tell that something was awry. Whatever had convinced Hattie to leave London must be more than the desire for a change of scene. On the third day, when Kate knocked at her customary time, Hattie was slow to answer. When she finally did, her thin face wore a mask of pale green.

"Oh, Hattie, you're ill. I'll come another time. Can I get you anything?"

Hattie shook her head and beckoned Kate inside. "No worries, milady. What I have isn't catching." She let out a crack of laughter. The dull look in her friend's eyes worried Kate a great deal more than her sallow face.

"You really aren't well, Hattie. Shall I call into town for a physician? We have a telephone in my husband's study, you know."

"I'm preggers, milady."

It took Kate a full minute to absorb the shock of that news. Hattie, despite her youthful appearance, must be forty or near to it.

"I know what you're thinking, milady, a woman of my age and all. But he had the shiniest dark eyes and the loveliest smile I've ever seen and . . . Well, sometimes at nights when the house is locked up and the chores done, a woman finds herself lonely."

Though Kate didn't say so, she more than understood. How many nights now had she spent alone in the big four-poster, imagining what it would be like to feel her husband's strong body pressing her down into the mattress, his callused hands caressing her, his beautiful mouth kissing her in places she'd never before thought to allow a man's mouth to stray?

Shaking herself to the present predicament, she said, "I'll do whatever I can to help. I meant what I said the other day. You are welcome to stay as long as you like."

Hattie shook her head, the sunlight streaming through the window catching the silver strands threading through her golden hair. "A pregnant housekeeper will never do. I'll go back home before I start to show."

Kate wrapped her arm about the woman's shoulders. "You'll do no such thing. You'll stay right here where I can see you're cared for."

Hattie sent her a sad little half smile. "That's what you say now, but your husband may have other ideas."

Kate was so used to making decisions on her own that she hadn't considered Rourke might have an opinion on the matter until now. Many a housemaid had been let go without references once a baby bump began to show. Kate was determined that wouldn't happen to Hattie. So far Rourke hadn't interfered in her management of the house, and Kate meant to keep it that way. In the meantime, what he didn't know wouldn't hurt him—or anyone else.

"Don't worry, Hattie. Things have a way of working out."

The latter was her father's saying. He'd repeated it on her wedding morning. Kate grudgingly admitted that for once he might have been on the mark. So far her marriage hadn't proved to be the leg shackling she'd envisioned. In point, she found herself wishing she might spend more time with her husband, not less.

Hattie subsided into her seat. "Try as I might, I can't find it in my heart to be entirely sorry things worked out as they have. I don't expect you to understand, milady. You're still so very young and lovely and used to having packs of gents trailing after you like lovesick pups. And now there's the master, so sick in love with you he can scarce stand to let you out of his sight."

Rourke sick in love with her? Kate felt as if her heart skidded to a halt, and then started up again at full gallop. Was it possible Hattie in her short stay had seen something Kate had missed?

Heart pounding, she slid to the edge of her chair, hoping the hunger in her heart wouldn't show on her face. "What did you say?"

"That you're used to—"

"No, after that. It had to do with my husband." *My husband.* How strange and yet how utterly smoothly those two words rolled off her tongue. "What makes you say he loves me?"

Hattie flushed. "That was wrong of me, milady. I spoke out of turn. It isn't my place to make personal remarks, only I can't help it. I've seen the way he follows you with his eyes when you're busy about your work. I do believe he loves you, loves you with his whole heart, though he's too prideful and wary to say so."

Kate's mind cycled back to a conversation they'd had just the other day at breakfast. She'd popped up from her chair to refill the coffee, and he'd growled at her and bade her sit back down.

"Why is it you always keep yourself so busy? Afraid if you sit still long enough, someone might find you out?"

Suddenly nervous, Kate had held her water glass up to the light to inspect it for spots. "Find me out? I'm sure I don't know what you mean."

"I'm sure you do." Emerald eyes locked onto hers. "That you're human after all, as human as the rest of us."

As human as the rest of us.

She hadn't thought much of it at the time, but now it occurred to her that his snappishness might be a clue that he was as unhappy about their separate sleeping arrangements as she was. She heartily hoped so.

Kate turned back to the maid. "You really think Mr. O'Rourke cares for me?" She knew she was fishing shamelessly, but it couldn't be helped. If there was hope, she had to know.

Hattie rolled her eyes as though Kate had posed a silly question, indeed. "That man would move heaven and earth for you if only you'd toss a smile his way once in a while. But then, you know what they say about catching flies with honey—and not vinegar."

After the past torturous week and a half, Kate was more than ready to let the honey flow. She only hoped she wouldn't get caught in a sticky mess of her own making.

Late that evening, Kate downed a glass of sherry for courage before leaving her room to seek out her husband. The silence on the other side of the dressing-room door assured her Rourke had not yet retired for the night. That wasn't unusual. He often stayed at his desk in the library late into the evenings, not drinking as her father did, but poring over his railway reports and investor portfolios.

Before leaving, she glanced one more time into the dressing mirror before sliding her arms into the sleeves of her silk wrapper. It and the matching nightgown beneath were the only items she'd purchased for her "trousseau." The gown's low-cut square bodice was beaded with seed pearls and paste diamonds, the slender skirt molding to her hips and thighs, the silk palest pink, almost translucent. She'd left her hair down and had spent the past quarter of an hour brushing the light brown waves to a high gloss. With the lamps turned low, her eyes appeared bright and her lips and cheeks a pleasing pink; whether the latter owed to the sherry, the excitement, or both, she couldn't say. Unlike her wedding day, she looked more bridelike than spinsterish, or so she hoped.

She prayed her husband would find her pretty.

Padding down the staircase, candle in hand, she told herself this nightly standoff of theirs was absurd, childish even. It was silly to keep it up. They were married, after all. Their wedding might have had the feeling of a farce, but the proceedings were quite legal. Now that they were married, they might as well make the best of it and "be fruitful and multiply" as the Bible counseled. Rourke made no bones about having married her to beget blue-blooded heirs. Though Kate had never admitted it aloud, she would like to have a child, children, in fact. Until now, she'd told herself that being a doting spinster auntie to Bea's future children would suffice, but she no longer believed that lie.

She stepped off the landing and darted a quick look about. The household was bedded down for the night, but then it was almost eleven. She cinched the belt of her wrapper tighter and headed for the library at the back of the house. As castles went, Rourke's was a small one, but even with the additional staff, they still only used a fraction of the rooms.

Outside the library door, she rapped lightly, the gingerly knock barely perceptible beyond the blood drumming her ears and the gavel-like thudding of her heart. When no call to enter came, it occurred to her he might have gone out, but no, the strip of light showing from beneath the door confirmed he had been within, even if he wasn't still. Certainly someone must be. She'd impressed upon the servants the necessity of dousing any unattended fires or lamps before retiring for the night.

When a second louder knock went unanswered, she opened the door and entered. Snoring drew her attention to the desk. Rourke sprawled in his leather desk chair, his cravat balled on the blotter before him. Several shirt buttons were left undone, the starched white collar lying open to reveal his muscle-corded throat, and the sleeves rolled up to reveal powerful forearms dusted with reddish gold hairs. She lifted her gaze to his face. His auburn hair was mussed as though he'd raked it with his fingers not once but several times, and his wire-frame spectacles had slid past the bump on his nose. The eyes behind the glass lenses were firmly closed. Approaching, Kate sighed. How could she have ever overlooked how purely magnificently beautiful he was?

She set the candle down on the edge of the desk, half-hoping the sound would wake him. It didn't. Her attention drifted downward to the discarded neckwear and the open book lying facedown beside it. Unlike the untouched books lining the library shelves, this one wasn't new. Far from it, the leather binding was weathered and the hand tooling on the spine had lost most of its gilding. Like her idol, Isabella Beeton, Kate had a great respect for books and definite opinions about their proper care. To leave a book lying open thus ran the very real risk of cracking the spine. Were it to slide off and fall to the floor, precious vellum pages might be irreparably bent.

By habit, her gaze went to the title on the spine. The tooled leather lettering had lost most of gilding, but it was still legible. *The Taming of the Shrew*. How odd. Kate wouldn't have pegged Rourke for a reader of either Shakespeare or plays. From what he'd told her, until his friend, Gavin's wife, Daisy, had made her Drury Lane debut as Rosalind in *As You Like It* that past spring, he'd never set foot inside a proper theatre. Resolved not to wake him, she leaned over, picked up the book, and closed it properly. As she did, a vellum note card fluttered out.

She picked it up and glanced at the precise, bold script. Whomever had penned the note was a fair hand and most definitely male.

What to give the man who has everything? Daisy and I pondered that dilemma and for good or for ill, we settled on this. Read it as a play or employ it as a marital-advice manual, however you see fit. Either way, I hope you'll pardon the unconventional wedding gift. We are only trying to do our part to smooth out the course of true love. Congratulations, Gavin and Daisy.

Marital-advice manual? It had been years since Kate last read the classic play, and her memory was foggy at best. Flipping through the musty-smelling pages without regard for their age, she felt as if the pieces to a bizarre but embarrassingly obvious puzzle were fitting together. The ridiculous clothes Rourke had worn to the church and his whisking her away before the bridal breakfast, the lost luggage and miserable trek from the train station to the castle, the wedding-night supper that wasn't sufficiently savory to be partaken of, at least not by her—each scenario had been borrowed from the Bard to bend her to his will, to tame her. Marital-advice manual, indeed! Her husband wasn't only reading Shakespeare's play. He was adapting it to play her—for a fool.

We are all fools in love.

The other night she'd been too muzzy-headed to recall the author of the popular line, but now she did—Shakespeare, of course.

She glanced up at his face, so innocent in sleep, and seriously considered slamming the book atop his head. But no, with a thick skull such as his, the only thing dented would be the book. Mrs. Beeton would be turning in her pristine grave.

Kate stuck the note back inside the pages and set the closed book back down on the blotter. She was furious and more than a little hurt. Inside her, some remnant of the foolish, romantic girl she'd once been had believed Rourke might truly care for her. Hattie's words earlier that day had stoked the flames of her fledgling hopes. Finding the play and note confirmed he was no different from Dutton or the other so-called gentlemen she'd dodged back in London. Like them, he saw her only as a conquest to be wagered on and won. No, not won—broken.

Backing away toward the door, she felt her hurt

hardening into steely resolve. She would best Rourke at his own game, make herself so disagreeable, so *disobedient*, that he would be more than happy to put her on that London-bound train. Following in the footsteps of other fashionable couples, they need not see each other more than once or twice a year. In truth, they need not see each other at all.

She stepped out into the hallway. Resisting the urge to slam the door, she pulled it quietly closed. She'd come downstairs with the hope that she and her husband might begin the next chapter of their lives as friends, lovers, and one day, parents. Now she knew that it would never come to pass. They were a closed book, she and Rourke, and Kate resolved that this time neither Shakespeare nor meddlesome friends would write the final scene.

Rourke awoke with a start, nearly tipping over in his chair. He'd been dreaming of Kate, but then that was nothing new. That night's dream, however, seemed different somehow, achingly vivid. Even awake, the memory stuck with him. Mad though it was, he could almost believe she'd stood there in the study with him. He'd always thought hallucinations to be tricks of the mind that affected the sight, and yet he swore he detected the orange blossom scent of her hair.

But given the breakneck pace she kept up by day, his

bride would have retired to bed long ago. Kate must be the most industrious woman Rourke had ever known. Catching her alone during the day was proving all but impossible. The woman operated like a factory machine, her slender hands always engaged in some busy, worthwhile task. In a little over a week, she'd transformed his castle from a ramshackle ruin to a gracious home, winning over his servants and tenants and neighbors alike. So much for the spoiled, selfish termagant he supposed he'd married. Whether patiently repeating a new receipt to his hard-of-hearing cook, delivering a basket of food to a bedridden tenant, or overseeing the concoction of an herbal remedy to ease his elderly neighbor's gout, Kate was the most giving, least selfish person he'd ever encountered. Her scolding tongue she seemed to reserve for him alone, though their bouts of bantering were more amusing than annoying.

His gaze fell to the play lying on his blotter. The odd thing was, he had no recollection of closing it. He must have done so in his sleep. Once again he'd fallen asleep reading, or rather rereading it, searching the paragraphs of prose for suggestions or even clues on how to go about wooing his lady wife. Unfortunately, in the play, Petruchio's seduction and the shrew's surrender occurred offstage. Nor did Master Shakespeare trouble himself to explain how the fictional Kate came to be a shrew in the first place.

When it came to the real-life Kate, Rourke fancied

he had that part figured out. Seeing her as a person and not a conquest, he more than suspected her caustic comments and flashes of temper weren't really shrewishness as much as they were the defenses of a lonely and vulnerable woman. When the other day she'd let slip that her father and sister called her Capable Kate, Rourke had glimpsed the hurt beneath the pride she affected. Thinking of it now, he felt a rush of guilt when he considered that perhaps he wasn't so very different from her feckless father or spoiled sister or the London swells who'd pursued her. Like them, he'd used her, in his case to further his social ambitions and bolster his pride. Small wonder she wanted him nowhere near her at night. Ever since she'd moved into the adjoining room, he'd slept with one ear cocked, but so far he'd not heard one wee tap upon that connecting door.

Rourke rose to round the desk. Crossing the carpet to the first of several bookshelves, he shoved the copy Daisy and Gavin had given him on the shelf beside its mate. He wanted his bride in his bed, but more than that, he wanted her in his life.

Until now he'd convinced himself that taming her was a sort of rehabilitation on par with the transformation he and his fellow orphans had undergone at Roxbury House. Casting his efforts in that noble light, changing her had seemed as much for her good as his. Once she left off her wildness and settled down to her duty, they could be happy, he knew it. But for the first time since he'd whisked her out of the churchyard and onto the train, he doubted the purity of his motives. He'd stalked her like quarry and then trapped her into a marriage she'd made it clear from the very beginning she didn't desire. Kate's happiness had never been his primary consideration. Until now he hadn't considered it—or her—at all.

Now that he did, he found he no longer cared about taming her. To change one thing about Kate struck him as the height of hubris. But he still meant to win her.

And for that, the play was most definitely not the thing.

The next morning Kate sailed inside the breakfast room, looking so fresh and pretty in a new habit of hunter green that Rourke felt his heart lifting at the sight of her. "Out for a ride, are we?"

"I can't speak for *we,* but that is certainly my intention." She picked up a china plate from the sideboard and set about filling it, scarcely sparing him a glance. When she sat down beside him, he fancied a chill wind had entered the room.

He reached out to lightly touch her arm. "Shall I come with you?"

She jerked away as though he'd touched her with a hot brazier rather than his bare hand. "No." Beneath the short filmy veil of her riding hat, she glowered at him. "And I'll thank you not to paw me at table."

Her scornfulness took him back to that day almost two years ago when he'd taken her riding in Hyde Park. She'd accused him of pawing her then, too. Had they really lost so much ground overnight?

Just the other day he'd taken her on a tour of his stables, and he'd proudly pointed out all his stock, including Zeus, his prize Arabian. Rourke had a trainer coming in from Derby. Until the man arrived, the horse wasn't to be so much as touched by anyone other than himself or the stable manager. Kate had glanced at the beast stomping in his stall and declared she would be quite content to ride Buttercup or a similarly docile mount.

She must have woken up on the wrong side of the bed. Either that or it must be her woman's time of month. He was as yet hardly in a position to know. When he'd come to bed late last night, he'd actually considered knocking on the connecting door. But setting his ear to the panel, he hadn't heard so much as a peep coming from her room.

His dog lumbered over to her. Crooning sweet nothings, Kate reached down and scratched the beast's ears. Watching the slow, gentle movements of her fingers, fingers he'd yet to feel on his bare skin, Rourke owned that he was jealous, actually jealous, of a dog.

She set her plate down on the floor and pushed back her chair to rise. "I'll be off, then."

Rourke started up. "Are you certain you don't want

company?"

She hesitated and then lanced him a look, *their* aristocratic look, that straight-through look that said he was invisible to the likes of her. And then she sniffed, *their* sniff, as if to indicate he was dirty or certainly not as sweet-smelling as she. Finally she lifted one side of her mouth in a sneer—*their* sneer—the twisted smile telling him that no matter how much money he made, he would never be worthy. And then she cut him, cut him like a prized diamond slicing through common glass.

"Quite certain I don't want yours."

His own wife had given him the Cut Direct.

Stunned, Rourke wandered into his study to work, but instead found himself staring blindly at the ledger. The rows and columns of numbers might as well have been Egyptian hieroglyphics for all the meaning they held. All his life, he'd had a gift for ciphering, but now he couldn't say for sure that one and one still equaled two.

It was no use. He slammed the ledger closed and mentally reviewed the bizarre breakfast episode once more in his head. Kate's waspishness reminded of the time when, as a boy at Roxbury House, he'd let Harry and Gavin goad him into poking at the wasps' nest with his shoe. Like opening his heart to Kate, it had seemed a good idea at the time, but in the end he'd gotten badly stung.

He'd thought they were becoming close, or certainly *closer*. Over the past weeks, their verbal sparring had become more thinly veiled flirtations than declarations of war. A current of unchecked desire undercut their every gesture, glance, and touch. Like the explosive fuses he'd once set to carve railway tunnels from sheets of solid rock, it would be only a matter of time before one or both of them imploded. There was no help for it. Whether she was wooed or not, Rourke was going to have to bed his wife.

When the knock sounded outside his study door, he was grateful for the intrusion. Though he should hold his gratitude in reserve, the thought occurred to him it might be Kate.

"Come in."

The door opened, revealing not his wife but Hamish Campbell, his stable manager. Tamping down his disappointment, Rourke beckoned the servant inside. Hamish doffed his tweed cap and made a study of the tops of his boots.

Impatient, Rourke prompted, "What can I do for you, Hamish?"

Hamish lifted anguished eyes from the cap he twisted between his hands. "I don't rightly know, Mr. O'Rourke. I'm not so certain I should have come."

"My door is always open, you know that. Now tell me, what is the trouble?"

Hamish blew out a breath. "Coming between a

man and his wife, carrying tales, well, it's not ordinarily my way, sir. You know that."

His heart kicking into a canter, Rourke said, "Out with it, man."

"It's your lady, sir. She marched herself out to the stable a short while ago and asked that Zeus be saddled for her. I tried telling her your orders are that no one is to go near Zeus without your permission but . . . well, she wouldn't hear of it. Saddled the beast herself and took off like cannon shot."

Fear fisted Rourke in the gut. The horse showed great promise, but for the time being he was a wilding. He had kicked his way out of his stall and jumped the paddock fence to freedom a good half-dozen times.

"You did the right thing in coming to me." Rourke was already on his feet, rounding the desk and halfway to the door. "How long ago did she leave?"

"Ten minutes, give or take."

Rourke considered reprimanding him for waiting that long, only he hadn't the time to spare. Kate already had ten minutes' lead on him, assuming she'd managed to keep her seat. If not, she might be lying on the ground injured or worse. It was the prospect of what counted as "worse" that had his pulse pumping and his heart threatening to hammer a hole in his chest.

His hand found the doorknob. The brass slipped in his slick grasp. One foot out into the hallway, he didn't bother with looking back. "Have my horse saddled at once."

When I get my hands on you, Kate . . .

He left the thought unfinished, the alternative too frightening to bear.

Sod off, Rourke.

Kate pressed her knees into the stallion's sides, and the animal took off through the open barn door. She crouched low and hugged the horse with her knees. Her hat whipped off, and rather than worry about it, she gloried in the fingers of wind raking her hair and the tepid winter sunshine on her face. The paddock, carriage house, and several other dependency buildings whizzed by on either side of her head. A fallow field lay to her left. To her right was the drive leading past the gatehouse and out to the main road.

She turned the horse toward the field. The low fence would be an easy jump, and beyond it the terrain was flat. From the estate map she'd glimpsed in Rourke's study, she could ride for several leagues and encounter nary a hill. With any luck, Zeus would exhaust himself eventually and let her lead.

"Kate. Kate!"

A man's shout sounded from behind. She didn't have to look back to know who it was. Rourke.

"Halt, Kate. I said *halt.*"

By now Kate considered she'd more than proved her

point. She would have been only too happy to end her husband's object lesson then and there, only the stallion clearly had other ideas. He headed for the road at a fast gallop.

Fear struck her, replacing the wild exhilaration she'd known but a few seconds before. The main road was no place for a wild horse. Carriages, hedgerows, and other riders all presented likely risks. She brought the reins up hard, hating to hurt the animal's sensitive gums, but having no choice if she wanted to rein him in. Zeus let out a screech and reared, forelegs leaving the ground and thrashing at air. Kate's world upended. For a dizzying few seconds, her gaze met with the sky, her foot slipping from the stirrup.

The animal righted itself. Amidst the stomach-pitching motion, somehow she managed to keep her seat, holding on with her legs. The episode would give her bragging rights for life, provided she didn't end the morning with a broken neck.

"Kate!"

Rourke was beside her, his bay running neck and neck with Zeus, the animals' exhaled breaths forming twin frost clouds. Kate risked a quick sideways glance at her husband. Sweat streaked the side of his face from forehead to jowl, dripping into his shirt stock, already banded by a wet ring.

"Rein in before you break your bloody neck or I'm minded to break it for you."

"I'm trying!" She said so at a scream, but she didn't

think he'd heard her.

A hedgerow rose up faster than she'd judged. Rourke snapped out an arm and caught her reins in a fist with his and yanked hard. Reaching over, he slapped her hands onto her saddle pommel. "Hold on!"

Kate was trying. Zeus, though more than half-wild, slowed to match the bay's gait. Several more circuits about the field were required to slow the horses to less than a full gallop. The next thing she knew, Rourke's arm wrapped about her waist, pulling her off the stallion and onto the saddle in front of him. Seconds later, Zeus tore off.

Hamish Campbell slipped under the fence and ran over to them. "Are you all right, missus?"

It took Kate a full minute to be sure. "I . . . Yes, I think so. But the horse . . ."

She looked off to the dust clouds rising up from the lane and felt her heart sink. A horse run amok was not only a danger to himself but to others. She'd never meant for anyone to get hurt, man or beast.

The stable manager took off his cap and ran his hand through his thinning hair. "Several of the lads have gone off after him. Dinna worry, like as not we'll get him back eventually."

Rourke's voice was a hard hiss in her ear, his arm about her waist a vise that permitted no escape. "Were I you, Katie, I'd save my worrying for myself."

CHAPTER ELEVEN

"Though little fire grows great with little wind,
Yet extreme gusts will blow out fire and all.
So I to her, and so she yields to me,
For I am rough and woo not like a babe."
—WILLIAM SHAKESPEARE, Petruchio,
The Taming of the Shrew

That afternoon Kate stepped out of the hip bath and wrapped the towel around her. The long, hot soak had proved just the thing for sore muscles. If only a bruised heart might be as easily remedied.

The dressing-room door flew open, crashing against the wall. Rourke stood in the portal, the breadth of his shoulders filling the frame. Kate wasn't all that surprised to see him. He'd been stomping about his bedroom ever since they'd gotten back to the castle and parted ways at the top of the stairs.

She held her chin high and kept a firm grip on the towel. She might be dripping wet, but he looked wild, indeed. His rumpled white shirt hung open to the navel as though he'd been in the process of taking it off and then changed his mind. Her gaze fixed on the queue of reddish brown hair leading downward to his trouser waistband, and her lower belly thrummed.

He braced a hand on the door frame and raked her with his gaze. She was keenly aware of the bathwater pearling on her skin, her nipples firming to hard points beneath the towel, and that her legs were bare from the knees down. And suddenly the room, large as it was, didn't seem to contain nearly enough air.

"You might have knocked."

He snorted, bringing to mind the stallion. Both were arrogant beasts used to having their way with females. "Aye, I might have, only I'm no feeling so verra civil toward you at the moment." He shoved away from the door and stalked over to her. "You might have obeyed me, Kate. Your disobedience caused the loss of a valuable animal and put those who must go after him at risk. Beyond that, you made me seem a laughingstock in front of my own men. No one respects a man who canna control his own wife." He drew up beside her, so close that for a moment Kate thought she might fall backward into the bath.

Kate shrugged, sending the towel slipping. "I suppose you chose the wrong wife, then."

"Whether I did or not, the deed is done. I'm your husband. That makes me responsible for you."

"The hell it does." She shoved one arm inside the silk sleeve and held onto the towel with the other hand. "Husband, yes; lord and master, no."

Bold words, and yet his nearness was like a drug, making her dizzy, making her wet. His musk filled her nostrils. She wanted to taste him, trace that queue of hair down his chest first with her fingers and then follow with her tongue.

"The vows you took before God and man say otherwise. Obedience, Kate, was only part of what you promised. Those vows you took of your own free will, I might add."

"Free will, ha! A fat lot of choice I had with your holding Papa's marker over all our heads."

His emerald eyes narrowed. "We struck a bargain, you and I. You promised to obey me, Katie, and in turn I swore to protect and provide for you, to worship you with my body and to keep myself unto you alone. We've neither of us been verra good about upholding our end of the bargain, but that, dear wife, is about to change."

His arm shot out. The towel came off. Kate stared down at the pool of it at her feet, and then swung her gaze up to his. "What the devil do you think you're doing?"

"Giving you what you've been asking for ever since we met."

She tried covering herself with her hands, but he hauled her against him, pinning her arms. Her breasts flattened against him. He smelled of starch and sweat and bay rum and man. The stiffness of his shirt and the coarseness of the curls on his chest chafed her nipples. Lower, his hardness and heat bore into her belly.

Warm breath struck her cheek. Emerald eyes seared her skin. His fingers dug into her flesh. "I want you on your hands and knees. On the bed. *Now.*"

Breath hitching, she shook her head. No matter what he did, she mustn't lose control, she mustn't lose herself. "I will not."

He swung her up into his arms. The bed was only a few feet away. He carried her over to it. Panic flared, and she struck out, her nails scoring the side of his face. He jerked back and cursed.

"You've claws, haven't you, my wild Kat?"

He dumped her in the center of the mattress and stepped back. Kate landed on all fours. She tried scrambling up, but he was too fast for her to escape and far too strong. He dropped down on the bed beside her, the mattress swinging like a hammock.

"Come here, Kate." He grabbed her, dragging her across his thighs. "We've unfinished business, you and I. Business I mean to see settled here and now."

Her face was afire, her sex weeping and strumming in turns. Her cheek pressed into the mattress, she tried levering herself up, but his arm cinching her waist held her firmly down. "Let me up."

He ignored her. "When I was a lad, I was tied to the whipping post, mind. Fifty lashes with the scourge,

Kate. Surely you can take half as many from the flat of my hand."

Twenty-five strikes! She'd gathered he meant to spank her when he'd turned her over his knee, but she hadn't thought much about what that meant before now.

His hand cracked down. "One." Furious, she tried shoving up on her forearms, but it was no use.

"Two." His hand came down again, harder this time. Kate gritted her teeth against crying out.

"Three!"

Wetness spurted between her thighs. The dull ache ratcheted to pounding.

"Four. You've a bonny bottom, Katie. It's pale as moonbeam and ripe as melon. My handprints look well painted on such a canvas." He smoothed a soothing hand over the sting and skittered light fingertips between the lobes.

Kate shivered. She bit back a gasp. A mental picture of his hands shot to mind—scarred knuckles, callused palms, thick fingers that knew just where to press, how to touch. He was spanking her as though she were a naughty child, a wicked girl, a slave. He was spanking her, and suddenly Kate couldn't seem to get enough. She turned her face into the mattress, her hands fisting the sheets, her hips rocking back and finding a rhythm with his hand. He wasn't only spanking her. He was marking her, marking her as his.

And the shame of it, *her* shame, was that she didn't

think she could bear for him to stop. Twenty-five strikes no longer seemed nearly enough. Each successive strike lifted her to a new level of dark pleasure, a deeper understanding that surrender could be sublime.

She needed this.

As if sensing the shift in her, he slid the hand holding her around to her front. His palm took possession of her mons. He gave it a light squeeze. "Ah, I am giving you what you want, aren't I, Katie? I thought as much." He tunneled a finger inside her, pressing on some previously undiscovered, exquisitely sensitive spot.

Kate's head lifted. She moaned and twisted back to look back at him. The act of control being taken away was surprisingly thrilling. "Please . . . more."

"I'll give you more, love, as much as you want, as much as you can take."

He stood, bringing her with him. They hadn't made it to twenty-five strikes, at least she didn't think so. This time he laid her on her back and came down atop her. His straddling thighs locked her hips in place and his big hands banded her wrists, pinning her arms high above her head. Wetness streamed her inner thighs, the hidden throbbing heavy and liquid. Her bottom felt raw, if not exactly blistered. She shifted on her hips, savoring the stinging.

He brought his face down close to hers. Perspiration beaded his forehead, and blood from the scratch she'd given him streaked down his jaw in a thin line. She'd marked him, too, marked him as hers, and seeing the evidence brought a heady pride.

"Tell me you want this, Kate."

Kate opened her mouth to answer but couldn't bring herself to give more than a low moan. Her body knew what she wanted, needed, even if she did not. And so it seemed did Rourke. He wedged a knee between her thighs, pried her legs apart, and plunged a second finger into her slickness.

Kate sucked in a sharp breath. His fingers worked scissor-style inside her, spreading her wider, driving the ache deeper. She thought about how open she was, how utterly trapped and yet completely free, and a grateful sob broke forth from her lips.

I need this.

When his one hand left her wrist to unbutton his trousers, she had no thought of trying to pull away. Her gaze riveted on the open flap—the long, thick cock, the thatch of coarse reddish brown curls, the shadowed testicles. Later once her hands were free, she would want to palm and lick him, to suckle and taste, but for now those sensations were too overwhelming, too rich.

He held himself and met her eyes. A sliver of milky moisture leaked from the slit and down the side.

"Tell me you want this. Tell me you want me." His voice was a husky demand, his breath a warm breeze settling into hair.

This time Kate found her voice. "I want this." *I*

want you.

He fitted his head to the throbbing spot between her thighs and thrust, his entry brutal and beautiful, hard and deep. The stab of pain told her he was all the way inside. She was glad. He stilled, perspiration beading his face, a long ripple sliding down his throat. "Kate?"

By now she knew what he wanted from her, knew her way to that place inside her soul that allowed her to surrender, to give. "Please."

And then he was on top of her, moving in and out of her, and through the fog that clouded her consciousness she understood that she was moving, too. Not against him or away from him, but with him. The rhythm into which their joined bodies had mutually fallen was building toward some sort of crescendo, something magical and earthy, wonderful and terrifying, that promised to carry her to a place so foreign and exquisite that she may have visited before but only in her dreams.

At some point, he'd freed her hands. She sank her nails into his shoulders, cinched her knees about his hips, and held on for dear life. Above where they were joined, his finger flicked and teased and stroked and played. An ache, a different sort, was spiraling to some sort of glorious end. Reaching for it, Kate lifted against him. Her bottom burned, her vagina burned. Oh, such lovely, scalding heat.

"You're mine." He let out a groan and slid an arm beneath her hips, bringing her high against him. "Say it."

He pulled out of her and then thrust hard and deep.

Dancing on the knife edge of that lovely pleasure-pain, Kate bit her lip. She lifted her head, hoping if she did he might seal her baptism by fire with a kiss. "Yes, I'm yours."

He didn't kiss her, but he smiled a smile of feral eyes and bared white teeth. "That's all I wanted to hear."

He reached down between them. It was his thumb this time, or so she thought, the flesh at the tip thick and sandpaper rough. He chafed the hard little nubbin she knew was there but had so far never seen—once, twice, thrice . . .

Kate fell back against the pillows and screamed.

They lay side by side on the mussed bed. Confessions came between hitched breaths.

Kate's was the first. She looked up from tracing circles on the dark matting of his chest—he'd yet to take off his shirt—and said, "I really am sorry about the horse. Do you think you'll get him back?"

He turned his head to look at her. "Hang the horse. You might have been injured, maimed for life, killed even. *Jaysus*, Katie, why did you do it? If you'd only wanted to defy me, surely you might have settled on some safer way."

Kate swallowed hard against a telltale tightening in

her throat. She'd hoped the hurt would have dissolved by now, but so far it had not. "Last night I came downstairs . . . looking for you. I found you asleep at your desk, but you weren't all that I found. I found the play and the note from Daisy and Gavin. Rourke, how could you?"

His eyes widened. "You risked life and limb on account of a play?" He swore and scoured a hand across his brow. "I didn't know how else to reach you, woo you."

"Woo me!" Reminded it wasn't the play at fault, but him, she elbowed her way upright, bringing the sheet with her. "Am I to believe that subjecting me to starvation, exhaustion, humiliation—public *and* private—was all done in the spirit of equanimity?"

He went stone still beside her. "I spanked you, which under the circumstance was a good deal less punishment than you deserved. And confess it, Katie, you enjoyed what happened here. Within these four walls, you liked setting Capable Kate free for a time and owning me as your master. You liked my hand on your arse and my thumb on your pearl and my cock in your cunt. Admit it, or better yet kiss me, for nay worries, I'll tame you yet, my Kate."

The last was the absolute worst thing he could have said.

Her face heated with shame. Nothing between them had changed. He still saw her not as chattel, little more than a slave. She'd played into his hands, abased herself in the very vilest of ways. She'd begged, actually *begged* him, to do those things to her. He'd turned her into a craven creature, a person she scarcely recognized as herself. And she'd let him. More than let him, she'd begged for it—for pleasure, for punishment, for *him*. For that, she could easily hate him all her days.

She yanked at the wrinkled sheet and swept it about her like a cape. "You may have taken advantage of me this once, but I'll not let you ill-use me again."

Kate had never before felt so truly naked, so achingly raw. He hadn't only marked her body. He'd stripped bare her soul, peeling away the civilized surface layer and exposing every secret fantasy and dark desire.

He sat up beside her. Knowing emerald eyes met hers. "There's no shame in showing you're a woman, Katie, with a woman's heart and a woman's needs, including the occasional desire to be mastered." He reached for her, but she jerked away.

"Get the hell out."

"Katie?"

"How many times must I tell you, my name is *Katherine*."

Kate didn't come down to dinner that evening, nor supper, either. Rourke took both meals alone in the big dining room, though he mostly pushed the food about his plate. Even his dog had shunned him, preferring to dine with Kate in her room. From the sounds that had filtered through the door earlier, Toby must be savoring a fine feast.

I'll tame you yet, my Kate.

If he'd mastered his wife as he'd boasted, then why was he lying abed alone nursing a brick-hard cock stand, aching balls, and a gouged cheek? But those physical discomforts couldn't touch the ache in his heart.

He'd set out to teach her a lesson, but it turned out he was as much pupil as she. Never before had he so lost himself in a woman, not only her body but her soul. For a time reality had dissolved into a series of impressions—Kate's nape, so slender and white, her honey-drizzled hair sliding over the side of the bed; her slight weight and beautiful curves covering his thighs; the slapping sound of first his hand striking her bottom and later his cock striking her creamy quim. He hadn't known a woman could become so scalding hot, so mouth-wateringly wet. When he'd finally spilled himself inside her, he'd come harder and longer than ever before.

Hours later he could still taste the brine of her on his tongue and her orange blossom scent on his skin. Her hair, he mused, smelled like warm sunshine. A moment later he shook his head to think what an idiot he'd become. Mooning over a woman, his sharp-tongued wife, as though he was some love-smitten swain straight from the pages of one of Shakespeare's damnable plays, what the devil had come over him?

Bloody hell, I love the woman.

Patrick O'Rourke, erstwhile purse snatch, top-notch bamboozler, and railway pirate, was in love—head over heels, over the moon in love. Who could have guessed that one pocket-sized woman would be the one to bring him to heel, to steal his heart as surely as once he had snitched gentlemen's purses?

Looking back to their wedding day, though he'd been deliberately late and had donned his queer costume to vex her, his heart had felt feather light, his mood genuinely merry. As much as he'd tried telling himself he was marrying her to settle a score for the humiliation in the garden, now he owned the truth: he'd quite simply wanted her.

Unfortunately Kate didn't want him, not anymore if, indeed, she ever had. She'd sent him away, thereby entering the league of loved ones who'd been rejecting him all his life. Never before had he felt so splintered, so aching, so absolutely close to coming apart.

Oh, Katie, I'll break you yet.

The trick would be not to allow his own heart to be broken in the bargain.

The next morning Rourke sat alone at the breakfast table, nursing his cold coffee and pushing his food about his plate. His folded newspaper, still warm from the iron, lay unopened beside him. In the bright light of day, he admitted that spanking and bondage were no ways to go about bedding a virgin bride. And yet he'd sensed Katie had both wanted and needed the raw honesty of a hard, fierce taking, and so, he admitted, had he. These past weeks they'd been circling each other like hissing cats. The episode with Zeus had pushed him beyond the edge of patience and civility. Thinking how easily her slender white throat might have snapped sent ice water trickling through his veins. By the time he'd flung open her bedroom door, he'd buried his fear in blistering rage. And yet before last night, he'd never laid angry hands on a woman, not even Felicity. His wee wife most definitely brought out the beast in him.

Kate entered the room, dressed in a riding habit of hunter green and bowler pinned to perfect place. To the casual observer she would appear elegant and self-possessed, a fashion plate from *Harper's Bazaar* come to life, the perfect picture of upper-crust English womanhood. But her shadowed eyes and less than springy step told Rourke otherwise. It seemed he was not the only one of them to come out of the previous night's tumult the worse for wear. He fingered the scab on his cheek. Surely she couldn't mean to ride?

Surprised and pleased to see her, he stood to draw out her chair. "Good morning, Kate. Did you sleep well?" He'd only slept in snatches himself.

She gave a quick glance to the chair and then moved

270

to the sideboard. "You needn't bother. I shan't be sitting." Spooning buttered eggs onto her plate, she glared back at him. "Unfortunately I've never been particularly adept at sleeping on my stomach."

He opened his mouth to remark on the bonny view that must have been, but for once better judgment prevailed. Instead, he said, "I hadn't expected to see you downstairs so early." He hadn't expected to see her at all.

"I'm headed to the stables to make my apologies to Mr. Campbell." She slammed the lid down on the rasher. "So, if your intention was to starve me—again—as well as beat me, I'm sorry to disappoint."

"That's not . . . Oh, hell, Katie, can't we call a truce? It's not as if you didn't manage to get in a few good licks yourself."

"Speaking of which, how *is* your face? That scratch on your cheek must sting dreadfully." She sent him a sweet smile, her first since entering.

He touched the cheek she'd marked and grimaced. "Shaving this morning hurt like the devil—and dinna look so pleased with yourself."

She came over to the table and plunked her plate down. "But I am pleased with myself, about the scratch at least. Come at me like that again, and I'll give you one to match on the other side."

Exasperated, he raked a hand through his hair. "Christ, Kate, how can you speak to me so? Last night we made love. Last night I was inside you."

Her gaze darted to the open door. "Kindly lower your voice. The servants, now that we have servants, will hear you."

Temper rising, he threw his napkin down like a gauntlet. "I don't give a damn if the whole bloody castle hears."

"Well, I do. I'd just as soon we forget last night ever happened."

Of all the things she'd said, the insults she'd lobbed at him, that last remark cut the deepest. He rounded on her. "Can you do that, Kate? Can you forget the feel of my fingers playing with your button and milking the cream from your cunt? Can you forget how you moaned when I thrust into you with my two fingers and you wiggled that bonny arse of yours as though begging for a third? Can you forget how you came for me, not once but twice in a row?"

Like a thoroughbred filly, a pulse beat high in her sculpted forehead, square between her eyes. She swallowed hard, the ripple traveling the length of her long, elegant throat. "A gentleman wouldn't throw such a private moment in my face."

"If by gentleman you mean that lot of pasty-faced pansies who courted you back in London, nay one of them would have been man enough to bring you to your knees." He reached out, lifting her chin on the scarred knuckles of his hand. "Nay, you canna forget, Kate, and you canna make me forget, either. Like it or no, I'm in your blood now, as you are in mine."

Later that day, Kate sat on a pillow in Hattie's room, nursing a sore bottom and hurt pride in equal measure. In truth, she was more saddle sore from her breakneck ride on Zeus than she was from her husband's spanking. Fortunately the stallion had been recovered, and the groomsmen who'd gone after him had returned with only a few bruises.

"That man, that miserable, infuriating man. Who does he think he is, adapting a play, a famous play by Shakespeare, to get one over on me, to *tame* me, no less? What cheek!"

Hattie sat across from her, stitching what looked suspiciously like baby booties, the picture of serenity. Barring the embarrassing bit to do with the spanking, the housekeeper had heard the story of Kate's discovery of Rourke's scheme, not once but several times.

She looked up from the stitch she'd just made. "Some might find it rather romantic. And you must admit it did work for a while. I've never seen you looking so happy."

Kate took another sip of tea, steam rising from the cup and, likely, from the top of her head. "Huh! I rue the day I ever agreed to dance the waltz with him. My life has gone to rack and ruin ever since."

Hattie bobbed a nod. "And well you should. Why, it was a regular paradise he took you away from. Between your father's drinking and gaming and your sister's tantrums and whining, only think of the happy times you're missing by being here—in your castle . . . with your husband . . . who happens to be mad about you. The short end of the stick, that's your lot, and I for one don't blame you a bit for being bitter."

The sarcasm wasn't lost on Kate. All at once, she felt sad and lonesome and more than a little sick of it all. Until now she'd railed against the state of affairs that had conspired to place her in her current untenable position—her father's gaming, her sister's selfishness, her long-ago promise to her mother to see that everyone and everything was taken care of and made all right—everyone, that is, but her.

Sitting in Hattie's room, thinking of all the luxuries and security she had that the housekeeper did not, it occurred to her to wonder from what marriage to Rourke had supposedly taken her away. Waiting hand and foot upon her father until he was in his dotage and she well and truly past her prime? Reading romantic novels and gorging on chocolate because there was no romance in her life or any real sweetness?

Thanks to Rourke, she no longer need fret about her family. Worries over her father's unbridled gaming and the need to secure a suitable dowry for her little sister were for the moment held in check. Not only was he rich, but he was wise. Unlike her father, he wasn't going to lose the roof over their heads in a game of cards or stake her like a serf in some absurd wager. His one great "crime" since they'd met had been to wager that he could coax a kiss from her in public. At this point, she'd gladly let him kiss her just about anywhere.

She ran her tongue along her lower lip. That was what Patrick was like—all steely control on the outside and carefully harnessed chaos within. Kate wanted him to lose control. She wanted to lose control with him. She wanted to not only embrace the chaos of her feelings, embrace him, but become one with it. She wanted them to walk hand in hand into the eye of the storm without fear, recriminations, God help her, or looking back.

But they were still a long way from that level of letting go. Trust must be earned. It wasn't her husband she didn't trust so much as herself. Until meeting Rourke, her entire existence had been predicated on maintaining control. Living with a drunkard, matters could spiral out of control at the snap of fingers. Her role had been to anticipate everything that might go awry and then take steps to make sure that it did not. She was very good at it, but the weeks of freedom from that household had shown her just how exhausting playing her father's keeper had been. She had lost something precious in all those years, something less tangible than her pony, Princess. She had lost herself. At eight-and-twenty, she wasn't sure she even knew who she was, but whatever her authentic self was, it seemed to come out, to shine, when she was with Patrick.

He hadn't tamed her. He'd rescued her.

That evening, Kate took a bracing breath and knocked on the adjoining door to her husband's room. She hadn't seen him since that morning at breakfast. She knew he was within because she'd heard him come up earlier. Heart beating fast, she listened for his footfalls cutting across the room. Given the silence, she wondered if he might be asleep.

The door opened partway. Rourke appeared in the opening. He wore only a shirt and waistcoat, both buttoned this time. His eyes, she thought, looked a bit hollow.

She fixed on what she hoped was a bright smile. "I've come to invite you to dinner. A private dinner in my room," she added, and then stepped back to give him a better view, not of the room but of her.

She'd exchanged her customary practical shirtwaist and skirt for a fashionable dinner gown. The sherry-colored satin shimmered in the candlelight and made a delicious rustling sound when she moved. According to Hattie, it also brought out her hair and eye color in a highly flattering way. The gown's daring décolletage was more suited to a formal than a family dinner. Then again, when one's purpose was to reconcile with one's husband, it was perfect, or so she hoped.

He ran his gaze over her. She thought he looked

wary. After that morning, she supposed she couldn't blame him.

At last he spoke. "To what do I owe this unprecedented honor?"

She shrugged, but her heartbeat quickened. He wasn't about to make this easy for her, but then she'd expected as much. "Think of it as a truce, an olive branch. If you'll cease trying to tame me, I'll cease searching for ways to vex you. Fair enough?"

He blew out a breath, and then nodded. "Fair enough." He reached to take her hand.

Kate held back. She'd hoped for more than a handshake to seal their bargain. "Aren't you going to at least . . . kiss me?"

"I considered it, but I'm minded of your dislike of such rough Scot's ways."

Kate would have given a great deal to be the recipient of his "rough Scot's ways," but she reminded herself that it was as yet early in the evening. She took him by the hand, not to shake it but to lead him inside before he could refuse.

She didn't drop her hold until they reached the small round table Hattie had helped her set up. Following her fellow conspirator's suggestion, she'd purchased a single red rose from the flower seller in town and set it in the center. And instead of the gas lamps, she'd lit candles about the room.

Several covered dishes had been set out on a cloth-covered side table. "It's a simple supper. I didn't want to have to worry with carving. I hope you don't mind."

Now that she'd got him this far, she was nervous. She found herself eyeing the wine, a bordeaux she'd had Mr. Sylvester fetch from the cellar and that she'd just decanted mere minutes before.

He lifted serving-dish lids and peered inside. "That wouldn't be oxtail soup, would it?" He gave an appreciative sniff.

"Indeed, it is. There is also a beef à la mode, butter beans with almonds, roasted jacket potatoes, and a ginger cream for dessert." Instead of ginger cream, she hoped her husband would be having *her* for dessert.

He lifted his eyes to her. "All favorites of mine."

"I know."

She served the soup while he poured out the wine. He tucked her into her chair, and then took his place beside her.

Picking up his spoon, he paused, "You've not peppered it, have you?"

"Don't be ridiculous."

"Dosed it with some emetic, then?"

"Hardly."

"Poisoned it? I hear arsenic can be verra hard to trace."

She smiled at that. "I'll have to remember that, but for the present, no." So long as he teased her, there yet might be hope. "I suppose you'll just have to try a bite and find out."

They ate in silence for the next few minutes, or rather Rourke did. Kate drank wine and pushed her spoon about her bowl. When her glass was empty, she reached for the decanter to top off his glass, and then refilled hers.

He looked up. "If I didn't know better, Katie, I'd think you were trying to get me drunk."

This time she didn't object to the nickname. In fact, she was coming to rather like it, at least the way it sounded rolling off his tongue with his soft Scot's burr.

"What if I am?" she asked gamely, the wine sending a pleasant languor trickling through her limbs. "Would you mind terribly?"

"You might mind."

Kate rather doubted it. She could see she wasn't the only of them who fancied holding on to self-control. "You're not much for keeping up the reputation of Scotsmen, are you?"

He pushed his empty bowl aside. "If I hold back from having to brace myself up by my elbows, as my wife I'd think you'd not have cause to complain of it."

"I'm not complaining, only . . . curious."

It was nearing eight o'clock. Excellent vintage or not, her father would be three sheets to the wind long before now. No, her husband's moderation didn't bother her. It but gave her one more reason to respect him, to like him—to love him. Despite having gotten off on the wrong foot in their marriage—several wrong feet—she knew she would always be safe with this man.

He hesitated, looking not at her but deeply into his glass. "Railway work is hard on a man, hard on his body and even harder on his soul. My da was fond of the whiskey and the gin. Overfond, you might say."

So his father was a drunkard, too, yet another commonality they shared. For two people who on the outside couldn't be more opposed in background and breeding, it was amazing how very much they had in common, how truly alike they were.

Appalled, she said, "Was he violent when he drank?"

Her father had never once raised his hand to her. She must give the devil his due. Still, there were other ways to wound. Not all scars were on the surface of skin.

He hesitated and then shrugged as though being beaten was of no consequence, and it occurred to her that she was making him remember things he might well rather forget. "A hard hand had my da, though he had goodness at his core. He was always sorry afterward, for what it was worth. I dinna hold it against him, at least not much, though I swore when I grew up, no matter how bad things got, I'd not follow him down that path. My wife and children would never have cause to fear or flee me." He lifted his eyes to her. "The other night with you, I broke that rule. I'm sorry, Kate."

"I'm sorry, too." On impulse, she reached across the table and clasped his big, rough hand. "I know you wouldn't really hurt me." Though she wasn't yet prepared to admit it aloud, being overpowered by him, and yes, feeling that hard open palm slapping her backside had excited her—powerfully.

She rose to clear the bowls and serve the second course. Blunt-speaking and rough-hewn though he was in many ways, with her he had the loveliest manners.

Taking the opportunity to shift the conversation to a lighter topic, she said, "So, why a castle?"

"What do you mean?"

Kate set their plates down and took her chair. "It seems a great deal of space and upkeep for one person."

He sat as well. "There are two of us . . . now."

By "now," she wondered if he implied there might one day be more than the two of them, and her heart skipped a beat. She so wanted a baby—*his* baby.

"I can't help but think of Sir Walter Scott's glorifying the so-called Dark Ages in the Waverley novel *Ivanhoe.*" Catching his blank look, she hesitated and then clarified, "Have you read any of Scott's work?"

"I havena, though I'm sure I've the books on my shelves. I don't read much, mind."

She couldn't resist. "Well, you read plays, certainly. Perhaps you'll want to branch out to other forms of fiction."

She shouldn't have said that. His gaze dimmed, and he focused on forking up his food.

Taking another sip of wine, she leaned forward, just enough to give him a teasing glimpse of cleavage. "Still, I think you rather fancy it here, the mystique of being master of your medieval domain and all that." The word *master* was a deliberate choice. "Have you a dungeon? Surely you must. What is a castle without a dungeon?"

His gaze slid upward, resting on her breasts before returning to her face. "What, indeed? In this case, what was the dungeon is now a wine cellar."

She reached over and brushed back the lock of hair that had fallen over the small white scar on his forehead. So many scars, and yet she'd be hard-pressed to say she'd ever met a more handsome man.

"Do you suppose previous lairds who lived here ever took their naughty wives down to the dungeon, hmmm?"

She was flirting, openly, outrageously, but she was too tipsy and randy to care. She only hoped she was going about it properly. In the past, she'd warded off suitors by being as sharp-tongued and displeasing as possible. Coming up with innovative cuts, direct or otherwise, had become almost a point of pride. She'd never given much thought to her flirting skills before now, but then she'd never before had so very much at stake.

"I couldn't say."

He set his cutlery neatly alongside his plate and looked over at her. The heat of his gaze scorched her, setting her skin prickling and her sex pulsing.

"I take naughty wives to bed."

CHAPTER TWELVE

> "Now, Kate, I am a husband for your turn,
> For, by this light, whereby I see thy beauty—
> Thy beauty that doth make me like thee well—
> Thou must be married to no man but me."
> —WILLIAM SHAKESPEARE, Petruchio,
> *The Taming of the Shrew*

When Rourke swung her up into his arms, this time Kate didn't struggle. She didn't kick. She didn't scratch. Instead she rested her head on his solid shoulder and draped her arm about his strong neck, and savored the delicious, buoyant feeling of being utterly cherished and cared for. She'd supposed he would carry her to the bed, but instead he crossed the room and set her down before the dressing mirror.

Standing behind her, he reached around her, settling his hands on her hips. "Beautiful Kate, Katie mine, so lovely betimes it hurts my eyes to gaze upon you." Kissing the side of her neck, he smoothed a callused palm over the well of her belly, sending small shivery shocks rippling through her.

He nipped at her ear, the side of her neck, the edge of her collarbone, his arousal pressing into her backside. Kate leaned into his muscled strength, his searing heat. The thought of taking all of that, all of him, inside her again made her skin prickle and warm.

He slid a hand into the back of her hair, letting the strands slide through his fingers. "Kate, sweet Kate, you're a temptress and an angel."

She stared into the mirror, fascinated with watching his hands. "I can't say as I've ever been accused of being either before."

Layer by layer, he peeled her clothing away until even her stays and panties lay atop the puddle of shimmering dress. Watching him lay her bare bit by naughty bit was a foreign and erotic sensation. He still hadn't removed so much as a stitch of his own clothes. Looking at their joined reflections in the glass, Kate was seized with impatience. She wanted to see him, too. She wanted to see him now.

His arms slid around her. He palmed her breasts, played with her nipples. "It's long, lovely nipples you have, lass, and ripe as berries." What they were was exquisitely sensitive, especially in his expert hands. Watching him roll them between his thumb and forefinger, Kate couldn't shake the sense that she was an instrument being played.

"Rourke, I—"

His lips found the sensitive spot at her nape again and licked. "Hush, Katie."

"But I . . . I don't know how much longer I can bear it. I don't know how much longer I can stand."

It was no more than the truth. She felt as boneless as an eel, her legs a breath away from buckling.

His soft laugh warmed the shell of her ear. "Dinna fret, Katie mine. If you fall, I'm here to catch you."

If you fall, I'm here to catch you.

He slid his hand down over her belly, his blunt fingers combing through the triangle of curls, stirring a slow-building ache. "Easy, lass, it's gentle I'll be with you this time. We'll go as slow as you like."

Her voice was lost to her for the moment. She managed a nod. Whatever response she gave, he seemed satisfied because he didn't stop. He sank a thick finger all the way inside her, rousing a longing that until the night before was as foreign as it was fierce. Kate started, but he still had one arm wrapped about her waist. She wasn't going anywhere, not that she wanted to. The mad fever was upon her, pitching higher, closing, muddling her thoughts and doing wickedly delicious things to her body. She wanted Rourke. She wanted to make love with her husband. He might be the enemy, the man determined to master her, but in this they were united. She wanted him in a very physical way, and the hard length of him pressing against her backside told her he wanted her, too.

She twisted her head about and caught his mouth in a clumsy kiss. A rumble rose from his throat, equal parts laugh and groan. Inside her mouth, his tongue swirled like a cloud, and she couldn't help wondering what it might feel like to have him kiss her like that, only lower at the oh-so-sensitive spot between her legs. He turned her in his arms, and she clung, his shoulders her anchor, his dark emerald gaze her guiding star in a world that suddenly seemed cast adrift, lost at sea. Reaching around, he caressed her buttocks, his big strong hands warm and sure. All at once, she felt safe and cherished, wanton and free. She moaned and arched against his hand, wanting more, wanting all.

His voice was a warm rumble against her fevered cheek. "Sweet Kate, Katie mine. Dinna fash, I'll ease you. I'll do anything you want. You've only to ask." He dragged the rough pads of his thumbs across her nipples, raising her shiver and a hot liquid ache.

She smoothed a hand over his chest, palming his pectorals. "What I'd most like is to see you, too. All of you," she added, lest there be any doubt.

"That eager, are you?" He grinned, but his expression turned wary.

Her face warmed, but she didn't look away. "I've never even seen you without your shirt. I'm beginning to wonder what you might be hiding, dragon's scales perhaps?"

She'd been in his arms enough times to imagine that beneath his shirt he must be splendid, spectacularly muscled in all the proper places. But she was no longer content with imagining. She wanted to stand skin to skin. She wanted to suckle his flesh and feel his bones.

He fixed her with a stark gaze. "Some things are best left to the imagination."

"You're my husband. I want to see you—*all* of you." And then she said the single word he liked hearing from her above all others. "*Please.*"

Candlelight flickered over his face. His resigned expression told her he would deny her no longer. "Very well, Katie, but mind afterward, you were the one who pressed, not I."

Fixing his gaze on her face, he started down the queue of buttons fronting his shirt. Though it might have been a trick of the shadows, she thought she caught his hands trembling.

She reached up to help. "Let me."

He dropped his arms to his sides and let her. Crisp hair teased her fingertips as she made short work of the line. She unhooked the last button and slid the shirt from his shoulders—his beautiful, broad shoulders. He was pale as she was. A smattering of freckles dusted his shoulder tops. The same dark reddish hair she'd glimpsed from the dropped uppermost button of a shirt collar matted his upper chest and dusted his pectorals, narrowing to that tantalizing queue she'd glimpsed the other day. There was a tattoo on his left bicep, some bird of prey it was too dark to clearly see. His belly was flat and rippling with muscle, his trouser front tented. Remembering what he'd looked like there, she palmed him.

He bucked against her hand. Smiling, she kept it there. There would be time enough later to learn the touch and taste of him. For now, she brushed the back of her hand over the flat disc of one brownish nipple and, leaning forward, sucked the nub into her mouth.

Rourke jumped as if she'd burned him. She drew back and smiled. "You're beautiful," she said, both because she suspected he might not know and because it was entirely true. "No dragon scales, as far as I can tell."

He shook his head, his arms still down at his sides. "No, Katie, you were right the other times. I am coarse and a beast, not nearly fit to touch someone as fine as you, though my wife you be."

"You are not coarse, and you are most certainly not a beast. What you are is tense. Here, let me help with that."

She slid her hands over his shoulders and back, marveling at what lovely skin he had, especially for a man. Not that she'd ever touched a man's bare chest before, but she couldn't imagine they were all made in so perfect a fashion. Her hands found the back of his neck. He *was* tense, she could feel it, and the flesh there wasn't quite so smooth, but rather ridged.

When I was a lad, I was tied to the whipping post, mind. Fifty lashes with the scourge, Kate.

"Oh, Rourke." She drew her hands away and stepped back.

He grimaced. "Satisfied?" He reached for his shirt to put it back on.

"Don't."

Kate stepped behind him. The webbing of thick white scars put her in mind of the intricate spiderweb she'd seen hanging from the hallway rafters on her wedding night. She reached out to touch a particularly deep cross-hatching.

He flinched away. Turning back to look at her, he grimaced. "Mine isna a gentleman's back anymore than these are a gentleman's hands. And yet you like them well enough in the dark, don't you, Katie? They may be coarse, ugly even, but they're the same hands that tease and toy with you until you cry out and beg me to let you come."

The anger in his voice took her by surprise. When he'd been courting her, she'd used the calluses on his hands to taunt him. She'd lashed out by seizing on what she'd sensed would hurt him the most. His hands hadn't bothered her even then, not really, but his self-consciousness of them, always shoving them into pockets and hiding them inside gloves, had told her they bothered him. Now seeing his poor scarred back, she'd never felt so thoroughly ashamed. Her shrew's tongue had cut him as surely as the whip that someone had wielded to lay open his back, and only actions and not words would heal the rift and salve the hurt.

"I don't find your hands ugly or your back, either,

for that matter."

To prove it, she leaned in and laid her lips upon his shoulder. Rourke sucked in a heavy breath. "Oh, Kate."

She opened her mouth and laved one angry mark with her tongue. His skin was slightly salt-flavored and scented with bay rum and mint soap, and his own special musk. Kate moved to kiss his other shoulder, deliberately dragging her nipples along his back. Ah, lovely. Who would have thought that in giving pleasure there was such a bounty returned, too?

He turned about. "I think you must be a brownie or some other fairy folk."

She made a face. "Because I'm so small, I know."

He shook his head. "Nay, it's no your size of which I speak. There's a magic about you, Katie. When I'm with you, it's as though everything has a sparkle, a glow. Now kiss me, Kate. Kiss me as a wife who loves her husband would kiss. Pretend if you must, only kiss me. Kiss me as if you mean it. Kiss me as if you can't *not* kiss me, and give all that thinking a rest for now."

Kate rose up on her toes, wrapped her arms about Patrick's neck, and matched her mouth to his. Tongues met, tangled, and twined. Bottom lips were nibbled, traced with gentle fingers, and abraded ever so lightly with fingernails. Corners of mouths were kissed and probing digits licked and laved and suckled. And throughout, deep in her heart, Kate owned the truth she didn't dare say.

She loved him. She didn't have to pretend.

His hands found her waist, and he lifted her off the floor. Kate wrapped her legs about his torso. Without breaking the embrace, he carried her over to the bed and laid her gently in the center of the counterpane.

Patrick turned away to finish undressing. When he turned back to the bed, he was fully, gloriously naked. Kate rose up on her elbows, gaze running over him from broad shoulders to powerful thighs, amazed to think that such a splendid male was her husband, all hers.

He straddled her. "Open your legs for me, Kate."

Kate opened her legs. Denying either of them was a notion she was no longer able to contemplate. He spread her inner lips with his fingers, sat back on his haunches, and looked at her—*there.*

"Kate, beautiful Kate, it's so pretty you are there and everywhere else. Another time we'll take a hand mirror to the bed, and I'll show you just how lovely you are, but for now tell me what you want, Kate. What happens in this bed is between you and me and no one else."

Lying back against the banked pillows, Kate wasn't sure how to answer. In her eight-and-twenty years, she could count on the finger of one hand how often she'd been asked what she wanted.

He slid a finger slowly inside her and then drew it just as slowly out. "You're so small, I can scarcely credit how it is I fit inside you." He lifted his gaze from her open thighs. "And you feel like warm, wet velvet." He traced her labia with a single slow-moving digit. "And

I'll vouchsafe you taste delicious."

He slid down to the bottom of the bed, his head disappearing between her raised knees. He kissed the inside of her thighs, stroking and caressing her buttocks. And then he found her with his mouth, touching that part of her where his fingers had played.

Kate's head shot up from the pillow. "Oh, Rourke." She reached for him, her hand sifting through his hair, her hips lifting.

He looked up, grin lopsided and eyes aglow. "You taste of oysters shucked fresh from the shell and tangy from the sea. I could suckle and lick you all the night and never grow weary of your texture, your scent, your taste. I just may."

Kate wasn't sure what to say or how to respond. Until now, pleasure—happiness—was a scarce commodity that must be measured, doled out, and above all, held back in storage for a future rainy day. Never before had she known such a bounty of bliss, such a feast of feeling. It was almost overwhelming. It *was* overwhelming. And frightening. And exhilarating. And . . . wonderful beyond words.

"Tell me what you want, Kate."

Kate lifted her head from the pillow. Meeting Rourke's heated gaze, she reached for boldness that before now she'd buried beneath scolding, shrewish ways. "I want you, Patrick. I want you to make love to me with your mouth and your hands and finally with your big beautiful cock. I want all of you, Patrick, and I promise to do my utmost to give you all of me in return."

Kate had called him Patrick, not only once but several times.

It was late. They'd made love for hours. He should be tired, exhausted. He wasn't.

He couldn't seem to get his fill of his beautiful wife, and that included looking at her.

Kate lay on her side, her back pressed against his chest. Her eyes were half-closed, her lips sweetly parted. Like as not, he should leave sleeping wives lie, and yet he had to know.

He lifted his head from the pillow. "Happy?"

She hoisted the lid of one eye and mustered a lazy nod. Even with one side of her pretty face turned into the pillow, he could see the half smile broaden. "Hmm, I like it here."

He tamped down his disappointment over not receiving the hoped-for response. "Scotland can take some getting used to, the winters especially, but it boasts some of the most beautiful scenery on earth. When spring comes, I'll take you north to the Highland country."

Her eye, the one he could see, opened the rest of the way. "No, I meant I like it here with you . . . in your arms."

"Oh."

He thought about that a moment, not certain of what he should say in return, if anything. Odd how in business his instincts were fair near impeccable, he always knew what to do, but in his dealings with his wife, he was very much a ship cast adrift from its anchor. Lost, hopelessly lost.

He leaned over and touched her shoulder. In the dying candlelight, her skin looked like alabaster. "Kate?"

No answer.

He levered himself up on his elbow and looked down at her. A soft purring, a ladylike snoring, but snoring all the same, confirmed she was asleep.

He smiled. It was just as well. Declarations of love, or at least the hope of hearing that sentiment returned, would keep for another day. It wouldn't do to push.

He lay back down and slid an arm about her waist, drawing her close. Her bottom pressed into his middle so that they lay stacked like two contented spoons. Even now that he'd memorized every square inch of her, it amazed him how neatly her slight frame fitted to his big one.

Closing his eyes, it occurred to him that though he'd been with other women, some of whose names he couldn't recall, none of those encounters could begin to compare to the joy of bedding his beautiful firebrand wife. It wasn't in his nature to give up easily or at all, but drinking in the sunshine fragrance of her hair, he conceded that taming his wild Kat might well be a lost cause. Against all reason, he'd fallen in love with his headstrong wife—and without altering a single thing about her. Well, mayhap one . . .

She called me Patrick.

Smiling, Rourke fell asleep.

The week that followed was a honeymoon in truth. Rourke and Kate spent most of it behind the bolted door of their bedchamber. They made love in every way Kate had ever imagined—and a few she'd never even considered. If her husband had any inhibitions at all, she'd yet to discover them. By the week's end, there was no part of her he hadn't touched, tasted, or otherwise explored. Every time she thought she'd sampled the entire platter of carnal delights, he found some new way to please her.

Lying abed one morning, Rourke's head tucked into her shoulder, she traced the outline of the bird tattoo on his bicep. In the light of day, it looked to be a rook. "What does this tattoo signify?"

Her husband turned his mussed head and looked up at her with lazy-lidded eyes. She loved his eyes, but then she'd come to love everything about him—the scars, the big hands that seemed more gentle than coarse, the Scot's burr. But beyond any physical trait, what she loved most was the brilliant, good-hearted man beneath.

"The crow was Johnnie Black's. Black's Boys was

the rookery I belonged to."

"Rookery?"

"A flash house, mind. I snitched purses and stole from street vendors anything I could get my hands on and hide in my pockets. Anything that wasn't nailed down was fair game in those days, and we had a weekly quota to fill. Any boy who didn't pull in his share was subject to punishment, to be decided by the group. It was dog-eat-dog, and I did whatever it took to stay fed and alive, but I never murdered anyone nor inflicted hurt for the sport of it. I'm not proud of my past, but I'll no lie about it, either."

She pressed a kiss to the crow's beak because she loved kissing him anywhere and everywhere, but mainly because she wanted to show him it was all right. "How did you escape getting caught?"

"I didn't. I was brought up three times on charges—vagrancy, thievery, and robbery. Robbery is with a weapon, mind. The last would have meant prison for me. Only the man I'd stolen from spoke on my behalf."

She'd started down this path because she'd grown to love the sound of his voice with its Scot's burr and deep timbre, but now she found herself wanting to know the rest of the story. "That sounds noble of him. Surely that can't be usual? Who was he?"

"You wouldn't believe me if I told you."

"Try me." *Trust me.*

She ran a hand through his hair. The auburn locks

falling through her fingers weren't coarse at all, but wondrously soft.

"William Gladstone."

She angled her face to his, wondering if he might be joking despite his solemn tone. "You robbed the former prime minister!"

"Aye, I stole his money clip, but he was wise to me, and in getting away, I accidentally knocked him out. There was even talk of adding treason to the charges."

"And still he testified on your behalf." Kate had always had a fine feeling toward "the People's William," as Gladstone was known. From what she'd read of him, he struck her as a principled man, hard but fair. Now she found herself liking him even more.

"More than that, he put up a thousand-pound surety on my behalf and had me sent to Roxbury House instead of jail. It was the first time anyone ever really believed in me. Of course, once there I met Gavin and Harry—Hadrian, I mean—and Daisy."

"And you've stayed friends all these years."

How ironic that she, born to the upper crust with the proverbial silver spoon in her mouth, would find herself in awe and envy of a quartet of orphaned ragamuffins, but she was. She envied them their wits and their street smarts, but mostly she envied them their genuine, no-holds-barred friendship. Because of the nine years separating them and the maternal role Kate had been called to play, Bea was more of a daughter to her than a sister or confidante. She hadn't had anything like that in her own life, and dear Lord, how she envied it.

He nodded. "We lost track of Daisy for fifteen years. It wasn't until we three happened upon her in the Palace music hall that we found her again, but the other three of us were never out of touch for more than a few years."

Kate traced the curve of a crescent-shaped scar on his brow. "Getting back to mapping the terrain, what about this one?"

"One of the bobbies who collared me was overzealous with his wee club. Gave me several good cracks, did Officer Taggert. My one eye wasna ever quite the same."

Kate drew back, outraged. "That's awful. Did you press charges, at least? Was he punished?"

He snorted. "He had the law on his side, and betimes no one fancies a rat."

Small wonder he must find her quaint, shallow, a snob. "And this one." She touched a gauge atop his left shoulder, not a whip mark, or at least she didn't think so. The scar was deep but not terribly long.

His smile flattened. "The buckle of my da's belt."

A hard hand had my da.

Kate shivered, her heart aching for the brave, lost little boy he once was. Other than the small scar on her cheek, all her scars were on the inside.

He stroked a hand down her arm from shoulder to elbow. Dear Lord, how she loved the way he touched her, gentle yet firm. "I'm hacked like an old badger, but you, my beauty, are smooth as porcelain, only warm, not cold."

Not cold at all, but warming by the moment and very much looking forward to making love again. Kate smiled. "You most certainly are not hacked, as you say. You're quite perfectly beautiful." She leaned over and pressed a kiss atop the bump on his nose. "And I love your nose. It's a fine nose, a noble nose. I can't imagine a more handsome nose on any man. In point, I cannot imagine a more handsome man—period."

He cupped her face in his palm. "Handsome, am I? I think my bride must have donned an invisible pair of rose-colored glasses, or else she needs glasses." He grinned.

"No rose-colored glasses are required, sir, nor spectacles of any sort. I but speak the truth as I plainly see it, and you, Mr. Patrick O'Rourke, are a beautiful man. Beautiful *everywhere*." Feeling positively wicked, she slid a hand beneath the sheet.

He sucked in his breath when she found him and thrust. A small bead of moisture blessed her palm. She smiled, and so did he.

"Tell me, my lady wife, just how many men is it you've seen—*naked* men, mind?"

He had her there. Sliding her fingers along the length of him, Kate faltered. "Well, none before you. But I did once see a photograph of Da Vinci's *David*. Though he's wearing a fig leaf, I could glimpse sufficient to, um . . . use my imagination to fill in the rest." Her husband exceeded her most elaborate fantasies in that department, as well as every other way.

Rourke threw back his head and guffawed.

It was Kate's turn to blush. It seemed the natural order between them was once more restored, for she felt her face flame. "What? What did I say?"

Rather than answer, he flipped her over on her back and rolled atop her. A hand braced on either side of her pillow, he shook his head. "God, Kate, you do please me. You please me mightily. Not only are you beautiful, clever, and saucy, but as I've discovered of late, you're also ticklish." He leaned in to tweak her belly.

"Rourke, no! No!"

Giggling, Kate pushed against his chest, futile though that was. Her husband was solid as a stone wall and nearly as implacable. Not that she really wanted to budge him so much as an inch. If the past week's bliss had taught her anything, it was that she didn't have to be in complete control every waking moment. She'd taken the week off, leaving the reins of household management in Hattie's more than capable hands. Amazingly, the earth had managed to continue to rotate and the sun to come up in the morning and set again in the evening, all without her guiding hand.

Perhaps being married wasn't so very bad after all. It was good to have a helpmate, a partner. Provided that partner was Rourke, she had little to complain of these days. She looked up at his grinning face, the rush of feeling, of love, she felt almost frightening her. It did frighten her. Experience had taught her that loving someone was the surest guarantee that they would be taken from you.

Beyond that, love sucked you in, love drained you dry. Her father, and Beatrice to a lesser degree, left her feeling exhausted and empty, resentful and sometimes even angry. Why was it that their happiness and well-being always took precedence over hers? Why was it she felt as though she was always scraping for crumbs? For the first time it occurred to her that her happiness and well-being might be every whit as important as theirs. Damn it, it was as important as theirs, and so was she.

Was it possible to love someone, to love Rourke, and not lose herself?

Carriage wheels sounded from the pull-up below, cutting off that thought. Their heads turned to the window.

"Were you expecting visitors?" Kate asked.

He eased off her. "Nay, were you?"

"Not I. Scotland in the dead of winter isn't a terribly appealing prospect to other than native Scots." Curious, Kate reached for her robe and padded across the carpet to have a look.

Peering through the leaded glass, she saw the cabbie climb from the box and lower the carriage steps. Kate had no difficulty in recognizing the tall, lithe young woman stepping down first. It was her sister. A second woman of similar height but fuller figure climbed out behind her. Kate caught a glimpse of red curls from beneath a garish purple hat.

From the bed, her husband's sleep-husky voice called out, "Who is it?"

Heart dropping, Kate turned away from the window. She sensed their honeymoon idyll had just come to an end. "My sister is below, and it seems she's brought a friend."

Her gaze traveled the room. The bedsheets were rumpled, the floor strewn with clothes. A barely touched breakfast tray sat abandoned on the bedside table, a perfectly good chocolate croissant lying uneaten because even chocolate couldn't come close to the deliciousness of making love with her husband. It had all been so lovely. Oh, why did happy times always have to end so very quickly?

"Katie?"

Rourke sat up in bed, the sheet drifting to his waist. Even with her fine mood fading, she couldn't help but catch her breath at how purely magnificently beautiful he was. Kate wasn't given to displays of emotion, but the feeling of foreboding settling in her belly was too strong to be denied. She bounded over to the bed and threw herself down next to him, needing to feel his strength, his warmth.

Pressing her face into the warm crevice of corded throat and broad shoulder, she said, "Hold me."

His arms went around her. He pressed a kiss against her temple and tightened his hold. "What is, sweetheart?

What's the trouble?"

She sighed. "This past week, it's been so lovely, hasn't it?"

"Aye, it has, but, Kate, love, why are you acting as though 'tis come to an end? We have the rest of our lives before us, my heart, fifty-odd years and then some. We're only at the start of it all. Think of this week as the beginning of Act I of a verra long and verra happy play."

In that moment, Kate didn't only *think* she loved him. She knew it. "Promise me my sister's coming won't change anything. Promise that we'll still go on as we have this past week."

"Of course, we shall. Why wouldn't we? Surely it's only a holiday visit, and even if it werena, a castle is a verra big place, mind."

"Humor me and promise anyway."

He carried her hand to his mouth and brushed her knuckles with his lips. "In that case, milady, I'll do a good deal better than promise. I do solemnly swear."

CHAPTER THIRTEEN

> "My tongue will tell the anger of my heart,
> Or else my heart, concealing it, will break."
> —WILLIAM SHAKESPEARE, Kate,
> *The Taming of the Shrew*

h, Kat, do stop fussing. If I'd known you would ring a peal over my head, I never would have come. I wish I had not."

Bea faced Kate with arms folded. They were in one of the newly appointed chambers in the east tower. Bea's friend Felicity was in the room next door.

"I'm not 'ringing a peal,' as you call it. I'm simply trying to discover what is going on. But if you don't want to stay, you're free to leave."

Kate had not called her baby sister's bluff often over the years. Had she done so, perhaps Bea might not have turned out quite so self-centered and spoiled. Looking back, she supposed she'd tried so hard to compensate for a missing mother's love and a father's neglect that she'd erred too far in the opposite direction. But what was done was done.

Bea's shoulders slumped, and her chin dipped. Her bottom lip stuck out as it had when she was a very little girl. She poked at the carpet with the toe of one satin slipper.

Gentling her tone, Kate confirmed, "You haven't anywhere else to go—have you?"

Bea shook her head. "Aunt Lavinia is horrid. She wouldn't purchase a gown for me that was any color other than white. Papa drinks all the time—and gambles." She said the latter in a hushed voice as though it wasn't common knowledge. "After Hattie left to come to you, I couldn't bear it."

Kate didn't for a minute think that her father nearly losing the estate to her husband would be the catalyst for him turning over a new leaf. Gaming was like a fever firing his blood. It would only be a matter of time before he got himself into another scrape, and when he did, she wouldn't be surprised to find him knocking on her door, too.

"What of your new friend, Miss Drummond. She seems . . . pleasant enough."

In truth, Kate had an uneasy feeling about the young woman. Though her behavior had been decorous enough when Kate showed her and Bea to their rooms, there was something about her slanted green eyes, a serpentlike watchfulness that Kate couldn't like.

Because of it, she was moved to ask, "How did the two of you meet?"

"Papa's friend Lord Haversham introduced us."

Alarm bells sounded. "She is a friend of Lord Haversham's?"

Bea nodded. "Felicity's a lot of fun. She knows all sorts of clever things."

I'll wager she does.

"You and your, uh . . . friend may stay through the Christmas holiday, but in the meantime, you must write Aunt Lavinia and make apologies for running off. As for the other, I'll see if I can't convince her to let you expand your wardrobe beyond white."

Eager to get back to Patrick—odd, how she'd fallen into using his given name without thinking—Kate headed for the door. "I'll leave you to settle in."

"Kate?"

Kate turned about. "Yes?"

"Thank you for being my sister."

Sitting before the dressing-table mirror, Felicity pulled the stopper from the vial of *eau de cologne* and dabbed a liberal dose behind either ear. The jasmine scent once had driven Rourke mad, or the nearest thing to it. So far she hadn't seen him, though she meant to remedy that state of affairs and soon.

She'd gotten an eyeful of his very proper English wife, however. Pondering her rival, Felicity couldn't comprehend the attraction. She might be merely a squire's daughter, yet her looks easily trumped her rival's. The little brown woman was hardly a proper armful. A big, strapping Scot like Rourke needed a woman who could match him in every way, but particularly in the bedchamber. Like all men, he fancied females who told him what he wanted to hear. She would have thought Kate's brash honesty would have worn thin by now. Felicity was careful to coat her every word in honey. When honey wasn't enough, she outright lied.

Not only was Lady Kate stunted and fork-tongued, but she was old. From what Haversham had told her, her tight-arsed "ladyship" must be thirty or nearing it. How could she possibly hope to compete with Felicity's apparent sweet disposition, youth, and flamboyant good looks, looks that deserved to be showcased onstage?

From what the sister, Bea, so far had blabbed on the dreary train trek north, all was not as it should be between the newlyweds. Reports of blackmail, mad weddings, and missed bridal breakfasts had cheered Felicity considerably. She meant to exploit every weakness and seize every opportunity to widen whatever cracks there were so that she might insinuate herself back into Rourke's life. Assuming Lady Katherine could be dispatched, she really wouldn't mind marrying him, but beyond all, she wanted him to open that theatre for her.

She'd been a fool to release him in the first place, but when one was young and hungry for adventure, it wasn't always easy to know what to do. Fortunately all the signs pointed to the foolish act being remedied. There were cracks in this marriage that, if subjected to the proper amount of pressure, might lead to an irredeemable splintering in twain.

Felicity meant to exert pressure on each and every one.

Rourke was finishing dressing for the day when Kate returned from settling in her sister. The adjoining door stood open on purpose. He'd been hoping for another glimpse of her before they both started their days. Catching her eye, he beckoned her inside.

"My sister has run away from home after a fashion. I've told her she and her companion may stay through Boxing Day. She has nowhere else to go."

The little wrinkle appeared in the center of her forehead. By now he knew it only showed itself when she was worrying. "Of course, she can stay."

She regarded him, some of the wariness leaving her eyes. "You don't mind?"

He found his smile. "I didn't say that. Selfish lout

that I am, I fancied having you to myself a while longer, say the next fifty-odd years. But she is your sister, your blood, which makes her my responsibility, as well."

The gratitude shining from her beautiful eyes shamed him more than any spoken reproach ever could. Accustomed as she was to doing for others, to giving but rarely receiving, she was pathetically easy to please. He only hoped she liked the surprise gift he had planned for her. He was going into Edinburgh to pick "it" up.

She shook her head, eyes shining. "Oh, Patrick, you are good to me."

She stood on tiptoe, wound her arms about his neck, and pressed her lips to the side of his neck, surprising and delighting him with that one small, sweet kiss. The dazzling smile she sent him had him forgetting to breathe.

Patrick. She'd said his name yet again. His heart warmed; his chest swelled. "If I'm good to you, Katie, it's only because goodness is your due." He almost added "because I love you," but stopped before he might. He'd tell her when they could be private and not distracted by guests. "I have to go into Edinburgh to attend some business. I'm afraid it's going to be an overnight trip, but I'll be back by tomorrow afternoon."

Her face fell, but she quickly covered her disappointment with a smile. "I suppose I've gotten used to having you not only around but all to myself. I forget you have responsibilities, a company to oversee."

He pulled her to him, gratified she apparently didn't want

him to go. "Katie, I meant what I said earlier this morning. The honeymoon isna over for us; it's just beginning."

Kate was in the kitchen the next afternoon when Rourke returned from his trip. She looked up from the dough she'd been rolling on the marble counter to see him coming toward her. Forgetting the flour on her apron, she dropped the rolling pin and launched herself into his arms.

Behind them, one of the new kitchen maids tittered, and the cook cleared her throat. Kate was too happy to pay them any heed. Since knowing Rourke—Patrick—appearances didn't hold nearly the weight they'd used to in her life.

"You're back," she said, then marveled at what a simpleton love had made her. Still, she pulled back to look at him as though he'd been gone a year rather than a single day.

"I am, and I've come bearing gifts or at least a gift."

"You didn't have to buy me anything."

His emerald eyes twinkled. "Think of it as an early Christmas present."

"Early, indeed. Christmas is a fortnight away."

Two weeks was not much time. Hattie was even now directing the decorating of the great hall with bows of holly and evergreen. It would be their first Christmas together, first Boxing Day, first Twelfth Night. She wanted to do everything properly. His friend Gavin's birthday fell in December, too, and they'd invited him, his wife, Daisy, and Hadrian and Callie to come up and celebrate. Kate was looking forward to becoming better acquainted with Rourke's friends. She already knew Hadrian and had met and liked Callie. She hoped the other couple would become her friends, as well. Perhaps their "Roxbury House Orphans' Club," as they'd called it, would admit her as a fifth, albeit honorary member. She hoped so.

But in the main her focus was Rourke. She'd spent the past few days struggling over what to give him as a gift. What *did* one give the man who apparently had everything? What she really wanted was to give him her heart, the whole of it, but she didn't yet dare. She could be brave about many things, but she'd yet to shore up sufficient courage for that.

In light of her dilemma, his early gifting was a fortunate thing. She could take her cue from him and gauge her own gift accordingly. "What is it?"

He rolled his eyes. "If I tell you, it wouldna be a surprise, now would it?"

"Not even a hint?"

He shook his head. "My lips are sealed. You'll just have to come outside and see for yourself."

Kate wiped her floury hands on her apron front and stepped back from the block. A few weeks ago it never would have occurred to her to allow something as frivolous as a gift get in the way of completing a task. Spending time with her husband was having a positive effect on her in more ways than one. Rourke wasn't a shirker by any means; his industry was evident from long hours he spent in his study at night bent over his ledgers and business reports, but he also knew how to be spontaneous, how to play.

She lifted her coat off the wall peg. He helped her on with it, and together they stepped out into the walled kitchen garden. "Where are you taking me?"

He grinned and squeezed her hand. "You'll see soon enough."

They started walking in the direction of the stables. There was a thin crust of snow on the ground, and the air was what she'd come to think of as crisp rather than cold. Scottish winters took some getting used to, but Kate fancied her blood was beginning to thicken.

They drew up to the paddock. She glanced over at her husband. Apparently they had reached their destination. On the other side of the fence, Mr. Campbell led a small pony inside the gate. Even from afar, Kate could see the animal wasn't young. The swayed back and gambling gait were telltale signs of age, but the patchy coat and ribs protruding from her sides bespoke of neglect, even abuse.

One booted foot resting on the rail, Rourke turned to her. "What do you think?"

She cast a sideways look at her husband. He was

beaming. Who was it that said never to look a gift horse in the mouth? She glanced back to the horse. Mr. Campbell was walking her over to them. As the animal neared, understanding dawned. The white blaze; the big, intelligent eyes; and the nut-colored mane she'd once braided with multicolored ribbons fit for a . . .

"Princess!" Tears filled her eyes, spilled over her bottom lashes, and ran down her cheeks. "Oh, Princess, sweetheart, can it really be you?" She climbed up onto the top fence rung and reached out to the horse.

Princess sniffed, nostrils working. She nickered and shoved her nose into Kate's neck and hair, "grooming" her as if only a day had gone by rather than almost seventeen years.

Beside her, Rourke explained, "I telegraphed your father and asked after the neighbor who'd . . . acquired her. It turned out it was a local squire with lands just outside of Romney. From there, it was a matter of tracking the bill of sales to several owners. I put Sylvester on it. She'd ended up in Edinburgh as a costermonger's cart horse."

She looked up from the horse and over to her smiling husband. "I can't believe it! All these years I've dreamed . . . How can I ever thank you? You can't know what it means to me to have her back. She's a greater gift than diamonds or pearls."

More tears skittered down her cheeks, crystallizing in the cold. He reached inside his coat pocket and produced his handkerchief. Handing it to her, he said, "I'd shower you with those, too, if only you'd let me, but for now I'll leave you two to your reunion."

He turned on his heel and strode away. Watching him go, Kate had the silly thought he was nearly as moved as she. She turned back to the horse and confided, "Well, my fine girl, just as you were a princess disguised as a coster's hack, that big, rough-mannered Scot who just left us is my true Prince Charming."

Two happy hours later, Kate emerged from the stable, cold, covered in muck, and happier than she could ever recall being. Determined to make up for the years of neglect and abuse, she'd set out on a protocol of pampering, including brushing the dust and scurf from the horse's coat, mane, and tail, and taking a hoof pick to clean out her encrusted hooves. Princess wasn't only old, but she was in very poor condition. Years of abuse had taken their toll. The state of her teeth shocked Kate. It was in examining them that she came across the scarring on the animal's sensitive gums. Obviously someone in her long line of owners had used a cruel snaffle bit to excess. She also found white scars on flanks—crop marks. That her precious Princess had been used so cruelly brought fresh tears to her eyes, not happy ones this time. For the future, though, there would be no more snaffle bits or whippings or even the weight of a saddle to be borne upon that poor swayed back. Princess's retirement days would be filled with lumps of sugar and brushings, with pets over the paddock fence and sweet nothings whispered into her dear ears.

She was on her way to seek out her husband and thank him again when she crossed paths with her houseguest. Felicity came from the direction of the orchard. In the dead of winter, the orchard wasn't much to see, but then Kate was given to understand from Bea that her new friend had grown up in Scotland. The tall redhead still wore her carriage costume with the jaunty purple-feathered hat. The color made for quite a contrast with her flame-red curls.

Kate didn't really care to stop, but the woman was her guest. She couldn't be rude. "Did you have a pleasant walk, Miss Drummond?"

The taller woman raked her slanted green eyes over Kate from head to toe, making her mindful of the less-than-pristine state of her clothes. "Aye, and please, call me Felicity. Under the circumstances, I feel like we're old friends."

Kate found the remark odd, as they'd never met before that morning. "You must mean because Bea and I are sisters, of course?"

Felicity quirked her mouth as though she were struggling not to laugh. She shook her head, setting the dyed purple plume bobbing. "Actually I was thinking more so because of Rourke."

The foreboding Kate had felt ever since the hansom cab drew up increased tenfold. "You know my husband?"

There it was again, that sly, slanted look. "Oh, aye, we go back several years. We're old friends, Patrick and I. Ah, well, it was lovely chatting with you, but I must be getting back. I promised Bea I'd help her with her hair before the tea."

She swept past Kate on the path.

Kate stood staring after her, the surety of her conclusion rooting her in place. Felicity and Rourke had been lovers. For a horrible, heart-stopping moment, it occurred to Kate to wonder if Felicity's arrival with her sister might not be happenstance. Surely Bea must be in the dark, but what about Rourke? These past weeks, had he only been dallying with her, biding his time for his mistress to arrive? Perhaps *dallying* was too strong a word. Among the ton, it wasn't unusual for a gentleman to have a wife and mistress both. Was it possible Rourke saw taking a mistress into keeping as just another trapping of success, not appreciably different from keeping a coach-and-four or acquiring a castle?

Were he and Felicity lovers still?

There was only one person whom she could ask: her husband.

Kate found Rourke in the library. When he gave the call to enter in response to her knock, his voice sounded tight, annoyed if not precisely angry. She entered, determined to broach the subject of Felicity Drummond, though she wasn't quite certain how best to begin. Delicately, she supposed. Delicate or not, she had to know.

Her husband sat behind his desk, drumming his pen on the blotter. He seemed put out, angry. Gone was the warm-eyed man who'd left her at the paddock fence a few hours before.

He stared at her a long moment and then blurted out, "Why didn't you tell me our housekeeper is pregnant?"

He could have knocked Kate over with a feather. Not certain whether to be relieved or annoyed herself, she said, "I was going to tell you . . . eventually."

"*Eventually,* hmm?"

She swallowed hard. She could already see this wasn't going well. "I wasn't sure how you'd react."

"And you naturally assumed that, great ogre that I am, I'd turn her and the babe out to starve?"

Rather than answer that, she posed a question of her own. "How did you find out?" Servants' halls, country kitchens, both were notorious mills for gossip. If lesser servants were telling tales, Kate wanted to know.

"She told me herself a while ago."

"Hattie came to you!" Kate was stunned.

"Aye, *she* at least felt I'd the right to know."

The implication wasn't lost on Kate. Apparently she

wasn't as good at this marriage business as she'd thought to have become.

She sighed. "Will you let her, them, stay?"

He nodded. "Hattie and her babe are welcome for as long as she wishes to remain. But I'm your husband, for Christ's sake, the very first person you should turn to in trouble, not the last. Why didn't you come to me? Why didn't you trust me with the truth? Is it so very hard to believe I might be a reasonable human being? Do you think me a tyrant?"

Kate bit her lip against pointing out that their marriage had, indeed, begun with him presenting himself in a tyrannical way. She liked to think in the past week they'd moved beyond the play to establish a true marriage.

"It's not that. It's only that I'm used to managing matters on my own. The less my father knew of the workings of our household, the better it was for all concerned."

Staring at his wife, Rourke was torn between fury toward her scapegrace father and an odd tenderness toward the brave little soul he'd married. Poor lass, she'd fended for herself and her sister so long she was afraid to let anyone else in, to let anyone else lead, let alone help her to shoulder the burdens that life brought her way.

"Christ, Kate, we're wed, in case you've forgotten. What do you think a husband is for if not to protect and cherish you and be there in your time of need, as well as to help celebrate the good times, too?"

When she didn't answer, he rose and rounded the

desk. He found her shoulders with his hands and drew her against him. Even now, he was amazed that such a tiny body could house such a wealth of will, such a treasure of soul.

"Whatever else you may think of me, whatever my many faults are, they dinna include gaming or drinking to excess or purposeful cruelty. You can trust me to be there for you in your hour of need, be that hour in the light of day or the dead of night. I want to be the one you come to with your joys, your fears, and your troubles, too. I mean to be there for you always and forever. You can trust me, sweet Kate, not only with your confidences, but also with your heart."

What do you think a husband is for?

Kate stepped out into the corridor, closing the door behind her. Patrick hadn't seemed angry with her, so much as frustrated and hurt. Likely that was why she found herself giving serious consideration to the question. Other than the financial aspect of their arrangement, she hadn't given their respective roles all that much thought. She already knew how to supervise a household. Beyond knowing how, she was good at it. As for a husband's job, she'd never given it a great deal of thought. All her father had ever seemed to do was drink, hunt, and wager away their worldly goods. From what she could tell, he'd never been a helpmate to her mother, let alone a soul mate. To Kate he'd been a neglectful tyrant and now a burden.

That a husband might be a defender and helpmate, a lover and friend, had never entered her consciousness before now. Under the circumstances, she couldn't find it in her heart to quiz him about Felicity. Surely whatever "relationship" he and the buxom redhead had shared was in the past. So long as it was, Kate could put up with the woman for another few weeks. As her husband had pointed out many times, a castle was a big place.

It wasn't until she stepped out into the great hall to examine the decorating in progress that it occurred to her she hadn't told him his former "friend" was there.

Kate's not telling Rourke about Felicity was soon remedied—by the redhead herself. His study door had scarcely closed on his retreating wife when his former lover boldly stepped inside, the scent of jasmine floating in before her. Once he'd loved the way the perfume mingled with the scent of her freckled skin, but now he found it cloying.

"Surprise!"

Rourke looked up from the pencil he'd been grinding into pulp on his blotter and felt his stomach slide to his knees. "Felicity, what the devil are you doing here?"

She put on a pout. "Now, Rourkie, is that any way

to greet an old friend?"

He hadn't seen her in nearly two years. Running his gaze over her, he confirmed that other than the citified accent she affected to cover her native burr, she hadn't changed much—but he had. Like her perfume, her buxom body and freckle-dusted pale skin used to drive him mad. In bed, he'd made a game of connecting the "dots" while toying with strands of her flame-red hair. Until meeting Kate, he'd considered tall, buxom women like Felicity to be his type. How was it then that Kate's sun-drizzled brown hair, intelligent amber eyes, and tight little body now seemed all that was womanly perfection?

"Given you left me for London more than two years ago without so much as a line, I suppose I hadn't thought of you as much of a friend."

Her sudden desertion had left him equal parts angry and relieved. Seeing her again now, he confirmed he felt nothing at all.

She reached out to fiddle with the paperweight on the edge of his desk. The miniature railway car was a trifle Kate had found in one of the shops on High Street and picked up for him. The gift had likely only cost a few quid, but it numbered among his most precious possessions. He didn't fancy Felicity besmirching it with her touch.

She batted her eyes and looked up at him through her lashes. Such artifice once would have melted him, but not so now. How very much more appealing he found Kate's honest, head-on gaze to be.

"What was I to do? Opportunity knocked, and when you wouldn't come up to scratch and marry me, I decided to answer the door. But it seems you're the marrying sort after all." She tossed a glance at the plain gold band he wore.

Now that the shock of seeing her again was wearing off, the horrible thought snuck up on him like a boxer's sucker punch. "Don't tell me you're Kate's sister's friend up from London?"

She looked up and nodded. "Aye, I needed to get away for a while, and the chit, while dull-witted, can be amusing at times—and useful. Befriending her brought me here after all."

"You can't stay."

She greeted that statement with a snicker. "I'm afraid I can, and I will. Were I to suddenly decamp before the holiday, surely your lady wife would wonder why."

"You leave Kate out of this." Rourke pushed back his chair and rose.

She was nearly a match for his almost six feet, and his standing put them on eye level. "Whether I do or not remains to be seen."

"What is it you want, Felicity?"

She appeared to consider the question, though he knew full well she must already have her prize in mind. The woman was a first-rate schemer. "That is for me to know and you to find out. For now I'm off to take tea with your little brown bride and her dim-witted sister. Lord only knows what the three of us will find to chat about. Toodles." She blew him a kiss and turned to go.

Heart hammering, Rourke subsided into his seat. Despite his "rule" to look forward, never back, his former mistress was conspiring to drag him back—and down—with her.

"Felicity, not so fast." Shaking with anger, Rourke called her back.

Slowly she turned about, no doubt staging the gesture, as she did everything else, for dramatic effect. "Aye?"

"Kate means a great deal to me. Should you consider doing anything to cause her harm or distress, anything at all, know that you'll face dealing with me—and there'll be the verra devil to pay."

She smiled as though pleased to have gotten under his skin. "Dinna forget, ducks, the devil and I are old friends, too."

Leaning over the paddock rail, Beatrice offered a carrot to Princess, Kate's pony. The grand old girl greedily gobbled it up. From the looks of her, she hadn't received many treats over the years.

She turned to her handsome companion, the warm look in his hazel eyes sending a little flutter to her heart. "I think it's grand that you helped Mr. O'Rourke track her down. I don't remember her, of course. I was only two when she was, um . . . sold, but I know she means a great deal to Kate."

Ralph cast a sideways look to the tall young woman at his side. Lady Kate's younger sister was as fresh and pretty as a springtime lily and, he thought, just as sweet. It was a pity her youth and birth put her beyond his touch.

Still, for whatever reason, he found himself asking, "Do you ride?"

She dropped shy eyes to her gloved hands. The last carrot having been consumed, she'd folded them demurely over the fence rail. "No, I mean, not yet. I'd like to, though."

"I could give you lessons during your stay. Of course, you might prefer one of the groomsmen . . ." He let the offer die. Jesus, what was he doing?

Blue eyes the color of cornflowers lifted to his face. "No, no, I would love it if you would take it upon yourself to teach me, but only if you have the time, of course."

"For you, miss, I'll make the time if need be."

A throat being cleared had their heads turning toward the barn. Kate's brisk strides carried her down the path in their direction. Bea bit her lip. Speaking her thoughts out loud, she said, "Oh, dear, I know that look. She's angry, and whatever the cause, heads will roll."

She hadn't seen her sister scowl so since she'd arrived the day before. Even when Kate had scolded her earlier about her so-called running away, she'd worn a soft, dreamy-eyed look.

After leaving her husband in the library, Kate had decided to take yet another walk in the bracing air to clear her head. She hadn't meant to hurt Patrick's feelings, but clearly she had. Given the gift of hindsight, she couldn't believe that a few weeks earlier she really had feared he might turn Hattie out. It seemed household management, certainly the marriage part of it, was a great deal more complicated than the regimens and receipts set out in Mrs. Beeton's book.

Her footsteps carried her to the path leading to the stables. She might as well see how Princess was settling in. Who knew how much time they might have together—the pony was nearing twenty and had lived a hard life, but Kate meant to make the most of what time they had.

Voices, punctuated by her sister's giggle, drew her attention to the paddock. Bea stood at the rail, petting Princess and making calf eyes at Rourke's valet, Ralph Sylvester. She held back, sizing up the scene. To her way of thinking, they stood much too close for comfort, hers at any rate. She ran her gaze over the valet. He had his hat in his hands and one foot propped up on the fence rail. Before now she'd been too absorbed in her husband to notice much about the other man, indeed, any other man, but studying him now she saw that he was most attractive. He also possessed charming manners, a glib tongue, and dancing eyes, all tools in the well-equipped rake's repertoire. She recalled how his hazel eyes had sought out her sister's at the church and quickened her steps.

She sidled up beside them. Bea's flushed face and sheepish look confirmed her suspicions. Mr. Sylvester had a rather sheepish look himself, as though he'd been caught with his hand in the confectioner's jar. In this case, the succulent sweet to be had was Kate's baby sister, and she meant to make sure the valet kept his lecherous mitts clear of her.

Sliding her gaze to the valet, she said, "If you will excuse us, Mr. Sylvester, I'd like a word in private with my sister."

"Certainly, milady." His hazel eyes found Bea's face. "I bid you a good day, miss." He bowed low over her gloved hand.

Watching him walk off, Bea sighed.

Kate waited until he was halfway up the path before rounding on her sister. "You were flirting. Don't put yourself to the trouble of denying it. I saw you."

Bea shrugged. Her heart-shaped face wore a mutinous expression. "What if I was? Would that be so bad?"

"He's my husband's valet."

Bea's blue eyes narrowed. "We can't all make marriages of convenience, Kat. Some of us must follow our hearts and marry for love."

For the girl to speak of marriage and a man she scarcely knew in a singular breath raised Kate's protective instincts to full hue and cry. Her little sister must be smitten, indeed. Certainly worthy, pleasant-faced, if dull Mr. Billingsby had never put a twinkle in Bea's eye as the valet had. Unfortunately Mr. Billingsby, while lacking Ralph's good looks and charm, had something substantial to recommend him that a personal servant did not: an income.

Her thoughts veered to Bea's implication that she and Rourke had made a marriage of convenience. A few weeks before she would have agreed, but not so now. Before the arrival of her houseguests, she'd thought she and her husband were well on their way to building a true marriage. But her earlier encounter with Felicity had caused her to doubt herself.

Instead of letting the comment pass, she probed, "Why are you so certain I cannot possibly understand?"

Bea focused her attention on petting the horse. "It's obvious, isn't it? You and Mr. O'Rourke made a marriage of convenience. You are more business partners than man and wife. When I marry, it will be to a man whose soul aligns with mine."

Her little sister's superior attitude in the realm of love was akin to salting a fresh, sensitive wound. Kate snapped back, "I wonder how closely your and Mr. Sylvester's souls would align a year hence when you hadn't the funds for train fare, let alone the fripperies you favor."

It was a snappish, shrewish thing to have said, and Kate regretted it as soon as the sharp words were out. That she'd lashed out at all demonstrated just how on edge Felicity's presence had made her.

Bea's head swung away from the horse to Kate. Her bottom lip trembled. A tear splashed her cheek.

Kate reached out to put her arm about her sister. "Bea, baby, I'm sorry. I didn't mean—"

Shaking her head, Bea backed away. "That was a horrid thing to say. I think you are a horrid, horrid shrew." She turned and ran toward the castle.

I think you are a horrid, horrid shrew.

Her sister's words ringing again and again in her ears, Kate headed back to the castle. She'd made a hash of explaining things to Bea, but she still couldn't stand back and allow her little sister to disport herself with the valet. At Bea's tender age, she had her whole future ahead of her. Kate meant to do all she could to protect her from being compromised or, God forbid, ruined.

Once inside the great hall, redolent with the smell of pine and gaily decorated for the season, she didn't bother taking off her coat. She directed her stomping footsteps to her husband's library. It was her second visit of the day, a record.

The library door stood open. Since it was, she didn't bother with knocking. Rourke looked sharply up from the map of railway lines he had spread out over his desk. Standing behind, big hands braced on the desk's edge, he looked almost relieved to see her.

"What can I do for you, Kate?"

His tone held no trace of the earlier annoyance. No matter. Kate was annoyed enough for them both.

"You can take Mr. Sylvester aside and give him a stern talking to." Belatedly she considered she might have sounded rather peremptory.

He straightened to full standing. "Why is that?"

"He is dallying with my sister."

She'd expected him to be outraged. He glanced to the map on his desk as if eager to return to it. "That sounds like a private matter for the two of them to sort out. Betimes, she only just arrived the other day. How much dallying could they possibly have done in only twenty-four hours?"

"Not they, *him,* and the answer is more than enough. I overheard him offering to teach her to ride."

"Shocking, I'm sure." He rolled his eyes as though she was a silly woman wasting his workday.

Kate felt her annoyance ratchet up. A mere hour ago he had dressed her down for not coming to him with her problems, and now that she had, she found herself met with sarcasm and indifference.

Feeling the need to reach for her alter ego, Capable Kate, once more she crossed her arms in front of her. "He's in your employ. It falls to you to speak with him before matters . . . progress. Will you do so or not?" She tapped her foot to indicate that she awaited his answer and that her time was as valuable as his.

"Verra well." He sighed as though put upon, in-deed. "I will speak to him tonight, but if you ask me, the chit would count herself lucky to land him."

"I didn't ask you, in point, but since you bring it up, the man is your valet."

He glanced sharply up. "Aye, he is. What of it?"

"He is a servant in this household."

"As is Hattie, and yet you treat her more as a family relation than a servant."

She uncrossed her arms, wondering why he must be so very difficult about this. She knew he and the valet were friendly, but good Lord. "I'm not marrying Hattie off to my sibling."

His gaze narrowed. "Valet or housekeeper, either is honest work, is it not? Had circumstances worked out differently, I might have found myself shining your boots and carrying your bathwater to your room in tin cans."

"You are being ridiculous."

"Am I? Mark that Beatrice wouldna be the only Lindsey sister to marry beneath her, *milady*."

Suddenly Kate understood why he was being so very difficult—and becoming so very angry. She did her best to backpedal. "Your case is different."

His eyes darkened to a cloudy greenish gray, more London fog than clear-cut emerald. "Why? Because I am rich?"

Kate didn't have an answer for that, but she fumbled for one anyway. "Rourke—Patrick—I didn't mean—"

"You had the right of it the first time. A lady to the manor born such as you should know better than to become overfamiliar with her minions, let alone say vows with them."

The coldness in his eye and voice had her trembling. "What are you saying?"

"That I can think of far better ways to spend my life than leg-shackled to a woman with too much spleen and too little heart, a toffee-nosed, sharp-tongued . . . *shrew.*"

CHAPTER FOURTEEN

"Nay then, do what thou canst, I will not go today,
No, nor tomorrow, not till I please myself.
The door is open, sir, there lies your way."
—WILLIAM SHAKESPEARE, Kate,
The Taming of the Shrew

A Week Later

Kate had ended the argument by fleeing the library before tears might break. A week later, she'd yet to enter it. Likewise she and Rourke each kept to their own rooms at night. The adjoining dressing-room door was closed once more as if the battle line.

With a house, or rather a castle, full of holiday guests, she didn't have the luxury of moping. Rourke's friends Hadrian and Gavin, with their wives, Callie and Daisy, had arrived the day before. By unspoken consent, she and Rourke had agreed to put on their game faces for their guests. Fortunately the presence of guests meant their paths crossed even less than usual. In the tradition of country-house parties, many of the activities segregated the sexes. In honor of Gavin's birthday, Rourke had taken him and Hadrian into town, and the womenfolk had begged off in favor of entertaining themselves.

Taking tea in the parlor Kate had redecorated in pale hues of blue and cream, she looked between her two guests. Callie, of course, was a renowned suffragist, and Gavin's wife, Daisy, was a top actress. A famous social reformer and a star of the London stage made for august company. Kate had never before lacked for confidence, but being in the position of entertaining two such remarkable women for an afternoon was a trifle daunting—especially when matters between she and her husband had clearly gone awry.

Settled into a chair by the lamp table perusing a week-old copy of the *London Times,* Callie peered at them over the top of her glasses. Out of the blue, she said, "Rourke is a bit rough about the edges, but he's a good man, Katherine. The botched-wedding business aside, I believe he loves you with all his heart."

Seated on the settee next to Kate, Daisy piped up, "To quote Shakespeare, the course of true love never did run smooth."

Kate frowned. Apparently hers and Rourke's game faces left something to be desired. "If you'll pardon my saying so, I've had rather enough of the Bard's dubious wisdom."

Daisy's saucy smile turned sheepish. She dropped

her gaze to the script in her lap. "I expect you found out about Gavin's and my . . . wedding gift."

Kate nodded. "I expect so."

Daisy plucked at her gown's striped skirt. She'd begun her career as a cancan dancer in the music halls of Monmartre, and sometimes she seemed to have difficulty sitting still.

"Oh, dear, and now you must think ill of me, and just when I had such high hopes we might be friends. I didn't mean to meddle . . . Well I did mean to, but only a little and only to help. It seems another of my grand schemes has backfired yet again. At any rate, please don't blame Gav. It was all my idea, truly. He tried to dissuade me, but in the end I had my way, and he posted the bloody play for me."

Having observed the lively actress and her darkly handsome, if sober-eyed barrister husband since their arrival, Kate expected that Daisy's having her way was not at all an unusual state of affairs. It was blatantly obvious to any onlooker that Gavin was besotted with his unconventional bride. Equally obvious was that she was every whit as besotted with him.

Likewise, Callie and Hadrian were passionately devoted to one another. Since Callie's retirement from politics, they'd commenced a new project together: a photographic exposé of the plight of London's East Enders, many of whom endured horrific poverty. Being in the midst of not one, but two such extraordinary couples was taking its toll. Kate felt a little envious, but in the main she felt wistful.

For whatever reason, she suddenly found herself confessing, "I'd promised myself I wouldn't bring this up until after Gavin's birthday dinner, but the fact is, I am considering asking Patrick for a deed of separation."

It was the truth. She'd gone 'round and 'round in her head, and she could see no other way. She refused to live out her days with a man who viewed her as a leg-shackle, a shrew.

Nor would she share him with another woman. A sham marriage was worse than no marriage at all. Rourke had yet to own up to his and Felicity's "prior" relationship. If that was all in the past, what had he to hide?

Expression horrified, Daisy slapped a hand over her mouth. "Oh, dear, you and Rourke are parting ways, and it's my bloody fault."

Kate reached over and touched her arm to reassure her. Though it wasn't in her nature to be physically demonstrative with strangers, she found herself feeling very much at home with these women. "You mustn't blame yourself. Tempted as I might be to shift the blame for my problems onto others' shoulders, I cannot. Even were I so inclined, I can hardly pin the demise of our marriage on a play."

Callie folded the newspaper and set it aside. "Dearest Katherine, once not so very long ago, you gave me some good advice, albeit in the loo of all places. Do you recall it?"

Kate thought for a moment and then the memory returned, hazy but intact. "In the main, it had to do with not minding a single cruel word certain, er, bitches said, I do believe."

"Precisely, and now I should like to return the favor, if I may? By way of an example, Hadrian and I met when a political enemy bribed him to discredit me by taking an embarrassing photograph and leaking it to the press."

Kate recalled the very revealing boudoir photograph that had appeared on the front page of every London newspaper the year before, though she hadn't known the story behind its leak to Fleet Street. Now that she did, she wondered aloud how Callie could ever bring herself to forgive him.

Callie's answering smile was as enigmatic as the *Mona Lisa*'s. "I could forgive him because I loved him, and by the extreme actions he undertook to mend matters, I knew beyond a shadow of doubting that he loved me."

"But even so—"

"My dear Kate, circumstances—and people—are rarely what they seem on the surface. Love, however, deals not with the surface, but with the essence. It is as honest as it is eternal."

Fighting the lump building in her throat, Kate turned to Daisy. Kate recalled Rourke mentioning that the plucky actress hadn't been orphaned, but abandoned at birth.

"To pick up on Callie's point, I am a prime example of someone who is not precisely as she seems. I wasn't always a respectable stage actress, you know."

Kate nodded. She'd heard something vague about Daisy's reappearance in London as the leading act at the Palace supper club, the variety saloon Rourke now owned; otherwise, he'd been sketchy on details, and Kate hadn't wanted to pry.

"I began my stage career as a burlesque performer in Paris music halls. Beyond that, to say my personal reputation was tarnished would be generous. While some of the gossip was exaggerated, I will tell you frankly that for the most part, I earned every salacious snippet. My daughter, Freddie, isn't Gavin's natural child, but rather the offspring of a brief liaison when I was very young and very foolish. I had lovers before Gavin and I met again by chance, and by lovers I don't just mean a few. Once Gavin came back into my life, I was so afraid to let myself love him that I did everything I could think of to push him away. When he came upon a letter I was penning to Freddie and assumed she was a 'he' and my lover, I let him go on thinking so. And then later when his grandfather attempted to come between us, I let him think I'd accepted his bribe to walk away. That all seems madness now, it *was* madness, but at the time I was so very afraid of getting hurt again I couldn't see straight. Unfortunately, I didn't only hurt myself. I hurt Gavin.

For the most part, Gavin was very patient with me. He still is. He forgave me not one outlandish lie, but two. Had I been in his place, I am not certain I could have been so forgiving or so generous with my love. Still, if it weren't for Harry and Rourke and Callie abducting me from Drury Lane and taking me to that abandoned theatre where Gavin awaited, Lord only knows if Gavin and I would have ever managed to sort out our mess or our feelings."

Callie crossed the room and claimed the seat cushion on Kate's other side. To Daisy, she said, "I rather think you would have sorted it all out, though not perhaps in such good time, and by the by, I love that you've let your hair go back to your natural blond."

The conversation veered off to hairstyles and fashions, children and work and future plans. Kate considered what she'd so far heard. Salacious boudoir photographs, bribery and blackmail, abduction! She would have been hard-pressed to say which woman's story was the more extraordinary. And yet to the world's eyes, Callie and Hadrian and Daisy and Gavin appeared as two perfectly serene, perfectly respectable newly married pairs. But as her and Rourke's stormy union showed, who was to say what went on behind the scenes in any relationship?

As if sensing her withdrawal, Callie touched her shoulder. "The two of us have done quite a bit of talking. It occurs to me that it's Katherine's turn." She turned to Kate. "I don't mean to pry, but if there's anything you wish to get off your chest, I'm sure I can speak for Daisy when I say we will listen with an open mind."

Kate divided her gaze between the two women. "Though I don't know either of you well, in many ways, I feel more comfortable talking with you than I would to my sister or . . ."

She stopped there, unhappily aware that other than Rourke, she didn't have close companions in whom she might confide. Along with the extended novel reading and chocolate-cake eating, acquiring a set of female friends had been part of her plan for spinsterhood independence. She saw now how silly she'd been to limit her life as she had. Her isolation wasn't a state of affairs she could blame on either her father's gaming or her little sister's selfishness. It was no one's fault but hers.

"Then what is it, Katherine?"

"Rourke is your friend." Singling in on Daisy, Kate added, "In your case, you grew up together. I don't want to seem as though I'm criticizing him or otherwise speaking ill of him but . . . Oh, Lord, it hurts. It hurts so bloody much."

Embarrassed by her outburst, Kate turned away and dashed at a tear sliding down the side of her cheek. To think she'd always prided herself on her stiff upper lip, game face, and perfect record of never once showing emotion, let alone crying in public. Precisely when had she turned into a watering pot?

By the time she finished confiding hers and Rourke's as

yet unfinished story, the pot of tea with which they began the afternoon had been set aside in favor of a decanter of sherry, and there wasn't a dry eye among them. When she came to the part to do with Felicity, she choked up.

Callie waved the decanter aside. "I'm afraid I shall have to make do with tea until little Henry or Alicia makes his or her appearance." She smoothed a hand over the slight baby bump at her belly, and Kate found herself swallowing against a building thickness in her throat.

She was reasonably certain she hadn't conceived. The slight cramping in her lower belly and tenderness in her breasts indicated her monthly courses were due to arrive on schedule. Given their imminent separation, she should be relieved. Who knew, but perhaps she was barren. She was closing in on thirty, after all.

But the truth was, she desperately wanted a small human being to cuddle and care for, someone who would be truly hers to love. How ironic that she who had been taking care of others nearly all her life might be deprived of the gift of motherhood. Beyond creating a life, she wanted to create a family—a family with Patrick.

But accomplishing that aim required him to love her just enough, just a little.

The sound of a carriage pulling up out front announced that the men were returned. At Callie and Daisy's encouragement, Kate went off to speak with Rourke. As Daisy pointed out, there really was no time like the present. Birthday dinner or not, there was no point in allowing wounded feelings to fester any longer.

Watching Kate go off, Daisy let out a sigh. "Oh, I do hope they work it out."

Callie hedged a dark brow upward. "I was under the impression you weren't overly fond of Kate."

"I had my doubts at first," Daisy admitted. "She seemed so very plumb in the mouth and well, just a bit tight-arsed."

Callie smiled at that. "You might have said much the same of me had you met me a few years ago."

Rather than deny it, Daisy said, "They're meant to be together, I just know it. The way he looks at her when he thinks she doesn't see, the longing in his eyes, well, it fair near breaks my heart." Despite her years in Paris, Daisy's Cockney roots had a tendency to show.

"What do you make of Felicity?" Callie asked. "I thought she seemed rather full of herself at dinner last night with all that talk of her theatrical career."

Never one to hold back, Daisy scowled and said, "Actress, my arse. I've certainly never heard of her. I think she's scheming jade, a fortune huntress out to stir the pot and make trouble for our friends."

"Hmm, well put. But the principal question is, what does she want?" Callie thought for a moment. "Don't you find it odd that after two years in London she suddenly befriends Kate's sister and turns up here before the holiday?"

Daisy agreed it was odd, indeed. "Let's you and I keep a watch on her while we're all here and see what she might be up to." She lifted a corn-colored lock of her long hair, formerly dyed a stage girl's cinnamon, and added, "Present difficulties aside, Rourke and Kate are on the cusp of their own happy ending. I can feel it. We can't allow that flame-haired vixen to spoil all our hard work now."

Rourke, too, was passing a talkative afternoon in the company of friends. Somehow his intention to show Gavin and Harry the new railway-history exhibit had been subverted into a rescue mission. Claiming thirst, Harry steered them to a local public house just off the High. Before long the ale flowed apace with his friends' unsolicited advice.

Starting into their third round, Harry hefted his pint. "To Gav, my favorite barrister friend—actually my *only* barrister friend—many happy returns, mate." Lowering his glass, he wiped foam from his lip and pinned his blue eyes on Rourke. "Speaking of birthdays, you have one coming up soon, don't you?" Rourke admitted he did. "In that case, give yourself an early birthday gift and make it up with your wife. Kate's mad for you. It's as plain as the broken nose on that boxer's mug of yours—plain to everyone but you."

Rourke lowered his gaze to his glass of Scotch whiskey. "Kate is no more in love with me than I am her. We're a mismatch, plain and simple."

Gavin sipped his sherry, not terribly good sherry, but when one was rusticating in a Scottish backwater, one must make do. "I agree with Harry. If not love, why else would a woman go to the trouble of showing a man such spleen?"

Rourke lifted the shot of whiskey and tossed it back in a single swallow. Swiping his hand across his mouth—why bother with manners when everything he'd just come to care for was apparently lost to him?— he answered, "Because she's a bullocks-busting shrew, that's why."

Had another man, including either of his two best friends, said the same or even half as much, he would have driven his fist through his face with nary a thought. But having just had his balls busted—and his heart slashed in twain—by said shrew gave him a feeling of entitlement.

Unlike Hadrian, who'd been a confirmed bachelor until he'd fallen for Callie, he'd always supposed he would marry, that the right woman would happen along. Once she did, they would marry, have a family, and live blissfully ever after with scarcely more fuss required than the horses he bred.

So far, horses were proving a lot easier to manage.

Thank God, he'd held off on telling Kate he loved her. Every time he considered just how close he'd come to confessing it, he felt shame wash over him to rival any embarrassment he'd felt from the garden episode. His wife was a marvel, truly she was. Just when he assured himself she couldn't possibly hurt him any more, she came up with some new and creative way to crush his hopes and his heart beneath her slender slipper.

Apparently oblivious to the danger he courted, Harry leaned across the pub table and wagged a forefinger in Rourke's face. "Mark me, numbskull, I knew Katherine Lindsey before she was your wife, before you ever clapped eyes on her. She was as sharp as glass and about as warm as snow, a proper ice maiden for all that on the surface she was perfectly friendly and polite. Not once in all our sittings did I ever peer through the lens of my camera and see her eyes light and her skin glow and her scowling mouth soften as it does whenever she's near you."

Gavin, ever the calming voice of reason, raised his snifter and asked, "It seems to me that the fundamental question remaining to be answered is, what do you want most: to be right or to be happy?"

Happy—Rourke wasn't certain he even knew what that meant, but that honeymoon week with Kate, he'd felt himself come close to it—close enough to touch it, even visit for a while, but not stay—never to stay. The sex had been sublime, the best of his life, and yet what he'd felt for her surpassed the physicality of their joining. How he'd loved the trusting way she'd laid her head in the crook of his shoulder and snuggled up next to him, her petite body molding to his despite the differences in their sizes, her slender leg tossed across him, the latter a wordless act of sweet possession. And yet even during that idyllic week, he'd never been able to let down his guard and relax, not wholly. Even propping himself on his elbow watching her sleep, he'd been seized with the irrational fear that at any minute she might disappear— or be snatched away. Was that a normal newlywed reaction? Rourke didn't think so. When faced with any other sort of obstacle, his natural inclination was to dig in his heels, raise his fists, and fight for what he wanted, what he believed in. Why was it, then, that when it came to his heart's desire, Kate, it felt safer somehow to simply walk away and give up on her, them?

He shook his head and considered ordering another drink. "Why is it I have the feeling 'both' isna an option?"

Gavin answered with an ironic smile. "I can tell you, my friend, that making a marriage work has very little to do with being right, let alone emerging the victor. It has to do with caring and compromise and choosing to do the morally right thing, the selfless thing, above one's own self-interest. But above all, it is about love. Beyond who is right and who is wrong, it is love that will carry you through." As if sensing Rourke was about to interrupt, he added, "If you'll recall, I came close to breaking it off with Daisy when I thought she'd accepted a bribe from my grandfather. My stubborn pride almost had me walking away from her forever."

"Just as I very nearly walked away from Callie rather than face her after that damnable photograph came out in the papers." Expression thoughtful, Harry traced the wet ring his beer glass had made atop the table. "I tried telling myself I was doing the noble thing in walking away, that she'd be better off without me, but the truth was, walking away wasn't about being noble at all. I was bloody scared she'd turn me away, not that anyone would have blamed her, me included. But if I had walked away, only think what I'd be missing—the best lover, friend, and wife any man could ever ask for, and, God willing, in another five months, the best mother, too."

Gavin and Rourke snapped their heads up at once. "Harry?"

Harry looked up, handsome face breaking into a broad and prideful grin. "We're having a baby."

Rourke reached across and clapped his friend on the back. "That's bonny news, mate. Congratulations. This calls for another round." Swallowing against the lump in his throat, he beckoned to the barkeep.

Imagining Kate's taut, lithe body increasing with his babe, Rourke felt a funny pull in the vicinity of his heart. He'd seen her kindness directed toward tenants' children, the younger members of the household staff, and yes, even his mongrel dog. What a beautiful mother she'd make and a good one, too.

He waited for their drinks to arrive, and then lifted his glass to lead them in the requisite toast. Raising his glass, he offered, "To good friends and second chances—I hope."

They touched glasses. Gavin's solemn eyes met his across the table. "It'll work out, Patrick, you'll see."

Harry set down his glass and nodded. "It's always darkest before the dawn . . . or some such thing."

Swallowing, Rourke admitted, "I've never felt worthy of Kate, not really. She started out as this glittering trophy to be won, someone beyond my touch or very nearly so. Once I had her, I couldna credit my good fortune. I wasna sure what to do with her—well, I knew well enough what to do with her in some respects, but in others . . . She's a lady bred, after all, and I'm well, me. A bruiser such as I ought to count himself lucky the likes of her would let me near enough to touch her, let alone wanting more, but I did want more, not only her body but her heart. And then her sister showed up with Felicity, and everything we'd built over the week, the trust and the friendship and yes, the loving, crashed down upon our heads like a house of cards."

"Do you want my advice?" Gavin asked.

"Have I a choice?"

Gavin and Harry exchanged glances. In unison they shook their heads and answered, "Not really."

"I didn't think so. In that case, out with it, then."

Gavin sighed. "Go to her, Patrick. Go to her the moment we get back. If you tell her even half of what you've told us here, she'd be a fool not to at least meet you halfway. If she doesn't, then at least you'll know you did everything in your power. You can move forward with your life without looking back, without regrets."

Harry agreed. "Gavin's right on the money, mate. While you're at it, you might want to give Felicity her walking papers. Having your former mistress under the same roof as your wife can't be helping."

Rourke shook his head. "Kate thinks Felicity is only a friend of her sister's. She has no idea Felicity and I were ever more than passing acquaintances, and I'd just as soon keep it that way."

Harry snorted. "So say you. Women don't have to think about these things. They *know*. They've eyes like eagles and noses like bloodhounds. Take our advice. Send that particular baggage packing and go to Kate. Gav's right on the mark. If you don't at least try to mend matters, you'll regret it for the rest of your days. When it comes down to it, Rourke, regrets are a far more bitter tonic for a man to swallow than sins."

As soon as the men returned home, Rourke meant to take his friends' advice and go in search of Kate. Felicity's waylaying him was an unpleasant surprise. She must have been watching from an upstairs window because she stepped off the stair landing before the main door closed. She flounced into the front hallway wearing a garish, low-cut gown more suited to evening than day.

Slanted gaze tunneling to Rourke, she said, "I must speak with you—in private."

Gavin and Harry exchanged frowns but made their excuses to be on their way. Before going, Harry muttered, "Mind regrets versus sins."

Rourke blew out a breath. His friends' counsel had included sending Felicity packing. Apparently there was no time like the present. Resigned, he led her into his library and closed the door.

Leaning back against the front of his desk, he regarded her. "Very well, Felicity, I'm listening. Not promising, only listening. Out with it."

Slanted green eyes met his. She whetted her lower lip. "The other day you asked me what I wanted, and I'm prepared to tell you. I want another go of it with you."

"In case you havena noticed, I'm married now." He almost added "happily" but held off. The outcome remained to be seen, but his afternoon with Gavin and Harry had him feeling hopeful.

"Oh, Rourkie, you were always so good to me, only I didn't properly appreciate you back then." She batted her eyes and looked up at him through her lashes.

Such artifice once would have melted him, but not so now. How very much more appealing he found Kate's honest, head-on gaze to be.

Patience nearing its end, Rourke shook his head. "It's water under the bridge now."

And it was. If he'd to sum up the paltry feelings he still had for her in a single word it would be *pity*. He doubted Felicity would ever know the glory of loving another person with all one's soul. Though his own dabbling in matters of the heart hadn't worked out according to plan, not yet at any rate, loving Kate had made him a better man. He wouldn't trade their blissful honeymoon week for all the world's riches—which stood as quite a statement for such an acquisitive man.

"Since you can't have me, have you anything else in mind?" Knowing Felicity, he felt certain she had a backup plan.

She hesitated and then admitted, "The other night at dinner, I may have gilded the lily a bit about my theatrical career."

Rourke listened in silence. That didn't surprise him in the slightest.

"I can't go on dancing in that horrid club in Leicester Square night upon night, I just can't, but it's hard for a girl like me to get a leg over in a city like London. But if I had a place of my own where I could set myself up as the headliner, like your friend Daisy does, well, that would make all the difference."

Distracted with thoughts of Kate, it took Rourke a moment to reckon Felicity's game. Once he did, it was as if a lamp had just been turned up. "You want the Palace, don't you?"

She nodded. "With all your money, you'll never miss it, and it would mean ever so much to me."

Relief had him feeling generous. So it was only the theater she coveted. Surrendering a property he'd never wanted in the first place was a small price to pay to rid himself of a nuisance. "Verra well, I'll sign over the deed before you leave." The latter was by way of being a strong hint.

The property in Covent Garden had been boarded up for two years. Ordinarily he would have offered it to Gavin and Daisy, but they had unpleasant memories of the place. The Tudor-era theatre they'd just restored was the ideal setting for putting on the Shakespeare plays they both loved. The point was, the Palace was sitting fallow. Turning it over to Felicity seemed the solution to serve everyone. How she would finance its opening was her private affair. Given her talents for "getting a leg over" well-heeled swells, he expected she'd work something out.

"Truly!" She squealed and launched herself into his arms.

Felicity had always been a substantial armful and the past few years had not lightened her load. Reflex had him closing his arms about her. Before now he'd always fancied big-boned women with blousy bosoms and full bottoms, but now it was Kate's lithe, tight little body his arms ached to hold.

She laid a hand alongside his face. "I didn't say the theatre was all I wanted. Come to London with me. You and I together, we could take London by storm."

Rourke had had his fill of storms. He was ready to experience the equivalent of placid spring skies—with his wife.

Gently but firmly he eased her off his chest. The intimate contact brought back one or two pleasant memories but no real desire. "I wish you the best, lass, but we're done, in that way."

She arched a brow. "As I recall, we were quite good in *that way*. I could make you happy, Patrick. I did once, mind."

Rourke shook his head. "You never made me happy, Felicity. We had some grand times for certain, but that was all we had. You and I lusted, but we never loved. Now I must ask you to excuse me. I'm off to find my wife and tell her I'm mad for her."

Kate headed for the library at a fast walk. The afternoon spent with Callie and Daisy had bolstered her confidence and put her marriage into perspective. She and Patrick were not the only newlyweds to go through a rough patch—or even several. Hang her pride, this time she would find the courage to tell Patrick all that was in her heart, that she loved him and was honored to be his wife. If need be, she would cast herself at his feet like her Shakespearian namesake post-taming. What she absolutely refused to do was let him go.

The study door stood ajar when Kate approached. Surmising he must be entertaining Gavin and Harry, she tamped down her disappointment and turned to go.

Felicity's voice filtered out into the hallway, stalling Kate in her tracks. "Come to London with me."

Heart drumming, Kate stepped stealthily to the side and peered through the crack. Rourke and Felicity stood in a close embrace. Her husband had both arms about the redhead. Felicity's head was tilted upward as if anticipating his kiss, her hand bracing his cheek. He did not look like a man who had just said no.

Kate felt as if an invisible fist plowed into her belly. The pleasant warmth of the sherry coursing through her veins turned to ice water. For a handful of seconds, she feared she might be sick. Pride, or rather the shredded remains of it, was all that held her back. To be found not only eavesdropping but retching outside her husband's door would seal her humiliation. To think that she'd been prepared to cast herself at his feet and beg his forgiveness!

So far in her marriage she'd been twice a fool, but if Rourke fancied she was fool enough to stay while he kept a mistress in London, he had best think again.

CHAPTER FIFTEEN

"Come, my sweet Kate. Better once
than never, for never too late."
—WILLIAM SHAKESPEARE, Petruchio,
The Taming of the Shrew

Rourke left the library and Felicity behind, only too glad to close that chapter of his life. He would sign over the deed to the Palace after breakfast in the morning, and then put his former mistress on the first train back to London. Their business done, she'd declared she meant to have a lie down before dinner. She might have hung upside down by her ankles for all he cared.

He came into the front hallway as Daisy and Caledonia entered from the side parlor. Dividing his gaze between the two women, he sketched a brief bow and then asked, "Where is Kate?"

Frowning, Daisy spoke up, "I thought she was with—"

Callie's hand clamping down on her companion's arm caused the sentence to die. "I'm not sure," Callie answered for them both. "I believe she said something about going upstairs to have a lie down before supper."

Daisy and Callie were acting odd, indeed, but odder still was that Kate would be napping with guests in the house. His wife was the most industrious woman he'd ever known. He doubted that her idol, Mrs. Beeton, could have possessed more energy and enthusiasm than she. From what he could tell, afternoon naps were unknown to Kate. It occurred to him to wonder if she might be pregnant. Though it was a wild guess, and as yet unsubstantiated, it was certainly possible. Before the previous week's rift, they'd made love all but nonstop. Excitement seized him. He excused himself to the two women and bounded up the stairs.

He gained the minstrel's gallery and headed down the sconce-lit corridor to the master-bedroom suite. He considered knocking outside Kate's door, but prudence and pride held him back. This last week they'd hardly been on the best of terms. Instead, he entered his own chamber and headed for the connecting door.

He could hear her moving about. From the sounds of thrashing, she must be banging dresser drawers and stomping on floorboards. His heart leapt into his throat. Might she be moving furniture? Packing?

He opened the dressing-room door only to find her

standing on the opposite side, her fist raised. "I was just coming to speak with you." She lowered her hand to her side and stepped back for him to enter.

The room was at sixes and sevens, clothes strewn about, books and journals and bric-a-brac dumped onto the bed. For a woman who prided herself on her household-management capabilities, it was one hellish mess. Mrs. Beeton would most definitely not have approved.

He swung his gaze back to Kate, standing in the center of the room. "Going somewhere?"

"I've done a great deal of thinking this past week, and I've come to the conclusion there is indeed no point in our being leg-shackled to one another any longer than we can help it."

"Kate!"

"Why should we go on deceiving our friends, ourselves, when it is painfully obvious to all that we will never suit?"

His gaze bore into hers. "So it's a divorce you want, then? To obtain one, one of us would have to claim adultery."

Her eyes flashed wide. For a half second, it occurred to him to ask what she might be thinking. He couldn't imagine Kate being unfaithful to him.

She swung her head to the side. "Not a divorce, but a separation. You have only to have the deed drawn up and I will sign it."

"Is that really what you wish?" He felt as though she'd slashed open a vital vein and left him to bleed out.

She nodded. "It is."

Thinking of all the ways they'd made love in this very room, Rourke felt his throat tightening. "In that case, I will provide you with an annual allowance for your maintenance, enough to allow you to set up a household independent of your father."

Eyes bleak, she gave a sharp, quick nod. "That is generous of you."

He moved toward her, settling his hands atop her shoulders. As much as he loved her and wanted her to stay, what he most wanted for her was to be happy.

"I willna tell you what to do with your portion, but I will say privately and because I care for you that you're a fool if you give your father as much as a farthing. He's a wastrel, Katie, a drunkard and a gamester. He doesna deserve you. Dinna let him take from you any more than he already has. If it's freedom you want, then *be* free." He let his hands drop to his sides. "I'll ask Gavin to draw up the papers, only there's nay need to dampen tonight's birthday celebration. Our news can keep until tomorrow."

She nodded. "As soon as the document is signed and witnessed, I'll go. There is no reason I cannot be prepared to leave for London within the week."

Silence descended like a leaden curtain between them, cumbersome and heavy. Rourke fancied he felt the pall of it pressing down upon them both, burying all their unrealized dreams and cherished hopes.

Kate's gaze climbed to his face. "We never would have worked. It was a lovely dream, but we're too different. We never stood a chance . . . did we?"

Staring down into her lovely, sad face, Rourke felt as if a razor slashed at his heart. He shook his head. "Nay, we never stood a chance. Not a snowball's chance in hell."

Kate's determination to take the high road while they had guests under their roof was subverted by Felicity's seeking her out alone. She was in the dining room fighting tears and checking the table settings when the Scotswoman waltzed in.

Without looking up, she asked, "What can I do for you, Felicity?"

"I came to offer my condolences. You and Rourke are separating, are you not?"

Kate snapped her head upright. The spoon she'd held clanged to the floor. "Listening at keyholes is not an attractive quality."

Reaching the foot of the table, Felicity slid a dessert fork a fraction of a millimeter to the left. Kate felt her jaw clench.

"Were I you, I'd try for an annulment. With your reputation as a shrew, sure everyone will think you were simply too frigid to bear bedding."

Kate swallowed against the lump rising high in her

throat. The dam at the back of her eyes was a hairs-breadth from bursting. Rourke had called her out as a shrew the week before. Was Felicity parroting what he'd told her in private? Separating though they were, the prospect of her husband discussing her with his mistress made her sick inside.

"Get out, Felicity. Until dinner, you may amuse yourself in the parlor with our other guests provided you hold that forked tongue of yours in check. Tonight is Gavin's birthday, and our friends have traveled a goodly distance to celebrate. I won't have you ruining everyone's evening."

Felicity shrugged. "Nay worries, Katherine. I'll keep your secret so as not to spoil your wee dinner party. It may be meant as a birthday celebration, but it seems more in the way of a farewell dinner—yours." She turned and strolled out of the room, leaving Kate clutching the back of the chair and shaking in her wake.

Kate walked back to the table, dragged out a chair, and sat. She pushed a place setting of carefully laid Limoges to the side with the edge of her arm, planted her elbows on the table, and braced her head in her hands. Only then did she give herself permission to cry. She cried until she tasted the scalding brine inside her mouth, and then she cried some more. She cried as though her heart would break, as though it was broken already. It *was* broken, she felt sure of it. Bit by bit she felt it breaking away, releasing an avalanche of buried dreams, of pent-up pain. And how could it not be?

She loved Patrick with all her soul, with all that she was and had yet to become. She loved him for his failings, as well as for his finer qualities. She loved his humped nose and crooked half smile every whit as much as she loved his beautiful emerald eyes and perfectly planed chest. Loving him wasn't a matter of logic or convenience or, God knew, common sense. She loved him because she loved him, because she couldn't help loving him, because to not love Patrick O'Rourke was quite simply not in her realm of being. To settle on not loving him would be akin to choosing to have blue eyes over brown, to stop being who she was, to stop *being*. And yet as much as she loved him, the curse remained unbroken.

When Kate loved someone, they always, *always* went away.

Kate's encounter with Felicity set the tone for the dinner party that night. The couples paired off to go into dinner. Rourke held back from the door, and Felicity seized the opportunity to slip her arm through his. He cast Kate a look, but she refused to meet his eye. He and Felicity were humiliating her under her very roof, and there wasn't a bloody thing she could do about it. Not her roof for much longer, she reminded herself. After she and Rourke made their announcement tomorrow, she would begin making her arrangements to leave. Once she let a small house in the country with a stable, she would send for her horse. Given the trouble to which he'd gone to buy Princess back, Kate didn't think Rourke would begrudge her another few weeks of stabling and feed. Even with the proof of his infidelity sailing ahead into the dining room on his arm, she couldn't think of him as a bad person.

But house hunting and packing must wait. First there were the next few hours to be got through.

From the head of the dining table, Rourke called down to Kate, "If it isna too much trouble, pray pass the salt. It is at your end, I believe."

"No trouble at all, my darling. Would you care for the pepper, as well, or do you find the tart sufficiently spicy?" She cut her gaze to Felicity.

Felicity didn't look up. The redhead appeared engrossed by the veal cutlet on her plate. Among the eight of them, the Scotswoman was the only one doing justice to Cook's fine fare.

Rourke glared back. "The dishes are all perfectly prepared, though the company in certain quarters seems to have curdled."

That did it. Kate threw down her napkin as though it was a gauntlet. "No worries, husband. Ere long you shall have only honeyed words and syrupy smiles to grace your table."

The farcical dinner party seemed to be taking its toll

on everyone. To make matters worse, Bea shot dagger looks Kate's way every chance she got. Rourke had apparently spoken to Ralph, and the offer of riding lessons had been tabled indefinitely. By the time the fruit course was cleared, Harry declared himself stuffed to the gills, and the others echoed the sentiment. When Kate suggested they take their champagne and cake in the parlor, the company rose at once as if glad to escape the oppressive atmosphere.

In the parlor, champagne flutes were passed around and cake cut and served. Once the birthday toast was drunk, Felicity announced she would favor them with a song. Looking on with an aching heart as her rival sang a soulful Celtic ballad of unrequited love, a deliberate choice, Kate was sure, it occurred to her that soon Rourke would have almost all of what he'd set out to win two years before: a willing woman to charm his dinner guests and breed heirs for his railways.

Only it wouldn't be her.

<hr />

Callie and Daisy exchanged glances. Throughout the tense meal, they, too, had watched Felicity and the byplay surrounding her, and they did not greatly care for what they'd seen. As soon as the song ended, Daisy crossed to the piano and took firm hold of Felicity's arm.

"Felicity, I'd like a word with you——in the hallway,

if you please."

The girl scarcely looked up from the sheet music she flipped through. "I don't fancy going out into the hallway just now."

Callie appeared on Felicity's other side. "I'm afraid we insist."

Taking advantage of the confusion, they marched her out into the hall between them.

The Scotswoman divided her gaze between them. "What is so terribly important that it could not wait?"

Daisy came directly to the point. "My husband and I have considerable contacts in the theatrical world. W. S. Gilbert is a very great friend of ours."

Felicity's jaw slackened. "You know Gilbert of Gilbert and Sullivan!"

Daisy nodded. "I do. Sir Gilbert has been badgering me to star as Yum-Yum in *The Mikado* ever since he first saw me debut at Drury Lane. Were I to recommend another actress for the part, an audition would be all but guaranteed."

Felicity clapped a hand over her heart. "I know all the songs by heart."

"I'll wager you do." Tall herself, Daisy looked around Felicity's shoulders and caught Callie's eye. "But if you want that audition, you'll have to strike a bargain with us first."

Felicity's blue eyes narrowed. She looked between the two women. "What sort of bargain?"

Her quarry having taken the bait, Daisy continued, "I will write a letter to Sir Gilbert, recommending you for a private audition. In return, you will not only go away but stay away, and leave our friends Rourke and Kate in peace—permanently."

Callie broke in, "And first thing tomorrow morning, you must have a chat with Kate and explain to her that you are not sleeping with her husband."

Felicity screwed up her face. "And if I refuse?"

Daisy didn't hesitate. "I shall make bloody sure the only role you ever receive in a London theatre is as a member of the audience."

"All right, I'll do it."

Watching Felicity sashay back inside, Daisy and Callie could no longer hide their smiles. They burst out laughing.

Callie wiped her eyes and turned to her friend. "Do you think she has a chance?"

Daisy shrugged. "Whatever else she is, Felicity really does have a very good voice. And as we've just seen demonstrated, she's a decent actress, though her delivery could do with a bit of polish. With her flamboyant looks and obvious flair for drama, who knows how far she might go?"

Callie smiled. "So long as her success takes her far away from Rourke and Kate, I'd say it's a case of *bon voyage* and good riddance."

Rourke didn't sleep that night. Lying awake listening for sounds of Kate stirring in the adjoining room, he allowed that the impending separation was entirely his fault. In relying on a play to "tame" his bride, he'd built their marriage on a foundation of trickery and deceit. Small wonder Kate didn't trust him, not with her troubles and most definitely not with her heart.

Giving up on sleep, he rose, dressed, and headed out to the stables, boots crunching on the frozen snow, his dog darting ahead. Once inside the stable, some devil's impulse drew him over to Zeus's stall. The trainer had finally arrived, and the stallion was coming along nicely. He wasn't yet broken, though, not completely. Rourke could see the untamed passion in his eyes, just as he could see it in Kate's.

Kate. Pain fisted his heart, the aftermath making him reckless. The horse's wildness matched his mood. He took the lantern off the peg and went into the tack room. Saddling a wilding in shadow wasn't easy, but as determined as the beast was to thwart him, Rourke had the devil on his side. Before long, he was galloping across the snow toward the loch.

Halfway there, it started snowing. The first fine powder fast built to blanketing. Soon it was as though the Powers That Be were dumping buckets of the stuff over his head. His glasses fogged. He finally gave up on wiping them and shoved them inside his pocket. Beneath him, the horse reared. Rourke snapped his head upright, struggling to see. The white mass rose up before him like an Eskimo's igloo. Too late to turn, he tried jumping, but the horse missed. The stallion screamed. Foot slipping from the stirrup, Rourke vaulted headfirst over the saddle. He landed hard. Pain shot through his arm, centering in his shoulder. He rolled—down, down, *down*—the winter-white world whizzing by. He reached out, hands clawing at air, feet kicking to find purchase on ground. A protrusion from the snow broke his fall. He hooked his good arm about it, a tree branch growing out from the edge of the hillside. Panting, he held on. Even as he did so, he acknowledged he was going to die. Not from the blood trickling into his mouth that he dare not wipe away, or from his likely-to-be-dislocated shoulder, or even necessarily from falling to the ravine below, though that might well happen, too. He was going to freeze to death. The particulars might be sketchy, but the outcome was assured.

He was going to die, and his first thought—his only thought—was that he would never see his Katie girl again.

I love you, Kate.

He closed his eyes and waited.

Kate, too, spent a restless night. Wide awake, the sound of Rourke's bedroom door closing had her rocketing upright in bed. Toby's bark below her window drew her attention outside. It was still dark, but the sky looked more cream than pitch. A gentle snow started, tapping against the window's leaded-glass panes. Bobbing light pointed her gaze to Rourke's silhouette. He was headed for the stables. Her first thought was he must be going to meet Felicity. But no, Felicity slept in one of the east tower rooms. Trysting in the stables when there was a perfectly good bed to be had would be a long way to go to uphold a romantic cliché.

Time ticked by. Kate stood at her window, waiting. Finally he rode beneath her window, though she didn't think he looked her way. The dog didn't follow. The snowfall was steadier now, harder. Kate couldn't be certain, but she thought the mount he rode looked larger than the bay, his usual horse. Watching him ride away, she glimpsed her future. With no ornery Scot to spar with by day and make love with by night, the years ahead stretched out— lonely, desolate, and bleak. All the chocolate confections and romantic novels in the world would not come close to filling such a void. She didn't want a separation or a divorce. What she wanted was a marriage.

Decided, she turned up a lamp, stripped off her nightgown, and fumbled in her wardrobe for her riding habit. By the time she stepped into the main stable building, dawn was breaking. Reminded of that day when as a child she'd found Princess's stall empty, her heart sank. This time the empty stall was Zeus's. For the first time she understood the fear behind his tight-lipped fury when she'd taken Zeus out against his orders.

Oh, Patrick.

She hurried into the tack room and emerged with a saddle and bridle. Princess lifted her head and whinnied, but she hadn't time for more than a pet in passing. "I'm afraid this is one adventure you're going to have to sit out, old friend."

Instead she led Buttercup out of her stall and over to the mounting block. "Are you up to it, my girl?" Kate might as easily have asked the question of herself.

By the time Kate rode out, Toby running ahead, daylight was breaking. It still snowed, but the fall had subsided to a fine powdery mist. She came to a low stone wall, scarcely recognizable from the banked snow. Toby fell into a frenzy of barking. At first Kate dismissed it, telling herself he must have scented an animal he identified as prey, but when he wouldn't cease, she decided to have a look. She dismounted, and her eye caught on a small shiny object sticking up from the snow. She bent to have a look. Tunneling a hand into the snow, she picked the object up and brushed the snow off. Her heart slammed into chest. She held her husband's glasses.

She waded over to the ledge beyond the wall, the mare's hooves crunching in the snow, her own boots sinking to midcalf. She was reminded of her and Rourke's miserable trek from the train station. A lump rose in her throat. What she wouldn't give for the chance to step back in time and undo even the last few hours.

Toby raced ahead. She followed the dog over to where the hillside dropped off. Coming to the edge, she saw that a ravine of sorts lay below. Imaging her husband's big, beautiful body lying twisted and broken at the bottom, she had to force herself to look down.

A groan drew her attention to the far left. She leaned over to look, and her gaze snagged on the snowman dangling off the side. *Rourke?*

"Rourke!"

A scarlet streak slashed through the frozen mask on his face. It took her a few seconds to realize it must be blood. But he was moving, and if snowmen didn't move, then neither did dead men.

Grateful tears crystallized on her cheeks. "Rourke, don't move. I'm here."

He looked up. "Kate?" He was too far below for her to tell for certain, but she thought the expression on his face was gladness.

"Yes, yes, it's me. I'm just above you. Hold on. I'm working out a way to come down and get you."

He hedged his gaze downward, and following, Kate felt her heart chip away. The snow had iced over the hillside, rendering the terrain slippery as glass.

"Christ, Kate, stay put. Dinna dare take another step closer, and that's an order."

She made a tunnel of her hands and shouted down, "An order? If it's a biddable wife you want, you'll just have to wait until you're free to marry Felicity."

He cracked open his swollen eye and stared up at her. "*Jaysus*, woman, you must be daft. I'd sooner let go and jump now then spend the rest of my life leg-shackled to a scheming witch like Felicity."

"Are you saying she's not your mistress?" Madness to be trading shouts as they were, but then this might be her last chance to know.

"Jaysus, no, not since two years ago, not since I met you."

"Hold on, I'll be back."

She hurried over to the horse and unfurled the rope she'd brought for no reason beyond instinct. As she worked, she cursed her foolish, *shrewish*, prideful ways. Why hadn't she been able to accept that someone as wonderful as Rourke might truly love her? Why hadn't she confronted him with her suspicions about Felicity and given him the chance to explain? Instead, she'd assumed the worst. Doubtless there was a lesson to be learned, if not several, but certainly the present was neither the time nor place to ponder it.

Looping one end of the rope about her horse's neck, she called down, "Whatever happens, we'll see it through together, for I am most certainly not leaving you. If you want to throttle me for being a disobedient wife, you'll bloody well have to wait until you gain a foothold on solid ground."

Watching her, fear broke over Rourke, not for himself but for Kate. "Kate, I mean it, stay put. You can't save me. You'll only kill yourself, as well."

"So be it. If need be, I'll be Juliet to your Romeo—or haven't you read that one yet?"

"Kate, I mean it . . ."

He tried all manner of verbal threats to stop her, but in the end he was helpless to do other than watch, his heart in his throat, as she shimmied down the edge of the embankment, feet skittering on the slippage. Breathing hard and fast, he held very still while she looped the twist of rope about his waist and tied it into a knot that would do a sailor proud.

"Where did you learn to tie a knot like that? Surely not from the worthy Mrs. Beeton?"

She flashed a quick, tight smile and set to work. "I know how to do a great many useful things. I'm called Capable Kate for a reason."

"You're *my* Capable Kate," he whispered, only this time the sobriquet wasn't a disparagement but an endearment. "Hold. A kiss, Katie, for luck," he added, knowing it might well be the last kiss they shared.

Kate's eyes met his. Snow frosted her lashes. He could only imagine how he must look.

"Not for luck, Patrick, for love." She angled her face and brushed her mouth over his.

Rourke felt the last of his reserve crumble away, much like the snow breaking away beneath their feet. Tasting the brine of Kate's tears, looking into her beautiful, brave face, he knew that, whatever happened, loving her was worth it all.

Drawing back, he said, "If we make it out of this, Katie, will you swear to grow old with me?"

She didn't hesitate. "I swear it, Patrick. And though I can't promise I'll grow any tamer with age, I can promise to be your loyal, loving wife for all my days."

She turned and started her upward climb. As soon as Kate gained the landing, he sent up a quick, grateful prayer. She at least was safe, and provided she let go of the rope once she lost control, she would remain so. Watching her loop the other end of the rope about the mare and walk the beast backward, he called upon all his strength to keep his hold. Slowly, centimeter by centimeter, he was hoisted upward. Gritting his teeth, he tried not to think about the shards of rock tearing at his clothes and flesh or how the rope about his waist was showing signs of fraying. Instead he focused on the image in his mind's eye of his wife's beautiful, tearstained face when a moment ago she'd sworn to grow old with him. Using his good leg and arm to work with the rope, he was almost to the top of the embankment when suddenly the coil about his waist broke.

He hurtled downward, catching himself this time on an icy shelf of landing. Kate rushed over to the side and flopped down on her front. She stretched out her arms. Even wearing the bulky winter coat, they were slender as reeds. "Take hold."

"Nay, Kate, you canna lift me. You'll only be dragged down, too." He started sliding. She grabbed hold of his collar, refusing to let go. "Let go, damn you!"

Her determined gaze met his. "Not now, not ever. We do this together, Patrick."

It was no use. He was going to die. But he was not going to take Kate with him. After all the mistakes he'd made with her, the least he could do was to not drag her to her death.

Toby's barking sounded as backdrop.

"Hold on." Harry replaced Kate at the top. "We're going to rig up a hoist and pull you up."

"We?"

Gavin's dark head materialized beside Harry's blond one. "Hold tight."

They dropped the hoist down, and he caught it in his teeth. Holding on, he managed to loop it about his waist.

From above, Harry called down, "Ready?"

Rourke nodded. "As ready as I'll ever be."

"Heave-ho."

The next thing he knew, he was rising again. He reached the top, Gavin and Hadrian pulling him the rest of the way. Even with more than a foot of snow on the ground, *terra firma* had never felt quite so good.

His friends fell to the side. Kate left the horse and rushed to him, her slender arms wrapping around him and her head burying against his chest. Harry threw a blanket about his shoulders. From the roadway, he saw Callie and Daisy climbing out of the carriage.

Wiping perspiration from his brow, Harry said, "When Zeus showed up at the stables without Rourke—and Kate, too, was missing—we formed a search party to comb the area."

"Toby is the true hero among us," Gavin added, reaching down to give the dog a pat. "We were just about to move on to search elsewhere when he ran up and grabbed hold of my coattail. He wouldn't let go until we followed him back here."

Kate pulled her head from Rourke's chest and looked up. A look of silent understanding passed between them. Grateful as they were to their friends, the details of the rescue could keep until later. For now all they wanted was time alone to savor the miracle of the second chance that was theirs.

Their two friends exchanged glances. Hadrian spoke up, "We'll, uh . . . be in the carriage when you're ready to go."

Gavin nodded. "I'll walk Kate's mare back. She's a brave little lady, but she looks as though she could do with a rest from being ridden."

Kate turned to them. "Are you quite certain you

don't mind?"

Gavin smiled. "Quite. I could do with a walk to stretch my legs. City living has made me soft."

Alone, Kate rose up on her toes and brushed a kiss over her husband's swollen lips. Dropping back down, she said, "I meant what I said, Patrick. I'll never let you go again. Like it or not, you can count on being *leg-shackled* to me for the next fifty-odd years at the very least."

Smiling through his bruises, Rourke used his good arm to pull his wife's slender body flush with his. "It's counting on it I am, Katie girl. In fact, you might say I'm staking my life on it."

EPILOGUE

*R*ourke's New *Rules*

Rule Number One: watch, listen, and wait. Sooner or later you and the lady of your dreams are bound to cross paths, so mind you keep a sharp eye out and a canny ear cocked.

Rule Number Two: when your paths do cross, don't hesitate. Woo her, win her, but under no circumstances try to tame her (especially not with a bloody play).

Rule Number Three: once she's yours, take her hand, love her with your whole heart—and never let her go.

Never let her go.

For more information
about other great titles from
Medallion Press, visit

www.medallionpress.com